THE SONG IN THE SHADOWS

THE CHALAM CHRONICLES VOLUME II

LEGENDS
BOOK TWO

MORGAN G FARRIS

The Chalam Chronicles

Volume II

CONTENTS

PART ONE

Chapter 1 3
Chapter 2 4
Chapter 3 31
Chapter 4 45
Chapter 5 50
Chapter 6 66
Chapter 7 89

PART TWO

Chapter 8 93
Chapter 9 103
Chapter 10 108
Chapter 11 120
Chapter 12 131
Chapter 13 141
Chapter 14 158
Chapter 15 176
Chapter 16 187
Chapter 17 196
Chapter 18 209
Chapter 19 224
Chapter 20 237

PART THREE

Chapter 21 251
Chapter 22 264
Chapter 23 274
Chapter 24 283
Chapter 25 292
Chapter 26 310
Chapter 27 329

Chapter 28 336
Chapter 29 350

Acknowledgments 357
About the Author 359
Also by Morgan G Farris 363
Sign Up for the Newsletter 365

PRAISE FOR MORGAN G FARRIS

This is her best work so far. So deep, rich and profound. I can feel, smell, taste everything in Har-Navah.

— TRIPP, READER

Beautifully woven and divinely portrayed.

— MORGAN, READER

Authentic. Powerful. It's rare to convey trauma and abuse with the level of realism found in these pages. And yet there is a beauty to this book that gives it life and hope. This is an instant classic.

— EMMA, READER

This book is a work of fiction. The characters, incidents, and dialogue are drawn from the author's imagination and are not to be construed as real. Any resemblance to actual events or persons, living or dead, is entirely coincidental.

A hardcover edition of this book was published in 2022 by Minor 5 Publishing.

ISBN 978-1-7379479-6-7

To Westley and Buttercup, Hosea and Gomer, Rhett and Scarlett.
You taught me that love is magic even when it's messy.

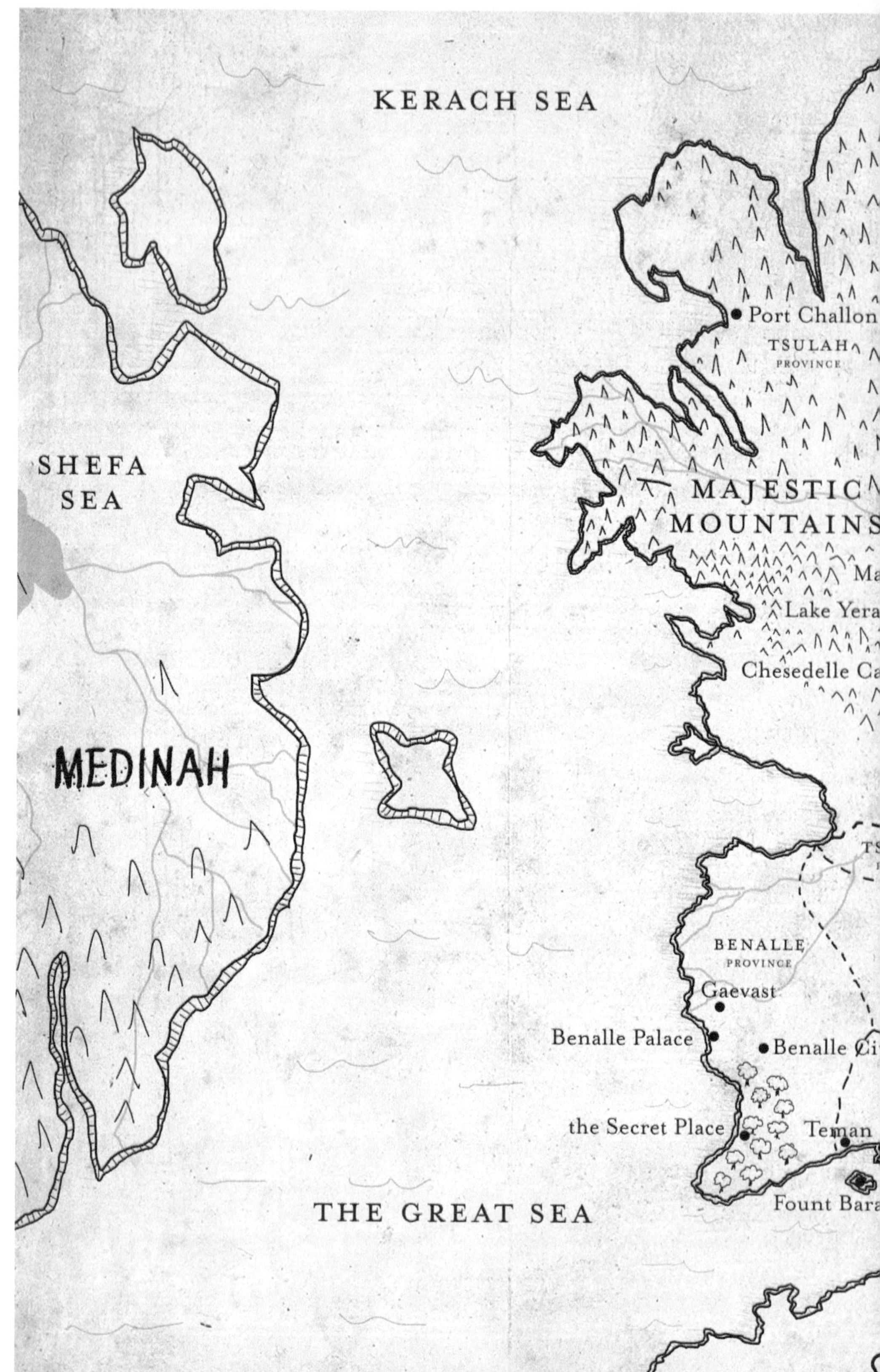
KERACH SEA
SHEFA SEA
MEDINAH
Port Challon
TSULAH PROVINCE
MAJESTIC MOUNTAINS
Lake Yera
Chesedelle Ca
BENALLE PROVINCE
Gaevast
Benalle Palace
Benalle Ci
the Secret Place
Teman
Fount Bara
THE GREAT SEA

N
W
E
S
Borras
BORRAS
PROVINCE
CHERETH
PROVINCE
EDEN OCEAN
HASAMAYIM
PROVINCE
AR–NAVAH
HINNOM
PROVINCE
NEHAR
PROVINCE
tle
em
KINNERETH
PROVINCE
delle City
Melamed Estate
Omer
Northern Pass
Ramleh
Dupree Estate
Adina's
House
Goleath
Palace
MIDVAR
Valley
QADIM
PROVINCE
WILD
WOOD
N'VEH
SEA

PART ONE

CHAPTER ONE

Her breaths burned in her lungs, her head pounded with the kind of pain that lingers in a relentless *thrum, thrum, thrum,* and her legs felt like marmalade, but she kept running.

She ran as long as her legs could carry her.

Her belly aching, her hips heavy with strain, her arms pumping with the pounding of her feet on the hard ground, Miriam ran as fast as she could. As far as she could. She did not stop.

She could not stop. It was better this way. For nine months, she had told herself as much.

He would understand one day. Even if he didn't yet.

Ezra was better off without her.

So Miriam ran.

CHAPTER TWO

Nine Months Ago

For the first time in a long time—longer than she could remember—Miri felt safe.

Settled.

She took a deep breath, the icy air stinging her lungs. Awakening her. Standing on the balcony that overlooked Lake Yerah, snow-capped mountains towering around, the wind brisk and chilly, Miri nestled into Ezra's arms, warm and strong around her. She basked in the warmth of his breath upon her brow, in the feel of his chest rising and falling steadily against her. She marveled at the thought that standing out here in the late autumn night, she could feel such warmth. Such safety.

But this was home, after all. Miri was finally home.

Not just physically. But mentally. Spiritually. She had found the place her soul longed for.

She breathed a deep sigh and let herself take it in. Let herself believe it.

"What is it, Wildfire?" Ezra asked. Snow danced on the gentle night winds, bits of white fluff that landed on his nose and eyelashes as she looked up at him. She smiled in lieu of answering, kissing him just to remind herself that this was real. That she was here, in his arms. That she had survived untold darknesses. That she had made it through thanks to this man. That he had made it through, too.

That maybe Ezra was right—she was brave and she was beautiful. So was he.

After all they had been through—all they had faced—maybe tonight was the start of a new story. Not a story under the dark shadow of Phinehas, but a story in the warm glow of Ezra's light. Ezra's love.

Maybe everything would be all right this time.

So she allowed herself to bask in it. To feel normal again. Like a person worthy of this sort of consuming, impossible, unbelievable love.

She would never stop wanting the comfort of this man's arms around her.

"Stay with me," she said, the thought wild, the words just as wild coming out of her mouth. "Stay with me tonight."

She did not know what he would think. What he would say.

Ezra was her husband—they had married on that rooftop in the village only a few weeks ago. But he had never touched her. Before tonight, the man hadn't even kissed her since bringing her home to Massahd Castle. He had been so careful. So very careful. Gentle. Patient.

She had needed it—that patience. As she healed not just in her body, but in her soul, she had needed Ezra's gentle, quiet patience and his steadfast love. But here in his arms she did not need his patience anymore.

She just needed him.

Ezra met her eyes, searching.

Embarrassment flushed her cheeks. "I don't... I mean, I just... I don't want to be apart from you," she amended. She had spent the better part of her formative years as a whore for a priest. She had known nothing but coy glances and brazen flirtation and the greed of a man's touch. But asking Ezra to stay with her tonight—it was not for the purpose of a game. It was not to tease and play and flirt. She hoped he understood that. She hoped he knew that her question was genuine, her need for him birthed from some place she had never explored before.

But she wanted to explore it. With him. She wanted to know his every secret. She wanted him to know hers.

A smile ghosted his lips as they met hers with a soft, tender kiss. She wondered if there would ever come a day when she would tire of the way he kissed her.

"Come on," he said, and moved not towards her bedchamber doors, but his. She hadn't even realized that their chambers shared this balcony until he had met her out here. In a way, she was glad she hadn't known. Once, before this, she might have been angry to know that he could come to her at any moment. That he had access to her whenever he wanted.

Now, knowing that he had been so careful, so considerate of her needs, she marveled that the man had never used those doors. Never insisted on his marital right.

A small, quiet part of her wondered if perhaps he didn't want to.

The night air was a sudden rush of cool, and when she moved to wrap herself more securely in her blanket, Ezra helped.

"Where are you going?" she asked, nodding towards his doors.

"To bed." He smiled. "Are you coming?"

"In your chambers?" She hadn't meant to intrude, to invite

herself into his private quarters. The chambers of the Grand Duke of Kinnereth.

Something in his eyes sparkled. “Well, I was hoping they'd be *our* chambers, Miri. This one has a much better view.”

He wasn't wrong. Around the bend of the balcony, the view from her chamber windows was beautiful, but it was nothing compared to this—the perfect spot to view the mountains and the lake and the stars. When she looked up to the sky, Ezra breathed a soft laugh and kissed the column of her neck.

“The best views for the Grand Duke, then?” she asked. Feeling light. Feeling playful for the first time in a long time.

“These are not the Grand Duke's chambers,” he said to her surprise. “Those are up about three flights and on the opposite end of the castle. These were my grandparents' chambers.”

“Weren't they the Grand Duke and Duchess?” she asked, tilting her head to one side.

“Yes,” he said, smiling. “But they preferred these chambers because of the view. When I became Grand Duke of Kinnereth, I decided to take over their chambers. My sister and John sleep in the Grand Duke's chambers when they are here.”

“I didn't know that,” she said, hating that, in all the time she had been here, she had never taken Ezra up on his offer of a tour. The castle was huge—much bigger than she realized.

“Well, I will show you. You need to get to know your estate, Your Grace.”

When she rolled her eyes and pursed a smile, Ezra huffed a soft laugh and kissed her once more. “Come on. Let's go to bed.”

Trembling softly, Miri took the arm he offered and let him lead the way.

Ezra's chambers were warm and vast, the fire in the hearth burning merrily, dancing along polished floors and lighting the whole space in golden splendor. Rich, plush carpets dotted the expanse, covering glossy marble beneath. Ezra slipped off his robe to reveal his crisp, linen nightshirt and drawers. Beneath the thin fabric, Miri could just see the darker skin of the scar that marred his stomach.

The wound he had taken for her.

Because he had nearly died to save her.

At Gian of Borras's blade.

A wave of regret washed over her. But she pushed—*shoved* it aside. She would not think about that right now.

Ezra smiled, watching her as he laid the robe carefully across the back of a nearby chair. He lifted a hand, and she reached out and took it. Lacing his fingers between hers, he led her to the vast, four-poster bed across the room. He moved the blankets down for her, revealing crisp, white linens. And at such a simple gesture, Miri trembled.

She had known darkness beyond even the most depraved imagination. She had whored herself for men who had promised the world. She had reduced herself to indignities too obscene to speak of. Yet here, standing beside this man as he prepared his bed for her, she trembled. Not from fear or shame. Not from nerves.

But from anticipation.

Like a virgin might tremble on her wedding night.

She trembled as she climbed into the bed. She trembled as she watched Ezra walk around, as she watched him climb in the other side. She trembled as he arranged the blankets over them. She trembled when he leaned close and ran a knuckle down her cheek.

"Are you warm enough?" he asked.

She could only nod.

Ezra's smile was as warm as his bed as he cupped her cheek

and kissed her softly, simultaneously laying her back on the down pillows behind them. He kissed her as he pulled her into his arms and tucked her into his side. He kissed her as he ran gentle hands down her side and to her waist, as he moved his hands to her hips and back up again. He kissed her, and she trembled at his reverent, consuming touch.

So unlike any touch she had ever known.

"Goodnight, my beautiful Wildfire," he said.

She hesitated when she realized he had no intention of anything more. His arm settled across her middle, his lips at her brow as he sighed. A moment later, his breathing deepened. Ezra had fallen asleep.

Without touching her. Without another word, Ezra had just fallen asleep. Even Miri's racing mind could not stop her from following him into a deep, dreamless slumber.

Bright light spilled across the bed, piercing Miri's closed eyes. She squinted them shut more tightly and rolled over, momentarily startled by the warm body at her side. Her eyes flew open again.

Ezra.

He slept soundly, his face relaxed and peaceful.

She had slept so hard, so deeply, that she had forgotten where she was and what had transpired. But one look at him sleeping peacefully beside her and it all came rushing back.

A smile ghosted her lips, and—as if he felt it—Ezra's eyes opened.

"Good morning, Wildfire," he said dreamily.

"Hello," she said, with a smile.

Ezra sighed and moved to tuck a strand of her hair behind her ear. "I think I've found my favorite way to wake up," he said.

She wanted to tell him that she felt the same—that she had never known such a sweet, simple pleasure. But the thought gave her pause, for to tell him that would be to remind him that she had been in the beds of many men. Had been Phinehas's most prized whore.

"What is it?" he asked, as if he could read her thoughts.

"I just—I want to tell you things. I want to share with you. But so much of my past is—"

"I do not fear the past, Miri," he said. "I do not want you to either."

And she believed him. The earnestness in his eyes, the way he said it.

She believed him.

So she spoke. "I've never slept with a man. I—well, I—what I mean is I've never slept *near*—er—I mean—" Heat rushed to her face so fast it felt like flame. She covered her cheeks with her hands.

Ezra took hold of her wrists, a grin ghosting his mouth. "You haven't?"

She could only shake her head.

That grin turned into a full-fledged smile, deepening the dimple on his cheek. "You know, neither have I."

She scoffed, rolling her eyes as her own grin spread across her face.

Ezra breathed a laugh and kissed her nose. "Tell me more. Tell me other things you've never experienced."

"Well," she said, feeling a little more at ease by his humor. "I've never woken in a man's arms."

"Again, neither have I," he added.

She chortled. "Yes, but you've woken in many women's arms, I'm sure."

"Are you so sure, then?" he asked with a conspiratorial grin.

"Positive."

He raised his brows, but did not say anything. She searched him for a moment, trying to read his face. And a thought occurred to her—an outrageous, ridiculous thought. She spoke it aloud anyway. "What, are you going to tell me you're a virgin, then, Ezra Kelach?"

"Is that so impossible?" he asked, simply.

"Don't play like that," she said, pushing his chest gently. "I don't understand your meaning."

"There is no implication intended, Wildfire."

"You mean to tell me that you've never slept with a woman?"

"I've slept with—er—*near* you, haven't I?"

"You know what I mean," she said, dismissing his joke.

Ezra did not respond.

Miri could have buried herself twenty feet below ground.

"Do you think less of me now?" he asked, a chuckle threatening.

"Less of you!" she scoffed. "I should think you would think a great deal less of *me!"*

"Why in the world would I do that?"

"Because you are a *virgin!"* she pronounced. Hearing it aloud... the absurdity of it rattled her... "And I am—*most decidedly not!"*

"Is virginity a measure of virtue, then?"

"Well, it's certainly more virtuous than I have been!"

"Miri," Ezra said gently, taking her face in his hands. "It's a matter of circumstance."

"Circumstance?" she balked. "Tell me, how is it possible that someone as gorgeous as you has never—" She halted, ignoring the grin flashing across his unfairly beautiful mouth and rolled her eyes. "You are impossible."

"Gorgeousness aside, the reason for my current state of chasteness has much more to do with the fact that I've spent the past fifteen years betrothed to one woman whose father made it quite clear—with rather vivid descriptions, mind you—what precisely would happen to me—or more specifically, my manhood—should she have found herself with my child in her belly before our wedding night. It rather put a damper on the mood, if you will."

"You speak as if she were the only woman in the world, Ezra. And don't pretend—John has told me that you did not avoid looking at other women."

Ezra barked a laugh. "I certainly did not," he said. "But unfortunately, I had no desire to support a gaggle of bastards and ex-mistresses, as it were."

"So you're twenty-six years old and you're still a virgin," she said flatly.

"You don't believe me," he said with a grin.

"I find it absurd."

"Why in the world is it absurd? I rather like my balls. I did not want to serve them on a platter to the king's dogs. And I told you before that I'm not one to take a lover for sport. For the men I know who do, it's not much of a sport once the fun has worn off."

She huffed. "I don't understand you at all."

"Why not?"

"Stop laughing!" she said.

"I'm not laughing. I'm amused," he retorted, chuckling softly.

"Stop—*being amused!*"

"What is it that you don't understand?"

"Why anyone like you would want—*someone like me.*" She added the last bit with a low voice, suddenly looking down.

Ezra did not let her, lifting her chin that her gaze might meet his. "Aside from the fact that you are staggeringly beautiful, aside from the fact that you are my best friend, I want you because I love you," he said. "I want you because I want this life we're making together." Then he kissed her so thoroughly that she could hardly keep any rational thoughts in her head. His hands found her waist, and he pulled her close to him, the warmth of his solid body spreading along hers. She shivered, reveling in his tender exploration of her back, her thighs, her waist.

"I never knew a virgin could kiss like that," she said when at last he broke the kiss.

A feline grin curled his mouth. "I'm glad you approve, my lady."

She blushed, suppressing a smile and shaking her head. "What a pair we make."

"Indeed," he agreed, and began exploring her neck and shoulders with his lips. But when her stomach rumbled, he pulled back with a grin.

"Perhaps we should fetch you some breakfast, Your Grace."

She bit the inside of her cheek and blushed. "I am a bit hungry."

"That's good," he said. "Now it simply comes down to which you prefer: breakfast in the dining hall or breakfast in bed."

She raised an eyebrow. "Breakfast in bed?"

A grin and a nod was his response.

"You, Ezra Kelach, are spoiled."

"Well, I would prepare yourself, then, Your Grace, for I plan to spoil you to atrocious degrees."

It was Miri who kissed him this time. She snaked her arms around his neck and kissed him fiercely, entwining herself with him. He obliged, wrapping himself around her like a blanket and trailing kisses along her jaw, her neck, just below her ear. She practically laughed with delight at his touch and let him continue his exploration as she said, "Well, then. Which should I choose?"

Ezra paused enough to meet her eyes. Toying, she tapped a finger to her chin and looked up as if lost in deep thought. Ezra huffed a laugh and kissed her jaw.

And then it hit her. "Ari!" she exclaimed, remembering that her beloved cousin was here. That he had stayed here at Massahd after having dinner with the family last night. That he was likely waiting for them.

Ezra laughed, pressing his brow to her shoulder. "Mother of kings, we are terrible hosts, aren't we?"

He moved to get out of the bed, and Miri followed suit. A moment later, as if she knew—as if she had been waiting, Kit knocked on the bedchamber door. "My lady?" she said. "Are you awake?"

"I'm here," Miri said, before she realized what she had said. "Should the servants know I'm here?" she quickly whispered to Ezra, who was slipping on a pair of trousers.

A grin met his mouth. "Whyever should they not?"

Kit opened the door, her cheeks heating at the sight of Ezra buttoning his trousers.

"Kit!" he said merrily. "Miri will need to be dressed. And today, I would have you bring her things here, please. She will no longer need separate quarters."

Kit nodded once and flashed a conspiratorial grin at Miri before whisking her off to dress for the day.

"What do you mean, he's not here?" Miri asked.

The midmorning light spilled rich and warm into the vast foyer of Massahd Castle as servants bustled about with their morning chores.

"I mean he must have left," said Thaddeus. The gangly butler looked simultaneously harassed by the question and confounded by his own answer.

"Why did you let him leave?" Ezra asked.

"I didn't," he said. "When the servants entered his chambers to bring him his morning tray, he was not there. We searched the castle and the grounds. He's not here."

"He just...left?" Ezra asked. He turned to Miri, his eyebrows knitting together. "Why would he do that?"

"It's...like him," she admitted. "Ari is different. He always has been. It doesn't surprise me that he would leave without saying anything. It's not as if this is the first time."

"Do you suppose he's all right?" Ezra asked.

"I don't know," she admitted. At her side, Ezra took her hand, lacing his fingers with hers. When she looked up, the butler was eyeing her with what looked like concern.

"I will send for General Albus," Ezra said. "Perhaps—"

He was interrupted by the butler. "Forgive me, my lord. I already have. None of the soldiers saw him leave."

"Soldiers?" Miri asked, confused.

"In the mountains," Ezra said. "The men placed there."

Vaguely, she remembered something about that. But she could not remember the purpose of soldiers surrounding the castle. "Why?" she asked.

Ezra met her eyes, but it was the butler who responded.

"For you," said Thaddeus. "To keep you safe, My Lady." When she looked again at the butler, she was certain now that it was concern she saw in his face.

That Ezra felt she needed the protection of soldiers only served as a sobering reminder of what Phinehas was capable of. That he had not attempted any kind of retribution yet only heightened her worst fears.

When would he come for her?

And what would be his revenge?

"Finally among the living, I see." Miri and Ezra turned their attention to the adjacent sitting room, from which the portly housekeeper emerged. "You must come and see this! Hurry, before it's too late!"

Helena waved her hands towards herself and was in the middle of turning around for everyone to follow her when Thaddeus said, "He's been there all morning, Helena. I doubt he's leaving anytime soon."

The housekeeper merely leveled a flat look at the butler over her shoulder and continued her hasty bustle through the sitting room. Ezra, Miri, and Thaddeus followed.

Across the vast room, a wall of windows looked out onto one corner of the lake, boasting an unfettered view of the open waters beyond. With the sun spilling across, it was clear just how broad and unending Lake Yerah really was. Like an ocean between mountains.

But Miri's attention, like everyone else's, soon landed on the subject of Helena's interest, and she froze. From behind her, she could feel Ezra halt in place, too. He put his hands on her shoulders but said nothing as Helena prattled.

"He's a beauty, isn't he? I've never seen the like!"

Miri could not say the same. And she knew Ezra could not either.

A stag.

A white stag, to be precise.

The very white stag they had once seen deep in these mountains. The same she had seen as a little girl, recognizable by the subtle glow from his moon-white antlers. He stood still and proud on the bank of the lake just beyond the windows. And as if waiting for Miri to see him, as if waiting for her to arrive, his emerald eyes met hers and held her gaze.

And then the stag bowed once and turned, disappearing into the forest behind him.

"Well, what do you make of that?" Helena asked, baffled as she placed hands on her wide hips.

"You probably startled him with your yapping." That was from Thaddeus. Miri watched them bicker, surprised by the casualness of their relationship.

"I am not yapping, Thaddeus!" Helena protested. "*You're* the one who insisted on having the rugs beaten out there this morning, despite the fact that I told you not to. Not until Ezra got to see!"

"Well, he didn't leave, did he?" Thaddeus retorted. "He has stood in that very spot all morning!"

"Not anymore!" Helena raised a single finger in emphasis.

Ezra chuckled softly. With his hands on her shoulders, he bent to whisper in her ear. "Feisty, aren't they?"

"Are they always like this?" she asked for only him to hear.

"They're particularly colorful this morning. But Helena and Thaddeus have always had a *special* relationship."

Miri huffed a chuckle. Special indeed. She looked back out the windows beyond the bickering staff to see if she could catch a glimpse of the stag again. But he was nowhere to be found.

"Why do you think he keeps finding us?" Ezra whispered.

"I don't know," she admitted. She leaned back against Ezra's chest, and he opened his arms for her, wrapping them around her waist and pressing a soft kiss to her ear. She thought of the last time they had seen that stag.

That night, they had jumped into a pond and found themselves in a pool of stars, færies by the hundreds clustered around. The stag had been there to witness it all. She wondered if Ezra remembered it, for it had taken her weeks to piece the memories together—a world, a galaxy beneath the water that wasn't water. Truth and light and love pulsing through her. She had felt the truth between them for the first time that night. She had not wanted to let it go. And Ezra had promised her that she wouldn't have to—that they could take it with them—the magic, the truth, the love in those stars.

A moment passed before either of them realized that the butler and the housekeeper had stopped arguing and were watching them in quiet bemusement.

"What?" Ezra asked, his tone light.

Thaddeus raised his eyebrows. "You've seen the stag before." It wasn't a question.

"Once, yes," Ezra admitted.

"Why didn't you tell me?" Helena asked.

Ezra chuckled. "I did not realize I was supposed to."

"It's the *stag,* Ezra!" she emphasized, as if the significance was obvious. "From the legends!"

"Oh, it is *not,"* Thaddeus grumbled, waving her off with both hands. Helena ignored him.

"What legends?" Miri asked.

"The legends. The ancient texts. They say even the halls of Benalle Palace in Old Navah are engraved with him."

"Helena, what are you talking about?" Ezra asked.

"Færytales," Thaddeus said, rolling his eyes. "She's been on about them all morning."

"Yes, exactly," said Helena. "Færytales. Folk stories. Legends. The stag!" Helena's tone implied that everyone should know what she was talking about. "The Promised One!" she exclaimed.

Miri felt Ezra go as still as a statue.

"Helena, what are you saying?" Ezra asked.

"They say the Promised One is a shifter," Helena said.

"Poppycock," Thaddeus grumbled.

"It most certainly is not!" The housekeeper shot him an impatient look.

"Shifters, Hel? Really?" Thaddeus said, crossing his arms. "There is no such thing as shifters."

"What about the wolves? What would you call them?"

"Færy stories," said the butler.

The housekeeper did not back down. "Why do you use that term like it's an insult? Færies are real. You've seen them with your own eyes. Why should their tales be false?"

"They're children's stories, Helena," said Thaddeus, uncrossing his arms. He held up a hand, counting off his fingers as he listed, "Cursed dragons. Shifting wolves. A magic stag. It's all a bunch of magical nonsense."

"Magic is not nonsense," Miri interrupted. From behind her, Ezra simply held her, saying nothing.

"Of course it's not, dear!" agreed Helena.

"Magic is not nonsense," Thaddeus conceded. "But all these tales are. Are you implying that the fabled son of Providence is a magic stag?"

"No, I am not implying at all!" Helena raised her voice to meet Thaddeus's. "I am stating it as a fact!"

"It is much too early for all this bickering," came a voice from behind them. Ezra and Miri turned to see Esther and John emerge, John Junior not far behind, skipping as he came into the room. John Senior held baby Leah in his arms and Esther took a seat near the fireplace, straightening the skirts of her simple yet beautiful dress. John sat beside her on the arm of the chair.

"Helena is filling young Miri's head full of nonsense." This from Thaddeus.

"Folktales aren't nonsense," said John, reasonably. "There's always truth to them."

"You know of the stag?" Helena asked hopefully.

"The Promised One," John said matter-of-factly. "Of course."

"The Promised One is a shifter?" Ezra asked. He walked back towards the furniture, waiting until Miri came to his side before sitting with her on a settee.

"So the legends say," John said. From his side, Esther leveled him a flat look, but said nothing.

Apparently, there were two clear sides to this opinion: those who believed in færy stories, and those who dismissed them as children's lore. Miri wondered why she had never heard such a story.

"Did you know of this?" she asked Ezra.

"No," he said. "I've never heard of it."

"You wouldn't have," John said. "It's not the sort of story the nobility tell their children."

Again, Esther rolled her eyes softly but said nothing. With a pursed smirk, she took the baby from John's arms as if she didn't want her influenced by such simpleton's tales.

"Exactly," said Helena, coming into the sitting area, but refusing to take a seat. Thaddeus came close to Helena's side in order to continue waging his verbal war. "They're not the kinds of stories the upper class tell."

"Well, now I feel like an elitist," Ezra said amiably, though Miri could hear a hint of disappointment in his words.

"It's silly nonsense, Ez," said Esther, her attention fixed on the baby she bounced in her arms. Miri watched the mother and daughter for a moment, the way Esther's eyes sparkled as she watched her daughter make her first attempts to express herself. Baby Leah made a small noise, and it seemed everyone in the room turned their attention to her.

"No one can deny that the stag was ethereal, at least," said Ezra reasonably.

"And you've seen him before?" Thaddeus asked, his arms crossed as he stood beside Helena.

Ezra looked to Miri for a moment. "Yes," he said. "At the pool in the mountains where Esther and I used to swim."

"I don't remember seeing a white stag there," Esther said.

"We didn't," Ezra agreed. "Miri and I did. A few months ago."

"What do you suppose he wants?" John asked.

"Wants?" Miri asked.

"Wants?" Helena interjected. "He's the son of Providence!"

From her side, Thaddeus scoffed again. But no one seemed to know what to say to such a declaration, and a palpable silence filled the room.

"Perhaps we should move on to more sensical topics of

conversation," said Esther, reasonably. "Like what we're wearing to the ball."

"The ball?" Miri asked.

"The invitation said to the Grand Duke *and Family,"* said Esther. "I'm going on the sheer assumption that it's a peace offering from the princess."

"I highly doubt that," John added. "Rachæl doesn't know the meaning of the word *peace*."

"What ball?"

"What with everything going on, I completely forgot to mention it," Ezra said. "The Harvest Ball. At Chesedelle Castle."

"It's a masquerade," Esther said, waggling her eyebrows.

"Esther and John have not been invited in...a long time," Ezra said softly, though Miri knew everyone heard anyway.

"Exactly," said Esther. "Couple that with the fact that for the first time in months, I do not feel like a beached whale, and I'm going to the ball."

"When is it?" Miri asked.

"Two days," said John.

"Oh," Miri said, deflating.

"What's the matter?" Esther asked.

"Nothing," Miri dismissed. She did not feel like explaining how much she did not want to go to a ball, especially considering *who* might be there. From her side, Ezra ran a gentle hand along her arm.

"You're going to have to let Helena dote on you, Miri," said Esther. "Considering you denied her the opportunity to give you an ostentatious wedding, I have no doubt she plans to make up for it with an exorbitant amount of ball gowns."

At Esther's side, John Senior chuckled. So did Ezra. Helena stood a little taller, lifting her chin proudly.

"Oh," said Miri. "I didn't realize—"

"Don't let them pester you, Wildfire," said Ezra, grinning. Miri nodded quietly, suddenly feeling a bit uneasy.

"Well, then," said the housekeeper, clapping her hands together. She practically shoved past Thaddeus as she stepped to Miri and eagerly held out her hands. Hesitantly, Miri took them. "We had better get started!"

Miri had spent the better part of the morning sorting through an array of dresses, all of which Helena had been making for her with a magicked sewing kit. Esther had not exaggerated—no less than ten formal gowns awaited in her chambers, all of which were stunning, intricate, and perfectly tailored to fit her. And if that hadn't been overwhelming enough, Kit had presented her with a gorgeous, handmade gift *just for the Harvest Ball.* Miri hadn't known what to say.

At every new gown, Esther had smiled softly. Helena had made *her* several gowns, as well. Esther had chosen a green gown covered in leaves made of the softest velvet and a crown of vines and matching flora. She would go to the Harvest Ball looking like the Goddess of Spring, and Miri was privately jealous at how gorgeous Ezra's sister looked—the rich colors of the forest a perfect compliment to her golden skin and dark tresses.

After a morning of gowns and planning for the ball, Miri had spent her afternoon touring the grounds of Massahd—the many rooftop gardens in every turret and tower, libraries on nearly every floor, and a grand ballroom complete with a golden pianoforte on the ground floor that Miri hadn't even known existed. Just off the lakeshore and tucked into the side of the mountain, the stables boasted dozens of horses, including a black stallion so majestic Miri nearly wept at the sight of him. In a valley on the edge of the grounds, Ezra's winged horse Ahadah roamed and grazed, as well as a foal he had sired only last year. According to Ezra, Ahadah did not stay in the field, but only visited when he felt like it, spending most of his time high in the mountains with the other winged horses. But somehow, as if on instinct, whenever Ezra arrived at the meadow, Ahadah always followed soon after.

And all of it—every bit—was hers. Ezra had reminded her today that the paperwork had been drawn up weeks ago. She was the Grand Duchess of Kinnereth by law, not marriage. Ezra had kept his word to her when they married. She would not be Grand Duchess because of marriage. She would have all of it—every bit of the Kelach estate—to herself. And this, he assured her, was something no one could take from her.

After giving her the tour of the grounds, he had stopped in his study, presenting her with the papers. Hoping she would not come to regret it, with trembling hands, she had signed the decree alongside Ezra, making it official. She supposed it didn't really matter one way or the other. They were married, which made him the Grand Duke by marriage—no different than before, really. But she obliged him anyway, for the sole reason that she couldn't help but feel as if Ezra had a bigger plan than he was letting on. Or maybe it was simply that she hadn't been able to resist the proud smile he had given her when he handed her the pen.

So they spent the afternoon talking and making plans for a spring wedding feast—a celebration to appease Helena and Esther, both of whom had made it abundantly clear that Ezra had denied them the joy of celebrating his wedding by marrying secretly on the rooftops of Shalem and that it had been quite rude not to consider how much the family would have wanted to celebrate and that he owed them this at the very least. Ezra had laughed and agreed, kissing the exasperated housekeeper on her forehead to placate her. They had made lists of the people they would need to invite and plans for a tour of the northern provinces after the thaw—a chance for Miri to meet her subjects, Ezra had said.

And the Harvest Ball. Ezra had stated that it would be the perfect place to formally announce their marriage, promising her that only nobility attended. "It's more of a party than anything," he had said. "No politics. No agendas. Just a celebration of the harvest and the bounty of Providence."

So Miri had reluctantly agreed to attend. When Ezra added that they would take several of his soldiers with them as guards, Miri felt a little less worried by the prospect of going into public for the first time since...

Since she had been dragged naked into the village square. Since she had been beaten within an inch of her life. Since she had had her womb ripped from her. Since her dignity had been stolen just as violently.

To go to the ball would be the first time she had left the sanctity of Ezra's home since...everything.

Maybe it would be good.

Maybe she needed it.

Maybe it was time to move on.

By the time night fell, Miri was so tired she could hardly wait to climb into bed. At least until she remembered that Ezra had had all of her things moved to his chambers. She would be sleeping next to him again.

The prospect both thrilled and terrified her.

She was not sure if she was ready yet.

She wanted Ezra. Providence knew it was true. Sometimes just looking at him was too much. And when he was near, when he would come up behind her and press a kiss to her ear or her neck... Sometimes she could barely take it, how much she wanted him.

How much she desired to give him everything. To have everything. With him.

But just the same, she was frightened. Unsure if she was enough. If she could ever be enough.

Worse, what if she was too much? What if her too vast knowledge of the intimacies between a man and woman only served to remind her *virgin* husband that she was nothing but a whore?

She had not been able to stop worrying about it all through dinner. Nor had she stopped pondering it as she dressed for bed in the quiet of her private dressing chamber next to Ezra's. She still hadn't stopped when she had crawled into his bed, grateful that he was still in the bathing chamber.

A snick of the door a moment later signaled Ezra returning to the bedchamber. She sat in the bed with the blankets pulled up under her arms, watching him as he crossed the room. She had left her hair down and soft, knowing that Ezra preferred it that way. Her heart thundered as she watched him doff his robe, revealing his sculpted frame beneath the soft linen of his nightshirt and drawers.

Providence above, the man was beautiful. Too beautiful, really. Her heart strained just to look at him.

He smiled, exaggerating the dimple by his lips. "I think the fire is probably warm enough tonight, don't you?"

She nodded, swallowing once. Ezra made his way around the bed, climbing in beside her a moment later. He did not hesitate to reach for her, to pull her close to him and kiss her with such devastating passion she could scarcely breathe. He laid her down gently, reverently, running a hand down her hair as he said, "You have no idea how much I love having you here, Miri. I feel like I'm going to wake up any moment and realize this was all just a dream."

"I know what you mean," she said.

"But it's not a dream, Wildfire." He kissed her softly, moving so that he was nearly on top of her. "This is real. This is our life now."

She trembled as he ran a languid finger down her leg, never once taking his eyes from hers. She practically purred at his touch, a sudden need, a rushing desire to have him taking over. She moved her leg, bending her knee in such a position that with one simple move, he could lift her chemise up her body and off of her.

Ezra's kiss was as languid as his hands as he explored her. And with every devastating touch, her body grew taut—a string on a viol tuned too tightly.

But she would wait. She would let him set the pace. She *needed* him to set the pace.

"Oh my love," he breathed onto the skin of her chest. "My beautiful Wildfire. I love you."

"I love you," she echoed. "I love you, Ezra. I do."

He pressed a lingering kiss to the base of her neck, letting his hands find her waist, her hips, her thighs with loving, languorous touches that set her skin ablaze. Wildfire, indeed. She threaded her fingers through his thick, raven locks and breathed a sigh.

His hand moved from her waist and up her torso until he reached her breast. He trailed his thumb in an unhurried movement along the underside, and all of her thoughts, all of her being focused on that thumb—on the sensation as it moved over the thin linen of her chemise. He bent and pressed a single kiss to the soft swell above his hand, and Miri hated the fabric that separated his lips from her skin.

And then he moved. Rolling away, Ezra settled himself on his side of the bed and rested his arm across her middle, shutting his eyes and releasing a very long, heavy sigh. "I think I could kiss you all night, Wildfire."

"I would not be opposed to the prospect," she said, trembling with anticipation.

He opened a single eye with a smile half-cocked on his mouth.

"I'll have to remember that." Then he pressed a kiss to her lips and said, "Goodnight, Miri."

And that was that.

"What is it that consumes your thoughts, my lady?"

Miri gave herself a shake, focusing on Kitty as she buttoned the back of Miri's dress. Standing in her newly minted private dressing room, Miri took a look at herself in the looking glass. The neckline of the dress was low and wide, falling just below her shoulders. The dress was of soft fabric with a bright, cerulean pattern—a day dress for a fine lady. And nothing like what she might have worn in the temple.

The stark contrast of it hit her so profoundly that she almost forgot Kitty's question.

"My life is so different now," Miri said absently.

Different, indeed. At the temple in Teman City, there was not a single man who would have refused Miri like Ezra had.

She did not know what to make of it.

"Kit," Miri said, looking at the servant's reflection behind her. "Do you have a beau?"

The servant's cheeks lit to such a bright shade of pink that Miri felt bad. "Sorry. I don't mean to pry."

Young. The servant was young. And innocent. Probably much too young to even show interest in men, much less know the first thing about them. Miri felt stupid for asking.

"I'm working on it," Kit said, to Miri's surprise.

She turned to face the girl fully. "What does that mean?"

Kit grinned, biting her lower lip. "Well, we haven't been formally introduced yet, as formal introductions go, I suppose. But the word is he's going to be escorting you and His Grace to the ball tomorrow. I'm hoping we'll get to know each other on the journey."

Escorting. Ah. "A soldier, then?"

Kit nodded eagerly.

"How old are you, Kit?"

"Eighteen. I'll be nineteen this summer."

"Eighteen? Truly?"

The girl did not look like she was only two years Miri's junior. Then again, she had not grown up a whore in a priest's unholy brothel. *Anyone* would look younger than Miri. Bile burned the back of her throat.

"I saw him last year," Kit said wistfully. "When he enlisted in the king's army. He joined His Grace's ranks and came to Massahd. He's absolutely glorious."

Miri wanted to laugh at the bliss with which Kit spoke of the soldier. She supposed it was not so very different from the way Ezra made her feel most of the time.

Except last night.

"I haven't felt this way in a long time," Kit went on, reaching for Miri's night chemise where it had fallen to the floor.

"A long time?" Miri chuckled. "You're eighteen. How many men could you have possibly had feelings for?" She hated that her answer to that question would be quite different than the servant's.

"Well, only one other," Kit admitted, folding the chemise. She turned and left the dressing room, walking across the bedchamber to a nearby wardrobe. "But that did not end so well." Kit placed the folded garment in the wardrobe with meticulous perfection.

"What do you mean?" Miri asked, following the servant, unable to keep herself from prying.

Kit's face grew dark. "I was stupid. And I gave him too much. He did not love me; he just wanted to sleep with me."

The declaration was so matter-of-fact, so abrupt, that Miri's jaw dropped.

"You've...been with a man before?" Miri asked.

Kitty shrugged, plopping rather unceremoniously into a nearby chair. "I thought I loved him. Served me right that he left."

"How in the world did that serve you right?" Miri sat down in the chair across from Kit.

"I should not have been so stupid," Kit said.

"Believe me, I know plenty about stupidity. I could dance circles around your stupidity."

Kit looked at Miri with pity. "Not anymore," she said, her eyes brightening.

Miri breathed a dismissive laugh, second-guessing her quest for wisdom from a naïve maidservant. "I see the way the Grand Duke looks at you," Kit went on. "If Vitas so much as glanced at me that way, I'm fairly certain I'd be in his bed within the hour."

"Kit!" Miri exclaimed, her eyes wide with shock. A few seconds later, both of them were laughing. "Vitas, huh?" Miri asked, glad for the lighthearted turn in conversation. "What is he like?"

"Gorgeous. Tall. As thick as an oak. And his eyes. Dear Providence, my lady, his eyes are perfect."

Miri donned a crooked smile. "It's just Miri."

"Oh no, I couldn't—"

"Just Miri," she insisted. Kit's smile lit her whole face.

"Miri, then."

Miri smiled back. "Why don't you talk to him?"

"I'm hoping to. Tomorrow." Kit stood abruptly. She whirled back towards the wardrobe and opened a different drawer from before. "That reminds me. I have something for you." She pulled out a piece of fabric, folded neatly and tied with silk ribbons, and handed it to Miri.

"What is this?"

Kit blushed again. "Something for you. Oh, who am I kidding?

It's His Grace who will like it the most, if I had to guess."

Miri furrowed her brows and untied the lace. Unfolding the soft fabric, she revealed a small piece of lace folded inside. A chemise—and a rather flimsy one, at that.

"Kitty! This is scandalous!" Miri said, half thrilled and half terrified at what she held. "Surely a proper lady would never wear such a thing!"

"Well, of course a proper lady would wear such a thing for her husband!" Kit said with an incredulous giggle.

Miri eyed the piece—all delicate lace and soft silk. It could not possibly be long enough to come to her knees. It probably barely covered her backside. She wondered just how scandalized her virginal husband would be at the sight of such a garment. It would certainly not do anything to keep him from remembering what she was. What she had been.

Kit put a hand on Miri's arm. "You've been through enough, Miri. I thought perhaps you might enjoy something luxurious. Something that makes you feel beautiful."

"You're very sweet, Kit."

Kit's smile was warm and bright, lighting her whole face. She was beautiful, in a simple, innocent sort of way. Miri couldn't help but think that any man who would fail to notice was a fool who didn't deserve her.

"Well, I had better get busy. There is much to do before we leave tomorrow!" Kit declared, whirling to leave.

"Kit," Miri said, stopping the servant, who turned to face Miri again. "Thank you for thinking of me." If any of the girls at the temple had even once thought of her, much less brought her a gift for no reason at all, she could not remember it. That a practical stranger had given her something just to make her smile meant more to Miri than she was sure she could express at the moment.

Kit's smile was as bright as it was mischievous. She winked and left the room.

CHAPTER THREE

Miri had been quiet all evening. Then again, she had been nearly mute since first arriving at Massahd weeks ago, so he supposed his pondering of today's contemplative silence was silly by comparison. Still, it was evident something weighed on her. He wondered if the same thing that consumed his thoughts of late also consumed hers.

"Miri, may I ask you something?"

From beside him in the oversized chair, his wife took her attention from the starry night sky and faced Ezra. "What is it?"

"I've been thinking a lot," he admitted. And with it, something in her face shifted—as if she were hanging on his every word.

"About the stag," he added.

Her shoulders fell softly, her countenance shifting, but she simply nodded.

"You told me once—at the pool in the mountains—*the stag is at hand.* What does that mean?"

"It was the færies who told me that. They visited me while I was in the temple. They told me the time was coming—and the stag was at hand. I did not know what it meant. I still don't. Not really."

Ezra looked down, tracing idle paths on the top of Miri's hand, unsure how he was going to pose the next question. "You said once—you mentioned your cousin... That he is strange. Different. How is he different, Miri?"

Miri let the question hang between them for a good moment before she answered. "He's...deep. A deep well, I think. When he speaks, it usually means much more than you realize at the time. Sometimes it's years before you understand it. There were so many times growing up that I felt as if he were speaking in riddles. Especially when he spoke of his father."

"Who is his father?"

"I don't know. I never met him. My mother always told me Ari was bastard born—that his father had never been in the picture."

"And what about his mother?"

"She died when I was young, but I remember she was kind and quiet. Much like Ari, she often spoke in ways that implied much more meaning than you realized at the time."

"But he speaks of his father in the present, as if he's alive."

"Ari has always been strange," she repeated quietly. "Speaking of his father the way he does, collecting trinkets."

"Trinkets?" Ezra asked.

Miri nodded. "He's always had a fondness for little oddities—gadgets and magical contraptions. He once gave me a crude necklace. Just a bit of stone but sometimes late at night, I could swear it glowed—"

"A bit of stone?" Ezra asked, tilting his head to one side.

"Yes. It's the reason I went back to the temple the night we were married. The thing I wanted to get." The night that everything had changed—the night he had not been able to save her. He saw her steal a quick glance at his stomach—and the scar beneath his shirt—and knew she was thinking the same. Something in his heart cracked at the flash of hurt in her gaze, there and gone again.

"Yes," he said, pushing the thoughts aside. "You said there something you could not replace."

"It was just a silly necklace," she said, but the way she said it made it clear she was admitting something she had never told another soul. "Just one of his curiosities. It's not beautiful or of any value, I'm sure. But Ari gave it to me. When I was a girl. Before —all of this. And I just... I wanted it. I wanted it to remember him."

"A rock, you say?"

"Yes. Just a broken rock."

"Broken?" he asked. It was clear from Miri's expression that she did not understand why the make of the necklace could matter.

She nodded. "In half. It was beautiful on the inside, shimmering with nothing but crystal. I remember as a girl, my favorite thing was how it sparkled in the moonlight. I guess that's why I thought it glowed. But it was lovely, and I just—Ezra, I know it's stupid, but I wanted it and—"

A broken rock.

A broken *crystal* rock.

"Miri," he said, taking her hand, his heart pounding. "I need to show you something."

He stood, helping her to stand with him, leading her to the other side of their chambers. His trembling fingers laced with hers just before he stopped in front of a wardrobe on the far end of the chamber, near the dressing rooms. He pulled open the doors and dug in the back, pulling an ornately-carved bone box from one of the shelves.

Turning, he faced her and pulled open the box. At the sight of its contents, Miri's eyes went wide as harvest moons.

"Did it look like this?" Ezra asked.

"Where did you get that?" Miri asked, reaching inside. Her trembling fingers held the half stone in her hand as she inspected it carefully.

"It has been in my family for centuries. Passed down from generation to generation. We came into possession of it before the Ramagi uprising. We've kept it secret. No one—not a single soul—knows that I have this. Not even Esther. My grandfather only told me of it on his deathbed."

"What do you mean? Ezra, this is my necklace. This is what Ari gave me. He—"

"No, Miri," Ezra said. "This is the *other half* of what Ari gave you. This is the Amulet of Haravelle. It is said to bear the protection of Providence himself. It was a symbol of the kings of Old Haravelle for millennia. But as the generations ruled in the wake of King Ferryl's reunification of Haravelle and Navah, it became clear that the amulets were more than just trinkets. They bore a sort of power—undiluted magic. And they made the bearer practically invincible.

"They became something of legend. Secrets and lies surrounded them, and their lore spread far and wide. Stories emerged of witches claiming to have harnessed the power of the amulets, offering tattoos with ink ground from the same Haravellian crystals. They said the magic was a means of protection. But no other magic ever truly matched the magnificent power of the amulets.

"It wasn't long before stories emerged that somewhere along the way, the kings of Har-Navah glutted themselves on the power from their talismans, and so Providence took the amulets and hid them away."

"The treasure of Hasamayim Province," Miri said, wide-eyed.

"Exactly," Ezra nodded. "It was rumored that the amulets had somehow ended up in the north, hidden by time and legend. But my family has protected this half for as long as we can remember.

We do not know the story of how we came into possession of it, but it is not something we speak of, Miri. No one knows we have it. No one except me. And now you."

"Why are you telling me this? Should I know it?" she asked.

He covered her hands with his, the amulet cupped between them. "You are Grand Duchess," he said, kissing her brow softly. "And you are my wife. I will not keep anything from you. Only truth between us, remember?"

She smiled softly, looking down at their clasped hands. "If this is the Amulet of Haravelle..." she said, and she did not have to finish her sentence for Ezra to understand.

"We have to find it, Miri. We have to find your half. We cannot let Phinehas find it. We cannot let him get ahold of it."

"What if he already has?" she asked, fear shining in her emerald eyes.

"I think we would know if he had," he said, trying to take comfort in the thought. "He would not hesitate to use it. To wield it. Against the king. Against me. Against you."

"We have to find it," she said. "We have to keep it from him."

"Don't you see it, Miri?" he asked. "You were right to go back that night. You had to. You had to find that amulet."

"But I didn't," she said. "I never had the chance. Providence only knows where it is now."

"We'll find it," he said, pulling her to his chest. He ran hands along her back. "We won't rest until we do."

"But what about Ari?" she asked, her head pressed against his chest. "Why were you asking me about him? About his strangeness?"

He took a breath to collect his thoughts, to make sure he was ready to speak them aloud. "The way he disappeared yesterday without saying goodbye," Ezra said. "I wonder..."

"Wonder what?" she asked, lifting her head from his chest.

"I wonder if he *did* say goodbye. Just—not in the way we expected."

"What do you mean?"

Ezra scratched his brow, wondering how he was going to say this, what she would make of his theory. "I just wonder, Miri—thinking of what Helena said—about the stag. The legends about the son of Providence say that—that he's a shifter. I wonder—"

"You think Ari is the stag?" Miri asked, cutting him off.

He thought of the man's white hair, as bright as spun moonlight, of those emerald eyes. The same as the stag's. What if it was true?

What if Ari was a shifter? What if Ari was the white stag?

Ezra merely nodded, searching her face. Wondering if he was upsetting her with his wild theories. But Miri's eyes merely darted to and fro between them, as if she, too, was putting the pieces together.

Ezra broke the silence. "If he had the other half of the amulet... Maybe he..."

She looked up, meeting Ezra's eyes, searching them for a moment. "Ezra, what are you saying—?"

Ezra kept his gaze intent upon hers. "Miri, what if Ari is the Promised One?"

Miri spent the better part of the next half hour in the bathing chamber. She hadn't seemed upset by his wild postulating. She hadn't even protested. She had simply gone silent and contemplative again.

It would change everything, to be sure. If Ari was a shifter...if Ari was indeed the long-awaited son of Providence...

Neither of them had known what to say about it, both of them falling into deep thought. And after a long bout of silence, Ezra had been privately grateful when Miri had suggested they finally go to bed. But then she had spent so much time in the bathing chamber that Ezra was beginning to worry he had upset her.

He was about to damn the consequences and barge in on her when she opened the door separating them, wearing a robe of silver silk. Her long, ruby locks were down and damp from her bath, and her face shone with an expression he could not read.

Providence help him.

Stopping himself would be damn near impossible tonight.

But he was trying.

He was trying to take it slow. To let her take the lead. He would never want to hurt her, never want to push her too hard or too fast. She had been through enough, had known enough pain at the hands of men. He would never forgive himself if he were the cause of a moment more. Even if it were by accident.

Miri moved towards him, slow deliberate steps that seemed much, much too fast and yet took an eternity. When she reached him, she stopped just short of him, looking down for a moment, playing with the sash of her robe before she spoke.

"I never thanked you, Ezra."

"Thanked me for what?" he asked, stopping himself from reaching for her, from pulling her close and stripping off that robe to reveal whatever was beneath. He didn't give a damn if it was a flour sack, he just wanted her close. He wanted to touch her. To feel her. To revel in her milky-white skin and silken locks. To find and kiss every single one of those cinnamon-flecked freckles.

"I never thanked you. For everything," she said, her words hardly more than a breath. "For saving me. For giving me a home. For giving me a life."

When she looked up again, she loosened the sash of her robe at the same time, doffing it in one fluid movement. What she revealed nearly knocked the breath from him.

He swallowed, utterly still.

Her chemise was...short. Extremely short. It barely covered her, revealing long, lean legs beneath a swath of lace that was anything but covering. Her skin shone through the fabric, revealing the shadow of her navel and the perfect pink tips of her breasts.

Ezra swallowed again, attempting to compose himself.

It wasn't working.

He took minor comfort that she was breathing as heavily as he was. But when she reached for the thin straps of fabric on her shoulders... When she pushed them down one arm, then the other... When that delicate swath of lace fell fluidly from her exquisite curves... Ezra fell to his knees.

She stood naked before him, trembling softly. He looked up at her, unable to stop himself from reaching out, resting his hands on the lush swell of her hips. He leaned forward, pressing gentle kisses to the long plane of her stomach, taking no small amount of pleasure from her little sighs.

"Sometimes I cannot believe you are my wife, Miri. Sometimes I can barely believe it."

She paused for a fraction of a moment, but before he could catch his thoughts to understand why, she was threading her delicate fingers through his hair. And he was done for.

Damn his restraint. It would not serve him tonight.

He stood, pulling her close until the length of her warm body was against his, running hands around to her back, gently caressing her skin, her shoulders, down to her backside. She did not stop him, his Wildfire. She did not flinch at his touch, and instead pressed even closer and kissed him with dizzying perfection. He could barely think past the sensation of her hands as she moved to lift his night shirt from his chest. She broke their kiss just long enough to slip the shirt over his shoulders. And the feel of her skin against his...

She was soft and she was warm and she was perfection and it

was all Ezra could do to remember how to use his arms, his hands, his mind again. He lifted her up, cradling her in his arms, unsure where he wanted to touch first, to taste, to explore as he moved them the few steps to the bed. He laid her back, hovering above her, kissing and tasting his way from her lips to her chin, from her neck to her breasts and Providence help him...

She moved as if she knew exactly how he wanted her to move. She touched him as if she knew his very soul, as if she knew exactly what he craved, what he needed from her. His glorious, impossible Wildfire. She would consume him, body and soul. And he would gladly burn. Burn and burn and burn for her. Until he was nothing but cinders and ashes. Nothing but hers to command. To rule. Like the queen—the goddess she was.

His goddess of the Wildfire.

His very being groaned and ached for her. He had just reached to work the fall of his drawers when she spoke, her words soft, almost indecipherable.

"Whatever you want," she said, breathless. "I will give you whatever you want. I owe you everything. And I am at your command."

He stilled, her words sinking in slowly.

"What?" he asked, trying to understand.

"I will do whatever you ask of me, Ezra," she said, her words a silken seduction. But it was not his sweet wife, his bright Wildfire who spoke those words. It was not the woman he knew and loved. Here was another Miri, dark and drawn into herself. As if she were not here at all.

Did she think she owed him this? That her body was some sort of penance? Did she want him at all, or did she only want to give him what she thought he wanted?

Ezra moved, settling himself beside her and pushing a shaking hand through his hair. He took a shuddering breath, needing to calm himself, to slow down, to think, to understand.

It was a good while before he realized that Miri hadn't moved, that she hadn't even spoken. When at last he turned to face her, what he saw made his heart stop.

Her face was hard, her eyes harder. Tears lined her emerald eyes, but there was no sadness.

No, it was something else there. Something much, much darker.

"Miri," he said, reaching for her.

"Don't touch me," she growled, jerking away from him. She moved from the bed so quickly he could not stop her. Bending to retrieve her robe and shift, she did not bother donning either, merely wadding them in trembling hands before marching across the room.

"Miri, wait."

She did not.

"Miri," he said again, unable to think for the desire pounding through his body like war drums.

"Please!" he begged as she reached the door.

She froze, her hand on the handle before she turned, rage in her eyes. "I did not understand. I could not make sense of you. Your hesitation with me. But I understand it now. I see it all clearly."

"I am certain that you do not," he said, moving from the bed.

She started, trembling against the door like a cornered fawn in a meadow. Ezra stopped, unwilling to frighten her further. He lifted his hands. "Miri," he said gently.

"Stay away from me," she warned, her words low, guttural.

"Miri!" he called again. But before he could move, she was out the door.

Gone.

"What in the world is going on between the two of you?" John asked, perching on the arm of a leather chair and crossing his arms.

Ezra rubbed his thumb and forefinger along the bridge of his nose, taking a deep breath. Sitting at the massive desk in the Grand Duke's study, he did not even know where to begin.

"She wouldn't even look at you at breakfast and hardly spoke three words to any of us. What happened, Ez?"

Books lined every wall in his study, floor to ceiling. Books his father, his grandfather, and his great-grandfathers for generations before him had collected and read. Wisdom from the many who had gone before him. Yet he doubted a single book in this trove offered advice on the subject haunting him.

"I messed up," Ezra admitted with defeat.

"What did you do to mess up so catastrophically?" John asked. There was a hint of humor in his question, but Ezra felt anything but amused. He hadn't slept a single moment all night. A breakfast of awkward silence with the family hadn't helped. He had hoped sorting through some paperwork would help, but it was a fruitless endeavor. Miri wouldn't so much as breathe in his direction.

"I refused her," he finally admitted, unable to look up from the ledger opened before him.

"You...what? Why in Providence's good name would you refuse her?" John asked.

Ezra looked up to his brother-in-law. "Because I'm an idiot, I think."

"Well, that much is obvious," John pointed out unhelpfully. But his countenance shifted as he stood and took a seat across the desk from Ezra. "What's going on?"

Ezra clasped his hands before him on the desk, rolling his thumbs, unsure where to even begin. "She offered herself to me last night. And Providence knows I wanted to, I—" Ezra stopped, giving himself a shake. He rested his forehead on his palm. "Something wasn't right, John. I couldn't. I mean—"

"You...*couldn't?*" John asked, and at the startled hesitation, Ezra quickly interjected.

"Of course I could! I just... I mean, I didn't want to. I mean, I *did* want to! Of course I did! I do, I just..."

John's furrowed brow didn't help, and with a frustrated sigh, Ezra explained, "She's been through so much, John. So damn much. I cannot hurt her anymore. I cannot. And the way she said it... The way she looked at me..."

"The way she said what?"

Ezra met John's stare. "She thinks she owes me. She... It was penance, John. She felt like she needed to pay me back. For everything."

"Oh," John said darkly.

"I cannot do that to her, John. I cannot take that from her. Not like that. She... Mother of kings, John, she nearly died! And now she feels like she owes me her body! What in Sheol am I supposed to do with that?"

Exasperated, Ezra took a breath and collapsed back against his chair. John, on the other hand, fidgeted with a loose thread on his cuff, thinking.

A moment of silence stretched between them, and John did not meet Ezra's eyes when he finally spoke. "What I am about to say, Ezra... You may not want to hear it. Considering my wife is..." John finally looked up. "I need you to forget that my wife is your sister for a moment, all right?"

Ezra nodded once, his eyes wide.

"She... Ezra, sometimes... I know you don't know this, because you cannot know this. Not personally. But sometimes the only way I can really speak to her, sometimes the only way I can really show her what she means to me, is when she is in my arms."

"I know that, John. I understand that sex—"

"No, you don't know, Ez. You think you do, but you don't. And you will not. Not until you experience it for yourself. My wife... She is the air I breathe. There are times when I can barely think just looking at her. And I certainly have never found a way to tell her what she really means to me. To put it into words. But sometimes... Sometimes, I don't have to. For just to touch her...to hold her...to feel her against..." John stopped, clearing his throat before he went on.

"Sex can be a weapon, Ezra. And it has been for Miri. It has been used as a vicious weapon against her.

"But, Ezra, it can also heal. It can speak where words fail. It can mend what no bandage can touch. It can build a bridge where there was none. And I think... I think she needs that. And I think you do, too.

"Maybe she came to you in the wrong way, Ez. So you fix it. You show her the truth. You show her love. And you show her in a way that no one else can.

"Maybe she thinks she owes you. But she also loves you. And you love her. And she's never known love like that. Neither have you. It's time to let the past be the past. It's time to heal. Together."

Ezra tried all morning to speak to Miri. But she would not answer the door. She had removed to her old chambers across the hall, and if it weren't for Kit appearing now and again, Ezra would have wondered if she was alive at all.

"She's all right, my lord," Kit said, passing him in the hall between their chambers for what was probably the dozenth time that day. "She's just...quiet."

"May I see her?" he asked, as helpless as a child.

"I—" Kit looked down, toeing something invisible on the carpet. "I don't think she wants that."

Ezra sighed, defeated. "What do I do, Kit?"

Kit's eyes lit up and she stood on the tip of her toes to press a kiss to his cheek. "She'll come around, my lord. Just give her some space for a while—enough space until she can hardly stand the space anymore. It won't take long. She loves you too much for that."

Ezra nodded once, and Kit disappeared into Miri's old chambers.

CHAPTER FOUR

"Well, well," said Esther, emerging into the foyer. "I never thought I'd see the day that you wore anything other than black."

Ezra looked down, running his hands down the crisp white lapels on his chest as he breathed a nervous laugh, wondering if his suit had been a stupid choice. He never wore white. He had always much preferred the dark sophistication of black. The quiet strength of it.

Now, standing in the foyer of Massahd Castle dressed head to toe in white with a domino shaped like a wolf's snout stuffed into the breast of his tailcoat, he wondered if he looked as stupid as he felt.

"The white suits you," Esther went on with a genuine smile. "You always dress like you're in mourning. Now you've a beautiful wife and no doubt a beautiful family soon to follow. It's time to find joy in life again, don't you think?" She rested a hand on Ezra's arm and pressed a kiss to his cheek.

He ignored his sister's predictions, appreciating that John had obviously not shared with Esther the finer details of their conversation this morning.

"And anyway, I think you look dapper," Esther added.

Ezra snorted a laugh.

"What? No quip about how *everything* looks dapper on you?" Esther added.

"He's nervous." John descended the final step in the foyer. Dressed in crisp gray tails, his suit was perfectly tailored for a formal affair. At his neck hung a gold-and-emerald domino waiting to be donned.

"Where are Leah and John Junior?" Ezra asked.

"With the nursemaid," Esther said. "They'll be along in a moment." Clad in a rich green gown of ripe, spring leaves, Esther looked positively stunning. She wore a crown of leaves on her head, her raven-black curls spilling soft and free down her shoulders and back. John took one look at her, and his eyes practically glazed over.

Ezra afforded them a bit of privacy, turning his back when he saw his brother-in-law reach for his wife. John murmured something for only her to hear, prompting a soft laugh from Esther.

"Are you done yet?" Ezra asked, crossing his arms with his back to them.

"Please," Esther scoffed. "You've hardly kept your hands off of Miri for days now. I think you can stomach a kiss now and then."

"The look in John's eyes would imply a bit more than kissing," Ezra pointed out. When he turned to face them again, he could not help the laugh that escaped at the conceding, mischievous smirk that adorned his sister's face.

"Perhaps *you'll* be the one with a little one on the way again soon."

"Och," Esther scoffed, shooing Ezra away with a hand. "Mind your own business." John, however, had found his wife much more fascinating, his eyes practically glazed with desire as they fixated upon her, uninterested in contributing to the conversation.

"We must leave soon if we do not want to be late," Esther said. "Is she almost ready?"

Ezra was about to state that he wouldn't know—he hadn't seen or heard from Miri all day. Now, well into the evening, it was time to depart for Chesedelle Castle, and he still had no idea if she even remembered today was the Harvest Ball.

A knock sounded at the front entrance, and Ezra turned his attention to the door. A moment later, Thaddeus emerged, opening the door with his shoulders back and his chin high.

A high whistle greeted them the moment the door swung wide. "You clean up nice!" came a raucous voice.

"Cosmas! Vitas!" John said, clasping the two soldiers on the shoulders. "It's been a while, my friends."

"Our extended mountain camping trip has surely proven a worthwhile endeavor," Cosmas said. Raising his pointer finger, he continued, "The business of keeping Massahd safe never ceases!"

Ezra ignored the sarcasm, knowing the smart-mouthed soldier did not mean it disrespectfully. The soldiers had always had a playful nature about them that he had enjoyed.

"You know that I am forever indebted to you both for protecting us," he said, tilting his head to one side.

"Yeah, we know. And now, thanks to the Harvest Ball, His Grace deemed us worthy enough to come in out of the cold," Vitas added, punching Ezra's arm once and hard. Ezra refrained from the indignity of wincing.

"You look...*interesting,*" Esther said to the soldiers.

Interesting indeed. The two soldiers had opted to dress in long white robes, tied at the waist with gold rope. But that's where the similarities ended. Cosmas wore a tall white hat adorned at the top with an ostentatious, gold eight-pointed star. At his neck hung a mask, painted to look absurd—almost intoxicated, obviously intended to mimic the High Priest of Har-Navah.

Vitas, on the other hand, had gold rings at the top of his arms and his lips were smeared with red rouge. He wore a matted blonde wig with a gold comb behind his ear.

An acolyte.

Ezra's heart pounded. "I'm not sure if this is a good idea."

"What's wrong? Jealous you didn't think of it?" Vitas asked, looking down at his robe.

"I doubt His Grace would be caught dead in such a get up. But I thought he might appreciate the satire, all the same." This from Cosmas.

Ezra's heart pounded. If Miri were to see them... "I don't think it's a good id—"

"It's fine," a voice said, the sound echoing slightly in the foyer.

Everyone whirled to see Miri standing at the landing of the staircase.

A high whistle from one of the soldiers behind him gave Ezra a start, but he didn't bother acknowledging it, too caught up in the vision standing before him. Miri stood stock still, clad in a silk gown form-fitted to her slender waist. Her wild, thick curls were down and free, spilling down her breast with reckless abandon, adorned here and there with pearls and diamonds along the glossy strands. One side of her hair was pulled back with a comb, embellished with feathers and butterfly wings. The gown flared from her waist into a wide skirt, edged in intricate, black lace at the bodice, sleeves, and hem. But that was not what made the gown remarkable. What began at her shoulders as a vivid, crimson red gradually faded to a rich, deep ox-blood red at the hem of the skirt. And at her back—those were færy wings spread wide behind her. Jeweled in onyx and diamonds, the wings were of a delicate, gauzy fabric, painted in a pattern to mimic a monarch butterfly.

She looked like an autumnal færy queen.

"Mother of kings, Miri," Esther said. "I had assumed you'd outshine us all. I did not realize you would blind us, too."

Miri looked down, fussing with her skirts as if she was reconsidering her choice of costume for the evening. As if of their own accord, Ezra felt his feet leading him across the foyer and up the few steps to the landing where she stood. He reached to take her gloved hand, to kiss it, but she moved it away before he could.

Another whistle from one of the soldiers. "Ouch. What'd you do to deserve that, Your Grace?"

Ezra turned and leveled a flat look at Vitas, who lifted his shoulders in innocence, the gesture accentuated by his absurd costume. A moment later, someone cleared their throat. Ezra turned to see Kit descending the steps behind Miri.

Miri turned to allow Kit room to stand beside her. The servant looked beautiful in a soft amethyst gown and matching gloves. On her head, she wore two ears fashioned out of delicate, white blooms, and her cheeks were painted with small freckles. She looked like an endearing young kitten.

"You look absolutely lovely, Kit," Ezra said. The maidservant blushed but said nothing, her eyes glancing past Ezra. She started, staring in disbelief for a brief moment before swallowing a throaty chuckle. It was only when he turned that Ezra realized *where* her gaze had settled: on the soldier dressed as an acolyte, who was oblivious. Ezra had half a mind to return the earlier favor and punch Vitas in the arm. Instead, he chuckled to himself.

"Shall we?" Ezra asked. He faced his wife once more, offering her his arm. She did not take it, did not even meet his gaze, descending the last of the steps on her own, her shoulders back and chin high. Ezra followed, swallowing once, doing his best to ignore the sinking feeling in his gut.

CHAPTER FIVE

The ballroom at Chesedelle looked like something out of a dream. Chandeliers floated above the crowd, the intricate gold arms glistening in the flickering candlelight, wax dripping from the edges. At every column, pumpkin vines grew tall, curling and wrapping around the marble. At the base of the columns, plump pumpkins grew in shades of vivid orange, crisp white, and mottled green. The bright, warm scents of cinnamon, cloves, and cardamom wafted through the air—the sign of autumnal cider served generously tonight. And in every direction, noblemen and women filled the room, dressed in their finest. Some wore dominos, some hats or crowns or great diadems of feathers and jewels and pearls. Bears and stags, caracals and wolves, færies and jesters. The court at Chesedelle was a myriad of color and costume flitting about the vast room.

Ezra and Miri led their party as they entered. Though she was on his arm, her nearness was no comfort. She was as cold as ice and had been the entire hour-long carriage ride to the castle. Behind them, John walked proudly with Esther on his arm, their first outing to a royal event in some time. If he hadn't been so preoccupied with figuring out what in the world to do about Miri, Ezra might have laughed at the look on John's face as he emerged onto the grand staircase. He was fairly certain his friend and brother-in-law could have burst with pride.

Behind the family, Kit walked in on the arm of one of the soldiers. Cosmas had offered to escort her, but it was Vitas that she had chosen. The young soldier had gladly accepted, though Cosmas had scoffed at being the only one at the party without a companion. Ezra knew the soldier well enough to know that such a state would not last long.

The page at the entrance to the ballroom gave a slight bow before ticking a mark on the parchment in his hand. Then he turned, his shoulders back and chin high, announcing to the crowd inside, "His Excellent Grace, Grand Duke Ezra Kelach of Kinnereth and Lady Miriam Sasson of Teman."

Ezra stopped the page, leaning past Miri when he said, "You read that wrong."

Somewhat affronted and certainly not used to being interrupted, the page raised a brow and said, "I beg pardon?"

"It is Her Excellent Grace Grand Duchess Miriam Kelach of Kinnereth and His Grace Ezra Kelach."

"I—" The flustered page seemed at a loss for words. "I am sure it was written wrong."

"No, it was correct," Ezra said. "I returned the response weeks ago. Now please read it correctly."

"Your Grace," said the page, clearly hesitant.

Miri let out a giggle that sounded obviously forced to anyone who knew her. "Ezra, dear, you shouldn't tease so. He doesn't understand your sense of humor."

Before Ezra could protest, she turned to the page and said, "He takes to the bottle much too early in the morning these days, wouldn't you say?"

The page's eyes were wide, his lips in a flat line. Clearly unsure what to say to that, Miri patted his arm. "It's fine, darling. Keep reading."

The page cleared his throat. "Erm... Mister and Missus John Rennius." John and Esther stepped proudly beside them.

Ezra leaned in, whispering sarcastically in Miri's ear, "Clever."

She did not deign to respond.

"Captain Vitas and Captain Cosmas of His Majesty's army," the page went on, his resounding voice echoing across the ballroom. "And Mistress... erm... Kitty."

He spoke the servant's name with a hint of snobbish disdain, but Kit didn't seem to notice or care, her eyes bright with delight and wonder as she stared around her. She was likely the only servant in attendance tonight. When Ezra had seen the way she fawned over Esther's gown, he hadn't been able to resist asking her to join them. The servant had been first shocked, then all too delighted to accept the offer. And when he had seen her descend his steps tonight, blushing and hopeful, he was glad he had invited her. Of course he was breaking about a dozen different societal protocols having her here. But then again, he had already done that the moment he married Miri. Much to his mother and father's chagrin, he had never given a damn about aristocratic protocol. Just like his grandfather before him. He wasn't about to start now.

Behind him, the party dispersed among the crowd, finding friends and acquaintances. From the corner of his eye, he saw Vitas and Cosmas take up strategic places on opposite ends of the room, their keen eyes scouring the crowd for any sign of problems. Ezra was confident tonight would not present any trouble. He would never have brought Miri here if there was a chance it would be dangerous.

No, this was nothing more than a dance. A party. Nothing political. Certainly nothing religious. No one but the nobility of the kingdom would be in attendance.

They hadn't heard a single word about Phinehas or Ambassador Phocas in weeks. Most of the rumors centered on Phocas, who was said to have gone into hiding since the day Ari had saved Miri from being disemboweled for all to witness in the Shalem village square. But as for Phinehas, he had lain low since that day, keeping to his duties as High Priest in the temple at Shalem, not bothering to hold any meetings of the Sanhedrin—the holy council—in weeks.

Which was the only reason Ezra had felt comfortable bringing Miri here tonight. The soldiers had been invited to give Miri a measure of peace, nothing more.

Ezra kept moving forward, deeper into the ballroom. Miri remained as silent as a statue beside him. Mother of kings, he wondered if she had any idea the spell she cast on him, what with those shoulders back, that chin high. She was perfection, even in her disdain. And he wanted her so badly he could barely stand it.

"It has been a long time since I've been to one of these," he said, leaning close to her. He was trying to make conversation, but Miri did not so much as nod. As they walked, her wings, which he had learned in the carriage ride were a handmade gift from Kit, tapped his back with each of her steps, as if encouraging him to keep trying.

"What can I do to apologize, Miri?" She did not answer. "Will you at least hear me out?"

Ezra thought perhaps she was going to respond, her chin lifting ever so slightly. But he did not get a chance to find out before they were interrupted.

"Your Grace," came a familiar voice. He turned his attention to the Crown Princess of Har-Navah standing before him, dressed in a gown of vivid colors and feathers. Next to her stood Gian of Borras, dressed as usual in leather pants and a plum brocade jacket adorned with far too many buttons down the front.

Considering how their last conversation had ended, he shoved down the urge to punch the bastard in the face and instead put on a smirk that he knew didn't reach his eyes.

"Your Royal Highness," Ezra said, then cut his eyes to her companion. "Didn't bother with a costume tonight, Gian?"

Gian smirked, the turn of his mouth wolfish and irreverent. "The lady prefers my usual attire."

Rachæl scoffed, rolling her eyes. "He's a caricature. But tonight, his insistence on ostentatious pirate fashion at least blends in."

Gian kept his smirk and took a bow. "A man aims to please."

At Ezra's side, Miri knitted her eyebrows, and he followed her gaze back to the princess, silently agreeing with Miri's reaction. There was something decidedly different about Gian here, the way he stood beside Rachæl. Something that looked a lot like... familiarity. Comfort. Casualness.

Ezra wondered what in all the realms of Sheol would convince Rachæl that Gian was a man to be trusted. Worse, had Gian become her friend? The thought made him sick to his stomach.

"Let me guess," Ezra said, turning his attention to his former betrothed. "A bird?"

"A bird of paradise," she corrected proudly, gesturing to the voluminous skirt of bright cerulean and amber plumage.

"A pirate and a parrot?" Miri asked.

As if the idea had only just dawned on Rachæl, her eyes widened.

Gian chuckled, crossing his arms across his chest. "You know I've always considered her something of a pet, after all."

"You're an insufferable ass," said the princess. Gian held her gaze, lingering on her eyes.

For far too long.

Ezra swallowed back a barrage of retorts, each less savory than the last and instead said, "You look lovely, Rachæl." He took her hand and pressed a perfunctory kiss to her brightly-colored glove.

Rachæl looked him over once. "A white wolf? How whimsical of you."

He nodded his head. "The legends of the wolves date back generations. I thought I'd pay homage to their importance in our kingdom's lore."

"I suppose it's only fitting, considering your family owns the legendary Adelaidian furs," said Rachæl.

At this, Gian's face shone with something Ezra could only define as a pirate's curiosity. He resisted the urge to inform Gian that he'd never get a chance to lay his hands on such a treasure.

Rachæl turned her attention to Miri. "And you must be the one everyone is talking about. Lady Miriam, is it?" The princess held out her hand, and Miri took it with a curtsey. Miri cut her eyes to Gian, who held her gaze with something heavy. Serious.

The man could have helped her. All those months at the temple in Shalem and Gian did nothing to protect Miri. Or any of the acolytes. Nothing.

Ezra's hand fisted at his side.

Rachæl flaunted a triumphant grin, breaking the spell. She looked at Ezra, then back at Miri. "So it's true. Our dear Ezra has at last deemed someone worthy to be his wife."

"His *wife?*" Miri asked. She let out a guttural laugh. "You seem to be severely misinformed, Your Highness. I am simply his whore."

Gian tipped his head back and barked a laugh. A cough erupted from the princess's throat before she said, "I beg your pardon?"

"Oh, was I not supposed to say anything?" Miri asked, raising a mocking hand to her breast. "Silly me. I forget which part I'm supposed to play these days. It's terribly confusing you know—being a duke's concubine can be a demanding task."

Rachæl's eyes grew as wide as harvest moons, but she could not seem to find anything to say. At her side, Gian could not stop the laugh that shook his shoulders.

Flabbergasted, Ezra moved Miri closer to him with a firm hand on her waist. "You'll forgive us, but I see someone I must greet. Have a lovely evening, Your Highness. Gian." With a slight bow, Ezra ushered Miri away from the crowd and to the side of the room.

"I suppose you think that was funny," he said, half tempted to shake sense into her, half ready to double over in a fit of laughter.

"Dear me, did I say something wrong?" Miri asked, raising her brows in false innocence.

"Miri." He leveled a flat stare at her. "What was the purpose of that?"

"You said tonight was the perfect night to announce what I am to you, didn't you?" She tilted her head to one side. "I thought I'd help things along."

"And so you are my paramour now, is that it?"

"What else am I?"

"Well, I had thought you were my *wife*," he said, emphasizing the word she refused to use.

"Oh, you just *couldn't* have me as a wife, Ezra. I'd ruin you. No, it's best if we call a spade a spade. After all, I've only ever been a whore. I cannot see any reason for that to change."

Ezra took both of her wrists firmly in his hands and forced her to meet his eyes. "Miri. I told you not to use that word."

"Whatever you want to call me, my lord. I am at your bidding."

"Stop."

"Whatever do you mean, master?"

"Miriam."

Something in Miri's face shifted. Gone was the feigned, wide-eyed innocence. In its place was something hard. Unforgiving.

"*You* stop. I'm tired of playing your damned games. And I'm tired of pretending like this is anything but what it is."

"And what is it?" he asked. The question came out more harshly than he had intended.

"A fool," she said, gesturing to his white tails and trousers. "Fancying himself to be a great white hero."

With that, she whirled, marching away and into the crowd.

"What the Sheol did she tell the princess?" John asked, standing beside Ezra as they fetched drinks from a long table.

"That she is my personal whore."

John nearly choked on his wine. "What?"

"Apparently, that's what I think of her. That I am a hero trying to save a whore."

"What in the world is she getting at?"

"I don't know," Ezra admitted. He didn't even know where to begin. "I just don't know."

"Everyone is talking about you and you haven't been here a half an hour. Why do you have a knack for bringing this kind of shit upon yourself?"

Ezra watched Miri across the room. She talked freely with Kit and Esther, sipping from a crystal glass of sparkling wine.

"I'll be damned if I know."

"All of this because you didn't sleep with her?" John asked, chuckling to himself. "Damn, Ezra. I thought your sister could be laborious."

Ezra leveled a flat look at John, who only raised his eyebrows and smirked. He reached out and clapped Ezra on the shoulder. "Good luck, my friend. That's all I know to tell you."

"ARE you going to dance with him or not?" Miri asked Kit, who stood shoulder to shoulder with her on the edge of the dance floor. Ezra stood engaged in conversation with some lord of this or that at the opposite end of the room, while John and Esther danced in the center of the room, not bothering to hide their delighted grins. Miri laughed to herself at their uninhibited exuberance.

"Even I have my scruples, Miri," Kit said with a giggle.

"Scruples?" Miri asked with a raised eyebrow.

"Oh, he'll have to ask me. Mother always told me it's no good for a woman to make the first move."

The side of Miri's mouth quirked up. "Oh really?"

Kit watched the soldiers just down the way. She hadn't been wrong in her description of Vitas. Or Cosmas. They were both about as formidable as an oak tree, all muscle and sinew, standing with their thick arms crossed as they assessed the ballroom.

She supposed she should have been offended by their choices in costume tonight. But she had found it humorous, if a bit off-color. Vitas's acolyte look was particularly absurd—as if polished, perfect Galina had taken to the bottle first thing in the morning and never stopped. Miri would have loved to see the look on the snooty acolyte's face if she saw the soldier's garb.

Cosmas's rendition of Phinehas hadn't bothered her either, considering the soldier looked nothing like the real High Priest. No, Cosmas looked more like a stone battlement standing guard. His mocking costume was in stark contrast to his watchful eyes and hard face as he scanned the ballroom from the edge.

Watching it. For Miri. To protect her. Just in case.

Ezra had given her a litany of assurances in the carriage that she would be safe tonight. Though she hadn't said a word, she had privately hoped he was right.

So far, the Harvest Ball had proven as uneventful as he had described it. Nothing more than a chance for the nobility to dress in costume and a mask and parade themselves about a ballroom, complimenting one another.

The masks did nothing to make her comfortable, since she couldn't see the faces beneath. But she reminded herself for the dozenth time that Phinehas would never reduce himself to costume. It wasn't in his nature. And he wasn't invited, anyway. Neither was the ambassador. Tonight was a party for the Har-Navarian nobility and no one else.

No one else.

"Everything all right?" Kit asked.

Miri turned her attention to her maidservant. "You look beautiful, Kit." The girl's cheeks turned a becoming shade of pink, but Miri went on. "You should at least talk to him."

The servant's eyes fell on the soldier across the way once again, a look of innocent longing on her countenance.

Without taking her eyes from Vitas, Kit said, "I could say the same to you."

"What?" Miri asked.

Kit smirked. "Don't pretend like the whole of the Massahd household isn't privy to your affairs, Miri. Whatever happened between you two...let's just say Ezra is not going to lose that pathetic look on his face until you speak with him again."

Miri glanced across the room at Ezra, still engaged in conversation with a nobleman. Even from so far away, she could see the slump to his broad shoulders, the anguish in his eyes.

"Was it the chemise?" Kit asked, her words small, her voice worried.

Miri looked at the servant again. "It was me. It will always be me."

THE SKY WAS CLEAR, the stars particularly bright as Miri leaned on the balcony balustrade. Unlike Massahd Castle, Chesedelle did not boast views of a vast, glassy lake surrounded by towering mountains. Instead, it was engulfed by mountains on three sides. The entire back end of the castle was nestled into the heart of one of those mountains, giving the feeling that the castle itself was part of it. It was beautiful—a færytale come to life.

But it paled in comparison to the towering majesty of Massahd Castle. Her home.

Still, the cool night was crisp, and the fresh air did her good.

She hadn't meant to set tongues wagging. She hadn't realized her antics would cause such a stir. But within moments of announcing herself as Ezra's personal companion, she was hearing the rumors about herself from other people. It was only then that she realized what a scandal she had created—that the former betrothed of the crown princess had shown up with a lightskirt on his arm.

She had not meant for it to go that far.

But she hadn't known how to stop herself, either.

Never once in her life had she been more hurt than last night. Never once had she felt more humiliated. More stupid.

More unwanted.

She had not been able to crawl out of Ezra's chambers fast enough.

Trembling, Miri gripped the rail before her, digging her nails into the ancient stone.

"Careful," came a voice from behind her. "You'll tear the castle down."

She looked over her shoulder to see Ezra emerging onto the

dim balcony. Quickly, she turned away, back to the vista of mountains that stretched on for miles before her.

"Am I allowed to join you out here?" he asked.

She shrugged.

Ezra breathed a sigh and rested his arms on the balustrade not far from her. He did not look her way, nor did he say anything else. She had wanted to tell him how perfect he looked tonight in those white tails and top hat. The wolf mask he wore over his eyes only added to the mystique, the splendor. He was beautiful.

Plain and simple, Ezra Kelach was beautiful.

But she had not told him. Because she had not spoken more than three words to him all day.

As the minutes stretched between them, she grew more and more antsy, waiting for him to say something. Anything.

He did not.

She knew she owed him an apology. But from where she stood, he owed her a much greater one. She wondered who would speak first.

"I'm not sure whether I should be amused or terrified by your ability to flay me so thoroughly."

Ezra's words were tinged with dark humor. She turned her attention to him once more, but he was not looking at her, his attention fixed on the view.

He did not speak again for long moments, and finally, she could not take it anymore. "I have never—not once in my entire life—been more humiliated than I was last night. I have never felt more ashamed. More foolish. I have never felt more like a whore than when you did that to me, Ezra."

At last, the Grand Duke of Kinnereth turned to face her fully. "Help me to understand," he said, but there was nothing placating or peaceful in his words, tinged with desperate frustration. "It is because I did *not* sleep with you that you feel like a whore?"

Miri fumbled, at a loss for words. “Don’t—turn this around, Ezra,” she said, flustered. “I—you—that was humiliating!”

“Miri,” Ezra said, moving towards to her. He stopped himself before he got close. “It was certainly not my intention to humiliate you.”

“Then what was your intention?” she demanded, crossing her arms. “I came to you. I—offered you everything. And you threw it away like trash!”

He moved again, a little nearer. Still, he did not come close enough to touch her. “That is not what happened!”

“I finally understand you, Ezra. It took me a while to put the pieces together—to make sense of you. But I see it now. I saw it clearly last night.”

“Pray, do enlighten me,” he said, crossing his arms.

So she did. “You want me, Ezra. I do not think you would deny it. But you are at odds with yourself. You are at odds because you cannot reconcile that wanting with who you are. And who I am. Because no matter how much you try to paint a different picture, nothing will change the fact that you’re a grand duke. And I’m a whore.

“And you know it. Deep down, you know it’s true. It will never change. You cannot change who you are. I cannot change who I am. You can dress me up and call me a duchess. You can call me your wife and paint an idyllic picture for the world. But they will never buy it. And neither will you.

“So when I came to you—when I offered myself to you, you wanted me. I know you did. But you know—deep down you know —I will ruin you. I will be the death of you. Your family name. All of it. And you should not have me. You *cannot* have me. Not as your wife. Not as your lover. Not as anything.

“Because I am a whore. And it is all I will ever be.”

Ezra stood frozen before her, searching. His eyes seemed to pierce right through her. “*That’s* what you think?” he said at last.

"Yes," she answered, hating that the word was not as confident as she had intended.

"Why don't you try this on for size?" Ezra moved even closer to her. Close enough to touch finally. Close enough that his breath caressed her face as he spoke. But he did not touch her.

"I love you, Miri. I am in love with you and I have been falling in love with you from the moment we met. And last night, when you came to me, yes, I wanted you. I wanted you so badly I could not bear it. I want you still. I want you right here, right now. And last night I might have taken you—I might have gone through with it except that I saw the truth. I heard it in your words, saw it in your eyes, in the way you touched me.

"You feel like you owe me something. You think you owe me penance for loving you. For bringing you into my life. Miri, you are not a charity case. You are not a project I'm working on. You are the love of my life. You are my heart and my soul, and I would die for you. A thousand times and a thousand times again.

"But I will not have you because you think it is something you owe me. I will not have you because you think you should repay me. When I have you—when I make love to you, Miri—it will be because you know that I love you. And because you know that there is no one else in the world that I could love like this. There is no one else I *want* to love but you. There is no one else I would fight for. Bleed for. No one."

He held her there with nothing but his searing gaze. His chest rose and fell with a steady, insistent cadence as he stood towering over her. Still, he did not so much as run a finger along her hand.

"I—will ruin your reputation," she said.

"It was ruined long ago. Any other protests?"

"You should not love me," she tried.

"I think we've already established that I do anyway. And I always will. Any others?" He moved another fraction, so close that his body was a living flame before her.

“I cannot give you children,” she said. The damning blow. The final straw.

She knew it would break his resolve. She was glad of it. She breathed in, shutting her eyes.

She felt his hands on her shoulders before she opened her eyes. “You do not know that. But regardless, I don’t care. I’m not in love with your womb, Miri. I’m in love with you.”

“You *will* care,” she protested, hating the tears welling, welling, welling. “When you have no heir, you will care.” A fat, heavy tear slipped down her cheek. Ezra leaned close and kissed it away.

“Then we’ll adopt. We’ll adopt a thousand children. There is an orphanage here in Chesedelle City, Miri. So many children that need homes. That need a family who will love them and a home filled with the kind of love we have to give.”

“No one—” She stopped, emotion consuming her. “No one will ever accept me as your wife.”

“They can all rot in Sheol for all I care. Any other objections?”

“I’m running out of them.”

“It’s about damn time.”

Ezra’s kiss was so consuming, so thorough, that she nearly swooned. But he held her close to his solid body and did not let her. He did not let her slip away. Did not let her believe her own lies. Her own demons. He refused to let her fall into the pit she had dug for herself.

So she kissed him back. She kissed him with every measure of the love she bore for him. She kissed him because she wanted to. Needed to. Because he was hers and she was his and no one could take that away. He wouldn’t let them.

He wouldn’t even let *her*.

When his lips parted from hers, his eyes were lit with a smile so big both of them laughed.

“Do you know what I want?” she asked him.

"You tell me and it shall be yours, Wildfire."

"I want our wedding feast. When we get home. I don't want to wait any longer to celebrate with the people we love. And give poor Helena a chance to throw the party she has been dreaming of."

Ezra laughed. "She would be forever grateful, I'm sure." He took her face in both of his hands and kissed her soundly again before he said, "Do you know what I want?" He wrapped her in his arms, running gentle hands down her back waiting for her answer.

She only shook her head, unable to stop trembling with anticipation.

"I want to dance with you. In there," he said, gesturing with his chin towards the ballroom behind them. "I want to tell the world that you are the woman I love."

She took the arm he offered, smiling broadly, and let him lead her inside.

CHAPTER SIX

"You should not kiss me so. A gentleman would never," Miri said biting her lip to keep from grinning like a fool. Ezra did not seem daunted by her half-hearted warning.

"You are my wife. I shall kiss you as often as I want. *Wherever* I want." He whirled her around him, lifting her at the waist as the music swelled. The white mask that covered the top half of his face hid what she knew would be a familiar crinkle near the edge of his eyes. But the short wolf snout of the mask did not cover the dimple by his mouth.

She laughed. "Wherever?" she asked with a raised eyebrow, and Ezra did not miss the scandalous implication. He twirled her once, her body flying effortlessly behind his lead.

When she spun back into his solid arms, he leaned closer than the dance necessitated to whisper in her ear, "Wherever. Whenever." Then he pressed a languid kiss to her neck and ushered her into the dance once more.

Around them, the people were a blur of color and sparkle as she danced with abandon. With a lightness she had only known with him. This man.

This insane, impossible, beautiful man.

She laughed with delight and let him spin her again and again.

Unsure if it was the effects of the dance or perhaps the wine she had sampled earlier, Miri felt a sudden chill in the room—a rushing sort of chill that gave her pause.

"Did you feel that?" Ezra asked. She met his eyes, narrowing her brow as she searched him.

"You felt it, too?"

"There must be a draft," he said, pulling her close before dipping her low. He stood her upright again as the song ended and the dancers clapped merrily. Ezra took the opportunity to kiss her soundly.

"I take it you made up." John held his wife close to his side as they approached from the other side of the room.

"She cannot stay away from me," Ezra said, tucking Miri to his side.

Miri pinched his side, and Ezra chuckled, but she did not bother to protest. It wasn't wrong, after all.

Across the floor, Miri spotted Kit in a conversation with Vitas. The soldier towered over her, but he bent low when she talked and laughed as if he were interested. Miri smiled.

Until another rush of chill brushed her cheek, burning along her skin like the harshest winter winds. On instinct, she pressed her palm to her face.

"What's wrong?" John asked.

"I—" Miri gazed blankly around her, but could think of no logical explanation. She looked to Ezra, whose eyes told her he had felt it, too. But when she looked back at John and Esther, it was clear they had not.

"I need to speak with Miri," Ezra said, pulling her aside almost abruptly.

"What was that?" he asked her the moment they had tucked into an alcove on the edge of the ballroom.

"I don't know," she answered, unable to stifle the chill that ran down her spine. "But something isn't right."

Ezra looked over his shoulder for a moment, scanning the ballroom. Everyone seemed oblivious to whatever she and Ezra had felt. Maybe it was nothing at all. But she could not help but feel otherwise. Trembling, she followed his gaze to where John and Esther had slipped back into another dance. He turned back to face her before he said, "I think we should go home tonight."

She had been about to suggest the same and was grateful Ezra had suggested it first. She did not want to ruin everyone's evening. "Yes," she said, nodding.

"I'll tell the boys. And begin the work of prying my sister and brother-in-law from the dance floor," Ezra said, nodding his head towards the other side of the room. He returned his gaze to her, kissing her softly. "Come," he said. "Let's go home."

EZRA THREADED the two of them through the throng of dancers like needles through heavy fabric. John and Esther were dancing a lively minuet that shifted partners like twirling dandelions upon spring breezes. When at last they reached a laughing Esther and John, stumbling haphazardly through the moves they clearly did not remember, Esther did not bother to hide her disapproval of her brother's interruption.

"I'm sorry," Ezra said. "But I think we should leave. Now."

John took a moment to appraise his brother-in-law. Apparently, whatever John saw in Ezra's eyes was enough for him to acquiesce. "All right," he said, albeit a bit reluctantly.

The four of them made their way through the crowd to the edge of the room where stood the two formidable soldiers and the maidservant flirting with both of them. Cosmas smirked at Kit's attention—a gesture that, coupled with his ostentatious costume, reminded Miri much too much of Phinehas. The thought of the high priest of Har-Navah only added to her sense of urgency.

Something was not right. Something was...off. She had not realized she was clutching Ezra's arm so tightly until his hand rested over hers, giving her a gentle, reassuring squeeze.

"Cosmas," Ezra said. "Tell the footmen to prepare the carriages. We will depart for Massahd tonight."

"Tonight?" Vitas questioned. "I thought we were staying here until the morning."

"Plans have changed," Ezra said. Cosmas did not hesitate to obey, disappearing from the ballroom a moment later while Vitas stayed behind, for their protection, no doubt. Miri did not miss the hand he slipped casually to the sash at his waist. It was only then that she spotted the cleverly hidden sheath and the hilt of a dagger just peeking out between the folds of the robe. She wondered how many more weapons the soldier had hidden in his clothes. Likely many.

It did not bring her the comfort it should have.

As if he sensed her doubt, Ezra's arm tightened around her and she leaned into his embrace.

It was not until several moments later that Miri realized how grateful she was for that arm around her, for had it not been there, she would have collapsed to the floor as a rush of something *other* swept through her whole body.

Darkness.

That was the only way she could describe it. A cold, hollow darkness.

She knew that darkness, that hollowness. She had known it in every grip of Phinehas's spindly hands on her face, in every hateful touch, in every fearsome gaze. In all the years she had known the man, she had never once equated that feeling with anything other than fear. Fear of him. Fear of what he might do to her should she disobey him.

But tonight, in the comfort of Ezra's arms, in the warmth of his strong yet reverent embrace, Miri understood something for the first time in her whole life.

Phinehas had used magic against her. Many times.

Dark Magic.

She knew it like someone had just lit a gas lamp upon the whole story. She knew it in the marrow of her bones.

And then she failed, collapsing on weakened knees. Only Ezra's arm around her kept her from cracking her skull on the marble floor.

Phinehas wielded Dark Magic. He had used it against her. For years.

Just as he was using it against her now.

"Look at me," Ezra said, taking Miri's face in his free hand while he held her up with his other. She felt like a rag doll in his arms, but she made herself meet his eyes. "What happened?" he asked. His question was quiet, though he knew it wasn't soft enough that John, Esther, Kit, and Vitas did not hear it.

Miri could not answer. Not with words, anyway. But at the terror in her eyes, Ezra's stomach turned as cold as ice.

"We need to leave. Now," he insisted.

John seemed to understand, wordlessly ushering his wife and the housemaid before him. Vitas waited for Ezra and Miri to go before him. Ezra nodded once at the soldier as he ushered Miri along. She could walk, thank Providence, but that was all. She seemed stunned to silence.

Heart pounding, every step through that ballroom seemed like an eternity. Ezra clung to the knowledge that it would all be fine when they got in the carriage and headed home.

It would be fine.

Halfway through the corridor that led from the ballroom to the main entrance of Chesedelle Castle, John stopped in his tracks at the sight of Cosmas running towards them.

"What is it?" John asked at the look on the soldier's face.

"The weather, my lord," said Cosmas. "Snow."

"Snow?" Ezra asked. "What snow? The skies are clear. Miri and I were just outside under the stars."

"No, my lord. There is a blizzard," said Cosmas, his eyes wide. "Too much snow to take the carriages."

"That's not possible," Ezra countered.

John and Esther turned to face him, their movement a little stiff.

"We cannot go home in this weather," John said. His eyes were almost absent as he said it, his voice distant.

"This is ridiculous," Ezra said. "It's not snowing." Huffing, he handed Miri to Vitas, who held her upright for him, before he marched across the corridor to a window that he knew overlooked the valley beyond.

But he did not see the clear, gorgeous autumn night he and Miri had just been enjoying on the balcony of the ballroom.

Outside, he saw only white—so much snow that the moon and stars were obscured completely. The only visible light that remained was the smattering of gas lamps on the cobblestone street below, glowing through the whirling snow like færies.

A blizzard.

Ezra paused, gaping at the view out the window, collecting his scattered thoughts.

"We will stay here for the night," Esther said, but her words were mechanical, just like John's had been.

"We're going home. Tonight," Ezra insisted with one look at Miri, who was visibly trembling in the giant soldier's arms.

He crossed the corridor in three steps before pulling Miri to his chest and holding her tightly. "I'll get you home. We're going home right now."

"All due respect," Cosmas said, "but you will die in this storm. I will not allow you to go."

Ezra could make no sense of it—the sudden change in the weather. The way everyone was acting strangely stiff and distant. He could have rationalized the cool air he and Miri had felt earlier as a result of the weather, except that he could not explain such a drastic change in such a short amount of time. And certainly not this early in the season.

He could make no sense of any of it.

And that's how he knew something was very, very wrong.

"Cosmas," he said suddenly. "I want you and Vitas to stay in our suite tonight. You can take turns sleeping in the common room, but I want one of you on watch all night."

"Are we in danger?" The question came from Kit, who looked like a child behind the giant soldier, Vitas.

"No, we're not in danger," said Cosmas. "It's just some snow."

"Nonetheless, you will stay in our chambers. All of us will," Ezra said. He turned to the housemaid, who looked as scared as she looked confused. "I'm sorry you'll have to sleep in the common room tonight, Kit. I will make it up to you."

Kit was eyeing Miri with concern as she said, "It's all right, my lord."

It took them several minutes to reach the suite of chambers reserved for the Kelach family for generations. Nestled deep in the heart of Chesedelle, the rooms were not vast, but plushly accommodating, with a northern view deep into the mountains. John and Esther turned their immediate attention to John Junior and the baby, disappearing into their private chamber and relieving the nursemaid of her duties.

Cosmas, Vitas, and Kit, however, stood silent in the common room that connected all of the sleeping chambers in the suite, watching a trembling Miri with wide eyes.

"I do not want you to stop your watch," Ezra said. "Do you understand? You can take turns on duty, but I want one of you awake all night."

"Should we be concerned, my lord?" Kit asked, watching Miri carefully. Ezra held her close to his side, afraid she would fall if he did not. She had not stopped trembling the entire walk back to their chambers.

"Everything is going to be fine," he said, mostly to reassure himself. "But I will not take any chances. Miri has been through enough. And there are enough people who would like to see her go through more—people deeply connected with the royal family—that I will not take the risk."

"The priest is not here, Your Grace," said Cosmas. "I've assured that myself."

"I know. Which is why we're all going to be fine," Ezra said. "But you will stay on watch regardless."

Ezra looked each one of them in the eye before he turned his attention to Miri. "Come, my love," he said. "Let's get some rest."

Ezra ushered Miri into the bedchamber, depositing her in the middle of the room. He had slept in this room a thousand times throughout his life when visiting the royal family, including when he was betrothed. Never once had he imagined he'd be sleeping here next to his wife—a woman who was not the princess.

Closing the door softly behind him, he turned and faced Miri, standing quiet and unreadable. "I promise you are safe," he said softly.

He was not sure, but he thought she might have nodded her agreement. He crossed the space between them and placed hands on her shoulders, feeling the tremble that had settled into her bones. He began kneading her shoulders softly.

"Miri," he said. He waited until she met his eyes before he went on. "Perhaps a warm bath would help."

This time, he was certain she nodded, so wrapping an arm around her waist, he ushered her to the adjoining bathing chamber.

Like most of the baths in Chesedelle, this one was not exactly a tub. The hollow center of a crystalline rock had been smoothed with time and a skilled hand to be an oddly-shaped, prismatic and pearlescent pool, vast enough for five or six people to rest comfortably. Utilizing the golden spout at one end, Ezra began filling the bath with steaming water and then turned to face Miri again.

She watched him silently, as if trapped in a spell. As if she, too, could not fathom what it was they had both felt in the ballroom.

Ezra did not want to know what it meant. He just wanted to keep Miri safe and warm, to comfort her until they could get home.

Home, where they could start their lives together as husband and wife. The thought brought a small smile to his mouth.

"What is it?" The question surprised him, and he stepped to Miri's side, lifting one of her hands to slide off the black silk glove adorning it.

"I'm just smiling about the fact that you are my wife."

A meek, hesitant smile found her mouth, too, and Ezra reached to doff her other glove. He laid both gloves carefully across a small table near the edge of the stone pool. The steam from the water began filling the space, casting a hazy, halcyon glow about them.

Ezra turned Miri around, working the delicate pins and

fasteners that held the intricate butterfly wings to her back. Once they were off, he began undoing the numerous small buttons that trailed down her back. His mind immediately flashed to the night before—to that silken robe and the lace chemise beneath and the way her skin had glowed in the candlelight of their chambers at Massahd. To the look in her eyes as she let that swath of lace fall to the ground.

He swallowed, willing his fingers not to tremble as he moved further and further down the glorious gown. The dress was loose and falling to the ground before Ezra realized it. But the corset beneath was a complicated weaving of ribbon, and Ezra could make no sense of where to even begin unfastening it.

Miri breathed a shallow laugh at his hesitation. "The stays are tucked beneath the corset," she offered, turning a bit to show him where and how to begin removing the last of her clothing. He stepped back, looking to where she pointed and wondering if she was trembling still from her fright, or from something else now...

Despite the complex lacing, the silk stays untied easily and soon Miri's corset was loose. She did not stop him as he reached around her to remove it. The chemise beneath was a soft, gauzy fabric that did little to hide the glorious curves beneath, the steam from the bath now filling the whole bathing chamber, surrounding her as if she had willed it from the heavens herself.

Miri herself removed her chemise, pushing the delicate sleeves from her shoulders and letting the fabric fall to her feet. For a moment, Ezra was not sure what to say. What to do next. What he had even begun undressing her for.

Miri turned, a soft smile ghosting across her mouth. "The bath is almost full."

Bath. Right.

Ezra abruptly turned, nearly tripping over his own feet, which had somehow grown cumbersome and clumsy, as if he had been sampling whiskey for the better part of a week. He turned the spigot and waited for the water to stop before he stood upright again and faced her. Not knowing what else to do, Ezra took her face in both of his hands and kissed her—a soft, tender kiss that simultaneously lasted much too long and ended much too soon.

Something in Miri seemed to relax at the sight of that vast, steaming bath, and she stepped towards it, dipping a graceful toe into the waters.

"Too warm?" he asked.

"Perfect," she said. She took the hand he extended and let him help her step into the pool. The ends of her lush curls had turned shiny in the steam, and they tapped the curve of her backside as she stepped deeper and deeper into the waters. It was only then that Ezra realized she still wore the comb fashioned of butterfly wings in her hair. He reached for it, pulling it free and letting the rest of her curls fall wild down her back. She smiled over her shoulder and lifted her heavy tresses as she at last sank into the depths, resting her head on the edge and spilling her hair behind her, the water lapping gently at her breasts. He watched her there for a moment—his goddess of fire and flame—as she closed her eyes and inhaled deeply before letting out a long, slow breath as if to expel every worry, even if only for a moment.

Then, turning towards the pile of her clothing nearby, he pulled a ribbon from her corset and knelt behind her.

"What are you doing?" she asked drowsily.

Gathering her curls into one hand, he threaded the ribbon beneath them, attempting to tie her hair as he spoke. "I thought you might like it out of the way." Her curls were heavy—thick strands with a mind of their own. After a few tries, he was able to pull her hair up, the result looking somewhat like a bird's nest atop her head. When he finished, she reached up, feeling his work and breathing a slight chuckle.

"Not bad for your first try."

"I'll get better at it," he said.

Miri smiled. And that smile... That smile could have started wars. And ended them. There was light and heat and joy and peace in that smile. So he knelt lower, bending over her so that his face was hovering upside down and kissed her again.

"I will leave you to it," he managed to say at last, standing again and gathering her things.

"Leave?"

He stilled, turning to face her, desperate not to mistake her meaning.

He had not.

Tenderness. Invitation. And somehow behind that vulnerability, a willful determination to not let worry win.

His Wildfire, burning bright and fearless.

His heart began to pound in his chest.

"I was hoping you'd stay," she said. And in those five words he did not hear seduction; he did not hear penance or remorse or apprehension. He heard a loving request—he heard the woman he loved.

So Ezra fumbled with his suit, the many layers a sudden burden as he unbuttoned and removed and dropped one piece after another. He reminded himself there was no need to rush. No need to hurry. No need to be shaking like a damned aspen leaf. But as Miri watched him, as her eyes slid to the scar that marred his belly beneath his shirt, he trembled. He could not help it.

When only his drawers remained, he was both surprised and slightly relieved when Miri turned her attention away from him. "Are you embarrassed, Wildfire?" he asked with a laugh.

"No, I—well, I've never seen you before, have I?"

"No, I suppose you have not," he said, slipping his drawers to the floor and stepping to the edge of the pool. He did not bother to test the water. He would not have given a fraction of a damn if it had been boiling. He would have gotten into it anyway—would, in fact, have jumped in if the occasion had necessitated it.

To his surprise, Miri turned her attention back to him, taking in his bare chest, his stomach and the scar across it, then lower... When she looked him in the eye again, she smiled softly.

Ezra smiled, too, at last sinking into the waters. And indeed, the temperature was perfect.

Only a small space separated them, but it felt like it might as well have been a mile. Shaking like a leaf in an autumn wind, Ezra did not know what to do, what to say next, where to begin.

But Miri did.

She moved through the water towards him, laying a warm hand on his chest as she craned her neck and kissed him soundly. And at the feel of her warm body against his, weightless in the swirling water, and her soft skin, somehow even softer in the bath, Ezra was a bowstring pulled taut, all of his thoughts focused in on her. On Miri.

On his glorious wife.

She broke the kiss and held his face with her hand. "I love you," she said. "Ezra, I do."

"I know, my Wildfire." He leaned in, pressing a kiss to her neck just below her ear. "I know," he said again.

She wrapped her arms around his neck and moved towards him so fluidly, so effortlessly that he did not realize her intentions. But as soon as he understood what she wanted, he shifted so that she might sit astride his lap. Trembling, he ran gentle hands along her back as she pressed her forehead to his.

"All of me... I want you to have all of me. I do not want to leave any part of me behind," she said softly, pulling back so she could look into his eyes. His hands stilled on her back as she went on, and he held her gaze intently.

"I realized something, Ezra. Something that took me a long time to understand. You see, I've always known that you were not like other men. You're different. Different because of the way you look at me. The way you treat me. The way you've always treated me. The way you love me.

"But I understand it now. Something I hadn't before. You see, you might think that in this moment I am the one with all the experience. That I am the one who knows just what to do. But the truth is Ezra, in this—in love—I am the virgin. I am the one who has never known it. Not before you. Not this kind of love, anyway. You're the one who knows it—who knows it well and gives it freely. You're the one who is teaching me."

Something in his heart cracked at her words, like a dam splitting open. He did not stop the tear that fell freely down his cheek. He took Miri's lips with his own and kissed her soundly, thoroughly, coaxing and tasting and touching her. Showing her what she meant to him, how much he loved her, how much he needed her.

John had been right. He had no words in this moment—no words to convey what he felt in his heart for this woman.

But tonight, he would not need words.

Breaking the savage kiss, Ezra reached up and pulled at the ribbon he had only moments ago tied into her hair, letting the curls fall freely down her back and arms. The humid steam had made them even more shiny and rich than usual. A smile turned the corners of her glorious mouth as he let her hair fall and she leaned forward, the warm water sloshing between them.

"I'll never understand why you like this mop of curls."

"They are a living flame, my love. I cannot get enough of them."

He ran his hands through the thick locks as she leaned forward and kissed him again. He reveled in the feel of her skin against his, her plump breasts pressed against him, her slender waist, her lush hips. She was his and he was hers and nothing would come between them again—he would be sure of it this time.

So he took hold of her hips, gently coaxing her to adjust, to move just enough that he might take her, body and soul.

She broke their kiss and met his eyes. “Ezra,” she breathed, her body trembling beneath in his hands.

He moved a fraction—just a fraction, her thighs on either side of his waist, her hands on his shoulders. And despite the warmth of the bath, the heat of her spread through him, consuming body and soul. Living flame, indeed. He reminded himself to slow down, to breathe, to savor every second. She deserved nothing less. He *wanted* nothing less.

Ezra held her eyes, taking in a breath as she seated herself onto him.

He could have shattered into a thousand pieces right then, but she stilled. Gentle. Patient. As if she understood that he needed to catch up to himself. She stilled long enough that he met her gaze. Held it. Her lips curled into a broad smile, and in that moment, he knew for certain—he would never have enough of her. Taste enough of her. Feel enough of her.

But he was certainly going to try.

She resumed her movements again—gentle, unhurried laps, like waves on Lake Yerah—and he held on to her hips, his only anchor in this sea of warm, foamy water and his even warmer wife.

He reveled in her beauty, gazing at her eyes, slightly closed, and her lips, slightly parted. She tipped her head back and took a deep, shuddering breath, squeezing his shoulder gently with her soft, delicate hands as she moved with expert grace—a dancer performing a flawless ballad. And he did not stop himself from moving with her, from matching her cadence with his own, leaning into her movements, pressing kisses along her shoulder, her neck, that inviting place below her ear where her curls tickled his nose.

And then as he felt her body tense, he could not help it. He leaned back again to watch her. To marvel in the moment as his wife took her pleasure in long, luxurious movements. To use every ounce of restraint to wait for his own until he finished watching her, until he knew she had found what he so desperately wanted to give. She cried out—utterly sated, utterly rapturous.

And it was his undoing.

He cried out with her—a dam breaking in a mighty, rushing wave. She held him through the throes of it, moving with him until he collapsed against the crystalline lip of the tub.

She leaned forward, pressing her lush breasts against his chest, and kissed him savagely, threading her long fingers through his hair and touching her brow to his, silent.

He rested heavy arms around her hips, clasping his hands behind her back.

After what seemed like an eternity, she sat up, her smile reaching her eyes as she searched his face. He could not help it—he smiled, too.

He took in a breath to speak, unsure what he was going to say. What could he say to something like that?

You're the love of my life.

Inadequate at best.

That was incredible.

A paltry word for such a moment.

I will never have enough of you.

Selfish and true all at once.

But before he could make a sound, something cold and unwelcome moved along his skin. Like a serpent in the grass, it slithered between them, rendering him frozen beneath her touch.

He could not move. He could not speak. But he could see her, and he watched the heady satisfaction in her eyes slowly melt into something like horror. He tried to move. To say something. Anything. To ask what was happening.

But he could not move.

And he could not speak.

Then he felt it—a draft—the same one they had felt in the ballroom earlier this evening. But it wasn't actually a draft. It was not the effects of the inexplicable blizzard outside. Not directly, anyway.

This was something else.

Something dark.

To the marrow of his bones, he felt that darkness spread. Capture. Seize.

He tried again to speak—desperately coaxing his throat and lungs to cooperate. They did no such thing. He wanted to writhe against the cold, the darkness encroaching upon him. He wanted to scream out against it. But he could not as the world around him slowly slipped into black nothingness.

Ezra's eyes fluttered closed and his head lolled back, limp like a rag doll. Miri reached down just in time to cradle his neck and keep him from cracking his skull on the unforgiving stone lip of the bath.

"Ezra," she said, shaking him gently. He did not stir. She bent down, pressing an ear to his bare chest. His heart beat steadily beneath his skin, his breast rising and falling with small breaths. But nothing more.

"Ezra." She tried again to wake him, panic welling as suddenly as a streak of lightning across the sky. That darkness, that cold that had slithered along her very bones. She knew he had felt it, too. She could see it in the way his whole body had stilled, frozen under that chilling draft that was no draft at all.

Tears slipped freely down her cheeks. "Ezra, please. Wake up," she tried. "Please."

With his eyes closed and his face expressionless from sleep,

Ezra spoke. “That’s a good girl,” he said. But his voice was not his own, as if two voices spoke at once. “Come to me, my dove,” he went on. “Be a good girl now.”

And Miri knew who was speaking to her.

Ice settled in her gut. She closed her mouth and breathed in once through her nose, steeling herself. Shoulders back, Miri rested Ezra’s head gently on the lip of the pool and stood from the warm waters of their bath, the water sluicing down her skin like blood. She did not bother with a towel or a robe. Nor did she bother to dry herself off. She simply walked, one step after another, towards that voice. The voice that had come from Ezra but was not his.

She crossed the cold marble of the bathing chamber towards the door that separated it from the bedchamber. She held her shoulders back and her chin high, emerging into the darkened room without a word—without even a sound.

Phinehas stood before her, a serpentine smile on his mouth.

“That’s a good girl,” he said, tilting his chin to one side. “How I have missed you, my little dove.”

“Get out,” she breathed, the words a growl in her throat.

“You aren’t even going to ask me how I got in? How careless of you,” said Phinehas. When Miri did not speak, he grinned and went on. “The soldiers were a nice touch. Too bad they’re ignorant of anything but brute force. I would have been here sooner if it weren’t for them. But in the end, they were, of course, no match for me.”

“Get out,” she said again, this time with a snarl.

“You left me, my darling. You left without even saying goodbye,” the priest said.

“You gave me over to him,” she said, memories of the ambassador, of his brutality, his rancid smell washing over her. Nausea roiled in her gut. “You let him brutalize me. You did nothing to stop him.”

Something in his eyes shuddered for a fraction of a moment, there and gone again. Then the High Priest steeled himself once more, raking cold eyes along her body, naked before him. But there was no lust in his gaze. Only chilling, hard possession.

She narrowed her eyes and gritted her teeth.

"So strong, my dove. How you've changed," he said.

"I am not afraid of you anymore."

A lie. But one she desperately wanted to believe.

A smile curled his mouth. "Pity. I like it better when you whimper."

"Rot in Sheol," she spat.

"I cannot, my darling. I am the servant of Providence."

"What do you want?"

"You know what I want. You've known since the day we met. But you keep it from me. You've lied to me—as long as we've known each other. You've lied and hidden from me. You've lied to your priest. To the high priest of Har-Navah."

She swallowed, squaring her shoulders and willing—no, *forcing* herself to retain her composure.

"Be a good girl now," he went on. "Tell me the truth."

"There is no truth between us. There never has been. Only lies. All of it was a lie."

Phinehas grinned. "Tell me where you hide it."

"I don't know what you're talking about."

He moved then. One step towards her, like a caracal on the prowl through tall grasses.

"Tell me where you hide it, my dove, and you can go back to mounting your precious duke."

She did not wince at his words; she did not let herself think on how he should know that. What evils had given him the power to overcome Vitas and Cosmas. To come in here undetected. To overcome Ezra without so much as touching him.

"Release whatever darkness you have on him and leave us alone," she said, her words more forceful than she felt.

"Oh, but you see," said Phinehas, "I cannot do that. Not until you give me what I want."

"I have nothing you want."

"Well, that is true. Except for one thing." He tilted his head to one side and stepped towards her with slow, deliberate steps. "Why do you think I went to all this trouble for you? Keeping you alive, fed, well? Why do you think I took such risk to eliminate your family? To eliminate anything that would stand in the way?"

Her breath picked up, a rhythm to match the pounding of her heart. "You killed them. My parents. There was never any debt, was there? No stranger came for my father's estate and holdings. It was you. You used my father's trust to get what you wanted. Then you killed him to use his riches to become High Priest."

Phinehas's face slowly curled into something horrifying—his brows low, his mouth closed and curled slightly at the corners, his eyes glowing with triumph. "Perhaps you're not as stupid as I thought."

"You can have it—every bekah you took from my family. I don't care. I don't need you anymore, Phinehas."

"What will you do, my little spider? When he tires of the whispers? Of the nasty things they say about him? About his little wife? What will you do when he finally admits that he made a mistake? Where will you go, my sweet Miri? What will become of you?"

"He won't," she countered, hating how the words found their mark and made her quail inside. Hating how much she feared them. "He promised."

Phinehas assumed a most unholy smile. "Promises can be broken, little Miri. Or did you forget that you broke your promise to me?"

"I made you no promises," she said, her words low.

He tilted his head to one side. "Didn't you? You promised to help me. And yet you lied to me. Over and over again." He moved toward her again. Closer and closer. "I know you have it. I've seen it. You bear magic, Miri. You used it that day—the day I rescued you from your father's brutality."

"You did not rescue me," she spat. "You enslaved me."

Another smile. "You have magic, Miri. A rare kind. The kind men have whored themselves, glutted themselves, bled themselves to get. You bear it. You wield it.

"Where did you get that magic, Miri? Where does it come from?"

"I—I don't know what you're talking about," she lied, the words pathetic and weak.

"Why do you think I kept you so close all this time, my little dove? Do you think I wanted you? That I loved you?"

"You love nothing but yourself," she growled.

A throaty chuckle was his response. "I love and serve only Providence. It is his calling that drives me."

"Bullshit," she spat. "You serve no one but yourself."

"Careful, darling. Blasphemy is a mortal sin."

"I hate you," she snarled.

He continued creeping towards her, his eyes alight with something dark, sinister.

"You hide from me, my dove. You've been lying all these years, haven't you? I figured it out. You hid from me the amulet of Haravelle. That's what you have, isn't it? It's the only explanation. It's the only way a nobody whore like you could bear such powerful magic."

"Get away from me," she said, hating the step backward that she took. But he was close. Too close. She did not want him to touch her. She did not want him near.

But still he prowled closer. Grinned.

When he reached her, he lifted a hand and ran it possessively down her breast and belly. "You are a lovely thing," he said, his eyes glazing over. "I confess, I've missed you: the way you give in to me so willingly, that little gasp you make when I take you."

She could not stop the tear that slipped down her cheek. Shutting her eyes, she bit her bottom lip to keep it from trembling.

"Be a good girl," Phinehas said, taking her chin between his thumb and forefinger. "Tell me where you hide it."

Miri did not—could not speak.

That thumb and finger tightened on her chin, and the phantom pain of bygone bruises thrummed beneath her skin. A slithering, biting cold spread from his fingers, down her neck and body, out to the tips of her fingers and toes. She froze, unable to move, her eyes still closed, shutting him out.

Silence stretched taut between them. When at last she dared open her eyes again, all she could see was Phinehas's wicked grin.

He gripped her throat, and she could not stop him as he choked the air from her lungs. It was an odd sensation, to tremble inside without the ability to move. He fisted her curls at the back of her neck and yanked so hard that tears spilled involuntarily down her cheeks. But she could not speak. Could not move. Could do nothing to stop him.

Bending slightly, Phinehas licked the column of her throat, all the way up to her chin and mouth. She could do nothing to stop him as he invaded her mouth with his tongue.

Pulling her against him, she could feel his desire beneath the thick robes. Nausea, commanding and unwelcome, turned her stomach, and—unable to stop it—she retched violently down the intricate embroidery of his priest's bib. The sick splattered up the column of his neck, even across his mouth and chin.

Phinehas snarled, shoving her away and down to the floor. She collapsed in a heap of bones, frozen and unable to move. But not from fear.

Magic. His dark magic held her captive on the carpets.

"Filthy whore," he ground the words through gritted teeth, lifting the bib off of his shoulders, wiping his face with a grimace before tossing it aside. He was on his knees before her a second later, simultaneously shoving her knees apart as he lifted the hem of his robe.

"Let's see if your precious duke still wants you when I'm through with you."

Miri shut her eyes and plunged headfirst into darkness.

CHAPTER SEVEN

She was naked. Lying on the bed, her rich, cinnamon curls strewn about her face like kelp washed ashore, Miriam lay face up, her eyes wide and staring blankly into the rafters of the vast bedchamber.

"Miri," Ezra called softly. "My love. Talk to me."

She did not. He tightened the towel slung around his hips, shivering softly in the cold, wintry night air, and took a seat beside her on the bed. His weight shifted the mattress, but Miri did not acknowledge his presence. For a moment, he watched her breasts rise and fall with her breaths, her alabaster skin wan and pale in the shaft of moonlight spilling across the bed.

A moment ago—no, a lifetime ago—he had been in the adjoining bathing chamber with her. A moment ago, they had been tangled in each other's arms in that vast, pearlescent tub, her skin supple beneath his fingertips, her lips eager against his. They had finally reached that threshold between one world and the next—they had crossed the bridge from friends to lovers.

But the moment had been snuffed out.

Like a candle in a wind storm, their intimate bath had faded to blackness. One moment he was in her arms, and the next moment he awoke alone and cold in a glassy bath of what felt like ice water, Miri nowhere to be found.

He had called her name several times to no avail. Slinging a towel around himself after hastily drying off the cold water, he slowly made his way back into the bedchamber of Chesedelle Castle, the faint sounds of the lingering Harvest Ball revelry distant through the crystalline walls. In the chamber, he found the love of his life lying across the bed they were to share tonight.

Awake. Silent. And afraid.

He could not understand the meaning of it.

Had he hurt her? Had he done this to her?

"Miri," he said again, running a gentle hand along her arm. She did not blink, did not flinch. She just stared straight above her, silent and unmoving. He pulled a thick fur blanket up from the foot of the bed, covering her with its warmth before moving to lay beside her underneath it. But when he draped an arm over her middle, she turned away, rolling onto her side.

With her back to him, he could not see her face anymore, could not know what haunted her. But dread, sure and unrelenting, pooled in his gut, forming a lump in his throat. He did not bother to wipe the lone tear that fell down his temple, wishing he could understand. Wishing he could know what she felt, what horrors kept her so distant after such vulnerability, such raw honesty only a little while ago.

But he did not know. He did not understand. Instead, he kept his arm at her waist and tucked her body close to his nonetheless, trembling softly and swallowing hard against the cold darkness that settled into his heart.

PART TWO

CHAPTER EIGHT

"You are expected to attend," said Queen Gelleia. Dressed in a fine gown of rich cerulean silk, Rachæl's mother flung her arms akimbo and lifted a single eyebrow. The tasteful diadem on her brow glittered in the golden sunlight streaming through the windows of the corridor at Chesedelle Castle.

Rachæl sighed. "Mother, this is ridiculous, and you know it. The whole spectacle of it. Why must we parade about like mares at auction?"

"Unfortunately," said the queen, looping her arm through her daughter's, "that is exactly what you are at the moment."

Walking along the corridors outside the king's small council chamber, the morning light spilling in glorious swaths of gold silk along the stone, the queen of Har-Navah ignored the passing courtiers. The crisp silk gown she wore sighed as she walked, a familiar cadence to Rachæl, since it accompanied her mother's every lecture. "It's a woman's role, darling, to breed and smile and throw parties for our kings." As if on instinct, the queen nodded, acknowledging one of the passing courtiers who stopped to curtsey. Once the courtier passed, she donned a false, toothy smile for Rachæl's benefit.

The princess puffed a breathy laugh. "I knew this would happen," she admitted. "The ridiculous spectacle to find me another suitor. I do hate Ezra for it, you know."

The queen leveled a flat look at her.

"What?" Rachæl demanded.

"Hate?" The flat look remained as the queen and princess strolled casually down the corridor as if chatting about the weather. Then again, conversation about the current status of Rachæl's love life was as casual to most at court these days as the weather. She had overheard no less than six conversations about it last night at the Harvest Ball.

"Love and hate, darling, they are masterpieces painted with the same brush, are they not?" asked Queen Gelleia.

Rachæl barely held back a snarl at the question.

She had watched them—the way Ezra and that redheaded whore had smiled and laughed together. The way they had not been able to keep away from each other last night. Despite whatever game the girl had been playing by calling herself Ezra's whore, it was clear to anyone paying attention that she was consumed by Ezra. Deeply in love with him.

And he with her. Maybe more so than she was.

Had he ever looked at Rachæl like that? Even once?

She could not remember a single time.

"Mother," Rachæl said, in lieu of answering her mother's perceptive observation. "Shouldn't you be knitting somewhere?"

The queen of Har-Navah chuckled. "Alas, I've never been very good at all that gentle, quiet submission. Much to your father's chagrin."

Rachæl laughed softly, but the queen leveled her daughter a look that let her know her distraction had not succeeded.

"Do you want me to be in love with him? Do you wish me to

pine over a man who didn't want me?" The words burned like bile in her throat. But it was true, wasn't it? He had chosen another—a whore over a princess. That much was clear last night with the way he could not keep his eyes off the girl.

Nor his hands.

The queen did not relent. "I want you to be honest with yourself. For if *you* cannot be, who can?"

They turned a corner, headed towards the royal chambers. "Why should I love a man who cannot love me?" Rachæl insisted. "I never understood such simpering females, wasting away, brooding over the wrong match." It was the truth, even if, upon facing the prospect for herself, she had found she was not quite as resolved as she would have preferred.

The queen huffed a small laugh. "Wars have been fought over men who did not love the right woman. And over women who loved the wrong man. Never forget that, my darling."

Rachæl pursed her lips, opting not to respond to the unsolicited wisdom.

But the queen's mouth turned up on one side, as if she found her daughter's stubbornness humorous. "I'm not sure I'll ever forgive him for it. He was a fool to let you go."

"Any man would be," said Rachæl, smoothing the front of her dress and squaring her shoulders.

"That's the spirit, my darling," she said, patting Rachæl on the shoulder. "Now cheer up. It's only a ball."

"We just had a ball. Most of the guests are still sleeping off the wine in their guest quarters."

The queen donned a conspiratorial grin. "We haven't had a ball in *your* honor. And now that Ezra has officially announced his wife, it's time you find a husband of your own."

Rachæl scoffed, but the queen ignored it. "Besides, you love to dance."

"Not when I'm chattel to be sold. It's not as if this my season and I'm coming out. It's an excuse to dress me up and parade me before a gaggle of desperate candidates."

"It's an excuse to parade about as the envy of every woman in the world and the object of every man's desire." The queen kissed her daughter's cheek and turned to guide them into the king's private dining room.

Rachæl chuckled. "You are ruthless, Mother."

The older woman looked over her shoulder at her daughter, a gleam in her eyes. "Is there any other way a queen should behave?"

Breakfast was exhausting.

Sitting around the table with her father, mother, and a few mouthy noblemen prattling on and on about the success of the Harvest Ball, Rachæl had been ready to excuse herself, but then the conversation turned to more pressing topics: the treaty with Medinah, the *glorious* empress, and worst of all, the upcoming ball.

But the discussion of those pressing topics still contained nothing to hold her interest, and Rachael sighed to herself as she left the dining room and again traversed the corridors of Chesedelle. She was exhausted already and it was only midmorning. Fortunately, thanks to today's schedule, she faced the prospect of a few hours of peace and quiet in her chambers. Alone. Before an afternoon of meetings, meetings, meetings, with yet more discussion of the same topics that had not enlivened the breakfast table.

She was being an ingrate, of course.

She didn't really care at the moment.

"My lady!"

Rachæl paused, her hand on the door handle, allowing herself a single sigh before turning towards the unfamiliar voice at the other end of the corridor.

The voice called again as she turned to find a man marching towards her, waving a hand as if hailing a cab on the busy city streets of Chesedelle. "I beg your pardon, Your Highness!"

To be called after like a dog—

"You will regret your insolence," she said flatly, crossing her arms. "This is my private corridor."

The man approached, his immaculately waxed mustache looking like a caricature drawn by a circus carney. Dressed impeccably from head to toe, he wore a set of tails adorned with gold fasteners that glistened in the gas lamps along the corridor. His wingtip shoes were freshly polished, made of two different shades of fine leather, and he carried a walking cane as if he were an old man.

Except he wasn't old. Perhaps in his late thirties or so, if the few gray hairs at his temple and in his mustache were any indication.

"My lady," said the man again, bowing when he reached her. A bit out of breath, he stood upright again and smiled toothily. "I am Lord Duriel of Nehar. I was hoping I could meet you before all of the hubbub."

"Hubbub?" Rachæl asked despite herself.

The lord ignored her question, taking her hand and pressing a far too long kiss to the top, the whiskers of his mustache scratching her skin.

"Of course, your father seems to prefer for all of this to remain secret—at least until the time is right. It is a bit like star-crossed lovers, slithering around in the night!" He breathed a throaty chuckle. "Though I cannot say I fully agree, I suppose I can understand his intentions," he added with a chortle. "Nonetheless, I was hoping I would catch you after your breakfast. There is much to discuss. But first things first—an introduction!"

Rachæl pulled her chin backward, pondering which of his absurd declarations to attack first, until she realized she did not have the energy to address a single one of them at the moment. Gods help her, was this what it would be like until she was betrothed again? She could strangle Ezra for leaving her to deal with this.

Defeated, she turned her back to the man, reaching to open her door. "If you would like to be formally introduced, you may present yourself at court like everyone else."

She heard his throaty chuckle, so haughty. "Oh, I believe we're past all of that."

"Excuse me?" she challenged, turning to face him again.

The man didn't seem rattled at all. "What with our impending betrothal, of course."

She raised a single eyebrow. "Your confidence is impressive, I will give you that."

A sleazy smile spread across his dry lips, turning his perfectly-waxed mustache with it. "There will be an official announcement soon, no doubt. And of course, a formal introduction. My family is most delighted to be joining yours. But for now, I thought it best that we meet one on one. I'm sure you agree it's much more romantic this way." He added that last bit with a laugh that set her teeth on edge.

"I am not your betrothed."

"Well, not *officially,* of course. But I am quite certain the king and I will finalize the terms soon. Your dowry is rather more than any of us had realized! And, of course, it would not be right to be cheated, even if I am not a Grand Duke." He twirled his walking cane once, as if the thing were a toy. She noticed it was topped with a gold handle, shaped to look like a strange, hairy creature with great tusks.

"My lord," Rachæl said coolly, breathing an aggravated sigh. "Until my father informs me of such news, I'm uninterested in your speculations. Good day." Turning away from him, she reached for her door handle once more so she might enter the refuge of her chambers. But the arrogant peacock was undaunted and continued his insufferable prattling.

"Oh, all of this pomp—it's only for show. The ball, your presentation. It's just a formality, of course."

Slowly, the princess turned back to face him. "I would not agree that the status of my marriage is a formality, sir."

Sir. An insult to a lord. An honorific for a knight, at best. Not a highborn lord.

He didn't seem bothered by the insult. The lord just laughed. "Your father told me you were in need of a bit of breaking in."

"Breaking in?" She balked. "I am not a horse, sir."

"I am not the first to make the comparison, I'm sure."

Rachæl balled her hands into fists at her side. "Excuse me?"

"Ah! There you are!"

Rachæl turned towards the voice coming from the other end of the corridor.

"You are one difficult princess to track down," said the newcomer.

"Gian," she said, thankful to see him. The irony was not lost on her—to be relieved to replace a presumptuous bastard with an irreverent one. Then again, Gian was practically a saint compared to the peacock currently invading her space.

"I've been looking everywhere for you," said Gian. A grin with a promise of mischief spread across his sensuous mouth.

Rachæl rolled her eyes. "You have?" she asked flatly. Good gods, the men in this kingdom.

"I seem to have misplaced my rum." He completely ignored Lord Duriel, who stood by in a state of affront at the interruption. Rachæl resisted the urge to smirk.

"It is not yet midmorning, Gian, and you go in search of

drink?" When Gian seemed undeterred, she added, "You are honestly a walking cliché."

He crossed his arms, the many silver buttons of his jacket glistening in the gaslight. "I happen to prefer the term traditional," said Gian, bowing at the waist with a grand wave of his arm. "Is it such a crime that a pirate should love his rum?"

"Excuse me, sir," said Lord Duriel, tapping Gian on the shoulder. "I believe you interrupted our conversation."

Gian turned rather dramatically, as if just noticing the lord for the first time. Rachæl knew damn well it was faked—a game he was playing well if the look on Lord Duriel's face was any indication. Rachæl did not miss the smirk that threatened Gian's mouth as he said melodically, "Oh, I did not see you there."

With that, he turned his back to the lord, looking at Rachæl again. "Please say that you will help me, Princess. You know how helpless I am without you."

"You are ridiculous," she said, unable to help the snicker that escaped at his words, so full of melodramatic alarm and implied scandal.

Gian's smirk turned into a wicked smile, his back still brazenly turned to the affronted lord.

"Sir, a gentleman would never interrupt a private conversation," said Lord Duriel. "And he would certainly never ask a lady to go in search of his libation."

"Oh, you needn't get your delicate little underthings in a twist, Your Saintliness," said Gian, deigning to look over his shoulder again to address the lord. "I am the son of a whore. And certainly no gentleman." He faced Rachæl once more, not giving her the option to protest before reaching around her and pushing open the door to her private quarters. Lord Duriel did not get a chance to protest either, his mouth having fallen so far open he resembled a codfish. Gian flashed his teeth and shut the door in the lord's utterly appalled face.

"I do not need you to fight my battles," she warned as he turned to face her again.

He gave her an artful, satisfied grin. "Good, because I left my sword in my chambers."

She crossed her arms, staring him down. "You do not need help finding your rum, you idiot."

He grinned, pulling a bottle from inside his jacket. "A pirate is never without it."

She rolled her eyes, turned away from him, and marched into her sitting room, plopping unceremoniously onto her settee. Gian followed without invitation and sat beside her, the leather of his black pants groaning as he did.

"I thought you gave up piracy," she said, watching him as he pulled the topper from the bottle of amber liquid.

"Oh, I'll never give up piracy, love. I simply found better treasure to hunt." He offered her the bottle, but she only eyed it skeptically.

"Have you ever tried it?" he asked.

"No. Nor do I intend to."

He winked and took a healthy swig from the bottle. "I'll corrupt you yet, Princess."

"I do not recall inviting you in here. And there are about a dozen different reasons why you should leave. Now."

"Your reputation included?" he asked, indifferent to her warning.

"You're a nuisance."

He took another drink before offering her the bottle again. When she refused a second time, he said, "Believe me, not even the scandal of a pirate in your private quarters will keep that man from pursuing you. He's a hound on the hunt."

"You make no effort to hide that you were listening in on my private conversation," she pointed out, crossing her arms and leaning back against the settee.

“Darling, everyone in eight corridors was listening to that conversation. And everyone else is waiting for the gossip about it. You’re the talk of the castle these days.”

“I’m thrilled to know that my love life is so entertaining.”

That wicked smirk returned. “Well, if you’d like some pointers on how to make it even more entertaining, I would be happy to oblige.” He tipped the bottle her direction once again.

She pushed it away. “Stop trying to get me drunk.”

“All other efforts to convince you to come to my bed have failed. What’s a man to do?”

“Get out of my chambers, Gian,” she said, standing. She took him by the collar and practically dragged him from her settee.

He stood at her insistence, but that ridiculous smirk never left his face. “All right, all right,” he said, lifting his hands in a show of innocence. “But you could at least kiss me as a thank you for rescuing you from that pompous goat.”

“How about I hand you to the guards instead.”

“You want to put your hands on my guard? If that is your furtive attempt at some bawdy threat, I heartily accept.”

“Good day,” she said, nearly shoving him out of her door.

But Gian did not protest further. Instead, he pranced out into the corridor, turning to deliver a dramatic bow before saying in a loud singsong, “You’re welcome, by the way.”

CHAPTER NINE

"You look like you had a rough night," said John with a roguish grin. He elbowed Ezra in the ribs, and when the grand duke did not respond, John kept teasing. "It seems rather contradictory that you should have such a scowl on your face this morning, Ez. I saw the gleam in your eyes when you followed her in there last night," he said, nodding toward the bedchamber.

Ezra had understood John's implication perfectly, but it did not improve his mood. He bustled about the common room between their guest chambers in the castle, waiting for everyone to wake up, silent with frustration. He just wanted to get home. To get out of here and sort through whatever the Sheol had happened last night.

Interrupted intimacy aside, something had happened last night that he could not place. Could not understand. The fragments of memory were not fitting together properly in his mind, like pieces from the wrong puzzle.

"Has the snow cleared enough?" Ezra asked.

"What?" John asked, tilting his long, narrow face to one side.

"The blizzard. Is it cleared enough that we can go home?" Ezra marched through the common room to the windows beyond and yanked open the heavy emerald curtains. A sudden assault of golden light flooded the space, causing the soldiers sprawled across the furniture to groan in disgust.

"Wake up, boys," John chortled, taking a seat on the arm of a nearby chair. "I think His Grace is ready to leave. Apparently, he didn't have as much fun last night as you did."

"How is this possible?" Ezra asked, staring dumbfounded out the windows.

Vitas rubbed his eyes. "Some of us know how to make a night of it, Ez," he said. He kicked his fellow soldier to wake him.

Cosmas gave Vitas a particularly vulgar gesture before sitting up from the rather awkward position in which he had been sleeping. "The sun is barely up," he grumbled. "Can't we wait another hour?"

"I'm not talking about the party," Ezra said. "I'm talking about the weather. From the way it was snowing last night, I'd have thought there would be several feet on the ground."

"What are you talking about?" John asked, standing. He walked to the windows. "We didn't get any snow last night."

Ezra whirled to face them. "Of course we did!" he protested. "The blizzard, remember? It was the reason we couldn't go home."

"We didn't go home because Cosmas and Vitas were too drunk to remember their names," John said, chuckling.

"What are you talking about?" Ezra barked. "We couldn't leave! The weather was terrible!"

"We might have had a few flakes of snow, but it was a nice night, if a bit cold," John said, patting Ezra's shoulder. "Sounds like you were a little distracted last night, my friend." He winked, chuckling. Ezra ignored him, facing the impossibly sunny day through the windows once more.

"Speaking of your distraction, where is she this morning?" Cosmas asked, tucking his shirt into his trousers with a sly grin.

"He must have worn her out," Vitas offered.

"I'd have thought it would be the other way around," Cosmas countered.

John and the soldiers shared a laugh.

"Enough," Ezra said, at last taking his eyes from the bright morning. It made no sense, the snow. It should have been blanketing everything in sight after that storm. Instead, the late autumn snows had only just begun to dust the world around them. Nothing at all like the aftermath of a blizzard. And nothing at all like the storm that had made it impossible for them to get home last night, impossible to escape from the fear, the cold, despondent darkness that had crept over both him and Miri in the ballroom.

And then again in that bathtub...

"What's got your drawers in a twist, Your Righteousness?" Vitas asked, slipping on his uniform jacket. He buttoned the toggles as he smirked. "Where's your lady fair? Don't tell me you've already found a way to piss her off." The soldier winked and grinned, but Ezra did not respond. Instead, he strode back through the room to his bedchamber door.

"Where is Kit?" Ezra asked.

"In our chambers. She's helping Esther with the baby this morning," said John. "Ezra, what's wrong?"

"I want everyone ready to go in an hour," Ezra said, and then disappeared into his and Miri's room.

Whatever had or hadn't happened last night, it was time to get out of here. Now.

"You're awake," said Ezra, snicking the door quietly shut behind him.

Miri did not turn from her vigil at the windows. Her fiery curls hung loose down her back, and her simple, cream dress glowed particularly bright in the morning light.

"Where is the snow?" she asked softly.

"You remember it, too?" Ezra asked, walking to her side. He put a hand at her back, and though she flinched softly, she did not move away from him.

"I asked John the same question. No one else seems to remember that we had a blizzard last night."

Miri faced Ezra, her emerald eyes sparkling in the morning sun. "Of course they wouldn't remember," she said. Something flickered in her countenance—something dark and cold. It tore at Ezra, and he turned to face her fully, resting his hands at her waist.

"Are you all right, Wildfire?" he asked.

Miri breathed deeply, moving to rest her head on his chest. He took the opportunity to wrap her in his arms and pull her close. It was only then that he could feel her trembling.

"My love, please tell me what happened. Did I..." He swallowed once, finding the courage to ask the question that had been gnawing at him since he awoke in that cold bath last night. "Did I hurt you?"

She looked up, meeting his eyes with that dark sadness in hers. "I didn't think you could."

He ran a gentle knuckle along her jaw. "I confess I do not remember. Did I fall asleep in your arms?" The absurdity of it... hearing it aloud... A vision danced in his mind—her body astride his, surrounded by billowing steam. How could he have fallen asleep in the midst of such a moment?

She did not answer, looking at him, although the blank distance in her eyes told him she wasn't really seeing him.

"Yes," she finally said. "Asleep."

"Miri," he said in disbelief. "I—"

"It's fine."

"It's not fine," he protested. "I hurt you."

"You could never hurt me."

The way she said it—he was not sure if it was meant to comfort him. If he had fallen asleep… Could she ever forgive him? Could she ever trust him?

"Wildfire," he tried, but she pushed out of his arms and turned away.

"I want to go home, Ezra."

CHAPTER TEN

"Is it really true?" Helena did not give Ezra and Miri a moment to breathe before smothering them with suffocating embraces the moment they re-entered Massahd Castle. Her hands on Ezra's face, she held his gaze, and he knew she would not release him until he answered—whatever her question was about.

"You'll have to be more specific, Helena," Ezra said, laughing.

"Am I arranging a wedding feast by week's end?" Helena clarified.

"Good news travels fast," said Ezra.

"Kit told her," said Thaddeus, making his way into the entry hall. The butler took Ezra's hat and coat and Miri's bonnet and cloak. "She started prattling about it the moment she set foot out of her carriage."

Ezra heard Miri puff a small chuckle, but he did not know what to say, how to answer Helena's question. Only last night they had decided to hold a celebration at week's end. But that was before whatever had happened to Miri and to him.

"We're not going to have a grand affair," he said after a pause. "There is no need to fret, Helena."

"That's what I told her," said Thaddeus. The butler turned his attention to Miri, quietly assessing her. "Are you all right, my lady?" he asked.

Miri took a moment to answer. "Simply tired, that is all."

Ezra did not miss the concern that shone on the butler's face —like a father might look over his daughter.

"Nonsense." Helena dismissed, resting her hands on her wide-set hips. "You are the Grand Duke and Duchess of Kinnereth. We shall celebrate with the whole province!"

"She doesn't want that, Hel," Thaddeus said, frustrated.

"Of course she does!" Helena protested to the lanky butler.

"Just family," Miri interjected before the two of them could bicker any more. "Just us. And Ari."

Ezra faced her, wishing he knew what to say. Instead, he took her hand. To his relief, she did not stop him, holding on tightly.

"Are you sure?" Helena asked skeptically.

"I don't want a fuss," said Miri softly.

"Where are John and Esther?" was Helena's next question.

"They went home for a bit to gather a few things," Ezra answered. "They will be back before dinnertime. Esther wants to be here to help with preparations."

"Well, I should hope so!" said the housekeeper. "There is much to do!"

"Please don't make a fuss," Miri repeated. "I just want the people that matter, that's all."

"Are you sure, child?" Helena pressed. "We could at least have the council lords, their wives, and—"

"Hel," Thaddeus practically growled. The portly housemaid huffed, shooing the butler away.

"Just us. And Ari," Ezra echoed what Miri had said, stifling a chuckle. It was good to be home.

"I'll write to him," said Thaddeus.

"Thank you, Thaddeus," said Miri.

The slender butler offered Miri a smile as he nodded once, turning to head deeper into the castle.

Helena, acquiescing with visible disappointment, turned and followed him.

"You could always wear my mother's dress if you wanted to," Esther told Miri as a servant spooned potatoes onto her plate. "I wore it when I married John. I know it's not your wedding, and it's not the same as having your own dress made, but on such short notice—"

"I'm sure it is lovely," said Miri, fiddling with the food on her plate. She hardly had an appetite, but she did not want to be rude.

Under the table, Ezra rested his hand on her knee, giving her a gentle squeeze. He had been worried since the moment he had woken, cold and alone, in that bathtub. The worry was obviously eating him alive.

But she could not tell him. She could not even bring herself to admit what had happened.

Still, the images danced in her mind incessantly. Phinehas's slender, brutal hands, his cold eyes, his mouth on hers, his body invading her. Invading every part of her. Demanding. Ripping the last shreds of dignity from her, insistent that she was hiding something from him.

She could not bring herself to tell Ezra that he had been cursed by the High Priest of Har-Navah, all so that the monster could have his way with her. So that he could rob her of any vestige of hope that she would ever escape him. So that he could ruin her once and forever.

She could not bring herself to tell Ezra what had actually happened.

So she let him wonder. Worry.

It was better than knowing the truth. For the truth would shatter him. It was shattering her, one concerned look at a time.

She scooped a bite of peas onto her fork and forced herself to chew them, only to realize that the conversation about their wedding feast hadn't stopped.

"Don't you think so, Miri?" Esther asked.

Miri looked up from her plate. "What? Oh, I'm sorry. I—"

"I was just saying that the ballroom would be lovely. Or the west wing library. Either room would work, don't you think?"

"Oh. Yes," she agreed. But she was failing. Failing at being a blushing, hopeful bride. At pretending like she was paying attention.

Failing at being worthy of any of this.

She was nothing. A nobody.

A whore.

"I thought we could marry on the mountainside," Ezra said.

Everyone looked at him.

John looked from Ezra to Miri and back to Ezra. "You're already married. This is just the feast."

"I know," said Ezra. "But none of you were there to witness it. I thought it might be nice—to promise our lives to one another on the knoll overlooking the castle."

He looked to Miri, a quiet hope kindling in his eyes. She had to look away from that hope lest it destroy her, fiddling with a pea on the tines of her fork in lieu of a response.

"Ezra," Esther said flatly. "It's almost winter. You cannot be outside. On a mountain. It's impractical."

"It's where I knew I was in love with Miri."

Despite herself, she looked back at him, furrowing her brow for a moment, trying to recall—

"The horses," she said, unable to stop the memory from flooding her mind. "When you took me to see the winged horses."

Ezra smiled, squeezing her knee again.

"That's when you fell in love with me?"

"No, that's when I admitted to myself that I was falling in love with you," he said. "I was in love with you long before that."

Miri, desperate to stop those words from sinking in, desperate to stop herself from allowing this man to love her so naïvely, swallowed the lump in her throat and turned away from him again.

"I knew I was in love with Esther when I caught her building a færy house in the stables," John said, laughing amiably.

"I was thirteen. You knew you were in love with me when I was *thirteen?"* Esther asked skeptically, taking a sip from her wine.

John grinned. "You were just so innocent, building that little house. You wanted to catch a færy so badly. I couldn't help myself."

"You are incorrigible," Esther said, but despite her disapproving reply, Miri could see that Esther very much did *not* find her husband's admission ridiculous.

"I used to build færy houses all the time," Miri admitted, thankful for the change in subject. "Little rocks and sticks and matchboxes...whatever I could get my hands on."

"Did you ever catch one?" Esther asked before taking a bite of her roast.

"My father always tore them down before I could," Miri said.

It was John who spoke into the sudden silence, a note of disdain in his question. "He tore them down?"

"He said they were childish," she admitted with a shrug.

"Your father sounds lovely." Esther stabbed her next bite with obvious distaste that had nothing to do with the food. "I am told Ezra built you a færy house, didn't he?"

Ezra did not look up from his meal, and Miri was glad. She had never thanked him for that little færy house he had made her. She had never once told him what it had meant to her.

"Miri has met færies," Ezra finally said.

"You've met færies?" Esther parroted, incredulous.

Ezra nodded. "At the temple. The færy king and færy queen came to her," he said, looking at John and Esther.

"Fa and Meren?" John's voice held surprise.

"Those are the ancient king and queen of the færies, my love," said Esther. "I'm sure there are new ones by now."

"No, that's right," Miri said. "Fa and Meren. That's who I met."

Esther put down her fork, dabbing her perfectly rosy lips with her napkin before going on. "How is that possible? Fa and Meren were the king and queen of the færies over a thousand years ago."

"They're perdurable," said Ezra. "The magic of Providence makes them immortal."

"It's love," said Miri. "Isn't that what Ari told us? Love is magic." She did not allow herself to look at Ezra at the mention of the word.

"How did you meet them?" Esther asked.

"They came to me. They told me that my cousin was alive, though I did not understand it at the time. And they said *the stag is at hand.*"

"The Promised One," said John, in awe.

Miri nodded. "They told me who is the Promised One long before I understood what they meant."

"Who *is* the Promised One?" This from Esther.

The table fell silent, and Miri finally allowed herself to meet Ezra's gaze before she spoke. He nodded once as if to encourage her.

"My cousin," she finally said. "I think my cousin might be the Promised One."

"The son of Providence?" Esther asked, but it was not skepticism. It was awe in her question.

"You did not know," John said slowly, sounding like he was putting pieces together in his lawyer's mind. "Growing up, you did not know who he was."

"He never told me," Miri said, shaking her head. "Though looking back, I should have known."

Magic. He had given her the gift of magic. And she had not realized the significance of it.

A gift. Rare and pure.

That's what Phinehas had wanted from her at the ball. The magic her cousin had given her when she was a girl. He thought she possessed it because of the amulet her cousin had also gifted her. He did not know that Miri had magic in her very veins.

Not that she had ever understood how to wield it.

That hadn't mattered to Phinehas. He had glutted himself on her last night, trying desperately to take that magic from her. Not the charlatan nonsense he used at the temple. Smoke and flame and silly words. But true, pure magic.

Magic like that, in his hands...

She shuddered to think what he would do with it. What he still might do.

"They say he attracts huge crowds wherever he goes now," said John. "The king is surely going to do something about him before long."

Miri shuddered, and Ezra took hold of her hand on her lap before he spoke. "We will not allow anything to happen to Ari."

"Careful, brother," said Esther. "Defying the king is bad enough. But defying both him and his high priest? You're likely to find your head on a platter."

"Thank you for the advice," Ezra said flatly. "I might have forgotten the danger otherwise."

Esther frowned but didn't respond, and an awkward pause ensued, broken only by servants coming in with dessert.

Even knowing she should not, knowing how selfish it made

her, Miri kept firm hold of Ezra's hand as the conversation around the table resumed, turning back to the wedding feast.

"Do you suppose they will try to hurt him?" Miri asked. Standing before the great glass doors that opened onto the balcony beyond their bedchamber, Miri watched snow fall lazily in the moonlight, clutching a thick, fur-lined robe around herself for warmth.

Ezra finished stoking the fire in the great hearth and walked up behind her, snaking his thick arms around her waist. He rested his chin on her shoulder before he answered. "We will not let them."

"That's not what I asked."

He sighed. "The king is not one to let his pride suffer. And if he views Ari as a threat, he will not suffer it."

"What do we do?" she asked, leaning back against him, ignoring the fact that she had no right to revel in his warmth.

"We make sure the king doesn't view him as a threat," said Ezra, simply.

She turned to face him. His arms tightened around her, but she ignored how close his lips were to hers and asked instead, "Can we do that?"

Ezra seemed distracted by their closeness as well, for his gaze dropped to her lips and lingered. "I'm certainly going to try."

She blinked and turned to face the snow again. She knew what message she sent with that simple move. But she could not bear it—how much he wanted her. And how much she wanted him, too.

And how much it should not be so.

He had not mentioned it once—the bathtub. Was it only yesternight? It seemed like it had been a thousand years ago. But he had not once brought up the fact that they had made love for the first time and then something had stolen their moment. Incapacitated him, like an autumn leaf frozen beneath a glassy lake.

He still wondered what had happened, that was obvious.

She knew it was Phinehas's dark magic. His censers and shimmering smoke and candles and ancient chants that he used in the temple—those were all for show. But Miri now understood the truth—Phinehas was well-versed in a magic dark and wicked. Like a cold draft in a dark corridor. And he had used it on both her and Ezra last night.

And she had been powerless to stop him.

The thought of that kind of magic combined with the amulet sent a flash of terror down her spine.

"Miri," Ezra said, his voice a gentle rumble against her back, bringing her back to the present. His arms were still securely around her, but he craned his neck to meet her eyes. She kept her gaze on the snow as he spoke. "I know you're not ready to talk about it. And it's all right. I just want you to know that I'm here when you are. I'm right here, Wildfire. And I'm not going anywhere. So when you're ready to talk about it, so am I."

She shut her eyes, swallowing hard against the lump in her throat. Ezra leaned and pressed a kiss to her neck—soft and lingering. Nothing possessive or seductive about it. A kiss of a lover; a kiss of a friend.

Her friend.

He was her friend. And so much more.

She wished she deserved him.

"We should get some sleep, Wildfire."

A FEW DAYS LATER, Miri woke alone. Ezra's side of the bed was already cold. He must have woken hours ago. She supposed she should not have been surprised that she had slept in, because yesterday had been a blur of fittings and flowers and decisions. So many decisions. For a small, family wedding feast, Helena had made a production of it, ensuring every detail had been considered at least thrice. Miri had privately wondered what a ceremony fit for the Grand Duke of Kinnereth would have been like if such a small affair was already so exhausting.

She had collapsed into bed for the past two nights, Ezra tucked securely beside her, his arm at her waist. But he had not asked anything of her. In the two nights since they had been home, he had just kissed her softly and fallen asleep beside her. Despite the fact that she knew—she could see it in his eyes, feel it in his kiss, his touch—how badly he wanted her, needed her, Ezra had not pressed the subject. And Miri had not been able to decide whether she preferred it that way or not.

She knew he would never push her too far or too fast. She knew that he knew she was keeping something from him. And she knew he would rather die than hurt her in any way.

And that kind of love, that kind of sacrifice...it tore her apart every moment she lingered on it too long.

She sighed, flexing her toes and stretching her arms above her head. She ran her fingernails along the intricate patterns on the mahogany headboard, patterns that climbed all the way to the canopy of the four-poster bed. It had been in his family for three hundred and fifty years—a wedding gift to the family from a subject in the province. Everything in Massahd Castle had a story like that: every chair, every table, every book, every curiosity contained a story of the history of the Kelach family.

And now she was a part of that family. Today, they would celebrate that she was the Grand Duchess of Kinnereth. Ezra's wife.

Miri's stomach turned—not out of disgust, but fear.

Fear that someone would figure out what a farce she was. Fear that her marriage would be forever tainted by the treachery she would never escape. For the last two nights, she had dreamt of that fear: scene after scene of the people of Har-Navah spitting in her face, laughing, mocking, taunting, calling her out for the fraud she was.

No matter how many times she reminded herself that Ezra knew her, knew her past, knew what she was, it did not suffice. For he did not know everything. And she did not know what she feared more: telling him so that he would hate her, or letting him find out and hating her all the same.

For he *would* find out. One way or another, her secrets would come back to haunt her. Perhaps not today, perhaps not tomorrow. But one day they would.

She did not know what would become of her when they did.

A knock sounded at her door, and Miri sat up abruptly. Before she could even answer, Helena and Kit bustled into the room: maids on a mission. Esther followed behind them.

"Up, up my dear!" said Helena, shooing Miri from the bed. "We must get you ready!"

From across the room, Kit snickered.

"So it begins," said Esther under her breath.

"Where is Ezra? I haven't seen him," Miri protested as Helena practically dragged her out of the bed.

"You cannot see the bridegroom on your wedding day! It's bad luck!" Helena said as she swept Miri along.

"It's not our wedding day, Helena," Miri pointed out. "We're already married."

Kit gave Miri a warning look. "Don't take this away from her, Miri. She's been planning your wedding to Ezra for months."

Miri sighed, shaking her head.

"Come now, child," said Helena. "There is much to do."

"But where is he?" she insisted. She wished he were here. Wished he could be a voice of reason for what she knew was about to be a barrage of Helena's well meaning yet overbearing opinions.

Kit was gathering a towel and robe and said over her shoulder, "He is with John. They're on the third floor in the Great Chamber."

"And Helena is right," Esther chimed in. "You cannot see him today. Not until the ceremony. It's tradition."

Miri did not think it would be wise to protest, so she let Helena usher her impatiently to her bathing chambers. But Esther stepped between them.

"Are you all right?" Ezra's sister asked, setting her slender hands on Miri's shoulders.

"Just nervous I think," Miri said, unable to meet her sister-in-law's concerned gaze.

"That's to be expected, of course," said Helena with a laugh.

But Esther did not seem satisfied, searching Miri a moment longer with her brow furrowed. When Miri said nothing else, Esther finally added, "I will fetch the gown." She turned and left the bedchamber without another word.

"Come, child, let's get you into the bath," said Helena.

The bath was scalding hot, but Miri did not protest. Sinking into the steaming waters, she welcomed the burn as it turned her skin pink and clammy. She welcomed the pain as it enveloped her body, a tingling sting that crept up inch by inch. She didn't bother to let Helena know it was too hot when the housekeeper asked. She deserved it. She wanted the pain to chase away her feelings.

After a moment, Kit and Helena left, promising to return soon so they might primp and poke and comb and brush.

Something twisted in Miri's gut and tears, feeling even hotter than the bathwater, fell freely down her cheeks.

She did not stop them.

CHAPTER ELEVEN

"What I'll never understand is why, hours before your wedding feast, you're walking around as if you're preparing for your funeral." John snickered, taking a drink from his snifter of whiskey, perched on the arm of the settee in the sitting room.

Ezra did not have a reply and took a drink from his own glass.

"Please tell me you've taken her abed by now, Ez. Otherwise, I'm going to have a litany of questions. Beginning with how in the Sheol you've found such unmitigated restraint."

Ezra puffed a sardonic laugh. "Yes, John. You needn't lose any more sleep over the subject of my virginity. It is no longer intact."

"I knew it," John said triumphantly. "At the Harvest Ball, right?"

"Why are you so interested?"

"Because!" John said, standing. He clapped a hand on Ezra's shoulder. "It's a big moment in a man's life when he takes his wife into his arms for the first time."

Ezra could not bring himself to share in the triumph.

John chuckled. "Ah. I see," he said, as if he had it all figured out. “You needn’t lament any lack of expertise on your part, my friend. That’s something you work out together over time,” he said with a wink.

Ezra didn’t bother to point out that there was nothing to lament—that being with her had been the single most incredible experience of his life. If it was supposed to *only get better,* he wasn’t sure he was prepared for such bliss.

“Cheer up, mate,” John went on. “You’ll figure it out the more you’re together.”

“There has not been a second time,” he said, hardly knowing why he was talking about this. He needed to sort through it all on his own. To understand. How could John understand when Ezra didn’t even remember the events of the Harvest Ball?

John stilled, as if he hadn’t heard correctly. “Really?” he asked, disbelief in his eyes.

Ezra sighed, fiddling with a thread on the arm of his chair in his parents’ old chambers, regretting that he had allowed John to broach the subject to begin with. “It just—hasn’t happened again.”

Ezra had no desire to go into why, no desire to explain that bathtub, the cold, slithering feeling along his skin just before he had apparently passed out.

John perched again on the arm of the settee beside him. “Well, surely you won’t be able to say that after tonight. After all, you never really had a wedding night. Not as wedding nights go, anyway.”

Ezra sighed, taking another drink of the whiskey, welcoming its burn.

John chuckled. “Don’t look so forlorn, brother. It will happen again.”

“I just want to be sure she’s ready.”

“And you believe she is still not?” John asked.

Ezra did not bother to meet his brother-in-law's stare. "She's just—been through a lot, that's all."

"True as that may be, she loves you, Ez. Everyone can see it."

"It's not whether she loves me that I worry about," Ezra admitted.

John stood, making his way to a nearby table and the decanter of whiskey. He poured two fingers into his glass before he went on. "It's your wedding feast, Ez. We should be celebrating, not lamenting the complexities of the gentler sex."

Ezra breathed a defeated laugh, lifting his glass to John. "I'll drink to that."

He downed its contents before a sound tore his attention from his drink and to the door leading to the hall. Through it burst a harried young maid.

"My lord!" Kit called, alarm in her voice.

"What's wrong?" he asked, practically jumping from his chair. The look on her face sent his heart racing, knowing it had something to do with his beloved.

"It's Miri," she said through sobs. "Please, my lord. You must help!"

Ezra did not wait for further explanation, nor did he pause to offer John his apologies. He was running—tearing from the room almost before Kit had finished saying the words. He took the steps to the floor below two at a time, running down the long corridor to his chambers. He burst through the door, not bothering to stop when Helena tried to explain the situation.

"I tried to stop her, my lord. I tried! She wouldn't listen! She—"

Ezra yanked open the bathing chamber door so hard it slammed against the wall. Miri sat in a steaming hot bath, her skin red and angry, but not from the hot water. No, those were scratches along her bare arms, her bare legs. And that was blood coloring the water.

"Miri!" he cried, clambering to her side, falling to his knees so hard they ached from impact with the cold marble floor. "Miri! Stop!"

She clawed at her skin, scrubbing with a rough sponge over and over again, as hard as she could, weeping as she drew her own blood.

"I cannot get clean," she wept. "I cannot get clean."

Ezra grabbed the sponge in her hand, needing a surprising amount of his strength to try to stop her from further harm. His shirt, sodden with bathwater, grew cold as he struggled against her. "Stop, my love. Don't do this!"

But she didn't. She did not stop struggling against him, clawing at her skin with her bare nails the moment he managed to take the rough sponge away.

He took hold of her wrists, pulling her hands away from her body, from the angry welts along her arms and legs and neck. He pulled until he had somehow managed to pull her from the scalding waters, collapsing onto the marble floors with her soaking body against him.

She continued her fight, struggling to wrestle her wrists free from his grip. But he did not let her, refusing to allow her to harm herself further. Her skin was as red as a hummingbird's throat, angry scratches along her bare thighs and belly. He held her close against him and rocked her there on that floor, back and forth, back and forth, letting her weep. Letting her release whatever had been bottled up inside her. She sobbed as she slowly stopped struggling, though she had not stopped chanting over and over again.

"Not clean.

"Not clean.

"I will never be clean."

"Wildfire," he said gently, pulling her against him, cradling her like a babe, soaking wet and clammy as he kept rocking. He kissed her brow and spoke her name again and again, a plea.

A prayer.

A hymn.

And she let him hold her; she let him soothe her. She buried her face against his neck and let him rock her gently until she lay as limp and weak as a newborn fawn. For a long moment, he held her there, weeping and soothing and rocking, her wet curls soaking through his thin shirt.

"Talk to me, my love. Please tell me what happened."

"I am unclean," she said in a weakened whisper.

"No, Wildfire. It's not true."

"I'll never be clean enough. Never enough."

"You're wrong, my love. So very wrong."

She looked up, meeting his eyes. He pressed gentle kisses to each tear as they fell solemn and salty down her cheeks. Her skin was soft in his hands as he soothed and touched and whispered comforting sounds. She sobbed quietly for a long while, the tension in her body slowly melting away with each new breath. When at last she released a long sigh, he met her eyes again.

They were clearer now, as if seeing him for the first time. Their emerald color shone radiant despite her unshed tears. And with her gaze, his heart strained, tugging and pulling within as it broke for her—for her pain and her loss and her fears and her shame. For all that had been stolen from her and all she thought she lacked. Ezra's heart broke for his beloved. And Miri held his gaze so intently, so full of fervent penance and desperation that he thought he would burn, combust with a need for her so strong, so sudden he was certain he would die from it.

So he kissed her. To comfort her as much as himself.

And she let him.

She wrapped her arms around him and kissed him so thoroughly he could not think of anything but her—her mouth, her hands, her bare skin beneath his fingers. Nothing but this wildfire who consumed him.

She whispered his name again and again as he pressed kisses down her neck and shoulder. Then she wrapped herself round him, her body a welcome warmth through his soaked linen shirt. She moved like an anthem, a song as she kissed him again, her lips an incantation against his.

"Mine, Wildfire," he said, barely breathing. "You are mine."

"Yes," she said. "Yes."

Ezra stood, lifting her in his arms. She was so light, her body made to fit in his arms. He carried her from the bathing chamber to their bedchamber, laying her down on the soft blankets of their bed as he kissed her, showered her with need and desire and affection. And Miriam did not hold back, kissing him fiercely, desperately.

She paused for a moment, taking his face in her hands. Her eyes were red-rimmed with tears, but her countenance was earnest. "Please," she said, her words little more than a breath. "Please, Ezra."

He could not refuse her. So he kissed her mouth. He kissed her neck. He kissed her breasts, first one and then the other. He kissed her navel, and he kissed the long, slender plane of her stomach. He fumbled for the laces of his shirt and pulled it over his head, the sound of the wet linen slapping as it landed on the floor. He found the fall of his trousers and worked it so deftly that, at any other moment, he might have stopped to marvel at the miraculous ease with which he removed them. In the span of a breath, he was above her again, body to body, the long, silken length of her stretched beneath him. His skin was against hers and his soul was bare before her and he was nothing and he was everything and time stood still and time rushed past him in a whirlwind of need and love and desire and hope.

His. She was *his*.

He would not let this darkness chase her any longer. He would chase it away with each new kiss, each new touch. He had felt so selfish, needing her like this. He knew if he was not careful, he could take and take and glut himself on her intoxicating body. But maybe she needed him, too. Maybe she burned for him as much as he for her. She certainly seemed to now.

So he made love to her there on that bed. For every kiss she gave him, he gave her two. For every touch of her fingers against him, he touched her again. With every sigh, he breathed her in. She was a wildfire and he the forest, the mighty poplar that burned and burned with every lick of her flames. He traced the swell of her hips with the tips of his fingers, relishing the little whimpers she made with every gentle movement, relishing the way she gave herself over to him. Trusted him. She was as unhurried as a falling leaf, and somewhere in the back of his mind, he thanked Providence that she had the wherewithal to savor the moment, for he was not sure he would have otherwise.

It was not long before her body began to tense beneath his, straining the tendons in her slender neck. How well he understood, for his own body was so tense he thought he would snap in two. But he held on; he held her through every breath, held her tightly as she gasped and arched against him. He held her, trembling with restraint until she was limp with what he hoped to Providence was pleasure.

When she met his gaze with heady, contented eyes, he knew he hadn't been wrong.

"Ezra," she said. And the way she said his name—such hope, such satisfaction, such adoration... Ezra could not restrain himself any longer. He was the wild, rushing waves crashing along the seashore until he, too, was limp in her arms, whispering her name against her skin.

He held her there beneath him for long moments. He held her until he could feel her heart beating at a steady rhythm again, until her breath had found a calm cadence. He relished the feel of her skin against his. With his head resting on her shoulder, he kissed her neck again and again, running tender fingers down her side.

"I'm sorry," she said, her words barely audible.

He pressed his brow to her temple but before he could find words, she went on. "I've been so scared, Ezra. Afraid that it's all going to end when you figure out..."

She stopped, her words catching in her throat. Instead, she shut her eyes. "I never imagined something like this for myself. I never dared to hope for it."

"Neither did I, Wildfire." He ran a gentle finger down her cheek, her chin.

She took his face in both of her hands and kissed him thoroughly. And that quickly, that easily, he knew he could let himself get lost in her again. He wanted to. Instead, he said, "Helena is going to murder us."

"Why?" she asked, horror flashing in her features.

"Because you should be getting dressed by now," Ezra said, chuckling.

"Oh," she said, slightly relieved. A tenuous smile found her mouth.

"But she will have to suffer our tardiness, because I'm afraid it's going to be rather difficult to pry me from your arms anytime soon," Ezra admitted, moving slightly. He become suddenly aware of the intimacy of her embrace as she cradled him with her legs.

But before he became too distracted, she asked, "Why, Ezra? Why would you want me at all?"

His heart shattered at the question. He took her chin with his hand, making her meet his eyes. "You're my best friend, Miri. Did you know that?" But he did not let her speak. No, he needed to tell her. Needed her to understand.

"You're the only person who has ever understood me. John

hasn't. Not fully. He was not born into privilege and expectation like you and I were. My grandfather didn't. Not fully. Maybe we were similar in some ways, but he was stronger than I am. He knew how to face the difficult things with grace. But you, Miri—you're the only person in the world with whom I can be fully myself.

"And I want to spend the rest of my life with my best friend. I want to spend the rest of my life with the only person who fully understands me.

"But that's not the only reason I want you. You are the kindest person I know. Despite all you've faced, all that you've had to endure, you're still kind. You're still selfless and beautiful and warm and loving. I want you because you've taught me what it means to be brave. You've taught me what the light is, for even in your darkest moments, you never let go of it.

"And there's more, Miri. I want you because when I think of what I want, when I wake up in the morning and think of my life, it's you. You're my life. You're the person I think of when I wake and the person I dream of when I sleep. You're who I want to grow old with and raise a family with and fight with and laugh with and dream and fail and hope and plan with. You, Miri. Only you.

"But there are still more reasons. I want you because I love you so deeply, so passionately, that sometimes I fear it will consume me. I love you so much that when I even think of touching you, of holding you, I can barely think of anything else. And when I get to kiss you, when I get to touch you, feel you in my arms, there is nothing but us. I cannot fathom anything but you. And us. Of holding you and touching you and needing you.

"Miri, I want to spend the rest of my life with you because you are my world. You are my everything. And you are my great love story."

Tears streamed down her face. Uninhibited tears he kissed away one at a time as he held her there on his bed.

"Will you meet me out there today?" He nodded towards the windows and the mountains beyond, towards the overlook visible from their windows. "Will you stand before our friends and our family on that rock where we watched the winged horses? With the people that matter most there with us? Because I want to celebrate that you are my wife today."

She nodded softly through her tears before she kissed him. Then he lifted her hand to his mouth, kissing it once before kissing the angry scratches that clawed her arm. He took his time, kissing each one, working his way up to her shoulder, her neck, the shell of her ear, tasting the tears that had fallen down her face.

"Ezra, I'll never understand why you love me," she said. "But I know that I love you more than I ever thought possible."

Ezra grinned, a rush of joy and need swallowing him whole when her own countenance melted into a tremulous but true smile. She moved beneath him, only slightly.

An invitation.

He did not decline.

He took her again, this time with a meticulous reverence that allowed him the luxury of reveling in her every expression, every little sound. And when he had given her pleasure again, when he had coaxed every bit from her, he gave in to his own with eager anticipation. She kissed until he collapsed in a heap beside her, spent and sated and smiling.

He might have even fallen asleep for a bit, it was hard to say. But when he felt her tender fingers exploring his arms and chest, he opened one eye and watched her for a long moment, running his fingers through her thick, glossy curls spilled around him.

"Your Grace?"

The question had come from the corridor outside their chamber. Ezra did not answer, but donned a grin as he watched Miri.

"We will have to explain ourselves now," she whispered.

"Helena is a smart woman. She'll figure it out."

"Is everything all right?" Helena asked from outside their door.

"Everything is fine," Ezra answered, swallowing back a laugh at the nervous trepidation in the housekeeper's voice.

"I beg your pardon, but—"

Ezra interrupted Helena. "Miri will be ready for you presently."

"It's just that the day is wearing thin, and—"

"She will be along, Helena. I promise," said Ezra.

Miri snickered, burying her face in his chest. He took the opportunity to curl her against his side and press a kiss to the top of her head. Her ginger curls spilled across his chest like liquid fire.

Mercifully, Helena did not press the subject further.

"I distinctly remember you telling her you did not want a fuss," said Ezra.

"The woman has been planning your wedding day for twenty-six years, Ezra. We stole it from her with our clandestine, rooftop wedding. Perhaps we should give her some grace," Miri offered.

"No, my love. You're wrong. She's been planning *our* wedding since the moment I came home gushing about you after seeing you in that theatre for the first time. Believe me, she did not have this fervor for any of my other marriage prospects."

"Well, we should not keep her waiting."

Ezra took a moment to run his gaze down the length of Miri's exquisite body. "It seems a sacrilege to leave this bed."

Miri smiled, a soft blush mantling her cheeks.

"It is only because I know that we have the rest of our lives together that I am even willing to consider it," Ezra told her.

"Look at it this way," Miri said, resting her hands on his chest and propping her chin on top of them. "The sooner we finish out there, the sooner we can come back in here."

"Indeed, my glorious Wildfire. Indeed."

CHAPTER TWELVE

Miri trembled. Watching her come up the snow-covered hill on John's arm, Ezra could see it was difficult for her to contain her emotion. Her face beamed with a smile, but even from a distance he could see she was desperate to stop her tears from falling. On the late autumn evening breeze, her fiery curls danced around her pink cheeks.

Once before on that rooftop, he had watched her tremble as she held back tears. He had marveled that the woman had chosen him.

But here, today, surrounded by those who mattered most, it somehow meant more. And he could see on her radiant face, those tears finally falling, that she felt the very same way.

He smiled broadly the moment her eyes met his, and he, too, could not stop the tears from falling freely down his own cold-kissed cheeks. He hoped the fur muff around her hands kept her warm enough. Perhaps Esther had been right—to hold a ceremony on a mountainside with winter just around the corner was a foolish choice. But Miri didn't seem to mind. And when she reached him, dressed in the thick, white fur-trimmed brocade gown his grandmother had worn on her wedding day, he did not care about tradition or superstition or any wedding protocol—he kissed her soundly. He could not help himself.

Beside them, Ari cleared his throat before chuckling softly.

"Now then, shall we skip straight to the feast, or will we get to hear the vows?" he asked with a wink.

Miri breathed a laugh that curled in smoky wisps before her mouth. Ezra removed her muff and covered both of her hands with his. "I want to tell the world how much I love this woman, if it's all the same to you."

Ari nodded and said, "Lucky for you, I only have this to say: I've known Miri my whole life. I grew up next to her. I had the privilege of sharing my childhood with her. She has always been a dreamer; the kindest soul I've ever met. She is quick to love and quicker to forgive. Needless to say, I was never willing to give her up easily. But when I met Ezra..." Ari smiled softly, and Ezra could see the tears he was holding back. "When I met this man, I knew that she had found her story, her destiny. I knew she had found someone who saw her for who she is and who loved her for every part of herself.

"I knew she had met the man who would choose her again and again, through sickness, through health, through darkness and through light, through the rain and through the sun. So to you, Miriam, I say that I will part with you only because I know I am giving you to someone who will love you as you ought to be loved.

"And to you, Ezra, I say I allow you to marry my beloved cousin only because I know how deeply she loves you and how much more beautiful you both are because of it.

"So today, before Providence and all of your family and friends, I will ask you to offer sacred, eternal vows; I will ask you to promise the eternal covenant. For in this, you show the heart of my Father in the simplest way: by giving fully of yourself to another, by promising to never give up, and by sacrificing the pleasure of solitude for the future that you will forge as one."

Ezra met Miri's eyes at Ari's declaration and smiled broadly, squeezing her hands softly. She smiled in return, and Ezra was quite certain it was the most beautiful thing a man had ever witnessed.

"There has never been a more beautiful bride," said Ari, holding Miri close and turning her in a gentle waltz in the ballroom at Massahd. The moment he had asked her to dance to the lone violinist Ezra had commissioned for tonight, she had been taken back to their childhood. To laughing and stumbling through dance after dance with Ari, practicing the moves he had never quite mastered, despite their many attempts.

"You've gotten much better," she said.

"I bribed Kit to practice with me this morning, just so I'd remember," he said with a soft laugh.

Miri kissed her cousin's cheek. "Thank you for the wine. Everyone agrees it is excellent."

Ari winked. "Only the best wine for the wedding feast, right?"

"And look at you. So dapper. Where did you get the tails?"

"Do you like them? John lent them to me." Her cousin smiled proudly as he looked down at himself.

That she had never seen him in tails only reminded her of all the things that her parents had denied her cousin growing up. He, the bastard, unwanted child. The nuisance. To her, he was anything but unwanted.

She kissed his cheek again as he turned her in the waltz.

"Thank you for tonight, Ari. It was perfect."

Ari looked past them to where Ezra danced with Esther,

laughing at something probably only the two of them understood. "He is good to you."

"I don't know why he bothers."

Ari turned his attention back to her. "You still don't think you deserve any of this, do you?"

"Does anyone?"

Ari tilted his head softly. "Love has nothing to do with what we deserve."

"You know, Ezra says the same thing."

"Wise man, that husband of yours."

She huffed a disbelieving laugh. *"Husband.* Can you believe it?"

Ari smiled. "You're an old married woman now, Mir. Next thing you know, you'll be filling this castle with a gaggle of little ones."

Something in her heart sank at that. For Ari did not know—*he could not know*—of her barrenness. That she would never give Ezra a family. Phinehas had made sure of it.

Ari must have noticed, for he stopped the waltz and held her chin in his hand. "Despite what the storybooks say, it doesn't end here. In fact, this is where the story truly begins," he said, nodding towards Ezra without taking his eyes from her. "And yours is a beautiful story, Mir. But you must learn not to fear it, for fear is a deceiver."

She looked down, unsure what to say.

"There is no fear in love. Not the kind you share with him. There will be days where you dance on mountaintops, and there will be days where you claw through the muck and mire. But you get to do that together now. That's the point, Mir. Marriage is the gift of two choosing to face the world as one."

"Choosing," she said.

"Choosing," her cousin echoed. "That's the gift, you see. That

you didn't have to, but you chose to anyway. That is how my Father's magic works."

She looked up and found a sweet smile in Ari's eyes. This time, it was he who pressed a kiss to her cheek.

"I love you, Mir," he said.

"I know," she said. "I love you, too."

"I would like to say that I regret it, but alas I have no qualms about insisting that I dance with my wife."

Miri turned her attention from her cousin to find her husband, bright-eyed and hand extended, his gaze fixed solely on her.

Ari smiled, breathing a soft laugh before quietly acquiescing to Ezra, stepping back without protest.

When Miri took Ezra's hand, he said to Ari, "You don't know what it means to us to have you here."

Ari smiled. "We're family now, aren't we?"

Ezra nodded. "I hope that means we'll be seeing you more often."

"I expect you will."

A moment later, her cousin having disappeared into the small crowd in the ballroom, Miri was dancing in her husband's arms.

"Hello, wife," he said with a grin.

"Hello, husband," she said with what she knew to be an equally uninhibited smile on her mouth. Ezra took a moment to kiss that mouth before sweeping her into a jaunty little dance that matched the liveliness of the fiddler's tune.

"Thank you for this. All of it," she said, nodding as she glanced around at the faces of their family: John and Esther, Helena and Thaddeus, the soldiers—Cosmas, Albus, and Veritas—and a giggling Kit, desperately trying to help Ari figure out the footwork for the dance.

"Everything is perfect," Miri said.

"Have I told you how beautiful you are?" Ezra asked.

She looked down at the dress he was eyeing. "I thought you might prefer this one."

"You have excellent taste, Wildfire."

"Lady Kelach had excellent taste." It was true. The gown Ezra's grandmother had worn for her own wedding was as exquisite as any Miri had ever seen. Classic lines and intricate gold embellishments adorned the hem and the sleeves of white brocade, whilst a thick white fur collar wrapped around her neck and shoulders. She felt like a Winter Queen.

"Judith," Ezra said. "Azriel and Judith Kelach."

"I don't think I ever knew their names," she said.

Ezra smiled softly. "I always wanted to name my son after him."

Her heart broke a bit at the declaration, but she did her best not to let it show.

"Thank you for wearing it," he went on. "You don't know what it means to me."

"I'll do my best to live up to their legacy."

"We'll make our own legacy together, Your Grace," Ezra said, and took a moment to press another soft kiss to her lips. "Do you suppose that's the proper honorific for me? Or am I just a *my lord* now? I can never remember the rules, much to my mother's chagrin," he said with a chuckle.

"What are you talking about?" she asked.

"Well, since I'm married to the Grand Duchess of Kinnereth."

She rolled her eyes and laughed. It didn't matter. Not really. She had never fully understood why he had bothered to give the estate to her. Not when marrying her would mean it was hers anyway.

She supposed Ezra was a romantic at heart. And nothing but the most grand gesture would suffice. But it was immaterial to her. She hadn't cared one bit about having any of it. Only him.

And now he was hers. Forever.

And in this, she knew she was the richest woman in the kingdom.

Hours later, exhausted from an evening dancing and laughing and sharing stories, Miri had not hesitated when Ezra had whispered in her ear that he wanted to retire from the festivities. She had taken his hand and felt a flutter in her stomach when he had winked and then bid his adieu to everyone, thanking them for being a part of their day. And then he had led her up the stairs to their chambers, nestled in a corner of the castle that overlooked the mountain where they had given their vows before family and friends only a few hours ago.

Ezra was in the attached bathing chamber and she, still in her wedding gown, had settled into a chair that overlooked the balcony and breathtaking view of Lake Yerah and the mountains beyond. She slipped off the delicate fur-lined slippers she had worn with the gown and nestled deeper into the comfortable, oversized chair, looking forward to the moment Ezra joined her.

The stars glittered off the powdery white snow outside, and their private corner of the frozen lake shone icy white in the moonlight. She took in a deep, contented breath and let herself smile, let herself forget her worries for a moment. Looking across the room, the small fern stand near the balcony windows caught her eye, so she stood, sinking her toes into the plush carpets.

When she reached the fern stand, she picked up the small færy house sitting on it. Intricate and rustic, it was lovingly handmade, built with a hodgepodge of stones, twigs, and wire. She smiled, a lump forming in her throat. When she heard the snick of the bathing chamber door behind her, she turned to find her husband smiling, too.

"I had Kit put it in here," she said. "I never thanked you for it."

In lieu of a response, he snaked his arms around her waist. She rested her head on his chest and asked, "Do you suppose we'll ever see them again?"

"I have a feeling, my love, that the færies, like most things of Providence, will come to you just when you least expect it. And just when you need them most."

"Not unlike you in that regard," she pointed out.

Ezra's responding kiss was thorough and unhurried. And when his hands began to explore her with similar headiness, she found she wanted little else than to get lost in this man's touch and kisses and tender affection.

It was so easy to get lost in him. To let his reverent affection wipe away her fears, to indulge herself on his touch until she was drunk with need, tipsy with desire. He was a drug, Ezra Kelach. And she welcomed his intoxicating, altering rapture. She welcomed the distraction of his skilled hands, his eager lips. She told herself that she would find a way to let it be enough. Forever. She could learn to forget the rest. If she could stay close enough to him, if she could let his love distract enough, she could learn to forget the rest. She could let the past finally die.

He lifted her in his arms and took her to the oversized chair nearby, where he sat down, perching her in his lap and brushing a thick strand of curls behind her shoulder.

"You are trembling, Your Grace," he said softly.

It was true. Though why, she could not quite say. Perhaps a touch of nerves and anticipation. Perhaps exhilaration. Perhaps for the simple fact that he had chosen her and she had yet to wrap her mind around it.

"You are trembling, too, you know," she whispered.

Ezra smiled. "I am married to the most beautiful woman in the world. A man cannot help but find himself a bit intimidated by the fact."

"I seem to recall a few hours ago you were not quite so intimidated." She leaned to press a languid kiss to his neck.

"Yes, well, extemporaneous circumstances and all that."

Miri giggled and sat up to meet his eyes. He was smiling as he traced the tips of his fingers in delicate paths along her back and arms. She suddenly wished there was not a swath of thick fabric separating his fingers from her skin.

His skilled ministrations, his expert affection—it was strange to think that only a few days ago, the man had never been with a woman.

"You are not a vestal man any longer, are you?" she asked.

He dipped his chin and shook his head, the corner of his mouth curling into a grin.

"Then perhaps you will be delighted to know that your expertise at this is unmatched."

He raised a single brow. "Unmatched?"

She bit her lips to keep from grinning.

"Pray, continue, Lady Kelach."

She could not meet his eyes, instead watching her own finger as she traced his Adam's apple, relishing the way his skin grew taut. "Perhaps you are unaware, but the act is not usually so...effortless."

"Effortless?" he asked.

She could not help her grin. "Yes."

"As opposed to?" he asked.

"Awkward."

"Awkward," he parroted, pulling at the pins that held up the top half of her curls.

As her hair fell, she went on. "And—dispassionate."

"Dispassionate?" he repeated, though it was clear his interest in the conversation was waning. He turned his attention to the sensitive skin just below her ear and let his lips explore.

"Fumbling," she said, her breath growing rather shallow.

Ezra moved his hands to the filigreed buttons that ran down her back, undoing them skillfully.

"And rarely so rapturous," she said, though the word was barely a breath. "Especially for a woman."

"Hmm," was his only reply.

Soon, the heavy gown was loose around her shoulders. With deft movements of his capable hands, he slid her free of the fur and brocade and laid the dress lovingly aside, and she perched upon his lap once more. She wore the delicate lace chemise Kit had gifted her beneath her corset, and upon seeing it, Ezra's eyes glazed over.

She kissed him as she slipped her hands beneath the layers of his own clothing—the intricate brocade tails, the ornate vest. When she reached his cravat, she stopped the kiss to meet his eyes, to watch him as she worked the knot. And in his eyes shone such adoration. Such affection. Such delight. She thought she might get lost in those eyes, as rich as burnished gold.

Of all the riches known to man, of all the treasures to be found in Hasamayim, she knew here, in the arms of this man, she had found the most priceless of all.

CHAPTER THIRTEEN

"Do you have a terrible pain, Princess? Or is that your attempt to look lively?"

The Crown Princess of Har-Navah did not bother to so much as blink in response to the baiting question, biting her tongue and only lifting her chin slightly as she stood on the edge of the grand ballroom at Chesedelle and overlooked the festivities with no small measure of disdain.

A ball. In her honor. As if she were sixteen years old and coming out for her first season. Instead, she was twenty-three, barely relieved of her betrothal to the Grand Duke of Kinnereth, reduced to watching a gaggle of desperate bachelors fawn *not* over her, but over her *father*.

"They certainly know the game they're playing, don't they?" he went on.

Rachæl deigned to look at the man this time.

Dressed in a white, ruffled shirt tucked into the waist of deep crimson pants and polished black leather boots, Gian had at least bothered to put on a jacket—crimson with gold embellishments—though he had not bothered to button it. Otherwise, there was nothing formal about his appearance. He hadn't even laced his shirt enough to hide that deep V of his golden, sculpted chest, or the tattoo on his skin. She could not be sure, with most of it obscured by the ruffles of his shirt, but it looked like it was round at the top with a dark center. A skull, perhaps?

When she realized she was staring at his chest—and that he had noticed with no small measure of satisfaction—she abruptly lifted her chin and offered him her most disdainful snarl. "You could have at least bothered to comb your hair. Or do you own a comb?"

Gian winked. "I must have misplaced it."

Rachæl rolled her eyes and turned her attention back to the ball. Suitors from all over the kingdom had come tonight, lords and knights and dukes alike all vying for her hand. Ever since she had been dumped from Ezra's life like a chamber pot, the eligible bachelors of the kingdom had been sniffing around, hoping to benefit from the Grand Duke's scraps.

"Are you going to dance with any of them?" Gian asked, a chuckle coloring his words.

"I see no reason to. I'm not the one they need to convince." Just as she said it, one rather ostentatious lord with whiskers growing thick and long down his cheek and chin bellowed a jolly laugh for the king's benefit, slapping a hand on his shoulder as if they were longtime friends reminiscing about the good old days.

"Well, you must admit they're resourceful," said Gian.

"Did you know that not a single one of them has spoken to me?" she demanded. Not that she had minded. But it *was* rather obnoxious when she thought about it. All of this was obnoxious. She scowled.

Gian looked out across the ballroom, scanning the crowd as the glittering chandeliers scattered flecks of gold across the dancers. "I noticed the queen is conspicuously missing from the grand affair this evening."

Rachæl shrugged. "Mother was not feeling well. Believe me, I gave her a piece of my mind."

"I've no doubt," he said with a throaty chuckle.

"This whole farce was her idea, and she dares to come down with an illness this very night? Does she relish throwing me to the wolves?"

"Darling, in a den of wolves, I'd place my bets on you any day."

Rachæl scoffed, but had no time to retort before—without invitation—Gian took her elbow and pulled her toward the center of the room.

"What are you doing?" she barked.

Gian did not answer, tugging her relentlessly in his wake and only facing her once he had swooped her into his arms.

"I do not remember agreeing to dance with you," she snapped, ignoring the pleasant feel of his taut arms around her.

"You should dance at your own ball," Gian said.

"The point," she said, her words razor sharp, "is to dance with eligible suitors. Not brazen, unkempt, washed-up pirates."

"Washed-up?" Gian asked with an affronted smirk. Rachæl's attention landed on a strand of his thick blond hair as it fell across his brow and played with his thick lashes.

"Everyone knows you gave up piracy to work for my father."

"Yes, that is the going theory," Gian said with a lazy grin.

He whirled her around the dance floor as if he had been formally trained in court decorum from birth, and though she was loath to admit it, he was rather good. Annoyingly good. His practiced hands guided her smoothly through the dance, his arms strong and solid around her, his footwork without falter. And the way he smelled—like salty seas and cool, summer rains—threatened to overwhelm her senses with its delightfulness.

"Are you going to tell me that you still pillage in your spare time?" she asked, lifting one eyebrow.

"Pirates do not pillage, darling," he said. "We simply reap untoward benefits."

Rachæl rolled her eyes. Deftly, he moved her through a rather complicated minuet, and she was struck by how effortlessly they had fallen into the dance, into each other's arms. As if they had danced a thousand times together. "I did not realize dancing was part of your duties where I am concerned," she said.

"I am a man of many talents, Princess." Gian inclined his head to her.

"So I've heard."

His face curled into a devilish grin.

Princess Rachæl sighed. "You certainly have one talent, Gian of Borras. Your ability to find a compliment in the most mundane conversation is unparalleled."

"I have found, as a rule, the gentler sex are eager to levy compliments in my direction," he said.

"Yes, I can see them lining up now."

Gian laughed, but Rachæl did not join him, her attention suddenly fixed elsewhere. Gian turned them enough to see where Rachæl glared.

"What-ho! The Lord of Desperation approacheth," said the pirate.

Indeed, Lord Duriel was worming his way through the crowds, pausing to smile and nod at his adorers. His mustache was waxed in a particularly obnoxious curl at both ends tonight.

Rachæl groaned.

"He can't be that bad," said Gian.

"No. He's worse," she countered. "And do not mock me."

Gian whirled her again, turning her back to Lord Duriel as they danced. A wolfish smirk curled his mouth.

She rolled her eyes, understanding his game. "You won't be able to stave him off forever."

"You underestimate me, my lady."

"No one would ever dare such a thing."

Gian winked, but Rachæl did not have time to respond, for Lord Duriel was only a few steps from descending upon them and utterly ruining her already useless night.

"You have a choice," Gian said, capturing her attention again as he whirled her through the jaunty minuet. "You can either stay here and let someone else determine your fate, or you can come with me right now."

"Wouldn't that make *you* the determiner of my fate?"

His lips curled at the corners. "I can think of much worse."

"*You* are the only wolf here tonight."

His grin only deepened.

Rachæl looked over Gian's shoulder once more. Lord Duriel was opening his mouth to speak to her, his mustache like a smear of black wax on his face.

She turned her attention back to her cohort in crime, whose smirk had never left his full lips and sighed. "I have a feeling I'm going to regret this."

Rachæl stood in awe not three steps through the door, trying not to gape at the trove of treasures and trinkets and *things* crowded into every spare inch of Gian's private quarters. Though the entrance to his chambers was far from her own, there was a secret few knew: his chambers shared a private castle garden with hers and hers alone. Gian, among his many other duties to her father, had been given these quarters to keep an eye on the princess of Har-Navah. In her father's words, to *protect* her. But Rachæl had always known the truth: Gian was her father's eyes.

Yet here, in the quiet privacy of his rooms, for the first time ever, Gian did not feel much like a guard. He felt more like a mystery to unfold.

The room was...full. Cabinets of curiosities lined every wall, crammed with bric-a-brac from all over the world: painted porcelain vases and ornate silver candelabra, intricate nude sculptures and engraved brass mugs. Shelves of bones and books and small chests. Cabinets of skulls and bottles and vials. And weapons. Rapiers and stilettos, fighting knives and massive ancient double-edged swords, the likes of which she imagined King Ferryl himself to have carried.

Gian's back was to her as she gawked, but when he turned, he handed her a surprisingly basic wooden mug, filled nearly to the brim. She lifted an eyebrow as she eyed it.

"I find life is better enjoyed when imbibing libation."

She sniffed the cup. "I don't drink."

"Yet," he amended, lifting a single finger.

She leveled him a flat look and turned her attention back to his trove of *things*. "What is all of this?"

"Are you truly so surprised?" he asked, cocking his head to one side before drinking rather heartily from his own wooden mug. "I am a pirate, after all."

"In five years of knowing you, I find you are much more of a cliché than I ever anticipated," she said. She intended the observation to be an insult. Instead, Gian smirked. Just as he always smirked. Gian was a walking, talking Smirk.

"I am nothing if not a man of tradition," he said with a bow.

Rachæl snorted and moved toward a nearby apothecary chest, reaching for a rather large object resting on a stand on the top of the chest. "A tusk?" she asked, eyeing the large ivory piece with a measure of surprise.

Gian nodded, moving to her side.

"I did not realize a boar could grow so large."

"That did not belong to a boar, Princess," he said, delighting in the horror that flashed through her eyes at the thought of a creature larger than loathsome, vile boars.

"Relax," he said, taking the heavy piece from her. "It belonged to a creature called a mammoth."

"A mammoth?"

He simply nodded, glancing down at the large piece of ivory in his hand. "They're mostly found in the western continent. But ever since Medinah began her ruthless exploration of our humble corner of the world, they have brought the giant beasts to many new regions. A display to awe their conquests, I suppose."

"Have you ever seen one?" she asked.

Gian smiled, but there was a darkness behind it. "Once. On the southern continent. A group of Medinians had been through one of the villages. A traveling carnival, full of the splendorous display only an empire like Medinah could afford. I think it was meant to entice the fools with the wonders that awaited them once her magnanimous holiness decided to grace them with her blessings."

Gian spoke of the empress with such disdain that Rachæl wondered what he wasn't saying about her.

"But once the pomp and circumstance had ended and the performance was over, the illusion of spectacle soon faded into stark reality."

"What reality?"

Gian's eyes grew distant, stories he either had never told or dared not repeat dancing in their darkness. "The Medinians are a special brand of cruel. The ringmaster was particularly—" Gian hesitated, the distance in his eyes fading to sobering honesty. "Let me put it this way: if you ever encounter a Medinian carnival caravan, run. Run away as quickly as you can and do not go anywhere near them."

"A circus? You would run from a traveling circus?"

"No, Princess. I would run from the cruelty of the Medinians."

She furrowed her brows. "My father signed the proclamation weeks ago. We're allies, Gian."

"Medinah does not take allies, darling. Only conquests."

Rachæl didn't like Gian's thoughts on the subject. But she did not pursue them.

He did not seem keen to keep talking about it, either, for he ran an absent finger down the long length of ivory, his mind far away before he said, "This beast—I'd never seen anything of its like in all my travels. He was—massive. Terrifying. And yet robbed of his splendor by the ringmaster's whips. Even in his size, his sheer brute strength, he was no match for that ringmaster. Not surprisingly, the beast died the very night the carnival ended—no doubt wearied by the whips and malnourishment. But the caravan disappeared without a word, leaving the poor beast behind to rot."

Rachæl looked down to the tusk in his hand, no longer as wondrous as it had seemed a moment ago.

"The people of the village plundered the carcass within the hour. I bought the tusk off a tinker the next day for far too much money."

"Why did you want it?"

"To remember, Princess."

When she looked up, Gian met her eyes and went on, a sobriety to his words she had never seen from the man. "To remember that cruelty is often clothed in beauty and wickedness is often drunk with pleasure. I never want to forget what the Medinians did that day. What they could still do. To any of us."

Rachæl swallowed once and looked around again, trying to dismantle the heaviness of the conversation. "And do all of your treasures have such sordid tales to go with them?"

The question seemed to break the spell over him, for he breathed a laugh through his nose and set the tusk back upon its stand on the apothecary chest. "Not quite so harrowing, Princess. You have an eye for the macabre, it seems."

She rolled her eyes and sighed. "Do you suppose she's going to be as cruel to us?" She knew he understood she was asking about the empress.

Gian did not answer for a long moment, taking a drink from his mug before finally saying, "Only if we are as naïve."

She did not meet his eyes this time, but stepped further into his chamber, running delicate fingers along his many, many treasures. "Is there anywhere in the world you have not been, then?"

"I have seen most of it."

"What is your favorite place you've ever been?"

"Here," he said simply.

She tilted her head to one side. "Har-Navah?"

"I've seen the wonders of the world, Princess. I stopped where I found the richest treasures." He smirked again and took another swig from his mug. "Are you at least going to try it?" Gian eyed the untouched mug in her hand.

"I told you I don't drink."

"I've never known you to be so pious," he said.

"It is not a matter of piety. I don't like it."

"Have you ever tried it?"

"Rum? Certainly not!"

"Why not?" Gian chuckled.

"Because it is unladylike."

Gian grinned, leveling her a mischievous look. He had a way of saying far too much without saying a damned word. As if he knew her better than she cared to admit. So she leveled a flat stare right back to him and then tipped the cup to her lips and drank heartily.

The liquid burned down her throat. Not an unpleasant experience, per se, but certainly one she was not expecting. She coughed.

"Careful, Princess," he said, taking the cup from her lips. "Rum is like passion. It is meant to be savored. Slowly."

Heat rushed to her cheeks, though she could not say if it was due to the rum or the comment. Probably both.

He took her empty hand and guided her across the room. When she realized they were making their way towards his rather large bed, something caught in her throat.

"I—"

But before she could finish whatever in all the realms of Sheol she was about to say, Gian pulled a chair from a small, round table she hadn't even noticed and gestured for her to take a seat.

"Oh," she said stupidly and sat.

Gian sat down opposite her and pulled a deck of cards from the breast of his jacket.

"I don't play," she said quickly.

"You don't drink either," he said, curling his lips into a grin.

"You, sir, are no gentleman."

"And here I was thinking you'd had your fill of gentlemen this evening." He shuffled the cards with practiced ease and began dealing them.

"I'm not joking. I don't know a single game."

He finished dealing and said, "Lucky for you, I am a shark."

"I thought we had established you are a wolf."

"A card wolf. I like that."

"Again, I must commend you for your uncanny ability to find a compliment in every turn of phrase."

"I am gifted in many ways," he said with a small, mocking bow.

"As the ladies will attest, no doubt."

A grin. "You're welcome to find out if the rumors are true."

"What, that you're a rake and a scoundrel?"

"Is that what they say?"

"Among many other things." If the rumors were true, Gian was a man of many talents with those of the gentler sex. Talents about which legend had spread far and wide. Indeed, there was not a woman in the castle who had not touted the finer qualities of Gian's *talents.*

Rachæl sneered, picking up the cards strewn before her and looking them over. A four with red hearts, a ten with a black symbol she did not recognize, a nine and eight with the same, and a young man dressed in finery. "What's this one?" she asked, showing him the card with the young man.

"A knave," he said, folding the card back into her hand. "You're not supposed to show me your cards, Princess."

"But what is that symbol?" she pressed on, ignoring his advice and showing him the card again. "I have four of them."

"Four?" he asked in disbelief. When she showed him the evidence of her apparently outlandish claim, he guffawed and said, "Of course."

"Of course what? Is there something wrong?"

"Only that I dealt you one card shy of humiliating me on the first hand."

"And is that such a bad thing?"

He chuckled. "Depends on who you ask, I suppose."

He walked her rather patiently through the finer points of the game, and—despite her better judgment—she placed perfectly good coin on the hopes that she would get the card she wanted in exchange for the card he assured her she did not need. Trusting that he wasn't lying, she gambled and sipped carefully of the rum in her mug.

Her gamble paid off.

Gian shook his head as he gathered the cards laid before him. "I have a feeling if we were playing for our clothing, I would be stark naked within five hands," he said.

Heat burned her cheeks without remorse at the bold statement.

He chuckled. "Do I offend, Princess?"

“Do you—do you often play—for your clothes, I mean? With ladies present?”

Gian laughed. “Darling, it would be rather pointless to play for such stakes with anything other than the finer sex.”

She folded her hands in her lap to keep from fidgeting, knowing full well that she was in over her head with this rogue before her. She had never met another like him. His bald comments. His ruthless flirtation. His complete disinterest in propriety or civility.

As pathetically nervous as a schoolgirl, she could not stop the tremble that settled in her fingers.

Perhaps her only recourse lay in the measure of dark liquid before her. So she took a healthy drink and played another hand. And another after that.

“What was it like being a pirate?” she asked, ignoring the fact that Gian occasionally glanced at her ever-growing pile of coin with correspondingly increasing disdain.

“Pirate-like, I suppose.” He dealt five cards and picked his up with such eager hope that it was all she could do to keep from giggling. Or perhaps that was the rum.

“Did you have shipmates?”

He placed a rather bold bet and then curled his upper lip in a soft snarl when she called the bet without hesitation. After she discarded only one card, he said, “No. I had a crew.”

“You were the captain?” she asked, surprised.

“Am,” he amended, never taking his eyes from his cards. He was determined to win a hand against her. She smirked and took another drink from her glass.

“You still have a ship?”

“I have a fleet, Princess.”

“A *fleet?”*

His attention rapt on the game, he made a noncommittal sound before placing his final bet.

He had won the hand, but only barely.

"Is this what they call beginner's luck?" she asked.

He dragged the small pile of coins toward himself and said, "In case you didn't notice, I just won."

"I noticed your win was lackluster."

He looked up, pausing the stacking of his pathetic amount of coins, his face frozen in disbelief for a brief moment before melting into an incredulous grin. He laughed. "Yes, my darling, this is beginner's luck."

"You did not gamble very aggressively," she pointed out.

"Yes, well, it's only coin, after all. If we were playing for your clothing, I'd have ensured you bet your corset."

It was her turn to stare at him in disbelief. When he laughed, she let herself laugh, too, and took another drink, feeling light and heavy all at once. An odd feeling, to be sure. Before she could make heads or tails of it, Gian refilled her mug and dealt again.

"You did not answer my question," she said.

"What question?"

"You have an entire fleet of ships?"

"I do." He placed his bet. She did, too.

"On what seas do you sail?"

"I do not sail the seas, Princess." He discarded only one card. She could see the impending victory in his eyes. But in her hand—

"What do you mean you do not sail the seas?" She doubled her bet. He met her with incredulous eyes before calling.

"I command a fleet of airships, darling. We sail the skies." He showed his cards. It was an excellent hand. Enough to win almost any game. Except this one.

She showed her hand and Gian scoffed most disdainfully. "How is that possible?" he cried.

She smiled. Five lovely red hearts, three of which were royalty. She did not fully understand what it meant, but it was surely enough to win again.

"I've been playing cards since I was a boy. I think I've had a legitimate royal flush three times in my entire life."

"Is that what this is called?" she asked, observing her cards innocently. Something flashed in Gian's eyes. But it wasn't anger or frustration. When his lips curled into a sensuous grin and his eyes narrowed softly, she knew it was something much more dangerous.

She set the cards down and took a healthy swig from her cup, for no other reason than to break his unflinching gaze.

"Careful, Princess."

She lifted her eyes and uttered a *hmm* before he went on. "You need some water."

"I have plenty to drink here," she said, lifting her glass. It felt surprisingly heavy, despite being nearly drained.

"Yes, well, if you don't pace yourself, I'll never convince you to come back." He stood, turning towards a table across the room and picking up a pitcher.

Surprised by the earnestness of his admission, she asked, "Were you planning to invite me back?"

When he glanced at her, his insufferable grin was back on his face. "You know I've been trying to convince you to gamble with me for years. If I am to be your warden, the least I can do is keep you entertained." He sat back down at their makeshift poker table and set a glass of water in front of her.

"You are determined to corrupt me."

"Corruption can be such a delight."

"I don't think that's what my father had in mind when he gave you these chambers."

"What do you suppose he had in mind?" Gian asked. The question was anything but innocent.

"You *are* his eyes and ears, are you not?"

Gian only waggled his brows.

"Are you going to tell him about this?"

"Pray tell, what benefit would there be in telling him that I commandeered you from your own party in order to gamble and drink with you in my private chambers?"

She swallowed. When he put it that way... "Then what is it you think you'll accomplish? Do you suppose we should be friends?"

His face turned a bit more serious, though still bright. "Perhaps I was hoping you'd figure out what I already know."

"And what exactly do you know?"

"That you and I are the same."

She snorted a laugh. "We are nothing alike. At all."

"Oh, no?" Gian asked, undaunted.

"You are a rogue, and a scoundrel at your very best."

"And a bastard-born nobody, I know, I know," he said. "It is not our breeding that is similar, Princess."

"Then what is it?"

Gian waited until she met his gaze before he said, "I think you, like me, see what others do not. And I think you, like me, do not quite fit into the mold from which you have been formed."

She folded her arms across her chest. "Are you saying I am strange?"

He grinned. "I am saying you are more than people think you are." He eyed her untouched glass of water. "Drink, Princess. You'll regret it if you don't."

She looked at the water, too. "I fail to understand the logic of needing to drink when I am already, as it were, engaged in the act."

Gian laughed. "You'll find out tomorrow, if you're not careful. Rum is a cruel mistress. One minute a delight, the next a nightmare. Not unlike a woman, in that regard."

She furrowed her brow over the rim of her glass, but did not get a chance to retort because he went on. "Relax, Princess. I was not referring to you. It was one of my crew who once told me a truth I should not soon forget."

"What truth is that?" she asked, taking a break from the rather welcome glass of water.

"That a drink of rum is akin to a woman's breasts. One is not enough, and well, three is just too damn many."

She rolled her eyes in disgust and downed the rest of her water without comment.

Gian grinned, of course.

"We are nothing alike."

He nodded, his brows raised as if he knew something she did not. She resisted the urge to fling the remnants of her water in his face.

"Well, I may not be a gentlemen, but I am curious to know what you plan to do about the one whom you spurned this evening?"

"I'm assuming you're referring to Lord Duriel," she said.

"Who else but the dashing young love interest?"

"He is anything but young," she said, nearly under her breath. Before Gian could retort with some baiting remark, she added, "I have no plans besides marrying him, if that's what my father wants."

Gian furrowed his brows. "That seems a bit incongruous of you, Princess."

"Incongruous? How?"

"In the five years I've been at Chesedelle, I have never seen you behave as anything but a bold, strong woman who knows exactly what she wants. I have witnessed a girl become a queen in the making. Never once have I seen you kowtow to convention. That you would choose to do so now—"

"What would you have me do? It is my duty to marry, to provide heirs to the throne, to secure the strength of my family dynasty and my kingdom's power."

"I never said anything about not marrying. But what ever happened to being the maker of your own fate?"

"Gian," she said flatly. "I have spent the better part of my life betrothed to one man. I have *never* been the maker of my own fate."

A shadow flickered in his icy blue eyes, there and gone again in a moment so fleeting she wondered if she had seen it at all. But all he said was, "Then perhaps it is time."

CHAPTER FOURTEEN

Miri woke to a heavy arm draped across her belly. At her neck, Ezra's breaths were warm and steady as he slept. Even so, a lazy smile found his mouth as if he had also woken contented at the thought of being in her arms.

"Awake, sweet wife?" he asked groggily.

She couldn't help the grin that broke across her mouth. "Something like that."

Slowly, languidly, his hand began exploring her side, her torso, her arm. And with equal leisure, his lips explored her neck, her shoulder, her jaw. Her skin grew taut at his touch, and she breathed a deep sigh, stretching out beneath the warm, heavy blankets. Toes curling, she chuckled when she heard her stomach rumble.

"Mmm," said Ezra. "I couldn't agree more."

"Pray, what could you mean, my lord?"

"Only that I've had little to no sleep and if I don't get something in my belly, I'm sure to expire."

"How utterly terrible. Why didn't you sleep?" she asked playfully, with a heated grin.

"Oh, you know," he said, pressing kisses along her neck, her chest, her jaw. "I just couldn't seem to find the time."

His kisses made their way down her body, a halcyon affair for this crisp, snow-kissed morning. When he reached her navel, he lingered, taking a moment to run his hands along her thighs. She could see a question forming in his mind, as if an idea had occurred to him. It was not difficult to figure out what he was too shy to say. For a single breath, she hesitated. She had never once been so vulnerable, so exposed...

Ezra met her eyes, searching her. The heat, the intensity of his gaze nearly robbed her of breath, but she said nothing. Neither did he. He would not force her. He would not ask anything of her that she was not ready for. But a part of her—quiet and hidden for so long—wanted to be bold. Wanted to be brave and fearless and free of the shackles that had been on her heart for so long.

So Miri gave him her answer, bending her legs so that she might cradle him in a most intimate embrace.

Ezra smiled, loving and bright, then bowed his head and kissed her.

A momentary shock was quickly replaced with utter rapture. His lips, his warm breath—she had never known anything so enthralling, and soon her entire body was little more than clay in the potter's hands. She wondered if he knew what his touch did to her, what his languorous graze did to her most intimate places. Judging by the way he lingered, she imagined he had an idea.

She threaded her fingers through his raven locks, a bright warmth spreading throughout her body as his kiss lingered, heady and devastating. Only when he had coaxed every secret from her did he slink back up the length of her body and collapse by her side.

"Breakfast, woman," he said, his words husky and near breathless. "I cannot survive another moment."

Miri tried to clear her head of the thrill of his touch, but the intoxication did not easily wear off. Instead, she sighed and stretched, folding lazy hands behind her head. Ezra chuckled from her side.

"What?" she asked.

"We are never going to get out of here." He stretched above his head, reaching for the ribbon that would ring the house bells, summoning the servants to bring them sustenance.

"Were you hoping to leave?" she asked.

"If we want to make the railcar, we'll have to."

Miri sat up. "Railcar?"

Ezra's eyes dipped to her body and all she had exposed, making her realize her impropriety, and she promptly covered herself with the blanket.

Ezra grinned and pulled the blanket from her hands, baring her to him once more. He ran lazy knuckles down her arm and breast as he spoke. "We can take the morning train or the evening train. But if we are to take the morning departure, we shall have to find a way to pry ourselves from this bed soon."

"Where are we going?"

He smiled. "That is for you to find out."

"But we'll take a railcar to get there?" she asked, trying and failing to hide her eagerness.

Ezra chuckled. "Yes, my love."

"I've always wanted to ride on one!"

"I know," he said, leaning to press a kiss to her chest. She could feel by his touch that he was not done here. That he wasn't as hungry as he let on—not for food, anyway.

"But why are we leaving at all?"

"Our honeymoon, of course," he said, and the feel of his warm breath along the sensitive skin above her breasts sent tingles all through her. "It's up to you whether we leave now or this afternoon."

She knew what he would rather do. The way he touched her, the way he doted on her, lingered on her skin as if he were a starving man at a great feast, she could be easily convinced to do the same and spend most of the day right here. But—

Ezra grinned and sat upright again. "The morning train it is."

"Are you sure? I don't mind."

He kissed her cheek, soft and swift. "And for that alone, I wouldn't deny you another second," he said. "Let's get dressed, my love."

Before he could leave the bed, she took his face in her hands, kissing him thoroughly, headily, making sure he understood she'd make it worth his wait.

THE RAILCAR STATION WAS BUSY, travelers passing to and fro, bustling about the platform. Some were greeting family with bright smiles and warm embraces. Some were boarding the carriages, alone and solemn-faced. Steam filled the air as the railcar whistled once, startling Miri. Her eyes were as bright as a child's on Yasha morning as she watched the hubbub around them.

Ezra squeezed her hand and chuckled.

"It's so big!" Miri exclaimed as they took their tickets from the clerk. Indeed, the railcar was massive. Heavy black iron and ornate gold accents adorned the train, whose cars linked one after the other so far that she could not see the end. The station itself was perched on the side of a mountain in Chesedelle City, overlooking the villages below. The tracks hugged the rocks and cliffs before turning off into open sky, buttressed by long, intricate latticed supports that towered over the city itself.

Ezra could see the moment Miri spotted those supports, for her eyes went wide with mute horror.

"It's not so bad," he said.

"You've been on a railcar before?"

Ezra smiled softly. "Only once. My grandfather was invited to the inaugural ride of the first train built in Kinnereth. Naturally, my family got to go, too. That was only a few years ago, but the tracks have been built much more extensively since then. They span most of the kingdom now."

"Was it as terrifying as it looks?" Miri asked, turning her attention back to the towering tracks.

"You forget you're so high up when you're in the train, I promise."

When she didn't look convinced, Ezra pressed a kiss to her cheek for good measure and guided her towards the carriage.

"Tickets," said a collector, standing by the door in a polished navy-blue suit with gold buttons. "Port Challon," he said, eyeing the tickets Ezra handed him. "A bit cold this time of year, don't you think?"

"Port Challon?" Miri asked. "Where is Port Challon?"

"About as far north as a man can be," said the collector. He tore the stubs from the tickets and handed them to Ezra. "Enjoy your trip!"

"Thank you," Ezra said, nodding. With his hand at the small of her back, Ezra moved to usher Miri ahead of him into the carriage, but stopped when he realized she had frozen in place, unmoving as a statue. He followed her line of sight, scanning the thick crowd for whatever had given her pause.

Amongst the throng he spotted a man, tall and slender, dressed in what appeared to be white robes. Ezra's heart stopped.

Phinehas.

It was sheer instinct that had Ezra stepping in front of Miri, blocking her from the man whose back was still to them. Let him turn; let him dare take a step towards them. Heart pounding, Ezra fisted his hand at his side and spoke in low tones over his shoulder, never taking his eyes from the man.

"Get on the car, Miri."

But she did not move. He reached behind, taking hold of her hand when he found it, and squeezed once, firmly. "Listen to me, Wildfire. Get on the car."

Before he could finish his sentence, Phinehas turned in their direction. For a blind moment, rage coursed through Ezra's veins, and it was all he could do to keep himself from launching through the crowd and pummeling the slender, brutal priest to the ground. Only Miri's hand in his kept him from doing just that.

Once his vision cleared along with his thoughts, Ezra heard Miri exhale softly and that's when he realized the man wasn't Phinehas. A lesser priest from some northern province, no doubt, but not the High Priest of Har-Navah.

Ezra breathed again, too.

"Is everything all right?" the ticket collector asked.

Ezra turned to face him once more, attempting his best smile. "Everything is fine." He stole a quick glance at Miri, whose face was flushed, her eyes wide with lingering terror, and ushered her inside.

THE RAILCAR FEATURED TUFTED emerald damask chairs along the windows and a table and two chairs just down from there. Fine chandeliers reflected light from the ornate tin arched ceiling of the car, and thick velvet curtains were tied back along each window. Intricate patterns adorned the plush carpets, and the dark wood shone glossy in the gaslight.

"Where is everyone else?" Miri asked, taking in every detail of the carriage. Following behind them, attendants carried in their trunks and bags. Ezra and Miri moved out of the way to let them pass, and Miri watched as they made their way to the end of the car, pushing past heavy brocade curtains.

"This is a private car, Your Grace," said one of the attendants with a small bow.

Miri whirled to face Ezra again. "A private car?"

"It's a three-day journey. I thought we might enjoy a little time to ourselves," he said with a shrug, unable to hide what he knew would be color flushing his cheeks.

Despite the utter terror he had seen on her face only moments ago, Miri's mouth melted into a smile, and she responded with a soft kiss.

"Is there anything you need before we depart, Your Graces?" asked the attendant, tearing Ezra's attention away from his wife. "Something to drink, perhaps?"

"Sparkling wine?" Ezra asked Miri. She smiled, and Ezra nodded to the attendant, who bowed at the waist.

"The railcar will depart momentarily, Your Graces. We will be attending you during your journey. If there is anything you need, simply ring the bell." He pointed to a ribbon hanging on the wall near the door of the carriage.

"Thank you," Ezra said kindly.

"Yes, thank you," Miri echoed.

The attendants both bowed at the waist and disappeared out the door to the next carriage.

"All of this just for us?" Miri asked, looking around and above, turning slowly as she did.

Ezra moved behind her, curling his arms around her waist and pressing a kiss to her neck before he said, "It is our honeymoon, after all."

Miri sighed, resting her head back against his shoulder. But after a moment of silence, Ezra finally said, "Miri, are you all right?"

She took in a long breath and released it before she spoke. "I thought it was him."

"I know," he said, gently tightening his arms around her.

"I don't know what I'll do if I ever see him again."

"You won't," Ezra said, his words sharp and final.

"I don't see how we can prevent that," she said. "He is High Priest, after all. And you—*we*—are on the same royal council as he."

"He is not on the royal council. He is the leader of the Sanhedrin. The religious council only consults the royal council when circumstance calls for it."

"And with the occupation by Medinah, wouldn't you think circumstance will call for it more often?"

Ezra decided not to mention the good it did his heart to realize how much she understood the politics around them. It seemed as good a sign as any that she was healing and genuinely looking to assume her role as Grand Duchess of Kinnereth. But he didn't comment on it. Instead, he simply said, "Even if it does, I won't bring him anywhere near you again."

"It's not our seeking him out I'm worried about."

Ezra didn't point out that it wasn't what troubled him, either.

THEY DINED on some of the richest food Ezra had ever eaten. Sitting in their private table as they watched the world whir by beneath them, they had feasted and drunk until they could feast and drink no more. Ezra decided it was the perfect way to commence their weeks-long respite together, for Miri looked as contented as a cat in a swath of sunlight as she relaxed in her plush chair, gazing out the vast window beside her.

"The sunset is so beautiful, isn't it?" she asked.

Ezra reluctantly tore his attention from his wife to gaze upon the riotous colors—intense shades of crimson and ochre and magenta stained the skies, a golden crescent of sunlight making her final stand as she slowly sank to slumber behind towering purple mountain peaks.

"Do you suppose Providence stops what he's doing every night just to watch the sunset?" Ezra asked.

Miri turned her gaze to him, but said nothing. And with swift clarity, he realized what was on her mind.

Her cousin.

If the prophecies were true, if it was all to be believed, then Ari himself might very well be the Promised One. The son of Providence—whatever that meant. It was strange to think of it—that the man Miri knew and loved like a brother, the friend Ezra had come to admire greatly was...well...

What was he? A man? A son of a god?

It was clear he was something more than a man. Something...*other*. A shifter. A færy, as the old stories went. A being rife with magic and mystery, able to take on other forms.

The legends of the Fæ were so rare, so steeped in mystery that few spoke of them anymore. They could only be found in old books and manuscripts. Folk songs had been written of the men with one foot in the forest—the shifters who had been bestowed with a special brand of the magic of Providence. But most of those tales, if Ezra remembered correctly, spoke of men who could turn into wolves. Not stags. Why, most legends these days claimed that it was one of those Fæ Wolves that King Ferryl himself had encountered on the mountain in Old Haravelle the night he saw the Light of Providence. And Ezra's grandmother had told him more times than once that the furs on her white blanket were that of a Fæ Wolf, too.

Still, wolf or stag, it was a rare, strange kind of magic that could turn any man into animal.

Was that what Ari was? Did he hold that kind of magic?

As Ezra watched the sky shift into night and the first stars began to twinkle softly above the mountains, he could not help but think that, indeed, if Ari really was some version of Providence —well he must be something magnificent, if something as simple as a sunset could be so moving.

Perhaps he took the time to watch it now and then, just to marvel at what he had done. The thought brought a wonderful sense of humanity to him.

When Miri yawned, Ezra abandoned his thoughts and turned a smile towards her. "Tired, Wildfire?"

"I've done nothing but eat and sit. I'm exhausted," she said with a soft laugh.

Eagerly, Ezra reached out his hand across the narrow table that separated them. "Then perhaps we should retire."

Miri looked back over her shoulder to the heavy curtains that separated the railcar. "I take it that's our sleeping quarters. Let me guess. Bunk beds?"

An image of a cramped sleeping arrangement, several beds stacked one above the other passed through his mind. Ezra grinned and simply said, "Perhaps you should see for yourself."

When Miri met his mischievous gaze, her face heated. But she stood from her dining chair and crossed the short distance to the curtains. When she pulled them back, she let out a soft gasp.

It had been a while since Ezra had seen a railcar. A few years ago, coming on the journey with his grandfather—the Grand Duke of Kinnereth—and his father, they had been offered a fine car, replete with all the luxuries the train could provide.

But it had not been anything like this.

When Ezra had booked passage on this train and selected the honeymoon car, he had no idea it would be quite this luxurious. For behind the curtain, Miri revealed a massive bed that stretched from wall to wall, with steps at the foot leading up into it. Covered in plush crimson velvet damask and rich furs, it looked large enough for four grown men. But it wasn't the bed that was the true wonder of the space; it was—

"The windows," Miri said breathlessly.

Yes. The windows.

Spanning the width of the train along the end, and arching over the bed completely, the end of the honeymoon car was practically made of glass, affording an astonishing view of the world outside. With the sun setting beside them, bathing the snowy expanse below in the last vestiges of gold, it seemed they had stepped into a vat of honey. The golden light spilled across the bed, warming the thick blankets and fat pillows. Miri took the steps and climbed across the bed until she lay on her back, looking up above them. She stretched her arms behind her head and breathed a contented sigh.

"Ezra," she said. "It's... I've never seen anything like this."

As Ezra made his way up beside her and stretched out by her side, he thought the same thing.

The sky passed lazily above them, errant clouds close enough to touch, turning purple in the waning sunlight. The first stars began to glitter in the twilight, and Ezra reached to take Miri's hand.

"I knew it would be nice," he said. "I didn't know it would be *this* nice."

"It's incredible," his wife said, never taking her eyes from the sky.

Ezra smiled to himself and joined her in silently observing the waning light. They remained thus for quite a while—a serene tranquility that settled deep into Ezra's soul as the train moved steadily along its elevated tracks.

Soon the sun had finished her journey across the sky, sleeping behind the towering mountains of northern Har-Navah. And with no light left to illuminate the landscape, only the skies could claim their attention now.

Ezra's heart stirred at the sight of those glittering stars and broad swaths of colorful clouds in the inky sky. Familiarity swept through him as if he'd known those stars, danced among them. But that was absurd to hold a memory of something impossible.

Regardless, one thing was for certain: he couldn't remember a night sky this vibrant in a long time.

"Do you remember the night you took me to the pond where you grew up playing?"

Ezra turned his attention from the sky above to look at his wife. "We found magic in that forest, didn't we?" he asked. Memories, like fog clearing from a mountain valley, began forming in his mind.

"Do you remember swimming?"

Ezra searched his memory. He remembered climbing onto the island that mysteriously floated above the placid waters of his childhood escape. He remembered sharing a fruit from the lone chalam tree that grew golden and splendid from the island. He even remembered Miri jumping into the water beneath them.

But he did not remember swimming.

"I know we must have," he said.

"The pond was not made of water," Miri said, and at her words, those bright, colorful clouds and glittering stars as numerous as sands on the seashore flashed through his mind once more, along with a picture of himself and Miri, tangled in each other, suspended in the midst of it all.

"Yes," he said. "Yes, I remember now."

"I've always wondered what it meant," Miri went on. "That night. The water that wasn't water. The stars and the sense of peace. Utter peace. It took me so long to remember what had happened that night. For it left me the moment we climbed out of the pond. But I've never stopped thinking about it. I've never figured out what it meant."

"It was magic," Ezra said reverently. "That's all I know. That forest had just been a regular forest when I was a boy. I did not take you there to see magic. I didn't know it was like that."

"It was Ari. That's where he went when he wasn't in the villages. I think—" Miri hesitated for a moment. "I think that's where he goes to...to be with Providence. To be with his father. I think that night he wanted us to see it, too."

"That's where he goes when he is the stag," Ezra said, surprising even himself hearing it aloud. He let himself consider it for a moment. That Ari was a shifter. Fæ. That he went into the forest as a man and came out as a white stag. That in that place, a man communed with the divine.

"Sometimes I am frightened," Miri said. "I don't know what is to become of him. I don't know what this all means. I don't know what's to become of us."

"I don't either," Ezra admitted, pushing a strand of her fiery curls behind her ear. "My comfort is knowing I get to face it with you."

Miri's smile was soft but genuine. Her kiss was equally as sweet. Ezra wasn't sure whether it was him or her who deepened that kiss, but when her arms came around him, when her legs entwined with his, he did not care anymore about stars or lingering questions or magical creatures.

All he cared about was her. All he wanted was to finish what had begun that morning.

He began unfastening the buttons that lined her back, kissing his way down every inch of the skin he exposed. Miri accommodated him when at last her bodice was loose, slipping her sleeves from her arms and abandoning the dress somewhere in the darkened train car. When he, too, was free of his clothing, he laid her back gently onto the thick bed and set about exploring her generous curves with his fingers and mouth.

Her answering sighs were like a sonnet on her plump lips, and he took delight in each one that she uttered. He was still reeling from it—what she had let him have this morning. A piece of her. A taste of her. That she had trusted him enough to be so exposed, so vulnerable. He had not stopped thinking of it for a single moment all day.

Her body was a valley of lilies in which to graze, an ocean of secrets in which to explore, to discover, to claim. So he explored. Touched. Savored. Tasted.

More. He wanted more. He wanted all of her. To claim her until their souls were forged into one, until there was no telling the difference between his body and hers, no division between one and the other. So Ezra moved until he was hovering above, watching her adoringly as she lifted glazed eyes to his and smiled lazily. He breathed a soft laugh. Joy. This was joy—deep and pure and true. He bent to kiss her, simultaneously nudging her thigh with his knee. She cradled him with her body, her skin delicate and supple against his. But before he could take what he so desperately wanted, he heard her breathe a little gasp.

"What's wrong, Wildfire?" he asked, hovering above her, surprised he could speak over the pounding of his own heart.

Ezra followed her gaze when he realized it was not on him, straining to turn his neck and look above.

The stars had been cloaked, not by clouds of color, but by sheets of silk in rich shades of green and blue. Rivers of riotous light spilled across the firmament in an ethereal dance.

"What is that?" Miri asked.

Ezra curled to her side so he could behold the spectacle with her. "Don't you know the stories?" he asked.

His wife only shook her head.

"They say up here, deep in the mountains, where a man is no

longer distracted by the modern world, this is where he can see the soul of Providence. And Providence likes to show off."

"Magic?" she asked in wonder.

Ezra nodded as he watched the splendorous dance of colors. "They say his magic never wavers. Never ceases."

"I've never seen anything so beautiful," Miri said.

Ezra ran a knuckle down his wife's cheek and smiled softly. "I've seen a few things."

Miri met his flirtatious smile and breathed a laugh of her own before turning her attention back to the skies. A long moment stretched in silence between them as they watched the sky dance with magic, Ezra gently running fingers down her arms as she contemplated the mesmerizing sight.

"I'm sorry," she finally said. "I just—I've never seen anything like it. I didn't mean to—"

"Keep watching, Wildfire. We have the rest of our lives to make love."

Her eyes were solely on him now, something deep and powerful in them. He thought he might not sustain his restraint if she kept looking at him that way. So it was to his utter relief and delight that she moved, pulling Ezra towards her with fluid grace.

"It's all right, Miri. I know you want to watch the sky," he said, wondering from where in all of the heavens he had found the ability to even say it, for her hands, her lips...

But he did not mind. He would truly be just as content to lay beside her and watch the sky all night if that's what she wanted.

"Do you know what I want, Ezra?" She waited until his gaze met hers again. "I want you to make love to me under the magic of the night."

It was all he needed to hear.

Ezra moved, laying Miri down gently, reverently beside him, kissing her passionately before he settled himself on her. She watched him intently as he moved, slow and steady, a rhythm to match the dance in the sky, and he marveled at her skin as it glowed turquoise and emerald in the light above them. Beads of sweat glistened like stars between her breasts and he took his time to kiss away each one, the salt of her skin like honey on his lips. Her body was soft and pliable, all gentle, rolling curves and exquisite warmth. Her curls glittered in the starlight, the fiery red muted to a rich umber. As she moved beneath him, her curls ebbed and flowed—a tide of sea kelp lapping along the shore.

Her emerald eyes danced with the fire in the sky while her fingers played skillfully along his back and arms. She was a song, a hymn undulating beneath him, a perfect harmony to the melody he made in her arms. He was the cello and she was the viola, entwining and playing off one another—a song of flame and light, of passion and abiding love. Soon that song had found its zenith, an intricate refrain singing of his need, his love, his unwavering desire for this beautiful creature.

His wife. Miri was his wife.

The thought undid him. To his utter delight, she came undone in his arms as well.

Ezra kissed her through the throes of it before collapsing beside Miri, listening to her pounding breath, a rhythm to match his.

"I did not want that to end," he admitted, breathless. "I couldn't quite help myself."

Miri smiled softly, her lips a glorious shade of cobalt under the magic skies. "I've never known anything like it, Ezra. What is between us. You— We—" She stopped for a moment, tracing delicate fingers along his chest.

"I know," he said, taking her fingers.

"I don't think you really do," she said, raising one eyebrow.

He chuckled, pulling her fingers towards him, kissing the tips. "You might be surprised."

"It's like...we already know each other. Like—"

"Magic?" he asked.

She stopped watching her fingers and stared at him, blinking once.

"Ezra," she said, glancing to the skies, still dancing with fire above them. "Magic, the things of Providence...you shouldn't compare them to sex. Magic is...sacred."

"And you don't think this is?" he asked, tucking her hair behind her ear.

"It's just sex. Great sex, I'll admit. But sex is just sex."

"No, Wildfire. I think there is *just sex* and there is what we share. I think if I had married the princess, as much as I might've enjoyed it, it would never have been like this. I think that even early on, when you thought Phinehas loved you, it was never like this, was it?"

Miri shook her head in mute shock, as if appalled at the candor of his thoughts on the subject.

"Do you know why? Because love, sacrifice, and faith, selflessness, hope, even friendship—they're all pieces of the same puzzle. They go together. And if a piece is missing between a man and a woman, sex might be nice, it might even be enjoyable, but it won't be whole. It won't be—this.

"Because this, Miri—this is magic. Love, Miri. Love is magic. Your cousin said so. And I've been thinking about that ever since. What it means. For us. For everyone. There is a gift hidden in that magic, hidden in love. Real love is given first, not received. And inside of that is a gift, hidden and quiet, waiting for those who would lay themselves aside. A gift that transcends language, that defies definition. I cannot tell you what it is. But I know you know it—I know you feel it, what is between us."

She held his gaze, taking in his words. "I did not know such a thing was possible."

"Neither did I, my Wildfire. Not until I met you."

Tears filled her eyes. Tears he kissed away, one after the other as they fell warm and salty down her cheeks. "I love you," Miri said. "Ezra, I'm so in love with you."

Ezra couldn't help it, the kiss he gave her. He couldn't help it when that kiss deepened, either. When her touch, her arms, her taste became a song in his blood. And when he lay spent beside her once again, finding his breath as he listened to her find hers beside him, he said, "I love you forever, Wildfire."

CHAPTER FIFTEEN

"Aren't we going to wait for the queen?" Rachæl asked.

Council members finished taking their seats around the long, polished wooden table at her father's command. Across the table, Gian lifted one eyebrow, but said nothing. The king ignored her question.

"Councilors," the king greeted them testily, pulling his chair close, tucking it under the end of the table. "You insisted on this godsdamned meeting. Now let's get on with it."

"Mother has not arrived," Rachæl tried again to speak. From the corner of her eye, she saw the other members of the king's privy council exchange significant looks, apparently aware of information she was not.

"The queen is not feeling well today," the king said. "The Grand Duke of Kinnereth will not be in attendance today, either. If I put off meeting every time one of you insolent bastards had an excuse to miss, I'd never meet with my council."

One of the councilors cleared his throat. "Your Majesty, our agenda today is to discuss our recent treaty with Medinah. It has come to the council's attention that there may be some facets of the finer details that you were not aware of at the time of signing."

"Finer details?" King Dægan asked, sitting back against his chair and crossing his arms.

"Yes, Your Majesty," said the councilor, a lord from somewhere in the south. Rachæl couldn't remember where and frankly didn't care. "It seems that in Her Imperial Majesty's haste to aid us in the transition, some details might have been overlooked."

"Are you questioning my judgment?" the king demanded.

Rachæl slid her eyes to Gian across the table, who was watching her with his eyes wide, his mouth set in his perpetual near-smirk. She rolled her eyes and looked away again.

"Of course not, Your Majesty," said the councilor. "As your privy council, we are simply eager to advise you, protect you and the kingdom, from any...surprises."

"I don't need to read every fine detail of every decree or treaty or plea that crosses my desk, Lord Barron. That's what I have a private secretary for. But you can rest assured that I am well aware of the important facets of the treaty with Medinah. Her Imperial Majesty made sure I was well informed."

Rachæl could have sworn she heard Gian snort. Or maybe that was her own private scoff.

"Of course, my lord," said Lord Barron. "We trust Her Imperial Majesty to be a woman of her word. Her track record with other kingdoms is without blemish. They are all thriving thanks to her generosity."

Rachæl did everything she could to ignore Gian's eyes, for they had widened, that smirk not so subtle anymore. Instead, she fixed her attention on her father, who seemed dismissive of the whole conversation.

"We are simply trying to understand some of the finer aspects of the agreement. Perhaps you could enlighten us," the lord went on.

"You were tutored as child, were you not, Lord Barron?" asked the king.

"I was," Lord Barron answered hesitantly.

"I trust your tutelage afforded you the luxury of learning to read."

Lord Barron froze, clearing his throat. "I simply mean that—"

"This is ridiculous," the king barked, slamming his hands on the arms of his chair. "If I didn't know any better, I might think that you were questioning me," he added, raking his dark eyes around the table. "Am I king or are you?"

"You are king, Your Majesty," said Lord Barron.

"Oh, good. I'm so glad to hear it," said her father, leaving Rachæl to wonder what had him so agitated. "Because instead of discussing inane land agreements and embargoes, perhaps we can discuss the problem of the godsdamned sedition forming right under our noses!"

"Sedition?" Rachæl asked.

"That rutting prophet, or whatever they call him. He's drawing crowds, inciting rebellion. He has scores of followers wherever he goes now. People by the hundreds gather to hear him talk of revolution. Of the New Kingdom or whatever nonsense he spouts. It has to stop!"

Gian's eyes were no longer on Rachæl, cutting to the lords gathered around the table—squirming in their seats and exchanging glances.

"My king," spoke another lord at the other end of the table. "We could not agree more that the prophet must be stopped. We—"

"Is that really what he is?" interrupted the king. "A prophet? What does the Sanhedrin say?"

The lord took a breath to speak. "They are quite perplexed as well, Your Majesty. But their official stance is that he is not a prophet, but rather some sort of charlatan. They, like us, are unsure as to his objective."

"There is no uncertainty. His objective is war," said the king.

Rachæl held her breath. Gian seemed to do the same.

"War, my king?" asked Lord Barron. "Do we have proof?"

"Have we need of proof?" her father retorted. "For a man who is raising an army of apostates under our very noses? We have all the proof we need, Lord Barron."

"We fear," said another councilor, "that making such a claim might only make things worse. Stir the hornet's nest, as it were. The people love him. Some are even calling for—"

The councilor hesitated, looking to his right at another man, who held his gaze with undeniable fear.

"Well. Say it, man!" said King Dægan.

"There are some, Your Majesty—not many, mind you, but some—who are saying..." He looked around again, obviously hating that he had been the one to bring up this news, whatever it was.

Rachæl wondered how bad it could possibly be, considering the king was signing treaties, no matter how minute, with a foreign country without so much as reading them. Was that not the worst thing for their kingdom?

"They are saying that the prophet is of the Adelaidian line. The...true successor to the throne of Har-Navah."

The king went utterly still, so much that Rachæl could not be certain he was breathing save for the small movement of his barrel-shaped chest beneath the thick, fur-lined brocade he wore.

The *Adelaidian line.* A phrase that had been all but banned at Chesedelle for more than three centuries. For that had been when the great uprising had occurred—when the nobles of the Ramagi family had decided that the descendants of King Ferryl and Queen Adelaide had become tainted. Their blood muddled. Their dynasty crumbling—the perfect storm for a new era. A new dynasty.

The Ramagi Dynasty.

Rachæl's dynasty.

And since the time that the Ramagi had laid claim to the throne of Har-Navah—and subsequently dispatched any who might speak against them—the term *Adelaidian line* had been banned.

The Ramagi dynasty was supposed to be the new era of Har-Navah. A promise of a better tomorrow, whatever that meant. Rachæl had never understood it. Never cared really. All she had wanted was to become the best she could be for her people, her kingdom.

If it was true that this prophet was gathering people against her father, citing an insurrection in the name of the original Har-Navarian royal line...

It could spell disaster. For everyone.

But mostly for her father.

"Three centuries," the king said, his words clipped and low, a growl coming from the back of his throat. "And I'm still having this fucking conversation about my family's claim to this throne."

No one moved. No one so much as blinked.

"And you are telling me now that it is a vagrant, a gods-damned vagabond who thinks he belongs here? With an entire army of followers who agree?"

"Not an army, sir," said Lord Barron, his words quiet, his eyes fixed on the table before him. "A few disorganized defectors at best."

"Oh, good," said the king. "And to think, only a moment ago it was a hornet's nest!"

The silence was as thick as molasses. Rachæl, impatient of the nonsensical lords, finally broke it. "Father, they are at best a band of uneducated peasants, easily persuaded. I would hardly call them a threat. You are a mighty king, and you have made for us a mighty kingdom. I wouldn't waste another moment's worry on vagrants and wanderers. Let us remain focused on what's important: namely the advancement of our kingdom and the terms of our treaty with—"

"The treaty is settled," he snapped, standing just as abruptly. His heavy chair scraped across the floors with a jarring shriek. "This meeting is a waste of my time."

With that, the king of Har-Navah turned on his heel and marched through the carven doors of his privy council chambers, leaving a table full of aristocrats to gawk at his empty seat and then at each other.

"Your father is in a particularly delightful mood today."

"I noticed you didn't bother opening your mouth in that meeting." Rachæl whirled to face Gian, who was only a step behind her. He shut the door to her private chambers and faced her once more, that insufferable grin on his full lips.

"You have a fixation with my mouth, Princess?"

"Once again, your ability to find an innuendo in the most mundane comment is unmatched," she said, turning her back to him and marching across her sitting room, finding her favorite chair and plopping down rather unceremoniously.

"Oh, I can find a lot more than an innuendo, Princess."

Rachæl scoffed as Gian took a seat on the chair next to her. "I do not recall inviting you to follow me here."

"I wasn't aware you were requiring invitations to your chambers," he said. "Pray tell where I can get one."

She leveled a flat look at him. "In Sheol. You should be well acquainted with the place."

"I've never been to Sheol," he said with his lip curled on one side. "But I've certainly known a few women who took me to its doorstep."

"I suppose I'm one of them," she said, picking at a thread on the arm of her chair.

"Quite the opposite, darling."

"I'm sorry," she said, sighing deeply and not meeting his eyes. "I don't mean to take it out on you. I just—don't understand my father these days." She looked up, meeting his gaze. Her companion seemed fixed on her every word. "You're his most trusted mercenary. Surely he tells you more than he's telling me. Do you think my father is intentionally ignoring the obvious, or do you think he's somehow lost his mind?"

Gian stood, taking the few steps to a sideboard across the room. Without invitation, he poured two glasses of wine, confidently, as if he owned the place. It had always been that way with him—in the five years she had known him, he had always treated her as if they were the closest of confidants, the best of friends. He picked up every conversation as if they had never finished the last. Every glance he exchanged with her made her feel as if they shared a private language no one else understood.

As her father's eyes and ears, she had tried to keep him at a healthy distance. But when Ezra had disappeared from her life, Gian had been there to fill the void in ways she hadn't expected. Nothing romantic, of course. But something better, if she was being honest with herself.

Gian had become something to her that Ezra had never been. As obnoxious as he was, and against her better judgement, Gian was becoming a true friend.

When she examined her feelings on the matter, she found she didn't mind, though she'd never stop giving him Sheol for being such an arrogant ass most of the time.

With his back to her, he said, "I'm assuming you're referring to your father's insistence on ignoring the finer details of the goings on of one Medinian Empress."

"It's like he's blind where she is concerned," Rachæl said. "I've never known him to be so willfully unsuspecting."

"Perhaps it is not with that cunning mind that he is thinking at the moment." Gian turned, walking back towards them, two glasses of dark liquid in hand.

"Then what is he using to think?" Rachæl asked, her cheeks heating the moment she heard the words come out of her mouth. "Don't answer that," she added hastily, ignoring his mischievous grin and taking the glass he offered, drinking without hesitation.

"For a girl who doesn't drink, it certainly seems you've found a taste for it."

"You speak as if I'm a lush."

"There is a half-empty bottle of port over there."

She swallowed her wine and narrowed her eyes. "Rot in Sheol."

Gian did not drink from his glass, waiting until she met his eyes again before he said, "Don't drink alone, Princess. It never leads to anything productive."

"I suppose your next suggestion will be that I should drink with you, should the need arise."

That grin returned as he lifted his glass. "I am nothing if not dedicated to my craft." He took a healthy swig of the sickeningly sweet wine.

She sighed and ignored his nonsense once again. "What if they're right, Gian?"

"Who?" he asked.

"The people," she said, deflating at the thought. All those people blindly following a madman who spouted unattainable ideals and lofty platitudes. In a matter of months, that prophet had acquired more followers than she had ever known any leader to gather. With a few words, he had turned the world on its head, challenging everything. And the people just *listened*.

"What in the world could they be right about?" Gian asked.

Rachæl sipped her wine before she answered. "All of it. The king. The throne. The Adelaidian line..."

Gian scoffed. "Bullshit, Rachæl. That's all this is. Complete and utter bullshit. This is what happens when a kingdom prospers—the people go looking for an excuse to whine and piss, and that's when they find someone to rally around. That godsdamned prophet was in the right place at the right time. Nothing more." He gulped the contents of his glass as if letting out his aggressions on the beverage.

"You saw my father today, Gian. It's like...it's like he's distracted. I don't understand it. But I tell you, he's signing away this kingdom, one decree at a time. Did you know he hasn't read a damned one of them? His private secretary told me he's signing everything without even reading them. Every statute, every decree, every order that the empress proposes, my father signs into law without question. It's insanity. Maybe that prophet is right. Maybe it's time for a new king."

"You listen to me," Gian said. Gone was his signature playful tone. Gone was his incessant flirtation. In its wake was a sobriety, a seriousness that she imagined few ever witnessed from him. "Your father is not himself, I'll give you that. I see it. We all see it. But don't you for one minute let that make you believe all this bullshit about the *rightful* king and the *rightful* heir.

"*You* are the rightful heir to this kingdom, Rachæl. You. Do you think I've stuck around here for my health? Do you think I've worked for your father all these years because it is such a delight to do his dirty work?"

Rachæl was stunned into silence, shocked at the words coming out of Gian's mouth.

"I stay here because of you, Rachæl. I stay because I see the woman you have become and the queen you will be one day. I stay because it will be a damned privilege to serve you. To bow to you. Because you will be a bloody good queen. Don't you dare let some ideal-spouting *twit* convince you otherwise.

"You are my queen. You are the queen we deserve. Anyone who says otherwise can go straight to Sheol. And I will be glad to send them there."

"Gian," Rachæl said, shooting him a flat look.

"What?" He huffed the question in an annoyed tone before he downed the last of his wine.

She couldn't think of what to say, how to respond. She had never met someone quite so passionate. That his passion was about *her*... She had never met anyone who believed in her like that. At least not anyone who'd had the stones to be vocal about it. She wasn't sure how to take it, what to make of it.

She finally settled for just saying, "Thank you."

He did not respond. For reasons she could not guess at, he actually seemed unable to come up with a response. Instead, he stood and said, "I leave in the morning."

"Where are you going?" she asked, standing with him.

He made his way to her sideboard and poured himself another glass from that bottle of port. This time, he filled his glass to the brim. He drank the whole thing in one swallow before he said, "A small village, just over the Tsulah border. A town by the name of Anan."

"What's in Anan?" she asked.

Gian refused to look at her. "Work."

"Work," she repeated flatly. "For my father, you mean."

"It pays the bills, after all."

"Gian, what's wrong?" She moved towards him, suddenly curious and concerned by his change in demeanor.

He whirled to face her before she could rest a hand on his shoulder. “Nothing is wrong, Princess. I will return in a few days.”

Without further explanation, he left her standing alone in her chambers.

CHAPTER SIXTEEN

Port Challon was like something out of a storybook. Towering mountains spilled into a sprawling crystal bay that opened her arms to the wide, blue ocean beyond. Glittering snow blanketed the rugged landscape and fat, crystalline icicles dripped motionless from every branch, every rooftop, every elevated surface. Homes stretched along the banks of the bay, their roofs smeared with fat snow, like icing on a decadent cake. Smoke puffed from the chimneys, floating lazily into bright, clear blue skies.

At the mouth of the bay, a bustling village sprawled across the long beaches. Ships docked along the shore, coming and going like ants on a busy mound. Their train car had begun to slow down a while ago, the towering tracks affording Miri an excellent view of the winter wonderland beneath them, and she had been nothing short of mesmerized by every bit of it for the better part of half an hour as she sat in the one of the luxurious chairs in the living space of their private car. Across from her, Ezra watched in equal wonder.

They had spent the last three days in a haze of decadent food, glorious views, and long conversations, interspersed between unhurried exploration of each other, as if discovering the other for the first time. She had been laid bare by Ezra's gentle patience, his carefulness to ensure she was comfortable at every turn, with every touch. She could feel his need for her with every tender caress, could see it in his eyes every time he looked at her. But he did not take, did not push her too far or too quickly. He only gave. She was not sure she could explain the distinction, much less put it into words. Whereas intimacy had only ever been a one-sided affair in the past, Ezra had shown her something entirely new. She marveled at the fact that a man without prior experience could be so learned.

But that tenderness, that selflessness had brought out a feeling in her that she had never considered before. To feel *comfortable* being so bare, so open with another—it was a possibility she had not entertained. The more Ezra touched her, the more he luxuriated in her, the more she wanted to give.

Slowly, kiss by kiss, touch by touch, piece by piece of her heart, as much as it terrified her, she could feel herself giving in to her husband's capable, tender care, trusting him more and more.

She could only pray she would not come to regret it.

THE VILLAGE WAS PACKED. People from all over the world moved about, hurried and intent. Shops and restaurants clustered up and down every street, tinkers selling their wares on the snow-lined cobblestone streets.

Miri pulled her fur collar closer and watched her breath cloud before her mouth as she said, "I did not think such a place would exist so far north."

"What did you think was up here?" Ezra asked, amused.

She looped her arm through the crook of his to steal some of his warmth as they departed the train station. They had opted to walk the short distance to the hotel where they would be staying for the next few weeks, just to do a bit of exploring. The cabbie had gladly taken their trunks for them, and Ezra generously compensated the man for his trouble.

"I suppose I thought the world ended somewhere at the edge of the old country," she admitted, laughing to herself.

"Of Old Navah?" Ezra asked. "You must have thought you were sentenced to the edge of the world when you moved to Kinnereth."

"I did," she admitted.

Ezra chuckled. "Port Challon is the hub of commerce and imports for Har-Navah. It's our window to the rest of the world."

"Why this far north though?" It seemed terribly out of the way.

"Geography, mostly," he answered. "The port is perfect for ships to come and go, and the surrounding mountains mean the weather stays generally calm."

She looked around at the snow and ice. "It's completely frozen, Ezra."

He chuckled. "I didn't say it stays warm. But the weather in this region is different than the rest of the north. Whereas blizzards and ice storms are a common occurrence in places like Chereth and even Borras Provinces, in Port Challon, it's just lazy snowfall most of the year. It has something to do with the mountains and wind streams, and I don't fully understand it all," he said. "But as a rule, it's cold but calm in this region of Har-Navah."

"And beautiful," she added.

Ezra kissed her cheek. "I was hoping you'd think so."

"You've been here before, I take it."

"My grandfather came here often when I was a child. He stayed actively involved in the trades and embargoes that affected Kinnereth in particular. But with the duchy, our obligations go far beyond our own province. He made sure that our people were being treated fairly, that taxes were collected properly, and that goods were readily available to the people of Har-Navah. This port does not just serve our kingdom, but the rest of the world as well. We trade with Medinah, Midvar, and many other countries as far as the Southern Continent on these waters."

"And so we are here for more than just a honeymoon, I take it," Miri said.

"No business this trip, Wildfire. But I thought you might like to see this place—see the commerce and the hub of our kingdom's industry."

She did like it—all of it. Busy and bustling, yes. But not in the way Teman City had become like a beehive of people, always agitated by something. No, Port Challon was a thriving hub of so many peoples from all walks of life and corners of the world. A great melting pot of ideas and creativity and progress. A wonder to behold, even if she was grateful for the quiet peace of a village like Shalem.

THEY DINED in a restaurant perched on a small cliff over the waters. Lauded as the best seafood in town, Miri could not resist when Ezra asked her where she'd like to eat. Having grown up on the coast of Teman, she missed the cuisine of the ocean: shellfish and bright, fresh herbs, oysters and crab fresh from the bay.

But this food was nothing like what she had grown up eating in Teman. Everything here was warm. Rich. Luxurious. Soups with heavy cream and bits of clam, spiced with cardamom, paprika and cloves. Dense, crusty breads served with giant shellfish tails, flavored with aromatic spices and butter. So much butter. One thing was obvious: in these northern climes, the locals did not hesitate to dine on fatty, soul-warming foods to counteract the constant chill in the air. And Miri had to privately agree: she was warmed to the bone by the time they finished eating.

"Would the lady care for dessert?" the waiter asked, a crisp, white towel slung over his arm.

Miri entertained the idea. She really did. But she was not certain she could eat another bite. She looked to Ezra, who wore an amused smile as he watched her.

"I think we will have to wait a while for dessert," her husband said.

The waiter nodded, satisfied, and turned to leave. Miri sighed contentedly and watched as Ezra signed a bank note, which he folded crisply and placed under a napkin. "Shall we?" he asked her.

Miri nodded and moved to stand, but Ezra was faster, coming around the table and pulling her chair out. He took her hand when she stood and pressed a kiss to her knuckles.

"My lord?" said a voice from behind them.

Ezra turned. "Ah, Lord Tarron!" he said amiably.

"What in Providence's creation are you doing this far north?" the lord asked.

"Honeymooning," Ezra said with a smile. "Lord Tarron, this is my wife, Lady Miriam Kelach."

She loved the sound of her new name on her husband's lips. She donned a broad smile.

"My lady," said the lord, taking her hand and bowing over it. "I did not know you had taken a wife!" he said to Ezra. "What a pleasant surprise. And what a beautiful duchess we have gained."

"Grand Duchess," Ezra said.

"Oh," said the lord. "I didn't mean—"

"It's quite all right." Ezra took Miri's hand. "She is Grand Duchess of Kinnereth now."

Not just duchess. Not just wife. Heir. Miri tried to hide her blush.

"How...wonderful," the lord said, obviously confused. He eyed Miri skeptically for a moment before he engaged Ezra in a conversation about trade and taxes and things about which she knew absolutely nothing. Looking about their corner of the room, Miri glanced at the note Ezra had folded under the napkin. Discreetly, she reached for it, lifting a corner of the napkin enough to see what he had written. The amount was extravagant.

Much more than a dinner should have cost—even one as glorious as theirs had been.

"Well, I have no desire to infringe on a bride's respite with her new husband," said Lord Tarron, bringing her back to the present. "I shall leave you to it. It was good to see you, Your Grace. Please give your sister my regards."

"I will, Lord Tarron," said Ezra. "It was good to see you, too."

"Do you know everyone, then?" Miri asked, taking his arm when he offered it, letting him escort her through the restaurant.

"My family—*our* family—has been serving this kingdom for centuries. I would hazard there are few we don't know, even if only by name."

Our family. *Her* family. Because she was a part of that legacy now. It was hers as much as it was his. She could only hope to live up to it.

Ezra pushed open the doors that led to a crude pathway down to the beach. Bustling with ships and merchants, it was by no means quiet and secluded. But it was fascinating—all of the people shouting and dealing and trading. She nestled more closely to Ezra for warmth as they walked.

"The note," she said. "I couldn't help but notice..." She hesitated.

Ezra didn't say anything, just tilted his chin, waiting for her to go on.

"You paid a lot. Much more, surely, than our dinner cost."

Ezra watched the sailors on a nearby dock as they hauled large baskets of fish onto dry land, but he did not respond immediately.

"You always used to overpay Joshua and Winona for our breakfast, too. Winona also once told me that you're the patron of the theatre in Shalem. Surely it wouldn't be so extravagant without you. Why do you do that?"

"Because all of this, Miri, everything we have is because of them. We were born into this privilege; we did not earn it. Not by work, anyway. So I'd rather earn it in other ways."

"Other ways?"

"By giving back," he said. "By taking care of the people. Our work is to manage well and keep things fair so that they can work and provide and create the wealth that keeps this kingdom going. Our job is to protect them so that they can protect their families. But if we ever forget, even for a moment, that our role is for *them,* not us, then we've forgotten our place.

"We did not choose the system in which we live. We did not choose how this world works. But we can choose how we treat others. And that choice is our ultimate privilege."

"I have a feeling," Miri said, leaning her head against his shoulders as they walked slowly, "That someone very special taught you that."

"Oh, yes?" Ezra asked. "And who is that?"

"Your grandfather."

Ezra stopped their strolling, turning and taking her chin so he could meet her eyes. He kissed her softly but fervently and then said, "That might be finest compliment I have ever received."

THEY CONTINUED their stroll along the docks of Port Challon, watching as the sun set, spilling riotous shades of gold and pumpkin across the ocean waters beyond. They walked through clusters of spice merchants, cloying scents assaulting them with a potency she would not soon forget. They walked past fishermen and tradesman, lumber ships and merchant ships, all of them either coming or going, unloading or loading wares.

The docks seemed to stretch on for eternity down here. From the city above on the hillside, it didn't look quite so vast. But down here, as they walked for what seemed like miles, the ships never ended.

"Tomorrow I want to take you to the caverns," Ezra said.

"Caverns?"

"Beneath the mountains, there are caverns that stretch on for miles. They were once mines for minerals and riches. But they were abandoned centuries ago when their bounty ran out. Now, they are a beautiful, haunting testament to bygone times."

"I would like to see that very much," Miri said.

"I thought you might," Ezra said, pleased with himself.

They walked on a bit further before Ezra finally pointed out that if they didn't turn around soon, they would be walking back to the town in darkness. Miri agreed, but before they could turn around, Ezra stilled, looking out across the last stretch of the bay.

"What is it?" she asked.

He narrowed his eyes, the waning light making it difficult to see.

"Ezra?" she asked again.

"That cannot be right," he said, almost to himself.

"What's wrong?" she asked, following his gaze out across the bay.

A line of ships were docked at one end, different from the rest. Not weathered with age and seawater, and clearly not stocked with crates and trunks. No, these ships were massive with obsidian hulls and towering black sails that stretched into the twilight. She couldn't be sure, but she thought she could make out the emblem on one of the sails.

A winged serpent.

"What is that?" Miri asked, a dark and foreboding chill crawling down her spine.

"A wyvern," Ezra said, his eyes fixed on the black ships.

"What is a wyvern?" she asked, afraid she did not want to know the answer.

"The symbol of Medinah," Ezra said ominously.

"What is Medinah doing here? Are those trade ships?"

"No, Wildfire. Those are not trade ships."

"Then what are they?"

She did not like the tremble that settled in her bones, one that had nothing to do with the wintry chill of this northern climate.

Ezra kept his eyes fixed on the shore, his gaze hard, his jaw set. She clung to her husband, her skin shivering with horror when he finally managed to answer.

"Those are Medinian warships."

CHAPTER SEVENTEEN

Anan was a shithole.

Gian hated everything about it. No commerce. No industry. Nothing of the modern world. Just farms. Farms and farmers and pigs and mud-caked snow. And the king had sent him on this shit mission to this shit town to do his shitty grunt work.

He used to love it—the dirty work. He loved the reputation that had come with it more. Everyone feared him. Everyone gave him a wide berth—the king's favorite weapon. No one really understood exactly what he did for the king. Mercenary or spy or assassin...the rumors had abounded for years. Gian had relished every one of them, for it was a chance to give the people of this world what they deserved and get paid to do it. It was a chance to see forgotten corners of Har-Navah for good coin. And a chance to pay the world back for all the shit it had put him through.

Now it was just another reason why it was all shit.

All of it.

When the king had assigned him to keep an eye on the High Priest in the godsforsaken village of Shalem months ago, Gian had grinned and borne it. Being away from the castle for weeks at a time had proven a much more taxing task than he had anticipated. And the High Priest had proven to be as slippery as the king had assumed. No wonder he had been laying low ever since that prophet had stood up to him for the sake of that redheaded whore. Everyone had seen the priest—and the ambassador—for what they were that day.

Liars and charlatans.

And, if the rumors of their clandestine operations were true, he could add murderers to that list as well.

So Gian hadn't minded keeping an eye on them, even if it meant being away from Chesedelle for weeks at a time.

Then that assignment was over. The High Priest had been laying low, so Gian had gotten several weeks of quiet with nothing to do but torment the princess.

Now, apparently, his unexpected respite was over.

Gian took a healthy swig of the swill this tavern called ale and slammed his mug on the scarred counter before him.

"Another," he said.

"We're out," said the barkeep without turning to face him.

Gian groaned. "Figures," he said.

He laid a bekah on the counter and turned to trudge towards the stairs on the other side of the taproom. He needed to sleep before he set about the king's work. He needed to get his mind off of what he had done with himself. The mess he had made of his life.

He had handed over a godsdamned *fleet* for this shit.

Worse, he had nothing to show for it.

An image rose in his mind: blonde locks, perfectly curled; a long, slender neck rising from a lush swell of plump, creamy skin; and eyes...gods, those eyes that were the color of wheat in sunset; that laugh any time he said something shocking. Or inappropriate. Or colorful.

Which was often.

Gods.

He shouldn't be thinking about the princess. He needed to stop thinking like a godsdamned schoolboy and remember his place. *Her* place.

Two very different places in this godsforsaken world.

Gian of Borras needed a lot of things.

Another ale would have been damn helpful.

Sleep would have to suffice.

Then tomorrow he could face why he was here—reminding some asshole why he wasn't worth his salt. He'd take more than taxes this time. Maybe a finger. Or a toenail. The king had always given him permission. "Do whatever is necessary, Gian. Your methods are of no consequence to me."

No consequence, indeed.

Perhaps getting back to what he loved would clear his mind and remind him of his place. So perhaps tomorrow, Gian would explore new methods of exacting his revenge on the world. In the name of the king, of course.

"Yes, milord?"

"I am no lord," Gian said, resting a casual arm on the threshold of the jamb that separated him from the pudgy woman before him. She was not unattractive as women went, but she certainly bore the telltale signs of motherhood—unkempt hair, a halo of perspiration at her collarbone and temple, a smear of the gods knew what on her apron. On her hip rested a babe, suckling at his fists between fits of whining.

"Apologies," said the woman. "Can I help you?"

Gian peered around her shoulder into the small excuse for a

cottage on the edge of the winter-bitten farm. "Is the master of the house at home?"

Something in the woman stilled at the question, as if she knew. As if she were putting the pieces together. "Milord," she tried, her voice shifting to something urgent. Harried. "If you would only give him a chance."

"I simply need to speak with him," Gian said. But his tone was anything but comforting. "On behalf of His Majesty."

"Please," the woman pleaded. The child on her wide-set hip began to fuss. "Please, milord. He is doing the best he can."

"His best is inadequate," Gian said, and pushed past her, not waiting to be invited in. Ignoring the whining babe she carried, he drew a breath to speak when the subject in question appeared from a door across the small, unkempt sitting room.

"Sweetheart, I—" The farmer—Gregory was his name—froze mid-sentence, his eyes landing on Gian. He did not move except to square his shoulders.

"Hello," Gian said with a smile that did not meet his eyes.

"Sir," said the farmer soberly. "I just need a bit more time."

"I believe you have been given more time than you need," Gian said, helping himself to a plate of pathetic-looking cakes on the scarred kitchen table before him. He managed to choke down one, licking his fingers before he added, "Or had you forgotten?"

The man did not move from the threshold. "I have not forgotten." His words were low, submissive. "Times have been lean on the farm."

"Yes, I know. You missed your harvest taxes, Gregory."

"Surely the king can spare—"

"The king can *spare,* you ask?" Gian's mouth turned into his signature smirk. But it was void of any humor. "You dare to decide what the king can spare?"

"The crops have not been selling as they once did. We cannot compete with the Medinian merchants, selling all those exotic dried fruits and vegetables for far less than they're worth."

"Are you making excuses for evading your duty to Crown and country?" Gian asked.

"No milord," the man said.

"I will say it again: I am not a lord."

"Forgive me, I do not know your station."

Gian's mouth widened into what he knew was a vulpine grin. "No one does. And that's what terrifies you the most, isn't it?"

"Sir, please. If you will only wait until spring, I am sure I can sell more crops and pay my taxes."

"And what about the taxes you owe from summer? And last spring? And the harvest before that? Have you forgotten, Mister Gregory, that you owe the king for a year's worth of your wages?"

"We can barely make ends meet," Mrs. Gregory interjected, bouncing the babe on her hip as she spoke. "And I'm sure the king has more than enough—"

"Chloe," the man said firmly, stopping her mid-sentence.

Wise man.

Just then, a little girl emerged into the room, peering around her father's thighs. She was small—no more than six or seven at the most, with long brown locks that fell straight around her smooth, pure face and cherub cheeks.

"Go back to your room, Sophie, sweetheart," said her father, placing a loving hand on her head. She did not comply, instead meeting Gian's eyes with her own, which were wide and lined with thick, brown lashes. She said nothing, and it struck Gian just how much she affected him without so much as opening her mouth.

Gian took his eyes from the little girl at last, meeting her father's pleading gaze once more. "Your taxes, Mr. Gregory," Gian said. "This is the last time I will ask nicely."

Mr. Gregory squared his shoulders. "Girls," he said. "Take the babe and go outside."

Mrs. Gregory began sobbing—great, unbecoming gulps between battering cries. The babe joined her almost instantaneously. "Please. Please, my lord. Please," she cried.

"Now," Mr. Gregory said again, never once taking his eyes from Gian. The little one at his thigh—Sophie—never took her eyes from Gian either. Not as she crossed the room to join her mother. And not as she dutifully followed her outside into the bright, snowy world.

"Now then," Gian said, the swagger in his words not matching how he felt. He crossed his arms and leaned against the pathetic kitchen table. "It's down to brass tacks, isn't it?"

"Make it quick," said Mr. Gregory. "That's all I ask. What will it be? A thumb? A finger? An eye?"

Gian wasn't sure why he was in such a foul mood—perhaps a combination of the lack of decent ale at the tavern, an uncomfortable mattress, and being away from the castle...away from Rachæl. But Gian decided in that moment that the unfortunate farmer would be the lucky recipient of his particularly uncharitable feelings at the moment.

"Now see, Mr. Gregory, I am not your first visitor," said Gian letting what he knew to be an unsettling grin curl his mouth. "I am sure you're aware that by the time the king sends me, negotiation is no longer on the table." Gian picked up another of the dry cakes, taking his time to eat it, to let the silence stretch long and damning between them before he said around a mouthful, "His Majesty requires payment in full."

To his credit, the farmer did not falter in his words as he said, "I don't have any money."

Gian tilted his head to one side. "So it seems." He pulled a dagger from a belt hidden beneath his jacket.

It was the first time he saw the farmer flinch. The man wasn't as much of a fool as he let on.

"Please," the man begged, his eyes wide. "If you kill me, they will starve. They will die."

Gian took a step towards Mr. Gregory, all wolf on the hunt. "You should have thought of that before you spat in the face of His Majesty."

Mr. Gregory took a step back. Just one. "I swear to you, I will find the money."

"It's too late for all of that," said Gian.

He turned the stiletto in his hand once and pounced.

For the first time in memory, Gian did not feel like drinking. In fact, he did not feel like doing much at all.

He had returned to the shitty excuse for a tavern after his visit to the Gregory farm, and spent the better part of an hour washing himself—his hands, his clothes, his body. The bath had long since gone cold, the blood long since disappeared, but he could not help feeling that it lingered.

It lingered in the look on Mrs. Gregory's face—in the look on little Sophie's face—as he had emerged from their cottage, wiping blood off of his blade with a towel he procured from their kitchen. Lingered in the heaviness that threatened to swallow him whole as he walked away from that farm, knowing he had changed their lives forever. That with one flick of his blade, he had robbed that woman and her two innocent children of a chance at normalcy. At wholeness. At peace.

He should know.

He had been robbed of the same as a boy of only eleven.

It should have felt more satisfying—the chance to bestow

some of that pain on someone else. It should have felt like retribution.

Instead, he could only hear one word in his mind, over and over again. An anthem, fitting for who he was. Who he had become.

Murderer.

GIAN SLEPT IN FITS. After several hours of tossing and turning on the lumpy straw mattress, he finally gave up, packed the few belongings he had brought with him, and departed the tavern in the middle of the night.

It was a fool's errand to travel in the dead, winter darkness with nothing but a horse and a few small blades. But it was better than lying there on that grievous excuse for a bed, running the look in Mr. Gregory's eyes through his mind over and over again. That look of resigned, muted horror as he ran his blade into the man's gut not once, not twice, but thrice for good measure.

And just because his mind was apparently in a particularly cruel mood, that blade became another one. Just as familiar. That face became the face of another. The feeling of sinking the blade all the way to the hilt, over and over again, the look on Ezra's face as he gave him a wound that wasn't mortal, but he knew would give him Sheol likely for the rest of his life.

He had lain in bed taking turns stabbing Mr. Gregory and then Ezra, over and over again for hours, until he was in a fit of restless unease.

Surely no horrors of the night could be any worse than what he was already living in his mind. So he set off towards Chesedelle City. It was only a few hours' ride away, anyway. He'd be there before dawn if all went well. And the moon was full enough, shining on the snow that he could see just fine. This was not his first nighttime excursion. And he was not a child.

He would be fine.

He was fine for about three-quarters of an hour.

He had been riding in blessed, quiet peace when he heard something in the thick brush along the oft-used mountain road. The horse stopped, too. Gian listened carefully, but soon wrote it off as nothing more than the innocuous wanderings of nocturnal creatures. He shifted in his saddle, trying to convince the horse to keep going. But the horse would not comply.

"Idiot," he said, kicking the horse harder. "It's an owl or a rabbit or something. Keep moving, you bastard."

The stubborn horse did no such thing.

Gian dismounted, muttering the most colorful language he knew before tying the reins to a nearby tree. He investigated along the road, the moonlight making it difficult to make anything out in the silvery darkness.

He peered along the brush, squinting his eyes as if that would help, but he saw nothing.

"You are a coward," Gian growled to his horse. "Where are your balls, you bastard?" When Gian eyed the horse's hindquarters, he huffed a laugh. "Ah," he said. "They took them from you, didn't they? Well, you're just going to have to trust me when—"

Within the span of a breath, Gian was on the ground, wrestling with something large, covered in dark fur. By the sound of its growl, he wondered if it was a bear. Crying out, he blocked the beast's snout before the damned thing tore out his throat. But when he realized that his hands were the only thing keeping him from certain death, he got a look at the teeth that were too damned close to him. And then he understood.

A wolf.

A massive godsdamned wolf. The size of a full-grown man.

He wrestled with all of his might to keep the thing from eating him alive or tearing him limb from limb. At one point he had even managed to roll the beast beneath him. But that victory was short-lived, for the massive, furry beast soon flipped him back onto his ass with an elegance any man would envy. The wolf snarled and growled, eager to kill. In the moonlight, a single canine gleamed white, ready to rip his flesh like a knife through warm butter. Gian wasn't quite sure where he found the strength to roll the damned beast off of him again, but he did, flinging the furry lump with all of his might.

The wolf yelped as it landed with a thud on the road, and Gian used the brief moment to grab a dagger from his jacket. In a breath too quick for his mind to comprehend, the wolf was on top of him again.

But this time, it was to its detriment, for the beast leapt right onto Gian's blade.

It took several thrusts before the beast finally fell, still and lifeless, spilling thick blood onto the silvery white mountain road. Gian stood over it for a long moment, panting, collecting his breath along with his thoughts. The blood, black in the dim light, dripped from his hand, from his dagger, from his clothing. And the sight was all too familiar. All too nauseating.

"Fuck," he breathed. He wasn't sure how long he stood over the wolf, watching it carefully, ensuring no sign of life remained before he finally wiped the blade on his jacket, wiped his mouth on his arm, and turned to face his horse once more.

"You could have said something, you know," he sneered to the horse, who merely whinnied as if to mock Gian. Using what was left of his strength, Gian dragged the heap of fur and blood and flesh off the road, dumping it rather unceremoniously into the thick snow.

When he faced his horse again, the damned bastard was staring at him. “What?” Gian asked flatly. “Do you want me to host a funeral?”

The horse merely whinnied again. “I blame you for this,” Gian went on. “You shouldn’t have stopped.” He untied the reins from the tree and mounted the horse, who complied this time when Gian nudged it. In a moment, as if nothing in particular had just transpired, they were off again.

They made it all of thirty paces before Gian realized something was following them.

He shut his eyes, sighing heavily.

Then he turned slowly on the back of the horse, looking over his shoulder hesitantly, not wanting to know what the Sheol was behind him.

What he saw surprised him.

He pulled on the reins of his horse until he stopped, lobbing himself off onto the road. Not three paces behind him stood a small, gray ball of fur, looking up at him with huge eyes that shone like onyx in the moonlight.

Gian knelt but made no move to touch the pup, who just watched him.

Finally, he understood. That had been no male wolf back there. It had been a mother. Protecting her pup.

“Shit,” Gian breathed under his breath. “Go home, little one,” he said to the pup.

The pup only stared.

Perhaps it was the guilt of all he had done today—all the senseless blood he had spilled. Yes, that’s what it was. Guilt.

Guilt had Gian standing again, turning to reach for his pack strapped to the horse. He fished inside until he found a bit of venison jerky. Turning back, he tossed it to the pup, who sniffed it once but did not partake.

It was too little, Gian realized. The cursed thing was too little to care. Probably still on the teat.

And he had just taken its mother from it. Its only chance at life.

Just as he had just taken a father from two innocent children.

Just as his mother had been taken from him.

Gian knelt and picked up the pup, breathing a string of colorful words before tucking it under his arm.

He mounted his horse and rode into the night, wondering what in Sheol was wrong with him.

The pup had slept for the remainder of the journey back to Chesedelle Castle. In fact, he hadn't roused once until they reached the stables and Gian had returned his horse to the groggy stable boy. Morning had not come yet, though it was not far off. The night was dark and still, the moonlight now gone, hidden behind the mountains.

Gian tucked the little bundle of fur inside his jacket and made his way into the castle, the guards nodding their greetings as he passed. None of them commented on the amount of blood on his clothing. Then again, the sight was not exactly an anomaly.

He made his way to his chambers as if on instinct, barely thinking as he pushed his way through his sitting room, past his bed and to the other side where a set of double glass doors spilled onto a veranda and snow-covered gardens beyond. He took the long way, walking around the perimeter so as to keep his tracks as clandestine as possible. Only he and one other had access to this garden, but it was not entirely invisible to other parts of the castle. So he moved in the places he knew could not be easily spotted before he finally made his way to another set of glass doors and knocked once.

When no one answered, he knocked again, more loudly this time. Still, no one came.

He knocked again, damning the consequences, and said, "Wake up, woman!"

A breath later, she stood before him, her blonde hair falling wildly down her breast. She finished tying a thick, ermine robe around her waist and did not bother to hide the scowl on her face as she pulled open the doors and growled, "What in all of Sheol is wrong with you?"

Gian did not wait for her invitation. He pushed past her, allowing her to close the doors and turn to face him once more before he pulled the little lump of fur out from under his jacket. "I need your help."

CHAPTER EIGHTEEN

"It is the middle of the night, Gian. What in Sheol are you doing here?" Only then did Rachæl take a moment to register what he held in his arms.

"You got a puppy?" she asked incredulously, crossing her arms across her chest. It was cold tonight, despite the fur of her robe. And Gian wasn't helping things by barging in here, letting the night air and bits of snow in.

Providence, he looked like Sheol. And was that…blood covering him?

"What happened to you?" she asked.

"It's not a dog," Gian said, turning to face her as she finished latching the glass doors.

"Why are you waking me in the middle of the night? It's freezing out there!"

"I don't know what to do with him," he said.

And Rachæl realized that for the first time in the five years she had known the man, Gian looked positively helpless.

"Why did you bring home a pet if you don't know what to do with him?" she asked.

Gian didn't wait for her invitation; he made his way deeper into her private bedchamber, sitting down on a nearby chair, pulling the pup out from the warmth of his jacket. He stroked the fluffy little head once.

"Please do come in," she said sarcastically, sitting down in the chair beside him.

"It's not a pet," he repeated, ignoring her comment. Not to mention completely ignoring a chance to say something baiting. Or inappropriate.

What was wrong with him?

"Well, then what *is* it?"

"It's a wolf."

Rachæl's eyes widened to the size of harvest moons. "Why—do you—have a—a wolf?" she asked, stammering. She leaned a bit away from Gian, as if that would somehow protect her from the beast in his hands.

"He followed me," Gian answered.

"So you—brought him home?" Rachæl asked. "I'm not sure I understand why a wolf pup would follow you."

"He lost his mother."

"How could you possibly know that?" Rachæl scoffed. But Gian didn't answer right away, and in his silence, the story unfolded before her. "Gian. How could you know that?" she repeated the question flatly.

"Because she was killed."

"And how do you know she was killed, Gian?"

"Because I killed her."

"You *what?*" she asked, leaping to her feet.

"I had to!" Gian said, exasperated. "It was self defense! She attacked me!"

"Why were you riding home in the middle of the night to begin with? Don't you know it's dangerous at night on the roads?

You could have been attacked by a lot worse than a wolf, Gian of Borras!"

"It doesn't matter. The point is: she attacked me, I killed her, and this thing followed me home."

"All the way home?" Rachæl asked skeptically, crossing her arms.

"I picked him up. I felt badly for the beast!" Gian confessed. "What else was I supposed to do? Leave him motherless?"

"It's a wolf, Gian. Do you have any idea how to care for it?"

"No," he confessed. "That's why I came to you."

"Because I am an expert at caring for wolf pups?"

Gian sighed, standing and cradling the pup against his chest as if it were his own babe. "I just—thought you might help. Never mind." He turned, moving towards her doors.

"Wait," she said, staying him with a hand on his arm. Her fingers brushed the fur of the little pup, and she took a moment to observe the helpless beast.

"I'm sure he's hungry," she said. "Have you fed him?"

"I tried to give him some jerky. He wouldn't eat it."

"He's a babe, Gian. He will need milk."

"Well, I'm fresh out of wolf's milk. So sorry."

Rachæl leveled him a flat look before she moved to the edge of the room and pulled on the ribbon that rang for her servant.

"Are you sure you should be doing that?" Gian asked. "I'm not sure how you'll explain to your servants that you have a man and a wolf in your bedchamber in the middle of the night."

She smirked. "I'm sure you'll come up with a creative explanation."

For the first time tonight, Gian grinned. And at the sight of it, familiar and irreverent, something comfortable settled in her heart.

"I can think of at least a dozen debauched excuses," he offered. "I'll even let you choose."

“How generous of you.”

Just then, a servant knocked on the bedchamber door. Rachæl crossed the room to answer, but she took care to only open the door far enough to speak, disallowing the servant to see inside the room.

“Yes, milady?” the servant asked.

“I am in need of some milk.”

“Milk?”

“Yes. Warm, please. And do hurry.”

The servant eyed Rachæl skeptically for a moment, doing her best to peer over the princess’s shoulder. When it was clear Rachæl would allow no such thing, the servant met her eyes again and said, “Yes, my lady. Anything else?”

“No, that will be all.”

Rachæl didn’t wait for the servant to curtsey before she shut the door and turned to face Gian and the pup again. He was sitting on the floor now, playing with the little beast.

“He’s a fluffy little thing, isn’t he?” Rachæl asked, making her way back towards them.

“A fluffy murderous beast,” Gian added.

“He can’t hurt you, can he?” Rachæl asked.

“Not yet, no. Give it a few months and it will be a different story.”

“A few months? You plan to keep him?” She sat down on the floor opposite of Gian and reached for the pup, who came to her willingly. He was soft and ever so warm, snuggling into her arms as if he knew her—even trusted her. She couldn’t help but smile.

“Well, I’m not sure what to do with him,” Gian said, watching them.

“You can’t keep him, Gian. He’s a wolf. Wolves belong in the wild.”

“Yes, they do. But he knows nothing of hunting or caring for himself. He's too young to have learned enough to survive on his own."

"So you're going to teach him, then?" Rachæl asked.

"No, but perhaps I could care for him until he's ready."

"Ready for what?"

"Old enough, I mean. To be on his own."

"Old enough with no knowledge of his own survival, you mean," she amended.

"Well, what was I supposed to do?" Gian snapped. "Leave him for dead?"

The servant knocked on the door again, and Rachæl stood, handing Gian the pup. "Not killing his mother would have been a better solution."

Before Gian could protest, she spun around toward the door, still opening it only a little way before taking the pitcher of milk from the servant. She procured a small saucer from a nearby table and poured a bit of the milk into it, setting it down on the floor.

Gian directed the pup, and within a moment, the fluffy beast was lapping eagerly at his meal.

"I didn't know she was a mother when she was attacking me," Gian said, but his comment lacked the bite of his original defense. In fact, he seemed downright remorseful. "And when I saw him—a poor, motherless beast just like me—well I couldn't leave him, could I?"

Motherless.

Something about the way he said made her realize what had happened. Why he had brought the beast home. "Gian," she said flatly. "If this is some attempt on your part to right the injustices you experienced because you didn't have a mother—"

Gian went very still but did not utter a sound. Instead, he met her eyes with a hardness in his that froze her in place.

"Never mind," he said darkly. He stood, scooping up the pup. "Sorry I bothered you."

Remorse washed over her in a wave. She had hurt him somehow. She wasn't even sure how. But she had never really known his story, his past. She never knew what had driven Gian to become the man he was today. Why he would feel the need to rescue a helpless pup in the middle of the night for no apparent reason.

Rachæl stood, too, reaching out and taking hold of Gian's arm. "I'm sorry," she said softly. "I was out of line."

Gian stopped walking but he did not turn to face her.

"I've hurt you. And that was not my intention."

Slowly, he turned to face her, though he did not meet her eyes.

"Gian, what happened to your mother?"

Something in his countenance darkened, but instead of answering, he kept his gaze on the pup in his arms, stroking his fluffy back. When after a good bit he still didn't answer, Rachæl laid her hand over Gian's.

He lifted his eyes to hers and held her gaze for a good while before he finally spoke. "She was a lightskirt. Did I ever tell you that?"

Rachæl nodded.

"I never cared. I never saw her as anything but Mother. She had a bright smile and kind eyes. Blue, just like mine. She always made sure to remind me of that." He looked down, fussing with the pup for a moment and breathing a soft laugh at the memory.

Rachæl pulled on his arm ever so softly, nodding towards the floor where they had been sitting before. Gian acquiesced, sitting down again. He released the pup, who nosed eagerly towards the abandoned saucer of milk. Rachæl sat down across from Gian and let him speak.

"We had a place on the water," he said. "The island of Borras is small—mostly sailors and merchants that come through. And Mother was always there for them. Waiting with a smile or a touch of the hand or a laugh at just the right moment. And those men looked at her like she was their world. And for a moment, she would look at them the same.

"I usually slept with her in her bed unless one of those sailors had called. Then I would climb into the rafters and read adventure stories by candlelight. Eventually I got old enough that I had to do more than read to distract myself from the things I heard below. Pillows over my ears most of the time. But always, when the men would leave, Mother would call to me and let me know it was okay to come back down. And always, she wanted me to sleep beside her. So I always did."

Gian grew very quiet, absently petting the lapping wolf for a good while before he went on. Rachæl drew a breath to ask him if he was all right, but he spoke again at last. "One night, a man came to our door who was not as pleasant as the usual callers. He seemed angry at my mother from the moment she allowed him inside. And my mother had a fear in her eyes I had never seen.

"I hid in the rafters as usual, listening to her pleas and apologies as he bickered and grew more angry, wondering what I should do to help. I was eleven years old, and I had decided that I was the man of our house.

"I remember there was a cold wind that night. A storm coming in. The wind cut through the walls, and not even the fire could overcome its chill. It whistled like a whisper, and my mind wandered to imagining ghosts and ghouls outside. I was frightened of that storm. But I was frightened more of the man below with my mother—of the way he shouted and cursed. I used my usual tactics to ignore them, immersing myself that night in a story of a lioness who saved a bird. Their arguing had finally stopped when I was drifting off to sleep.

"I think it was the sound of the door shutting that woke me up. Or maybe the rain and thunder outside. I'm not sure. But I knew the man had left. I didn't wait for my mother to ask me to come sleep beside her. I climbed down the narrow ladder from the rafters and climbed into my mother's bed.

"The rain leaked through the small house onto us, and I slept with a chill all night. But I held my mother close to me while she slept."

Gian stopped. He made no sound, spoke no words. He didn't even seem to see anymore. He just sat in the pale moonlight spilling onto the rug of Rachæl's bedchamber, still as a statue.

"Gian," she said, as quiet as a whisper.

His name seemed to pull him from his stupor. He looked up, meeting Rachæl's concerned gaze.

"You don't have to keep talking if you don't want to."

"It wasn't rain," he finally said. "It took the morning light for me to realize that there was no leak in our roof. It was her blood. Cold and thick. Pooling around her pillow. The angry man had beaten her to death. I never even knew why."

Too stunned to speak, Rachæl felt a silent tear slip down her cheek as she moved to sit beside Gian on the rug. She wasn't sure what to do, what she could say, what would help at all. On instinct, she ran her hand along his arm. He didn't stop her. He didn't even seem to notice.

A lump formed in her throat but still she could find no words. So she leaned her head on his shoulder. The pup, having finished his milk, crawled into her lap, eager for warmth. She obliged him, making a place for him to curl up and snooze, and she silently stroked his head as he drifted off.

They sat in companionable silence for a good while, the only sound their breathing. She had no words for him. But when she noticed a spot form on the thigh of his trousers, she tilted her head to see the evidence of a single tear that had fallen down his cheek.

"You're right, you know," she said gently. "We can't leave little Bear to his own devices. He needs us."

"Bear?" he asked.

She smiled softly, stroking the pup as he slept in her lap. "That will be his name. Bear."

Gian moved, and Rachæl looked up to see his blond eyebrows furrowed. "You can't name a wolf Bear."

"Why not?"

"It's absurd," he said.

"No, it's not."

"Yes, it is. You wouldn't name a horse Fish or a dog Cat. And you can't name a wolf Bear."

"Of course you can," she said. "He's fluffy and sweet, like a little bear cub."

"A bear is a vicious killer," Gian said flatly.

"So is a wolf. What is your point?"

"It's—*you cannot name a wolf Bear!*"

"Do you have a better name in mind, then, since you're such an expert on wolf naming habits?"

Gian looked down, taking the wolf from her lap as if to protect him from her ridiculous naming attempts.

"I do, actually."

She leveled a flat look and waited.

"Maximus."

"Maximus?" She scoffed.

"Yes," he said. "It's a strong name. A warrior's name."

"It's a Medinian name," she pointed out. Gian seemed indifferent. "He is *not* a Maximus, Gian."

"Well, he is certainly not a Bear."

She took the pup back from Gian and stood. Walking the short distance to her bed, she set the pup at the foot, nestling him in a thick blanket before turning to face Gian again.

"We are naming him Bear," she said.

"You speak as if we're keeping him."

She looked again at the pup, now sleeping soundly, and sat down beside him on the edge of her bed.

"Well, he's our responsibility now, anyway."

Gian strode to her side, watching her for a moment as she tucked the little beast into the thick blankets. When he finally took a seat, she could not help but notice how close he sat to her. They were silent a few moments, just watching the pup. Gian seemed he had no further arguments about her naming choice. Or perhaps he wasn't thinking about names at all. He had never shared that story with her—of what had happened to his mother. The horrors he had witnessed. She wondered if he had ever shared that story with anyone.

When he remained silent by her side, she leaned into his warmth, resting her head on his shoulder and yawning once. "I'm sorry about your mother."

"You've no need to apologize." His words were soft, pensive.

"All the same, I cannot imagine losing my mother. She is an anchor for me."

Gian didn't say anything, but she felt him nod.

"I suppose now you know why I'm such a bastard all the time."

Rachæl huffed a laugh and looked up, meeting his smile.

"Tell me what happened. After your mother—" She didn't finish the sentence. Couldn't bring herself to utter the word —*murder*. The darkness of the word. The utter destruction. She could not imagine the horrors Gian had faced as a boy upon losing his only family. But despite her not finishing her sentence, Gian understood well enough.

He sighed, looking down and fiddling with his fingers. "I took to pickpocketing for a good many years. It kept me alive. And I found I was rather good at it."

She smiled as she imagined a young Gian, alone in the world, darting in and out of crowds, pilfering purses and trinkets from passing nobleman and women. Yes, she imagined he had been quite good at such a thing.

"But then one day, some pirates docked their ship in town."

"An airship, you mean."

"Yes, darling," he said. "An airship. I took one look at that ship and was forever in love.

"I snuck on board to join them on their adventures. But they didn't take too keenly to a stowaway. A few of the crew beat me to within an inch of my life, but in those skies, so high above the world, there was no one to hear my screams.

"It was the captain who finally stayed their hand and let me rest and heal. He took a liking to me, for some reason. We became friends, I suppose. And when he died a few years later, he gave me the ship. Named me the captain.

"Most of the crew didn't like it, but they had no choice. The code is a sacred thing among sky pirates. They could not defy their captain's wishes.

"I spent the next few years adding ships until we had a whole fleet. We sailed the skies and visited every corner of the world. I saw it all before I finally came here, to Chesedelle."

"Why would you give all of that up?" she asked. "The freedom. The chance to see the world."

"Because I found something better."

She waited for him to explain his meaning, to go on speaking. He did not. When she looked at him, he did not meet her gaze, still fiddling with his hands.

A heaviness obviously weighed on him tonight. More than the memory of his lost mother. More than the memory of his lost fleet.

So Rachæl reached across his lap and took hold of his hands. "Tell me more about your life, Gian."

And he did.

Rachæl woke to the feeling of scurrying along her feet. She sat up abruptly to find the wolf pup nuzzling and sniffing the blankets at the foot of her bed. But that wasn't what stopped her heart for a moment.

A man slept soundly on her bed. Beside her.

Gian.

Fully dressed, he hadn't even bothered to remove his boots, which were sprawled rather irreverently across her down-filled blanket. He looked peaceful as he slept, even with his hard angles and dark clothing lying on top of crisp white bedding and his jaw-length blond locks spilling haphazardly around his face.

She did not remember falling asleep. She certainly did not remember inviting Gian to sleep beside her in her bed. But he had, apparently.

When the shock wore off, it was replaced by a need to laugh. The drool slipping slowly down the side of his mouth certainly did not help. She breathed a chuckle and reached for the pup.

"What are you doing, little one?" she asked as she fluffed the soft fur on his head. The pup squeaked what she assumed was his attempt at a bark.

She felt a stirring behind her and turned to see Gian sitting up, rubbing his eyes with a rather unbecoming yawn before stretching his arms high above his head.

"Sleep well, dear prince?" she asked flatly.

Gian offered her his most presumptuous smile. Then he nodded to the beast at her feet. "He needs to see to his needs."

"Well, then you should take him outside." She offered him the wolf.

Gian eyed her skeptically. "I think you should probably take care of that, Princess."

She looked beyond him to the garden outside, covered in a blanket of snow. "It's freezing."

Gian lifted a single eyebrow as he reached for the pup. "All right then, Princess. If you don't mind anyone seeing a man coming out of your private bedchamber first thing in the morning, I—"

She stayed him with her hand and took the pup promptly. "You are a nuisance and an ass."

Gian only grinned and folded his hands behind his head as he laid back in her bed.

She slipped on her fur robe before she took the pup to the doors of the gardens and set him down.

"Go," she said. "And do be quick about it."

The pup scurried off into the snow, and Rachæl shut the doors quickly behind him, keeping out as much cold as possible.

"Leaving him to his own devices?" Gian asked from her bed. He crossed one ankle over the other and watched her with his hallmark arrogance.

Rachæl rolled her eyes. "He cannot get out of the garden, Gian. It's surrounded by the castle. And besides, it's freezing out there. I am not going to stand outside to wait for *your* dog to see to his needs."

"He's not a dog," Gian said.

"Wolf. Whatever." She shrugged as she sat down on the edge of the bed next to him. "And you've certainly made yourself comfortable in my chambers, by the way."

The pirate sat up, tilting his chin conspiratorially.

"What?" she finally asked.

"I always knew you'd find a way to get me into your bed one of these days."

"Oh, you did, did you?"

Gian nodded, never letting his gaze falter.

Rachæl crossed her arms. "I suppose the whole of the Chesedelle court will know about this before noon."

"Oh, darling," he said, reaching out to run a delicate finger along her cheek. "It's likely they already know."

She elbowed him. Hard. "They had better not."

Gian grinned. But even behind his insufferable self-admiration she could see something else—a gratefulness. He had opened up to her last night. Told her about his whole life, his childhood. Stories she imagined he hadn't told often, and had thought of even less. And she had enjoyed every moment of it.

"I enjoyed last night," she offered. "And before you turn that remark into something inappropriate, I should like to point out that I'm being serious."

Gian offered her a smile, but it wasn't irreverent or baiting. After a quiet moment, he said, "I've never told anyone that story."

"Thank you for trusting me with it."

Gian held her gaze for so long she wondered what he must be thinking. He reached a hand out, tucking a strand of her hair behind her ears. But just when he drew a breath to speak, a servant knocked on her door.

Her eyes grew wide, and she stood as she called out, "Just a minute!"

Gian stood, too. "I should leave," he said.

"Yes, I think so," she agreed, though she wondered what it said about her that she did not want him to.

He stepped across the short distance between them, took hold of her face with his hands, and pressed a gentle kiss to her brow. His breath was warm on her skin, and he lingered longer than necessary for a chaste, friendly kiss. She did not know what to do with her hands, did not know what to say or what to do.

Gian broke the silence and pulled away from her, meeting her eyes before he said, "I'll see you later, Princess." And then he turned, leaving through her garden doors, taking care to stay close to the castle and out of sight of any prying eyes. He did it expertly, as if he had thought before about how he might make it unseen from her chambers to his own. She watched him, waiting by the windows as he called for the pup, who came to him eagerly. Gian scooped the wolf into his arms and disappeared around the edge of the gardens.

CHAPTER NINETEEN

The winds blew cold on Lake Yerah, banks of snow piling thick along the edges. Miri watched as it danced in wispy clouds along the frozen waters. She wrapped the thick wolf fur blanket around her shoulders as she leaned on the balustrade overlooking the massive lake and towering mountains at Massahd Castle. But it was a chill of a different sort that crawled down her spine.

Hands, brutal and slender. Grasping and forcing her. Eyes, angry and hungry. Devouring her. The priest's long neck, the tendons and veins straining as he forced himself upon her.

Over and over and over again.

She shut her eyes, a lone tear escaping. She quickly wiped it from her cheek lest Ezra see it. He was still in the bathing room this morning when she had slipped from the bed to step outside. To clear her mind from the dreams that still haunted her. Dreams she did not dare speak aloud.

Nightmares. The truth that would never escape her.

She still hadn't told Ezra about what had happened at the Harvest Ball. It had been weeks now. She was hoping the memories would fade. She had hoped that the whole thing had only been a nightmare. That Phinehas hadn't had his way with her.

But he had.

Ezra did not know. He did not need to know. She did not want him to bear that burden, too. She did not want him to worry. Or fear.

Phinehas would come for her again. It was only a matter of time. For he was convinced there was something she hid from him. Some magic secret she tucked away, deep inside.

She bit back a sardonic chuckle. There were too many secrets to count when it came to Phinehas. Too many lies. She didn't give a damn which one in particular haunted him.

Yes, it was the amulet he wanted. But more than that, he just enjoyed torturing her. Like a game. Like the night of the Harvest Ball. The timing of his arrival. The way he had come to her—at a time when she was most vulnerable. Yes, she had always been a game to Phinehas.

And she would carry the secrets of that night to her deathbed.

Ezra did not need to know.

Her husband emerged a moment later onto the balcony, dressed smartly in a black brocade jacket and crisp, white cravat—his signature look. She turned as he approached her, meeting his smile with one of her own.

"Aren't you cold out here, Wildfire?" He wrapped his arms around her waist when he reached her, pressing a kiss to her brow as she folded herself into his arms. They had arrived home from Port Challon only last night, having spent three weeks in the trade village. When they weren't exploring the wintry wonderland, they had spent their spare time finding out anything they could—any whisper of rumor—regarding the reason for those wyvern-adorned ships. Why Medinah would feel the need to have a military presence in a country that was supposedly their newest, greatest ally. But any time they spoke with a local, any time the subject was broached, they were greeted with silence and wary eyes. No one, it seemed, was willing to talk. So the journey home had been one of quiet contemplation and hushed conversation about it all.

Medinian warships.

Neither knew what to make of it.

"I'm fine," she answered, resting her head on his chest.

This. This...peace between them. This surety. She would lounge in it like a cat in a swath of sunlight. She would learn to get lost in it and forget all of the nightmares. The haunting darkness that whispered the moment she was alone.

You are not enough. You will never be enough.

"John will be here soon with Esther and the little ones. They are staying for a few days—until after Yasha. I'm fairly certain John Junior has asked for every toy in existence this year."

Yasha. She lifted her head and met his eyes, so warm and rich.

"Do we... I hadn't thought of it," she said. "Gifts. I haven't gotten anyone anything."

Ezra smiled and kissed her, soft and swift. "I've taken care of it, my love."

She tilted her head to one side, knitting her brows. Ezra only winked. "Let's get back inside. It's too cold out here!"

She willingly acquiesced, her fingers going numb in the biting cold.

Kit was in their bedchamber as they emerged again, waiting with a smile to dress Miri for the day.

"I'll be downstairs, Wildfire. Join me for breakfast?" Ezra asked.

Miri nodded, letting Kit fuss over her as Ezra disappeared.

MASSAHD ALREADY SHOWED the early signs of Yasha. Smells of warm, spiced breads—cinnamon, nutmeg, ginger, cloves, and citrus—wafted through the air. Entwined around the bannister were lush evergreen boughs laden with dried cranberries and pinecones. The hearth in the dining room was similarly adorned, with candles adorning every table and surface. The dining table itself was covered in evergreen and ribbons of the richest colors: wines, ambers, and plums. In the corner of the adjacent sitting room, a massive spruce stood tall and proud while servants affixed candles to the tips of its boughs and draped ribbon and strands of dried cranberries from top to bottom. Magicked baubles were scattered throughout the branches, floating of their own accord, tiny vignettes of winter scenes inside: snowy mountains; icy rivers; ice-coated branches.

She hadn't remembered a Yasha so extravagant since she was a little girl. Phinehas had never celebrated the holiday with much fervor, opting for a quiet candlelight ceremony in the temple on the eve of the holiday and little more. Then again, Phinehas had never been particularly keen on the Providential holidays that did not bask in the wonder of the priesthood. And since Yasha was about as ancient as it came—the holiday predating the priests themselves—Phinehas had little use for it.

But Miri remembered. Even with her father's ire and her mother's indifference, she had always loved Yasha. She had loved spending time by the festive tree, listening to Ari tell her stories of ghosts of the ancient past. Stories of Providence—of his victories in ancient battles. Of his provision in ancient famines. Of his magic weaving throughout the thread of history like a tapestry of the richest color. *That,* Ari would say, was the meaning of Yasha. To remind people that his evergreens never wither. That his magic never fails.

"Hungry?" Ezra asked, standing as she emerged into the vast

dining hall. He pulled a chair out for her as she approached, smiling broadly and accentuating that dimple on his right cheek.

Miri took the seat he offered next to him and nodded. "I shouldn't be. I ate enough for two people on our trip. But I confess, I am quite hungry."

Ezra grinned mischievously and offered her a large scoop of eggs and fried potatoes, as well as several thick slices of bacon. Miri marveled at just how hungry she was and ate every bite before going for seconds.

"A package for you, my lady." Thaddeus emerged into the room on silent feet, handing Miri a small box wrapped in brown paper and tied with twine. A small note attached read:

To Her Grace Grand Duchess Miriam Kelach

Miri eyed Ezra skeptically, but he just lifted both hands in innocence. Even Thaddeus offered no explanation. So Miri opened the box warily, her heart nearly stopping at what she saw inside.

"What is it?" Ezra asked. And by the way he asked the question, she knew it hadn't been his doing. He was just as curious as she.

Wordlessly, Miri handed him the box.

"How did you...?"

"I didn't," she interjected. "I don't understand."

"Who gave this to you, Thaddeus?" Ezra asked.

The butler watched Miri for a moment, his eyes lingering with concern. "No one I recognized, my lord," he finally said. "A young street urchin, by the looks of it."

Miri furrowed her brows, but Ezra's face had already melted from confusion to wonder. To hope. "Someone," he said, reaching inside and pulling out the heavy, ornate ring, "knows what this means to us."

His grandmother's ring. The signet ring of the Kinnereth

duchy. Ezra had given it to Miri the night they married. The night everything went to Sheol. Phinehas had taken it from her, and in the aftermath...after all that the ambassador had subjected her to, she had forgotten all about it.

But apparently someone hadn't.

"How—" Miri asked, unable to form complete sentences.

"It would seem, my lady," said Thaddeus, "that you have more friends than you realize."

She met the butler's eyes again. Yes, it was concern there. Concern and kindness. Almost fatherly. He placed a hand on her shoulder—a gesture she was fairly certain she had never witnessed from the man. Cold steel, that was Thaddeus. A man of conviction and principle. He spent his days running this house with meticulous efficiency and without apology. He never showed the slightest sign of humanity, much less affection.

In fact the most human thing about the butler Miri had ever witnessed was his incessant arguing with Helena. Aside from that, he was the consummate professional. So for him to rest his hand on her shoulder...

He squeezed once before he dropped his hand to his side again. "We're glad you're home, Your Graces," Thaddeus added. "We missed you."

"If you're not careful," Ezra said jovially, "we might start thinking you have a heart inside that chest, Thaddeus."

Miri could have sworn she heard the butler offer a throaty chuckle before walking away.

"Who could have found this? Phinehas—he..." Miri eyed the ring in Ezra's hand, swallowing once. "He took it when..."

"I know, my love. But I think," Ezra reached for her hand and slipped the ring on, "Thaddeus is right: you have a friend, and that friend is trying to give you a message."

"What message?" she asked warily, looking down to the ring on her hand. Who would have known about it? She could think of no one who would have bothered to notice except one of the other acolytes. She hadn't heard from any of them in the aftermath of everything, not even Kata.

Who could have found the ring? And more so, who could have taken the risk to take it from Phinehas in order to return it to her?

Ezra lifted her hand to his mouth, kissing the top once before he spoke again. "I don't know," he admitted. "Perhaps we'll find out."

A knock sounded at the front door, and Ezra stood promptly, a conspirator's smile on his full lips. Miri knew what that smile meant. She smiled broadly as a little boy came dashing into the room, crashing into her knees as he hugged her legs. She laughed and lifted John Junior into her arms.

"Merry Yasha, my lord," she said, pressing a kiss to his cherub cheek.

"Aunt Miri!" the little one exclaimed. Miri hardly noticed as John Senior and Esther emerged into the room a moment later, Esther handing baby Leah to an eager Ezra.

"I have something for you," the boy went on.

"What is it?"

John fished his small hand into the pocket of his knickers, pulling out a pinecone decorated with unruly globs of bright paints and tied with a lopsided ribbon on the stem. "It's an ornament! For you!"

"It's beautiful," Miri said, letting him place it her hand.

"He usually makes one for *me* every year," Ezra said with feigned affront, coming to her side with the baby in his arms. And at the way he looked holding the babe, something curled tight in Miri's chest. An ache sharp and keen. She willed herself to ignore it for the sake of John Junior.

Ezra maintained his mock frown. "I suppose I've been replaced as the favorite around here."

"Apparently." This from Esther, a knowing smile on her mouth.

"You did a lovely job, John," Miri said to the boy. "I love it."

"Do you want me to put it on the tree?" he asked eagerly. She nodded and set him down. The boy took the ornament and bounded to the spruce tree in the adjacent room, picking a bough somewhere near the bottom and hanging the gaudy pinecone. Miri smiled as she watched him.

"It's perfect," she said as he turned to face her, his little chest puffed with pride. "I shall treasure it forever."

Satisfied, John Junior bounded off, no doubt in search of Helena and her treats.

"Welcome home," said John Senior, taking a seat on the arm of a nearby settee. Esther seated herself on the cushion next to him. "How was your trip?"

"Well, that's something we need to discuss," Ezra said, sitting across from his sister and brother-in-law, still holding his infant niece in his arms while she snoozed peacefully. It still struck Miri how much the child looked like Ezra. The Kelach family resemblance ran true in baby Leah. And Miri wished, not for the first time, that she could give Ezra his own miniature to hold. To fawn over. To spoil.

She hated the idea that a man like him would never be a father. Never get to lavish his love, his kindness on his own son or daughter.

"Discuss? I'm not sure your honeymoon is any of my business," John said, his brow raised in a question that Miri had a feeling she understood completely. Ezra choked on his own chuckle, and Miri realized John's question was indeed a scandalous one.

"It isn't," Ezra said. "We...discovered something interesting."

Before John could ask Ezra to elaborate, a knock sounded at the front door again.

"Who now?" Miri asked.

Ezra stood, unsurprised, offering her a grin as he handed Leah to Esther. He reached his hand for Miri to take it. And when she did, he guided her into the front hall.

She broke into a sprint when she saw who stood at the door.

"Ari!" she exclaimed, slamming into his embrace without an ounce of decorum or manners.

Her cousin breathed a chuckle. "And a Merry Yasha to you, too, Mir."

"I didn't know you were coming," she said, pulling out of his arms.

"Ezra wanted it to be a surprise," Ari said.

Miri turned to face her family as they all emerged into the hall. She met Ezra's eyes, grateful tears welling in her own as she said, "It's perfect."

DINNER HAD BEEN a veritable spread of every delectable meat she could imagine, savory vegetables, warm, buttery breads, and piles of fresh fruits, some of them sugared to look as if they'd been kissed with freshly-fallen snow. She had consumed a full plate of the fare and still wanted more. Ezra noticed and gave her a grin, nodding for her to accept the second helping a servant offered. She obliged without a modicum of regret.

She had not felt like eating in weeks. Not really. She supposed her body was simply making up for the weeks of near-starvation she had experienced not so very long ago at the temple. So she drank her wine and munched on a crispy piece of pheasant and told herself that her body was healing.

Slowly. But it was. She supposed that was a good thing.

Ari sat just down from her, laughing at all of John's ludicrous jokes and surreptitiously aiding John Junior in procuring more and more sugared berries from a crystal bowl near them. It warmed her, how he fit here. How he sat at this table as if he'd always been a part of it. She supposed it hadn't been any different for her, really. Ezra, Esther, and John had welcomed her into the Kelach family as if she'd always been a part of it. Maybe it was inevitable they'd offer the same kindness to Ari.

She took another sip of her wine, warm and spiced to perfection. Somewhere between candied potatoes and pickled parsnips, the talk had turned from family stories to politics. Miri had sighed at the turn of conversation, but said nothing.

"Do you suppose His Majesty is aware of the ships?" This question came from John, who sat back in his chair as if to take a break from his dinner. Probably wise on his part, considering dessert had not yet been served.

Mother of kings, she was so very hungry.

"I cannot imagine he is ignorant of them," Ezra replied. "I think the ignorance is on the part of his subjects, who surely have no idea what lurks in the north. Or for what purpose."

"But why warships? We just signed a peace treaty." Esther asked.

That Ezra and John had always welcomed an open discussion of matters of import with the women of this family had never ceased to amaze Miri. Phinehas had certainly never included her in such discussions, had never wanted her opinion on anything.

"That is the question," Ezra said.

"Perhaps the simplest explanation is the correct one." That was from Ari. Miri looked down the table at her cousin, who sipped casually from his glass of mulled wine.

"And what would you say is the simplest explanation?" Ezra asked.

Ari set down his glass before he spoke. "Might and power. That is their mantra isn't it? Magic is power."

“You think the ships are there to intimidate? To make us feel weak?” John sat forward again, concern on his face.

“Har-Navah is anything but weak,” Esther retorted with disdain.

“I think the empress does nothing by accident,” said Ari. His tone was matter-of-fact. Simple.

The implication horrified Miri. It horrified her family, too, if the looks on their faces were any indication.

“And I think those ships have little to do with alliance and everything to do with her plans,” Ari went on.

“What are her plans?” asked Ezra.

“A new world.”

Miri could no longer stomach the table conversation. Her stomach roiled, either from the bounteous amounts of food she had eaten tonight, or perhaps from the fear that had washed over her regarding those Medinian warships. So she had excused herself from the table and made her way to her chambers before everyone else.

She found a smiling Kit turning down hers and Ezra’s bed.

“Hello, milady!” Kit chirped. She finished fixing the blankets before turning to Miri’s adjoining dressing chamber and retrieving a warm shift for the night.

“Did you have a nice dinner?” the maid asked.

“I did,” Miri answered. Taking a seat in a plush chaise that faced the glorious view of the lake, she began removing her boots, yawning most unbecomingly in the process.

“I’ll do that!” Kit exclaimed, coming to her aid. Miri did not protest.

“I don’t know why I’m so tired tonight,” Miri mused as the maid worked the button hooks and supple leather.

Kit didn't say anything, but a smile turned her pretty face bright.

"What?" Miri asked.

"The kitchen maids told me you had a third helping of candied potatoes tonight."

Miri raised an eyebrow. "You discuss what we eat?"

"Not usually," Kit admitted, a becoming shade of rose coloring her cheeks.

"Why in the world was it a subject of discussion tonight, then?"

The maid met Miri's gaze, a quizzical knit to her brows. "You haven't noticed?"

"Noticed what?"

Kit finished working the boots and stood to take a seat beside Miri on the chaise. "Your appetite is greatly increased."

"Yes. I figure I'm just trying to gain back what I lost," Miri offered.

"You're more tired lately," Kit went on.

"I did just return from a month-long vacation, you know."

"Yes, and I wouldn't think a thing of it except that your linens are still clean."

"What do you mean, they're still clean? Nothing about my courses has been normal since the moment I arrived here, Kit. You know that. And why are you paying attention anyway?"

Miri felt exasperated. This conversation... She did not want to have it. What Kit implied...

It was no use even thinking about that possibility anymore.

"Miri," Kit said, her voice softening. She put a hand over Miri's, which she realized was trembling in her lap. "All I'm saying is that the signs are good."

Miri stood abruptly and began pacing. "These aren't signs, Kit. They're coincidences. You heard what the doctor said. The chances that I am…" But she couldn't say it. Couldn't bring herself to utter the word.

Pregnant.

Was it possible? After all that had happened? After the broken mess Phinehas had left her in?

Kit stood as well, taking hold of Miri's arm when she paced by. "Miri," Kit said softly. Carefully. "All I'm saying is it's different. It's… I don't know how to explain it, but I can just tell. They say women glow and…"

Miri leveled the maid a flat look. "Kit."

Kit lifted her hands in innocence, smiling. "All I mean to say is that it's *possible*, isn't it?"

She wanted it to be. She did not want to admit to the maid how it tore a new ache in her heart—the possibility that she carried Ezra's child. And even more, she did not want to admit to herself how badly she wanted it to be true.

CHAPTER TWENTY

"Helena, if you bring out one more cake..." John sprawled next to his wife on the settee, sitting on a proper cushion instead of an arm or table for once. Ezra figured it had something to do with the amount of food the man had consumed in the last four days.

"You'll what?" the portly housekeeper asked. Her tone was half threatening, half amused. Thaddeus made his way into the room behind her, wearing an annoyed gleam just for her benefit. She paid him no heed, setting a platter of cakes before them—the third platter of the evening. These were cut into perfect, bite-size squares, covered in a thick layer of white frosting, and topped with bits of holly and berries.

"He'll eat the next one you bring. And the next," said Esther, cooing over a sleeping Leah in her arms as she spoke.

"It's true," John acquiesced with a chuckle.

"I keep telling her it's too much," Thaddeus said, his tall, lanky form stiff, his shoulders back. As if he alone held the line of propriety against Helena's ungodly fascination with Yasha treats.

"Oh, it's *not* too much," Helena spat at the butler. "They're all too thin. Need some meat on their bones, the lot of them. You most of all, you old miser." She faced Thaddeus at last, pressing a pointed finger to his chest. The butler only returned a glare. Then the housekeeper sauntered off, no doubt to gather more cakes and pies and treats, Thaddeus following testily in her wake.

Ezra chuckled, resting a hand on Miri's knee beside him. She had been pensive this evening. Quiet. He glanced around her to where her cousin lounged in the chair on her other side, smiling lazily as if he, too, had indulged perhaps a bit too much in Helena's Yasha smörgåsbord. It was good—so good—to be here. With all of them. To watch John Junior flit about the room like a bee in a clover patch, playing and singing to himself. To watch John Senior and Esther fuss over their little one and exchange proud parental glances at every little sound she made. To watch Miri listen to her cousin's stories with a light in her eyes that Ezra so rarely saw. They had spent the last four days that way. Sharing and laughing and eating and even singing from time to time. Esther had even offered to play a few Yasha tunes on the pianoforte in the main hall. She hadn't lost her skills despite claiming it had been years since she'd last played.

It had been the first Yasha since losing his grandparents that Ezra had felt whole again. Settled. He wondered if he'd ever get used to it: how good it felt to be with each one of them. How whole he felt with Miri beside him. It was a gift he did not intend to take for granted.

"I noticed Shalem has erected a tree in the town square," Ari said, breaking the companionable silence.

"Every year," John agreed.

"Does that come as a surprise to you?" Ezra asked Miri's cousin.

Ari looked at Ezra. "They have not erected one in Chesedelle City. Nor in Teman, or Benalle. Or in any of the major cities of Har-

Navah this year, if my sources are correct."

"Why not?" Miri asked, perking up a bit from where she lounged beside Ezra.

"Progress," was Ari's answer. "In the name of the new world. The new era of Her Imperial Majesty."

There was no disdain in the way he said it. No ire that Ezra could detect. But something else in Ari's words had the hair of his arms standing on end. Something...resigned. It made him wonder what Ari knew that the rest of them did not.

"It would seem that Her Imperial Majesty is intent on making many changes to our kingdom," said Esther. Ezra did *not* miss the disdain in his sister's tone.

"There are some who say you are the one to stop it," Ezra said to Ari. Careful words. A careful question. He did not want to imply anything of his own thoughts on the subject, which were numerous. But he was immensely curious to know what the man before him thought of those rumors. If he had even heard them.

"That is the going theory," Ari said with a small smile.

"Are you planning to stop her?"

Ezra smiled to himself at the bluntness with which Miri spoke to her cousin—a product of knowing each other a lifetime, he supposed.

"My Father's plans are as numerous as they are nuanced," Ari offered.

His father. Miri had insisted the man was the bastard son of her aunt. That none had ever known who had sired her cousin. But every time Ezra had been around Ari, the man had spoken freely and plainly of his father. And his plans.

Ezra abandoned caution. "Who is your father, Ari?"

Ari met his gaze. The depths of his emerald eyes caught Ezra. Held him. "I think you already know the answer to that question, Ezra."

An image flashed in his mind: the pool of starlight and unfathomable firmament; a stag glowing amidst a forest teeming with færies and fauna; a pale, silvery vine of light growing from his wife's hand and wrapping around his.

He wasn't sure why he hadn't asked before—why it hadn't occurred to him until this moment to just *ask*. All the books he had read as a child. All the prayer vigils he had attended with his parents and grandparents. All the talk of Providence and his coming salvation: the Promised One.

The son of Providence himself.

Something in Ezra's heart clenched tightly. He wanted to say it aloud, to explore the absurd words for himself.

Are you the son of Providence?

But he didn't have to, for when he gazed upon Ari again, the enigmatic man smiled, nodding once. "You see not with your eyes, Ezra. And by it, you will be blessed."

Ari.

The son of Providence.

So it was true.

Miri perked up beside him, observing their unspoken exchange with mute wonder. He would talk with her about it later. He could not wait to, actually. To explore all it meant—for him, for her, for the whole changing world around them. To muse about what it meant to be a son of a god. How had he been sired? Had his mother known? Had any of his family known?

Did anyone know who Ari really was?

Miri had told him once, many months ago, that Ari was a direct descendent of King Ferryl—that through his mother's line, he bore the blood of the fabled king. And while her late father had once tried to use Miri's own weak ties to that bloodline as an excuse to put her up for the throne, she had always believed Ari to be the true heir.

The heir to the Adelaidian throne.

That fact alone put Ari in a world of danger. If King Dægan

knew—if any in the Sanhedrin knew Ari's lineage—there would be many who would call for his reclaiming of the throne...and just as many who would call for him to be hung from the highest tree.

And that kind of controversy could spell war.

The word sobered Ezra. Brought him back to the present.

He would think about all of this later. Tonight was Yasha. Tonight was about family.

"Uncle Ezra!" cried John Junior, tugging on Ezra's sleeve. He looked down at his nephew and smiled broadly.

"Yes, dear boy?"

"When can we open our presents?"

"Patience, son," said Esther. But Ezra grinned and picked up his nephew, perching him on his lap.

"You've been so very patient, haven't you? How about we open them now!"

The boy's face lit up. "Yes, please!" He jumped down from his uncle's lap and dashed across the room to the evergreen in the corner, fetching every package his little arms could carry and bringing them back.

John Senior chuckled. "I remember when I was a boy, feeling like that. There is something deeply fulfilling about watching your own son do the same."

At Ezra's side, Miri shifted—a movement so slight he doubted anyone else noticed. But he knew what it meant. Knew the pang of sorrow she was pushing down, down, down. Sorrow for the son they might never have, thanks to the butchering Phinehas had inflicted on her months ago. The doctors had agreed: Miri would likely never conceive again. Her womb had been so severely lacerated that her body had taken weeks just to stop bleeding. The rest of the healing... Well, it would be a miracle if she were ever normal in that regard again. Even her courses had not returned properly.

And while Ezra held on to hope, fragile and fledgling, that one day they might have a child of their own blood, he could not help the pang of his own sorrow that pounded in his heart, knowing it was an unlikely prospect.

John Junior finished collecting the last of the gifts and settled himself on the carpet at the feet of his parents. He did not wait for permission before ripping into the first gift—the largest, of course.

"A winged horse!" the lad exclaimed. Indeed, Ezra had found a toymaker in Shalem weeks ago and commissioned the riding toy especially for the boy. He had even asked him to paint it to look just like Ahadah, dappled gray with a mane as black as a crow's feathers. Wheels were hidden cleverly in the wooden hooves so that when the boy mounted, he could easily scoot the beast around and set off on an adventure. Which, consequently, he did immediately, ignoring the rest of his presents.

John and Esther chuckled as the boy rode wildly through the sitting room.

"I suppose a new book and a new set of boots will pale in comparison," Esther said, though there was no disdain in the observation.

Ezra chuckled. "Sorry about that." At his side, Miri smiled softly, though it did not hide whatever heaviness plagued her thoughts this evening. He took hold of her hand and pulled it to his lips, kissing it once before setting it on his thigh.

After a few minutes, John and Esther opened their presents to one another—a book on ancient law for John and a thick, ermine muff for Esther, which upon opening, she kissed her husband with a look of utter delight.

Next, Ari reached for an oddly-shaped box, wrapped in pretty red paper and tied with a white bow. He handed it to Ezra and Miri. "For you both," he said with a smile before taking his seat again.

Knitting his brows, Ezra handed the tall, narrow box to Miri, who opened it with an equally quizzical look on her face. When she retrieved what was inside, her face melted into a bright smile.

"I'm guessing this is the same wine you brought to our wedding feast," Miri mused, observing the dark green bottle. There was no label to indicate its make or origin, but Ezra knew without tasting it that the wine inside would be exquisite. Ari had excellent taste.

Miri's cousin smiled. "I hoped you'd like it."

"Like it?" John chimed in. "That wine was positively divine!"

"You're going to have to share your secrets, Ari." This from Esther. "I don't think we've ever had such a fine drink."

Indeed, the wine was impossibly smooth with a spiced sweetness that was unlike any Ezra had ever tasted—including some of the eighty-year-old bottles his grandfather kept in the cellars.

Ari simply winked and said, "Happy Yasha, Miri."

Miri stood from the settee and crossed the small gap between them, planting a kiss on her cousin's cheek. "Thank you, Ari. Truly."

"Och," was Ari's only reply, waving her off.

Miri came back to Ezra's side, nestling a little closer into his arms as she took a seat again. He rested an arm over her shoulder and pressed a kiss to her temple.

"We wanted to get you something, too," he said. He picked up a small box John Junior had haphazardly thrown at his feet and handed it to Ari.

As Ari opened the present, a smile spread over his face, as warm as a sunrise.

Miri chuckled softly as her cousin pulled out a small, ornate golden box and placed it in his hand. He opened it carefully, his eyes widening with delight as music began to play—an ancient folk tune of the Fæ—while a white wolf leaped and howled inside.

Ari chuckled. "What a clever idea. Thank you!"

"Miri told me you had a love for curiosities," Ezra said. "When I saw this, I couldn't resist it."

"Do you know the lyrics of the song?" Ari asked.

Ezra shook his head. "The tune is familiar, but I don't remember how the words go."

Ari smiled, sitting up and clearing his throat with an air of pomp. Miri giggled as he began singing, his voice clear but not particularly beautiful.

Call, call, o ancient ones
Tell of the king who is to come
Draw your swords
Howl your songs
Tell of the ancient, mighty one

Everyone clapped, laughing as Ari finished the old, familiar tune.

"You didn't tell me you were such a singer, Ari." Ezra laughed.

Still sitting, Ari bowed. "I aim to please."

Miri could not hide her giggle. "You didn't think I forgot you, did you?" Ezra asked.

When Miri realized he was speaking to her, she perked up a bit, meeting his gaze with knitted brows. "Ezra, you just took me on a month-long trip. I don't need another gift."

Ezra winked and handed her a box. Quizzically, she opened it and peered inside.

She pulled out a set of ornate gold spectacles, outfitted with a number of changeable lenses and a handle on one side. "Opera glasses?"

"I figured since you and I are patrons of the theatre at Shalem, you should have your own set."

"I—oh," she said, and at her hesitation, he knew he had been right to get her the second part of her gift.

"There's more," he said, gesturing to a small parchment folded at the bottom of the box.

She pulled it out, reading the contents of the paper to herself. After a moment, she raised her brows and met his gaze with wide eyes. "You're bringing them? Here? To Massahd?"

Ezra grinned and kissed her swiftly.

"The opera?" Esther asked, tilting her head to one side. "You're bringing it here?"

"Just a small troupe," he explained. "We have such a lovely ballroom that never gets used. I thought you might enjoy seeing another show." And considering she probably wouldn't want to set foot in the village—or go near the temple—for a while yet, he had decided to bring the theatre to her instead.

"Ezra, this is..." But Miri did not finish the sentence, a tear glistening in her eye when she launched herself towards him, caring little that everyone watched as she kissed him with glorious ardor.

"You've been quiet tonight, Wildfire. Everything all right?" Ezra asked.

Miri pulled a brush through the strands of her thick curls, staring blankly into the fire that burned brightly in their hearth. Ezra finished fastening a thick robe around his waist and took the seat next to her in their chamber. "Anything on your mind?"

Miri kept at her brushing without answering.

"I hope it's all right about the opera," he said. "I just thought you might enjoy—"

"It's wonderful," she interjected. "That's not... I just..."

Ezra reached between them, taking hold of her hand and effectively stopping her from brushing her no longer tangled hair. He squeezed once, waiting until she finally met his gaze. "Whatever it is, you can tell me anything, you know."

Whatever she had kept locked up inside in the weeks since the Harvest Ball... Whatever haunted her... Maybe she was finally ready to talk about it. To share what he knew she guarded so fiercely.

A tear slipped down Miri's cheek, making Ezra ache. He reached to wipe it away, and had the motion not brought him closer to her, he was positive he would not have heard her words, barely a whisper above the crackling fire.

"I'm pregnant."

Ezra froze, his finger still on her cheek.

"What?"

"I... I think it's the only explanation. Kit seems to think so, anyway. For my appetite. My fatigue. I don't know what to think. Maybe she's wrong, but..."

"And your courses," he added, his heart pounding so wildly he thought it might beat out of his chest.

"My courses? You...pay attention?"

A small smile curled his mouth. "You're my wife, Miri. Of course I do. I've been wondering for a few weeks now. Hoping it could be possible." He moved his thumb to wipe another tear that fell. "Why do you cry, my love?"

"I'm so scared," she said. And the words seemed to break a dam within her, for tears began to tumble furiously down her cheeks. She shut her eyes and buried her face in her hands.

"Miri," he said, coming out of his chair to kneel before her. "My Wildfire, you don't have to be scared."

She only met his gaze when he gently pulled her hands from her face. Something shone in her eyes—something he could not read. Could not explain. That secret, buried so deep.

"Talk to me, Wildfire. Tell me what frightens you."

"I—" She tried to speak, but choked on her own tears. "I am afraid to hope. Afraid...of everything."

"I know," he said, lifting up onto his knees that he might meet her face to face. He kissed the end of her nose, salty with tears. He kissed one cheek, then the other. He kissed her lips softly. "I know, Wildfire. But it's going to be all right. I promise."

"I might not even be pregnant. It's too soon to tell, truly."

Ezra smiled. "Well, considering it could have happened as early as the Harvest Ball, I don't think it's impossible to know."

She froze, her eyes glazing. "The Harvest Ball?"

"We wouldn't be the first couple to conceive after their first time together, my love."

But she was not as amused by the notion as he was, something like dread widening her eyes as she sat before him.

"Miri?" he asked gently. "You don't have to be afraid. Even if you're not pregnant, it's going to be okay. I promise. But we're going to hope. Together. And we're going to let hope be a balm and a blessing."

She took in a stuttering breath, shaking her head gently. "I'm so afraid," she repeated.

"I know," he said, and pulled her into his arms. He rubbed a gentle hand down her back. "I know. But it's your turn, don't you see? It's your turn for some joy. For some light, Miri. You've been in darkness for so long. It's your turn to know peace and joy and love. And I for one am so thankful that we're here. That we've shared this holiday together. The first of many to come. We can put the past behind us. And we can let hope be our guide. Because do you know what I think?" He pulled out of their embrace, placing a gentle hand on her belly. "I think the future Grand Duke or Duchess of Kinnereth is in there. That's what I think."

She breathed a trepidatious laugh and wiped a tear from her chin. Ezra took it as a good enough sign. Lifting her into his arms, he carried her the short distance to their bed. Laying her down with careful reverence, Ezra made love to his wife, letting every touch, every sigh, every kiss fill him with quiet, precious hope.

PART THREE

CHAPTER TWENTY-ONE

The fires burned bright in the hearth of the king's dining hall at Chesedelle. A merry mockery of the night.

Yasha.

It was not quite the jovial holiday Rachæl remembered from her youth. Her father sat at one end of the long table, engaging in hushed conversations with a few of his closest councilors. Her mother was, once again, absent. The halls had not been trimmed in lush evergreens and richly colored ribbons as in years past. No Yasha tree stood tall and towering in the great hall. There had been no Yasha ball either. No merry songs of courtiers and musicians alike lilting throughout the castle.

Just silence. Peace, she supposed. But hollow. Too quiet.

Her father had said it was for the sake of progress—a new era of Har-Navah. No longer bound to the tradition of ancient religions, this new Har-Navah would be one for all peoples. All cultures: Medinian, Har-Navarian, Midvarish, and beyond. It had sounded wise. Forward-thinking, even. Most of his councilors had nodded in eager approval when the king had announced it not long after the Harvest Ball.

All Rachæl could think was that the palace seemed awfully cold and hollow without the decorations, the candles, the inevitable warmth that came with the memories of this time of year. The chill reeked of the Medinian Empress and her incessant sermons of unity. Oneness. Progress.

Rachæl picked at her plate: roasted boar, spiced pears, leafy, vinegary greens, and warm, sweetened potatoes covered in a rich, smoky-sweet sauce. Traditional fare for Yasha, the ancient Har-Navarian holiday.

It all tasted like ash.

She wished she gave a damn. She wished at least Gian were here to goad her with indecent propositions. But Gian did not attend dinner on Yasha. Never had. It was only for family and a few trusted councilors. Except that, this year, there was one extra guest at the family table.

The oh-so-glorious empress herself had deigned to join them.

And it was her with whom Rachæl's father was currently immersed in conversation, ignoring everyone else in the room.

Rachæl sneered at the woman; decked in a garish gown that practically swallowed the chair in which she sat, she was covered head to toe in her signature gold, adorned with black butterflies—or were those moths?—all over the bodice and skirt. Her skin was dark and rich—like coffee kissed with just the right amount of cream. And her hair was thick and glossy like a river of chocolate down her back.

She was nothing like the queen—nothing like Rachæl's mother. The Empress of Medinah was exotic and enigmatic—a picture of perfection and certainly more than Rachæl or her mother could compete with.

No wonder the king was entranced.

As if the empress could read Rachæl's thoughts, she turned her perfect face toward the princess, looking over one shoulder and meeting Rachæl's gaze with icy, cruel eyes. She tilted her head to one side, and her mouth widened into a toothy smile that did not meet her eyes.

The princess squared her shoulders, willing herself to hold the empress's invading stare. Willing herself not to blink.

She didn't.

Then again, neither did the empress before she finally, slowly turned her gaze from Rachæl and back to the king, who had been oblivious to the entire ordeal.

Rachæl hadn't felt so alone in...well, a very long time, what with her mother's absence, her father's indifference, and without the presence of her former betrothed... This year was the first Yasha she had spent exclusively at Chesedelle since she could remember. In years past, half of the holiday had been spent with Ezra and his raucous family. Even after his grandparents and parents had suddenly passed, Yasha remained a merry, joyous occasion with the Kelach family. One she had always looked forward to.

"Where is Mother this evening?" Rachæl asked, indifferent to the rudeness with which she had interrupted her father's *important* conversation.

He lifted his gaze from the empress and met her stare with ire in his eyes. "She is still unwell."

And that was that. He went back to his conversation. To ignoring her.

"Has she seen a physician?"

"She has the best healers in the kingdom looking after her," said one of the councilors. The king remained immersed in his conversation.

"Are you not concerned for the queen, Your Majesty? She is, after all, your *wife,*" Rachæl said pointedly.

The king lifted his head towards her again. Slowly. Too slowly. The empress kept her back to the princess, not bothering to acknowledge her presence. That alone would have had anyone else thrown into the royal dungeons.

The king met Rachæl's stare for an uncomfortable moment before he finally said, "She is in hands far more skilled than mine. I have full faith and confidence in her caretakers."

Rachæl resisted the urge to sneer. To continue to provoke him.

Instead, she stood abruptly, threw her napkin on top of her unfinished plate, and marched from the room. If her father noticed—or even cared—he made no indication.

Alone in her chambers, Rachæl took a seat before the roaring fire her servants had prepared for her, sipping from a glass of a sweet port that made her grimace every time it met her tongue. Some swill her servant had procured for her, thinking she would enjoy it, no doubt. She had come to the conclusion that she did not like sweet wine. She much preferred the smoky fire of rum. Accompanied with untoward gambling. And inappropriate commentary.

She sighed, letting the dance of the flames take her from this room, this empty place.

But that was no good either, for her thoughts drifted to Ezra. To Esther and John and their little one. To the merriment of Massahd Castle at Yasha. Wondering what they were doing tonight. Probably laughing and eating from a wide assortment of rich cakes Helena had insisted on making—too many for one family.

She wasn't in love with Ezra. She understood now that she never had been. Not when she saw the way he looked at Miriam at the Harvest Ball. That had been the moment she knew that he had not loved her. And that she had not loved him. At least not the way he now loved another.

But she had been jealous of it—those looks and quiet smiles

and whispered secrets. Jealous that he had never shared such a thing with her. Never even tried.

Ezra had never tried with her.

He hadn't wanted to. If last Yasha hadn't made that clear enough, nothing would.

She had spent the eve of the holiday with Ezra's family, laughing and sharing stories. But the holiday itself had been reserved for the royal family. Yasha at Chesedelle had been a long-standing tradition from the time she was young. Ezra had never minded. Last year, after a rich dinner with her father and her mother and some of the councilors, they had gathered around a crackling fire and exchanged gifts. She couldn't recall what her mother or her father had given her. Likely something inane and absurdly expensive.

But she remembered Ezra's gift.

And maybe it was the sickeningly sweet wine, maybe it was the too quiet peace of her chambers, but the memory of what she had tried to give *him* washed over her, unwelcome and without mercy.

Ezra's arm draped casually over Rachæl's shoulders as she watched her father, her mother, and a few close friends open small gifts in the royal sitting room. She had felt peace tonight. Companionship. She had always appreciated that about Ezra—how he had always made her feel like a friend. Someone who mattered.

She rested her head under his arm and breathed a sigh.

"That boring, huh?" Ezra asked jovially.

Rachæl chuckled softly. "Another set of crystal for Mother. I wonder when Father will ever remember that he's gotten her the same gift every year for the past five."

She felt more than heard Ezra's chuckle in his chest where she rested against it. "Men are hopeless when it comes to gifts, I think."

Something in her gut twisted at that—at what she had planned to give him tonight.

Later. She would give it to him later.

Ezra, to her surprise, slipped his free hand into the pocket of his trousers and retrieved a small box, tied with a bright crimson ribbon.

"What's this?" Rachæl asked, perking up. She grinned as she took it from him.

His response was a soft smile. "Hopefully, this is better than crystal goblets."

She opened the present to find a necklace inside. A necklace she had seen in a shop window in his village just last week. Simple. Elegant. Nothing extravagant. But lovely all the same.

"I knew you were eyeing it," he said. The unspoken image hung in front of her—he must have sent a servant back to the village to purchase the gift for her later that day.

"It's lovely, Ezra," she said. "Thank you."

He lifted it from its box and moved to clasp it around her neck. She lifted her hair and turned to afford him a chance to do so, pressing a kiss to his smooth cheek when he was done.

"Merry Yasha, Rach," Ezra said.

"You're not going to say anything?" she asked.

He tilted his head to one side, meeting her eyes with furrowed brows.

"About my not getting you a gift."

He huffed a chuckle. "You don't have to get me anything, Rach. You know that."

She cut her eyes to her family across the room, ensuring no one was paying attention. They weren't. Somehow, that sent her heart into a thundering gallop. "I did get you something," she said.

"Oh?" Ezra asked, but there was no intrigue in the question. Just simple curiosity.

So Rachæl stood and extended her hand. Ezra stood as well, taking it without hesitation, his hand warm and firm around hers.

"Merry Yasha," she offered to everyone and to no one. Ezra did the same, following her from the room without further comment.

He hadn't said much as they walked through the halls of Chesedelle. There had always been a quiet peace at the end of the night of Yasha. A reverence, a reflection of the day's festivities. Even the musicians who played jaunty Yasha tunes in the halls and corridors had slowed those songs to peaceful hymns and carols at this hour of the night. She had always found contentment in it. Which is why, she supposed, she had chosen now to offer Ezra his gift.

He still suspected nothing. She wasn't sure what to think of that, but she ignored the urge to worry as she ushered him inside her private suite of chambers.

"You kept the present in here?" he asked.

She did not answer, instead making her way across the room to an apothecary cabinet on the far end. From the top, she picked up a small vial and brought it back to Ezra.

She kissed him softly before placing it in his hands, her own trembling violently. "Merry Yasha, Ezra."

He looked down, observing the small label affixed to the amber glass. "A tincture?"

She could only answer with a nod.

A slightly confused smile found his mouth. "What's it for?"

"It's an herb," she said, willing him to understand on his own.

He did not.

*"*The *herb," she finally explained.*

Ezra looked up at that, meeting her gaze. Gone was the lazy smile, the light in his eyes. In its place was something else entirely.

"Oh," was all he said.

"I thought perhaps... I mean, I thought it was time. We've been together for years now. We marry in the summer and...I just thought we could..."

She winced, hating how she stuttered through a speech she had rehearsed ten thousand times in her mind. Then again, in her mind, Ezra's reaction had not been quite so...stunned.

"I...don't know what to say," he admitted, his gaze lingering on the vial in his hands as if he were holding a venomous snake.

"Don't you want this? Don't you want...me?" Theirs had not exactly been a passionate betrothal. But it hadn't been dispassionate either. Ezra had certainly made it clear over the years that he enjoyed her. At least he had kissed her often enough that she thought it meant something. And though she knew his reasons for never touching her, she was twenty-two years old and had never known a man's touch. She wanted it. Now.

He looked up, his expression unreadable. He hesitated, as if looking for the words to answer. "I—"

"Oh gods." She breathed out quickly. "Oh gods."

"I—of course!" he quickly amended. "Of course I want you."

She did not believe him, snatching the vial from his still open hand, as if he could not bring himself to close his fingers around it.

"Never mind," she spat. "This was a mistake."

"Can we talk about this?"

She turned, walking back towards the back of the room, embarrassment sluicing along her skin like a wave of ice. She tried to ignore it. Tried to steel her spine. "There is nothing to talk about."

Ezra followed her. "So after nearly fifteen years together, you decide now is the time to sleep together, and when I show the slightest hesitation, you decide there is nothing to talk about?"

She whirled, facing him with ire welling in her gut. "That was a bit more than slight *hesitation, Ezra."*

To his credit, Ezra did not back down. Did not cower at her tone that had sent most of the weaseling courtiers in this castle running with their tails between their legs. "What happened to tradition? What happened to protocol? I thought we were waiting!"

"Waiting for what?" she barked.

"Marriage!" he barked right back. "Your father has made it quite clear that there are lines. Even for us."

She scoffed, but it came out more like a snort. "We're betrothed, Ezra. It doesn't get much more married than that. And since when do you give even a fraction *of a damn about protocol?"*

He did not have an answer for that. And she should have reveled in the small victory over this man who had never once been intimidated by her. Never once backed down from her. Instead, his silence only gutted her more.

He didn't want her. He certainly didn't want to take her to his bed. She hated him for it—for the tears that threatened, for the lump that formed in her throat. But with the last remnants of her iron will, she squared her shoulders, cleared her throat, and leveled a glare at him. "Leave. Now."

"Rachæl. We need to talk about this."

"There is nothing to talk about. Get out."

He took a step towards her. A single step. When he reached for her, she flinched so quickly that his hand dropped immediately.

"Don't. Touch. Me."

Ezra did not disobey. And his steps as he turned to leave were like the pounding of a death knell as he strode from her chambers.

Rachæl stared at her fire, the glass of wine almost empty in her hand.

Ezra had not wanted her. She supposed she shouldn't have been so stupid. So blind. So...naïvely juvenile. But she had thought he would delight in her gift. She had thought he would accept it with something of an I-thought-you'd-never-ask smile.

Instead, he had lectured her like a child and left her alone on Yasha.

It had taken until the following Harvest for her to understand why. Ezra had not loved her. Ever. At least not in the ways that count between a man and a woman. Most days, it didn't bother her. So why tonight? Maybe it was the stupid, annoying quiet of the Yasha night, the incessant reminders of kith and kin during this time of year that had her feeling piteous. Like a simpering child.

She finished the last dregs of the wine and set her glass aside.

She had just risen to refill it when she heard a light *tap tap tap* on her door. Not her chamber door, but the door to her private garden.

There was only one other suite with access to that garden.

She made her way to the heavy, glass doors and pulled them open to find Gian on the other side. He lifted a green bottle with a lopsided smile on his mouth. "Hello, darling."

"Are you drunk?" she asked, crossing her arms.

He grimaced. "No. But I was hoping you could fix that."

She looked down, spotting a bundle of gray fluff sticking his head out between Gian's shins. She smiled, bending to scoop up the wolf pup. As she stood again, she rolled her eyes for Gian's benefit, telling herself she wasn't glad to see him. Never mind the lightness in her shoulders proved the thought to be a lie. She stepped back and gestured with a grand sweep of her hand for him to enter. He offered her a deep, mocking bow before stepping inside.

"Why aren't you still at dinner?" he asked.

"Apparently, I was more keen on wallowing in self pity this merry night." She fluffed the fur of the pup's head, letting him lick her hand as if it were a piece of barley sugar.

"Ah," Gian said, making his way to her settee. He plopped down rather unceremoniously before he popped the stopper from the top of his bottle. "'Tis a common side-effect of Yasha, I'm afraid."

"What a depressing pair we make," she said, draping herself into the chair next to him. She settled the pup on her lap and began scratching his ever-fattening belly. On the table between them sat her now-empty glass of wine, which Gian, of course, had not missed.

He eyed it with a knowing smirk. "Drinking without me, Princess?"

She ignored the comment. "Bear is getting bigger. I swear he's grown since yesterday."

"Yes, and he drinks enough milk for three grown men." Gian took a healthy swig from his bottle before offering it to Rachæl.

"Not bothering with glasses this time?"

"Rum is a social drink. Best enjoyed in the company of fine women."

She snorted and accepted the bottle he offered, taking her own healthy swig, letting the liquid burn a welcome path of fire down her throat and kill any lingering aftertaste of that abhorrent wine.

When she handed the bottle back to Gian, he took one look at the remaining liquid and swore colorfully. "That bad, huh?"

"Mother is still sick, and Father doesn't seem to give a damn."

Gian flicked her a look that was a mixture of disdain and pity. She ignored it. "I was tired of playing Practiced Princess. I decided to come back here for some solitude."

"And here I am robbing it from you without remorse." He took another swig, not making a move to leave, or even to feign worry for his impropriety.

She huffed a laugh and looked down at the wolf, who had turned over, offering her his back and head to scratch. She accommodated with a grin.

"You're spoiling him, you know," Gian said, cutting his eyes to her. "He'll never make it in the wild if he expects such luxury on a daily basis."

"He is a wolf of Chesedelle court. He will have all the luxury he requires."

"And with no idea just how lucky he is, the little bastard. Edging out every other male in this castle to have your undivided affections on this Yasha night."

She rolled her eyes, keeping her gaze fixed on the fire before them. It was only when she heard the soft thud of something beside her that she turned to look at him again. A small package now sat on the table between them.

"What is this?" she asked.

"Well, it is Yasha, after all," was Gian's response.

She furrowed her brows but reached for the package all the same. Pulling away the thick, brown paper, she found a beautiful, intricately carved wooden box inside.

"It's lovely, Gian," she said, inspecting it. Indeed, it was lovely. The work of a skilled hand. Although a bit random and sterile for a gift. Not unlike the sterile and thoughtless necklace she had received last year.

Gian snorted. "That's not your gift, darling. Open it."

She brought her attention back to the box, opening the delicate gold latch.

"Cards," she said with a grin. "You got me playing cards."

"I figure you should have your own deck."

She smiled, pulling them out. It was only upon closer inspection that she realized these weren't ordinary, press-printed playing cards. Not playing cards anyone could pick up at the local mercantile. These were something else; a work of art. "Gian, these are hand-painted."

He didn't answer, only watching her as she looked through each one. The expert linework. The vibrant colors. The intricate designs. Whoever had painted these was a skilled artisan. She thumbed through each one, stopping when she came across the first Queen in the deck. Her long, blonde locks; her vibrant, gold eyes; her gown, cut strikingly similar to the fashions Rachæl preferred...

She held it up to him. "And this?"

He offered a smirk. "I told him to make sure the Queens were the most exquisite of the deck. Nothing short of ravishing beauty would suffice."

She leveled him a flat look. "I am not a queen, Gian."

He did not back down from her gaze. "You are *my* queen."

She looked away quickly, her cheeks instantly warm, using the excuse of shuffling through the cards again just to avoid that branding gaze of his. Then she came across the Ace at the back of the deck. In lieu of the spade emblem, an exquisite rendering of her initials gleamed in gold and crimson and obsidian.

"And this?" she asked, raising the card for him to see.

He didn't even look at her, his gaze now fixed on the fire, his bottle resting lazily on his chest. "Everyone knows it's the most valuable card in the deck."

Something in her chest tightened and unfurled all at once. "Gian," she started to say. But words did not come easily. "No one has ever... This is the kindest..."

"It's nothing," he said.

But it wasn't nothing. In fact, it was the most *un*-nothing gift she had ever been given.

"I feel terrible," she finally managed to say. "I don't have anything for you."

His gaze at last met hers. He held it for a long moment before he said, "I tell you what. Let me stay here with you by this fire. That's all the gift I want."

So she did.

CHAPTER TWENTY-TWO

"You cannot seem to stay away from here, can you?" Ezra asked amiably as John emerged into his office. "Every time I look up, you and the children are back for a visit. If I didn't think it would insult your pride, I'd just ask you to go ahead and move in."

John huffed a dismissive laugh as he perched himself on the arm of a plush chair facing Ezra's desk. "Right."

Ezra raised a brow and watched his friend as he dug through his leather satchel. "I seem to recall the only reason you and Esther didn't take my grandfather's offer to live here to begin with was to prove to my father you were capable of providing for her."

John looked up from his satchel. "What's your point?"

"You've made your point, haven't you?"

"Are you asking me to move in with you, Ezra? It seems a bit presumptuous."

Ezra crossed his arms, dismissing the joke. "I'm serious, John. It's not as if we're hurting for space around here. Six wings of this place are entirely closed due to lack of need. It seems a waste that you and my sister must trek across the valley every time you want to have a conversation."

"I doubt you would feel the same once you realize just how loud my children can be."

Ezra huffed a laugh, a surge of joy welling from his gut. He'd soon know just exactly how loud children could be, wouldn't he? "The castle could use some mayhem. It's much too quiet now that we've grown up and stopped pestering Helena and Thaddeus."

"Oh, we still pester them, just in new and more sophisticated ways," John countered.

Ezra laughed, shifting his gaze to John's satchel and the book he'd retrieved from it, now resting on his lap. "You've been to the library," he said with a chortle. "What's this new conspiracy you've brought me today?"

John eagerly opened the book in his lap, his attention on finding the precise page. He hadn't dared mark it—nor would he. The book was old. Maybe even ancient. As a lawyer, John bore a healthy respect for old tomes: the secrets they bore; the mysteries they uncovered. Over the years, John had made it adamantly clear that wouldn't dare commit the sacrilege of marking a page in such a prize.

"Ah! Here it is," he finally exclaimed, turning the book and handing it, open and waiting, to Ezra.

Ezra scanned the worn pages but saw nothing to claim his attention. "Is this genealogy?"

"It is," John said, nodding. "The genealogical records of the royal families of the world, dating all the way back to before Haravelle or Navah existed."

"And Achim wed Emuna and begat Neshuan and Hasse. Neshuan wed Alona and they begat Chagiya and Jemina. Jemina wed..." Ezra looked up from the tome, his expression confused. "I fail to understand, John."

John leaned forward, pointing farther down the page. "Read this."

"Barak begat Midian, the first king of Midvar."

"Notice anything strange?" John asked.

Ezra scanned the page again. "Am I supposed to?"

"Who is Midian's mother?" John questioned.

Ezra read the passage again. "She is not mentioned," he admitted.

"Strange, isn't it? In all of the records, both the father and the mother are listed. Except for this one."

"What is your point? These are ancient records, John. Surely they won't get every name right. Maybe she was a prostitute. Or maybe she was a lover."

"That's not how these records work, Ez. They're for the purpose of historical record, not hiding family secrets. I find it curious that of all the charts, only this one lacks a mother's name," John said, taking the book back.

"You find everything curious, my friend," Ezra said with a chuckle.

Fishing again in his satchel, this time John retrieved a scroll tied in a worn leather thong. Placing it on the ornate desk, he unrolled it with near religious reverence, carefully moving the ancient paper until he found the section he was looking for. "Read this," he said, pointing to the ancient writing. It was barely visible on the parchment, the ink faded with time. Ezra squinted as he attempted to read the ancient handwriting.

> *"In the time of the judges, a woman emerged from the shadows. Her origin unknown, many believed she had come from the stars. A fallen one. Mother goddess divine, cursed to live among men. She roamed the*

lands in search of worthy seed, for from her womb would come the Eastern Star."

Ezra looked up. "What does this even mean?"

"Keep reading," John insisted.

"King Midian, gods-blessed with the blood of the ancients. Midian the Nephilim." Ezra stopped reading. "What in Sheol is a Nephilim?"

A light shone in John's eyes as he spoke. "I wasn't sure either. I checked several sources and most of them say something similar. In essence, the legends state that the Nephilim were an ancient breed of people, birthed from the womb of a goddess."

"Demigods?" Ezra asked.

John shook his head. "Demi-demons. The legends say that it was out of the blood of these half-bloods that the kingdom of Midvar was birthed. There is story after story, Ez. They were unbeatable in war. Gifted with preternatural strength, healing abilities, some even had wings. They remained undefeated in the eastern lands until the time of King Ferryl."

"The Golden Era," Ezra mused.

"Exactly. It was prophesied that a king and queen would rise to end the era of the Midvarish darkness. Which many say is what happened with King Ferryl and Queen Adelaide, ushering in the Adelaidian era of peace and prosperity in the lands."

"I'm not sure why you're giving me a history lesson, John. Most everyone knows at least that part of the story."

"I know. But no one seems to ask—from where did Midian gain his strength? Who was his mother? Was she really a fallen goddess? A demon roaming the earth? And if so, what happened to her?"

"How could anyone ever know the answer to that, John? And better yet, why are you asking impossible questions?"

"Because I found out," John said, sitting up, eager to share this little tidbit, apparently. "The King of Har-Navah is to welcome a visitor soon. The son of the Medinian Empress. Do you know what his name is?"

Ezra only raised his brows.

"Midian."

Ezra let the declaration sink in for a moment. "Coincidence, John. Nothing more. This world is ancient. Do you think there has only ever been one of any given name among its peoples? There have probably been thousands of Midians over the eons."

"True. But none with such an interesting story."

"How so? You said this ancient King Midian has no record of his mother's name in the annals. We know that this Prince Midian coming to visit us has a mother, alive and well, and her name is Lilith."

"Indeed. Empress Lilith. Whose genealogy is nowhere in the books."

"What are you implying, John?"

"Can you find her name anywhere in these books?"

"I don't know because I'm not going to bother sifting through them to find out."

"Well, I did," John said.

"Of course you did."

"And she's not mentioned anywhere. Not once. The only mention of the ancient King Midian's mother is 'a woman' or 'mother goddess.' Never once is her name mentioned. Nor is there a record of Empress Lilith's family, her heritage, genealogy. Nothing. It's as if she exists without existing at all."

"Maybe you're just looking in the wrong books."

"These are the definitive records of the ancient monarchs, Ez. If she's not in here, she never existed."

"So Empress Lilith is a phantasm, then?"

"No," said John. "But what if she is a fallen goddess?"

Ezra thought of the night he had visited Chesedelle Castle a few months ago. The king had called a last-minute, mandatory council meeting. Instead of discussing the matters of the kingdom, the council had gathered in the throne room to listen to Empress Lilith sing.

It wasn't only her song that had been curious that night. No, it was her appearance. For standing before the king's council, Ezra had seen a woman of fiery red curls and creamy skin, flecked with cinnamon freckles. He had thought the resemblance to Miri uncanny until another councilor had mentioned her looks—chocolate hair and caramel skin.

Had she appeared differently to Ezra than everyone else? Had he been missing his wife so much that he saw her in every beautiful woman?

Or had the empress perhaps appeared differently to everyone that night? Had her countenance shifted—an illusion of desire for any who beheld her?

The hairs on Ezra's arms stood on end, the words she had sung that night echoing in his mind. Her song had been ancient, the words those of the Medinian tongue. And while his knowledge of that language was broken at best, he had recognized some of the words. In fact, he had not been able to get them out of his head.

Alea iacta est.

Ad meliora.

Peace.

In newness of time.

The splendor of the earth and the heavens.

The power of magic. The magic of men.

No mention of Providence, or of ancient blessings. No mention of that ancient magic that had been revered and worshipped for as long as men roamed the earth. No, the empress's song had been about something else. Something new. Something...*other.*

If John was right... If this was true... Then perhaps it wasn't mere coincidence that she was making her move to imperialize now. Perhaps her quest for power was not happenstance, but precisely timed. If it was true that Lilith was an ancient goddess, fallen from the stars, then her timing was motivated by the presence of someone else. Another powerful player in this ancient story.

A chill shivered down Ezra's spine.

"What is it?" John asked.

Ezra looked up, realizing he had been staring at the scroll lain out before him. "Ari," he said.

John nodded soberly. "The Mashiach."

"We must speak to him. Tell him all of this. He will know what it means."

THEY FOUND Ari on the small lawn facing the front of the castle—the only part of the estate not sitting on the still-frozen waters of Lake Yerah. He was laughing at something John Junior had said, watching with a contented smile as the child skipped and hopped around the snow, searching for pinecones and squealing every time he found a large one.

"Ari," Ezra said pleasantly. "I take it you were conned into coming out here with him this morning." He nodded towards the boy.

Ari chuckled. "No conning necessary. One of the best things in life is to view the world through the eyes of a child."

"I couldn't agree more," John said.

Ari appraised them both for a moment and then said, "But you did not come out here to do that. There is something on your mind."

Ezra stole a glance at his brother-in-law before he nodded. "What do you know of the Medinian Empress?"

Ari's face shifted to something ominous as he held Ezra's eyes with his own, a piercing shade of emerald, articulated by the glistening winter sunlight. "I was wondering when you were going to ask me that."

JOHN, Ari, and Ezra had been in conversation for the better part of an hour, having ushered a reluctant John Junior back inside the castle before making their way to the downstairs library. Sitting beside a crackling fire in the oversized hearth, John perched on the arm of a chair while Ari took the settee. Ezra, however, had not been able to sit, pacing the floor to help him think as they discussed the missing information in the annals of history and the implications of the empress's visit.

"But the king seems...enthralled with her," Ezra said. "I saw it for myself when I was there a few months ago. He called a special council meeting. But there was no meeting. She just sang for us."

"Sang?" John asked, knitting his brows together.

Ezra nodded. "It was a strange song. Not one I've ever heard. It was in Medinian. I did not understand most of it, but I caught a bit of its meaning."

"In Newness of Time," Ari said distantly, staring out the great windows beyond Ezra. "It is not a song of my Father, though it is old. Ancient, even."

"You know the song?" John asked, perching a little closer to the edge of the chair arm.

Ezra stopped pacing, his eyes fixed on his new cousin.

“It was sung by the giants of old. The Nephilim. An ancient legend that began even before Haravelle and Navah.”

“What legend?” Ezra asked. “What is the Nephilim?”

Ari turned his gaze to Ezra, his face unreadable and cold. “The fallen ones. Banished from my Father’s kingdom for their defiance; they followed the star as it fell through the skies and came here. To this planet—to the seat of Providence’s creation. There are others, you see. But he started here. With you. Your people.”

“I don’t understand,” John said. “What do you mean others?”

“Other planets,” Ari said, as if it were not the most shocking news he could deliver. “Other peoples. Tribes. She wants them all. But she’s starting here.”

“She? The empress?” Ezra asked, heart pounding with dread.

Ari nodded once. “The fallen star. She considers herself a goddess now. But she is no such thing.”

“Then what is she?” John asked hesitantly.

“A demon.”

The room fell utterly silent, the words hanging between them like droplets of water cast from the wings of a færy. As if time itself stood still.

“There are few who know such things. Few who have lived with such knowledge,” Ari went on. “She has been careful to erase those details from the history books.”

“I noticed,” John said, his words strained.

Ari nodded. “This is not the time to let this information leave this room. But you must know if you are to understand why I am here.”

“Why *are* you here?” Ezra asked.

“I think you already know that,” Ari answered, another of his typical, roundabout answers. But Ezra pressed him anyway.

“You are the Promised One. The son of Providence,” he said, still not quite sure what to make of the words that were coming from his mouth. He could have sworn a shadow of great antlers shone above Ari's head—but if it was there, it was gone again in a flash. "Are you here to wage war?" Ezra asked.

Ari smiled, pursing a chuckle. "There is already a war, don't you see? I am not here to wage battles. I am here to usher in my Father's kingdom."

"To restore the Adelaidian line?" John asked.

"To restore the True Magic."

CHAPTER TWENTY-THREE

"I want to know what you have learned. I want to know who he is working with. Is it the high priest?"

The king was agitated. Markedly so. Rachæl hadn't seen him thus since...well, she could not remember a time when he had been this agitated. Certainly not over a prophet. The councilors around them remained obstinately silent, though she could not be sure if it was for the purpose of saving their own skins or some kind of collective defiance. Across the table, Gian's signature smirk was nowhere to be found, his attention fixed on the king as if he were a puzzle the pirate was trying to solve.

"My forefathers did not fight for this throne only for me to lose it to some vagabond!" her father's voice rose. "Where the Sheol is my high priest? Where is the Sanhedrin? Have they nothing to say?"

"My king," said one of the councilors. "We have spoken with members of the holy council. It seems His Holiness has been on sabbatical of late, but they assured me that he has not betrayed you."

"Sabbatical?" Gian asked. Something in his eyes darkened, but conspicuously, he looked everywhere but at Rachæl.

The king's undersecretary emerged just then, the sound of his steps on the stone floors echoing irreverently through the room. "Your Majesty," he said with a curt bow. He handed the king a stack of parchments and a pen. Without pausing to read a word, the king began signing the papers, one after the other.

"Father, what are you signing?" Rachæl asked.

The king didn't bother lifting his eyes from the parchment he was currently signing. "My dear, if you're so worried, why don't you read them for yourself?"

"Do *you* read them?" she asked.

"I read them for him," the undersecretary answered.

"So the daily business of this kingdom has been reduced to the judgment of an undersecretary?"

"His Majesty is burdened with much responsibility. He leaves reading through the finer details to me," said the man.

"I hadn't realized my father's schedule was so cumbersome that he cannot be bothered to read the laws of his own land. Perhaps a vacation would do some good."

The king set down his pen carefully, looking up to Rachæl at the same time. He set his elbows on the table, folding his hands before his mouth. A small, horrifying smile turned his lips. "I have never questioned my decision to hand the throne to you before."

Everyone went utterly still, Gian included. The king went on. "Perhaps in your infinite wisdom, you'd like to educate me in all the ways that you are more equipped to run this kingdom than I. Because from where I sit, we are looking at war with a band of proselytizing insurrectionists, and yet your focus remains on trade agreements and the price of spice. Forgive me if I fail to see the dizzying superiority of your intellect, dearest."

"Father, I—"

"Do not speak, child, lest you intend to make more of a fool of yourself. Your focus—everyone's focus—needs to remain on this prophet. Who he is working with. Who he speaks to. Where he goes when he thinks no one is looking. If my sources are correct, your former betrothed has become *remarkably* close to him," the king said, looking at Rachæl with a pointed stare. "I would hate to think that he set you aside to align with a vagabond and betray me. I noticed he still has not returned to council, despite the fact that he has been home from his so-called honeymoon for weeks."

That thought was too absurd. That Ezra could do something so devious. So underhanded. Surely he would not be so stupid...

"I want to know everything about this prophet," the king went on. "I am tired of hearing rumors of insurrectionists in the streets calling for the restoration of the GODSDAMNED ADELADIAN LINE!

"THERE IS NO ADELADIAN LINE TO THE THRONE. THERE IS ONLY ME. And I will do WHATEVER is necessary to ensure that remains."

"There will be no throne to defend if you keep signing it away, one spice trade agreement at a time." Rachæl knew she should not have said it, especially not in front of the council. But she had been unable to stop herself. The accusations he had made were too outrageous.

The king froze, his hardened gaze falling on his daughter. "Everyone out," he said half under his breath, his words dark and menacing.

But no one moved.

"Out!" the king cried. "Get out!"

The council could not seem to move fast enough then, chairs scraping along the stone floor and feet scurrying out of the room. All except for Gian, who did not move from his chair, his face hard, his eyes fixed on the king, simmering, like a beast on a short tether.

When the room was at last empty, the king's blazing eyes

narrowed. "You've grown arrogant, dearest," he finally spoke. "Confident in your claim to my throne."

"No, Father. It is not arrogance with which I speak, but with a great love for my kingdom and concern for your indifference towards it."

Though her gaze remained fixed on her father's, she could have sworn Gian's eyes flashed. He was probably shocked that she had said such a thing to her father. To the King of Har-Navah.

Then again, so was she. She did not know where the gumption had come from.

"You are not my only option, you know," said her father, a victorious if not feral grin in his eyes.

"What is that supposed to mean?"

He cocked his head to one side, still leaning over the table between them, his face mere inches from hers. "You think I've not been paying attention, don't you? You think I don't know that you've been fucking my mercenary?" Without taking his eyes from her, the king nodded to Gian across from them.

Rachæl dared to glance at Gian, whose face shone with white-hot rage. But he did not say anything.

The king chuckled, and there was nothing humorous in the sound. "I don't give a fuck what you do anymore, darling. I have plans for you."

"What plans?"

She was about to utter that question herself, but Gian had beaten her to it, his words a low vulpine growl.

The king at last turned his gaze to the man. "Where is your loyalty, Gian? Is it to me anymore? I do wonder."

Gian did not utter a sound.

The king grinned. "I don't care, you know. I don't give a shit if she is still innocent on her wedding night. It won't matter. Not anymore."

"What have you done, Father?"

The king turned his attention back to her, a smile spreading wide across his mouth. "Ensured the legacy of my dynasty."

"She's cursed you," Rachæl said wildly, damning the consequences of her insolence. She needed to say it. No matter what would come of it. "Don't you see it, Father? She's blinded you to what she is doing. She has convinced you that she is an ally, when she is taking this kingdom from you, from *us*—"

The sting of her father's hand did not manifest immediately, as if time itself had stopped from the moment he struck her to the time she felt the pain. And in that frozen moment, Gian launched himself across the table, as nimble as a wolf, taking the king down to the floor in a tumble of limbs and fists.

"Stop!" she cried as Gian laid into her father. But the king was no rag doll to be thrown about, and he soon landed a devastating blow to Gian's cheek. Blood sprayed from his mouth but the pirate did not relent, reaching for the king's throat and closing his massive hands around it. A treasonable offense.

"Don't. Ever. Touch. Her. Again," he said through his teeth. Blood dripped from his nose onto the king's cravat.

The king struggled under Gian's grip, taking hold of his wrists to pry them away from his throat. But he could not speak.

"Do you understand me?" Gian went on. "Never touch her again."

The king's eyes went wide from lack of breath, his face a dark shade of red, but Gian did not loosen his grip.

"Gian, stop!" Rachæl said again, louder.

He did no such thing.

"Do you understand me?" the pirate repeated, demanding.

The king was expiring. His face had changed from beet red to a dark, unholy shade of plum. Gian saw it, too, and as if released from a trance, the pirate suddenly let go of the king's throat and sat back on his heels, heaving gasping breaths and wiping the blood dripping from his nose and lips.

Standing to his feet, Gian reached down and offered the king his hand to stand.

To her eternal shock, the king accepted, allowing Gian to help him off the floor. As her father stood, his own chest heaving, he brushed his hands down his vest and lapels, straightening his clothes before looking at them again.

"You've taken your job a little too seriously, Gian," he said.

"Sir," was Gian's only response, his head down, unable to meet the king's gaze.

"It would be a pity for you to come to regret that one day." At that, her father turned and left the room without another word.

"What in Sheol is wrong with you?" Rachæl scolded the moment the king was gone.

Gian did not meet her eyes, either.

"He's not going to let that go, Gian."

"I know," he said quietly.

"He's going to make sure you pay for that."

"I *know.*"

"Then why did you do it? What came over you?"

"Why did you defy him? What came over *you?*"

"You know, I really hate the way you answer my questions with more questions."

"Afraid to answer me, Princess?"

Rachæl scoffed. "I defied him because I care about this kingdom. I care about what happens to it. I defied him because I love it and I won't stand idly by and watch him destroy it."

Gian nodded, sucking on his swollen lower lip for a moment before he said, "Now you know why I defied him for you."

She froze, letting the words sink in.

Because I care... Because I love... Because I won't stand idly by...

He turned to walk towards the door, but he only got a few steps before Rachæl said, "Are you hurt?"

He paused, turning to face her again. "I've had worse."

"Let me tend to you," she said quickly, not wanting to let him leave. What he had just done...for her...

He searched her, hesitating for reasons she did not know. But at last he walked towards her again, stopping just shy of her, his face a picture of shame.

She felt stupid when she admitted, "I...haven't a handkerchief."

Without taking his eyes from her, Gian reached into the breast pocket of his jacket and retrieved a rather haggard-looking cloth that she supposed was his excuse for a handkerchief. She took it from him, using it to gingerly wipe the blood from under his nose and the corner of his mouth that she might better assess the damage.

He sucked in a breath between his teeth at her touch.

"Sorry," she said. "You shouldn't have done that, though."

"He shouldn't have hit you."

He had a small cut at the corner of his lip where the blood pooled every time she wiped, so she pressed the worn cloth to the wound and said, "I should not have defied him in front of the council."

"That's not an excuse," Gian countered.

Her fingers trembling, she could not bring herself to meet Gian's branding gaze. "I don't think I'll ever forget the sight of you launching yourself across the table towards him."

A ghost of a smile curled his mouth, there and gone again with the pain it brought him. He winced. "He needed his ass kicked."

Rachæl could not help her grin.

"Though," Gian added, "I doubt when he asked me to look after you all those months ago that he ever imagined I'd be protecting you from him."

She met his eyes then, searching. "What exactly did he ask of you, Gian?"

A shrug. "He knew, after Ezra left, that you would be vulnerable to pricks like Lord Wax-a-Mustache sniffing around, looking for chances to take advantage. So he asked me to keep an eye on you."

"You had the upper hand. You could have killed him, but you didn't. Why?"

"I don't hate the man, despite how it may seem. I respect him most days. There is good in him. I have seen it."

"So have I," she admitted softly. "I just don't know what's wrong with him these days. He's had many lovers before. But none of them made him utterly indifferent to the throne, and certainly not to his own family."

"I know," Gian agreed. "But I don't think this is mere lust distracting him. I think you are right—I think he has been cursed."

"I don't know why I said that. I don't even know what that word means."

"Neither do I. Until all of this, I would have argued that magic is neither good nor bad, it's just magic. I'm not sure I believe that anymore."

"There is a darkness spreading in this kingdom. It's subtle, difficult to explain. But I can feel it, Gian. And I fear what it means. For all of us, but especially for him."

"Then we must pray to every god we can name to protect what is good in him," Gian said, and his tone was serious. Rare for him, and all the more important. "Because I know he still cares. Somewhere in there. It wasn't just a king protecting his dynasty the day he came to me. It was a father asking for my help. I respected the Sheol out of him for it."

Rachæl removed the cloth from Gian's mouth. The wound had stopped bleeding, at least. But the color blooming on his jaw and under his eye would not soon wane.

"He thinks we are lovers," she said, barely believing the words had come from her lips.

Gian breathed a dismissive laugh. "Silly, isn't it?"

"Indeed, considering you have every woman at court. I don't see why you'd have need of me." She hadn't meant for the words to come out sounding so pathetic. But there they were—out and between them. She wondered what he'd make of them.

"Funny, I was going to say it was silly because you have your pick of any man in the kingdom. I see no reason for you to bother with the rabble."

She looked into his eyes again, and he held her gaze without falter. Then again, so did she, not caring if it made him uncomfortable. There was an honesty there in Gian's eyes—an honesty she wasn't sure she'd ever known with another soul.

The momentary spell broke when she finally remembered what she was doing and said, "I think you will survive. It's all superficial, anyway. Nothing that needs to be stitched up."

Gian nodded, adjusting his jaw this way and that with his hand. "Thank you."

"Thank *you,*" she said. For protecting her. For being her friend. For jumping to her defense. She leaned a bit closer to him—it did not take much—and pressed a gentle kiss to his cheek.

When she pulled away, Gian held her gaze for a moment longer before he turned to walk away again.

"Gian," she said softly.

He stopped in his tracks.

She waited until he turned to face her and said, "It doesn't sound that silly to me."

She didn't wait to see his reaction, turning on her heel and leaving the council chamber, head held high.

CHAPTER TWENTY-FOUR

In the months that followed Yasha, winter began to wane, the snows slowly ebbing from the frozen shores of the lake, the ice thawing from patches on the ground, and the grasses emerging here and there on the forest floor. Spring was in full bloom at Massahd Castle. The snow only remained in patches of the most shadowy parts of the forest; the trees had exploded in bright, fresh green leaves; the skies hovered above in vibrant shades of blue; and the wildflowers... Miri hadn't gotten over the wildflowers blooming on the mountainside, all around the lake, and in every garden at Massahd. Tall, proud purple blooms with white centers; dainty yellow blooms like a carpet across the grass; clusters of white and pink and orange and red. Spring at Massahd was a bright, cheery occasion.

Early one morning, Miri rose and dressed quietly without waking Ezra and went out for a little exploration, hoping the symphony of color and new life would somehow permeate into her own soul.

She had grown considerably in the last few months, her belly protruding so that it was no longer hidden beneath her skirts.

There was no denying she was pregnant anymore. Somehow, despite everything, life had found a way—much like it bloomed all around her.

She had even begun to feel the little one inside moving around, though she hadn't told Ezra yet. She couldn't. Not with the knowledge that hounded her day and night.

The knowledge that would damn everything. Ruin it all.

The child might not be Ezra's.

Thanks to Phinehas—thanks to what he had taken from her the night of the Harvest Ball—the child could be his.

But it could just as easily have been Ezra's, a fact which she reminded herself again and again.

But every time that comforting thought gained any sort of footing in her heart, it was soon squashed by the damning truth that chased her wherever she went: she would never know.

She hadn't been able to bring herself to tell Ezra what gnawed at her day in and day out, though she knew he could tell. Sometimes at dinner she would look up to see him watching her with concern in his eyes. And sometimes at night, in the quiet of their four-poster bed, Ezra would kiss her brow and touch her cheek and say, "I'm right here beside you, Wildfire. I always will be."

Because he knew. He knew without her saying a word that she was lying to him. Hiding something.

In plain, ever-growing sight.

He was thrilled and overjoyed about a child that might not be his.

But she could not bring herself to admit the truth to him, knowing it would break his heart and likely his spirit all at once.

So she kept the truth hidden deep within and never spoke of it.

But this morning, with the sun beaming on the wildflowers outside the window, she could not help but to go to them, hoping they would soothe her. Offer comfort. Hope, even.

She ran her hands along the tallest flowers as she meandered around the front lawns and towards the lake's edge. The bees flitted among the blooms, their fuzzy bodies yellow with pollen. The hummingbirds visited the brightest flowers, hovering with their tiny wings as they fought with each other over the precious nectar.

But for all the color, the light, the life around her, she could find no joy.

At the water's edge, Miri knelt, the movement awkward thanks to her protruding belly. She reached down to touch the water, marveling at its crystal clarity that only a few days ago had still been a sheet of ice. The lake here had no beach, but seemed to plummet straight down between the mountains, its depth unknown. Brightly-colored fish darted between the ripples, feasting on flies at the surface. Algae and plants waved lazily in the lapping water, their colors made more vivid by the brightness of the sun. But after only a few feet of the clear waters, the lake turned too deep for the sun to reach, an inky darkness looming beneath the bright life above.

Miri ran her hand along the surface of the water. For all the life frolicking beneath, it was surprisingly cold. Ezra had once told her the lake was fed by glaciers, which explained why it remained so cold even in the heat of summer. She wondered what sort of creatures could stand to live in such perpetual frigid temperatures.

Then again, she supposed the creatures in this water had never known anything different, had they? Their lives had been lived in the icy waters, and though they could see the sun, those fish had never once felt its warmth.

Had she really been any different before Ezra came into her life? She had lived in a captivity of sorts from the time she was a babe, what with a father who sold her off to the highest bidder and a priest who had whored her for his own gain. She had lived in cold darkness for so long that, though she could see light around her, she could not fathom what it felt like.

Until she met Ezra.

A heaviness washed over her at the thought. He had been nothing but kind, nothing but loving from the moment they had met. He had seen her for who she was and had loved her anyway. A kind of love she had not earned and certainly not deserved.

And here she was, carrying a child that might not be his, throwing that love and devotion in his face. Mocking him with every day that her belly grew.

Miri shut her eyes, squeezing out a tear as she did. She moved to wipe it away, glancing across the placid lake, when something caught her eye.

She focused on the water just beyond the shore, trying to make sense of what she had seen. Something had moved, she thought. Ever so subtly and gracefully, but it had definitely been movement that had caught her eye.

Something large.

She froze, holding her breath as she watched the waters intently.

And once again, she spotted the movement.

Scales.

Dark and iridescent.

They crested the waters with effortless ease, there and gone again in a flash. The back of a giant creature.

One she had seen before.

Once Ezra had taken her out on this lake. A long time ago. He had taken her for a ride in a glass gondola on the very night he had asked her to marry him. And while in that boat, she had spotted a similar creature—with large black scales that shimmered in every color under the sunlight.

Ezra had recounted the tales of a creature cursed to live in the depths of this lake. She had questioned that day whether she had seen it at all, or whether it had just been a figment of her imagination.

But she saw it today. Clear as day. There was no questioning it now.

"Bound by the sea
For all eternity
Leviathan awaits her destiny.
By fire and flame
She sets the world ablaze
For the coming of the new age."

Startled, Miri turned and stood to find Ari approaching the lake's edge, a smile on his face as he recited the familiar verse.

"You remember?" she asked.

Ari nodded. "What were you, thirteen, fourteen when we read it?"

"Something like that," she said. "It was from an adventure book, right?"

Ari nodded again. "A rather good one, if I recall."

Miri smiled softly. "You always had good taste in stories."

"That wasn't just a story, Mir."

She tilted her head to one side. "What was it?"

"A prophecy," he said nonchalantly. "About you."

"What?" she asked, her heart suddenly pounding in her chest. "That's impossible."

"Is it, *Wildfire?"*

She froze, the name Ezra had given her strange and foreign on Ari's tongue.

By fire and flame
She sets the world ablaze

"Why did he give me that name? What does he know?"

Ari shook his head. "He did not understand its meaning when

he gave it to you, though I suspect that is no longer true. He originally named you thus for your curls."

"What do you mean, it's no longer true?"

"Your husband has been doing some research, cousin. He believes all of this is connected: that prophecy, the empress, my presence."

"Is it?" she asked, the question quiet. She wasn't sure she was prepared to hear the answer.

"As with all things of my Father, there is no such thing as coincidence."

"What does the prophecy mean?"

Ari looked out across the lake, as if he could still see the phantom shadow of the giant creature. "Leviathan awaits her destiny, Miri of the Wildfire."

MIRI NEEDED TO THINK. She had wandered about the castle grounds for an hour after her strange conversation with Ari, until she found herself in the stables. One of the grooms had kindly offered to prepare a phaeton for her, which she had accepted and before she knew it, before she realized where they were going, Miri found herself back in the village of Shalem for the first time since...

Well, since Ari had saved her and Ezra had brought her home.

For reasons she could not name, she did not ask the groom to turn around, though her heart pounded the closer they got to the familiar streets.

The sound of the wheels on the open carriage shifted to a familiar cadence the moment they met the cobblestone, the sound of the horse's hooves shifting from a muted thud to an echoing clip. The shops were as familiar as old friends: brightly-colored thresholds and vibrant wildflowers in every window box. Tinkers lauding wares along the way and people bustling in and out of mercantiles and apothecaries and bookstores. And there across the way, the bakery owned by Joshua and Winona. One she hadn't had the courage to visit, but from where Ezra had had their breakfast brought many mornings recently, just because he knew how much she loved their chocolate challah. Something tugged her heart at the sight and smell of that bakery as they approached—she remembered the many conversations she'd had with Ezra over breakfast on that rooftop, the months she had spent falling in love with him without even realizing it.

Her life had only truly begun in that place, nearly a year ago. She wanted to taste it again, to smell it, to experience it all over.

So she asked the groom to stop the phaeton. He pulled off to the side of the road, hopping down from his elevated seat to offer Miri a hand as she stepped down.

"Thank you," she said.

"My lady," he returned, offering her a deep bow at the waist.

"I plan to explore for a while. I'll send for you when I am ready to depart again."

"As you wish," he said with another bow before climbing back into his seat and snapping the reins once.

She watched the carriage disappear around the next corner before she turned her attention back to the bakery across the street. She was just about to cross when a familiar, slithering voice came from her other side.

Miri froze, willing herself to calm, to breathe at a normal pace.

But nothing could stop the dread that shivered down her spine when she turned to face the High Priest of Har-Navah.

"There's my good girl." Phinehas grinned. "It has been too long." His embroidered bib shone brightly in the spring sunlight, the vivid colors and glittering gold threads expertly sewn in symmetrical patterns on his chest. He did not wear his hat today, but his robes were particularly bright white against the brown cobblestone.

Miri took in a breath to steady herself and looked him in the eye, although she said nothing.

He raised a single brow. "Will you not greet me? After all we have been through."

"What are you doing here?" she asked.

"Worshipping Providence, of course."

"You've been in hiding."

Phinehas chuckled, but there was nothing lighthearted about the sound. "Hiding? Why would I need to hide?"

Because you tried to kill me. Because you violated me. Again and again. Because you gave me over to a monster. Miri kept her ire on a short leash and only said, "Because you are a coward."

Phinehas smiled, the gesture turning his mouth without affecting his eyes. "I see congratulations are in order," he offered, nodding to her belly.

On instinct, she covered it with her hands, snarling as she did.

"It looks as though you are a few months along now. Perhaps even a harvest conception?"

He knew. He knew without her having to say a word that she was unsure who the father was.

That it might be his.

She hated him for it. Hated him bitterly.

A lump formed in her throat, and tears stung in her eyes, but she kept her chin high and her shoulders back.

Phinehas laughed, stepping towards her. He stopped just short of touching her when he said, "Does he know? Your dear, precious husband. Does he know the child is not his?"

"The child *is* his," she said through her teeth. "He is the father."

"Is he?" Phinehas asked, tilting his head to one side. "You are certain?"

She hated that she could not answer him. Hated that the

words caught in her throat which had suddenly turned as dry as a desert.

Phinehas ran a single knuckle down her cheek. "You don't know how long I have hoped for this."

"Liar," she spat. "You never wanted a child with me."

"All I have ever wanted is for you to be mine. Forever. I suppose that's inevitable now, isn't it?"

"Ezra will never allow it."

"We'll just have to do something about that, won't we?"

"You stay away from him, do you understand? You will not hurt him."

Phinehas ran his knuckle over her lips. "My little spider, I have no need to hurt him. You'll be the one to do that."

CHAPTER TWENTY-FIVE

Rachæl entered her private quarters, thankful for the reprieve. After dinner and all the questions, she welcomed the solace her room offered. The night had fallen, leaving her chambers dark. Apparently, her servants hadn't gotten around to lighting the fire in the hearth or any candles either, because she fumbled around in the near-darkness for a match before she nearly tripped on something soft at her feet.

"Oof," she grunted, righting herself by grabbing the edge of a nearby table. The thing on which she tripped uttered a sharp little yelp.

"Bear!" she exclaimed, leaning down to scoop him in her arms. "How did you get in here?"

"I suppose he followed me," came the answer from the darkness, and Rachæl startled.

Light spilled immediately nearby—the flame of a match in Gian's hand, which he used to light the candle in front of her.

"What in the world are you doing in here in the dark?" She scowled.

"Listening."

"Listening? To what?" The pup in her arms nudged her neck with his cold, wet nose. She scratched his head absently.

"You can learn a lot from servants when they think no one is around," he said with a shrug.

She raised an eyebrow. "And what is it my father wants to learn from my servants?"

"This one was for my benefit," he answered with a smirk.

"I see," she said, understanding immediately. "Which one of them have you set your sights on this time?"

Gian balked, slapping a hand to his chest. "You offend me, Princess."

"Why?" she asked, shuffling past him with the wolf in her arms. "Because a gentleman never kisses and tells?"

She hated it, but she reveled in the chuckle he offered—the warmth in it. The familiarity. "Darling, you of all people know I'm no gentleman."

"Indeed," she said, taking a seat on her settee, settling the wolf in her lap and stroking his downy fur as a means of distraction. She did not want to think about how many of her servants he had been with. Likely most of them. She certainly did not want to think about the jealousy that rushed down into her gut at the thought. No, she did not need to think of that at all.

Gian did not wait for her to ask before arranging the logs in her hearth and starting a fire with little effort—something she'd rarely seen from any nobleman she'd known. She wondered how many fires Gian had made on his many adventures around the world. He'd certainly had no lack of adventure in his life. Adventures she would never be a part of.

"Father was not at dinner tonight," she said, changing the subject for her own sanity more than anything. She had to get her mind off this man with her servants, with anyone but . . .

He puffed the bellows at the base of the logs, encouraging the flame. "I heard. Where did he go?"

"Sachar River," she said. "With the empress."

Gian stopped fussing with the fire, turning to face her, his expression unreadable. "The spice trade?"

Rachæl nodded once. "Why is the king bothering himself with spices when he won't even bother to pay attention to the treaties he signs anymore?"

Gian seemed to think for a moment before he finally said, "That is an excellent question."

"Meanwhile, Mother is getting worse every day. Just this morning, she couldn't open her eyes, couldn't even speak to me. And Father seems utterly indifferent."

"And no word on her condition? What's causing it?" Gian made his way to a table topped with a decanter and two glasses. He poured wine generously for both of them before returning to the seating area.

"Nothing," Rachæl lamented, accepting the wine he offered and taking a sip. "No one can explain it."

"Perhaps that is because the explanation is not a natural one."

"What is that supposed to mean?"

Gian kept his gaze fixed on the hearty fire he had made. "I've been thinking about it. Ever since last fall when the Empress first visited. She sang to us, remember?"

"Yes, some Medinian song none of us knew," Rachæl sneered.

"Not just any song," Gian countered. He took a healthy swig from his glass before he continued. "I've heard stories of those with the ability to cast a spell with lyric and melody. A Shadow Song. It is said that those who can sing them bear an ancient, dark kind of magic, lost to most history books."

"You think she cursed us that day?"

He shrugged. "Well, see, that's the tricky part. I don't know what happened. I think she likely cursed your father. Perhaps the council. But I don't think she cursed you. And I could be wrong, but I don't think she cursed me either."

"Why not? Why spare us?"

"I don't think she intended to. Why would she?"

"Then how *were* we spared?"

"That's the question, isn't it?"

She could tell there was more to what he was thinking than what he was saying. Something he wasn't divulging. She could not imagine what. Or why.

But bursting through the door on the opposite end of the room, a servant emerged, wide-eyed and harassed, effectively ending their discussion. Gian stood immediately. "What is the meaning of this?"

Rachæl stood, too, letting Bear jump from her lap. Gian stood between her and the door, his shoulders broad and chin high, as if he would shield her from whatever atrocities this servant dared subject her to.

"I'm sorry, Your Royal Highness, but you must come. Immediately," said the servant.

"Come? Where?" Rachæl demanded.

"The queen," was all the servant could get out before Rachæl was tearing across the room, Gian behind her.

He had never seen her run. Then again, he supposed she hadn't had very many reasons to in her life, but one look at that servant and Rachæl hadn't hesitated. She had run from her chambers and through the palace corridors like a caracal on the hunt. Bear had followed them, his wolf instincts kicking in, despite his small size. Had he not been worried, Gian might have stopped to laugh at the sight they must have been: a princess, a pirate, and a wolf running through the palace halls.

She made it to the queen's quarters in record time, barely breaking a sweat. Bursting through the double doors that led to the queen's private bedchamber, Gian did not hesitate to stay close to her, never mind that he was not technically allowed in such hallowed rooms of the castle. At the moment, he didn't give a damn what they did to him. He wasn't going to leave her side.

"Mother!" Rachæl cried, launching herself towards the bed. But a physician stepped between the princess and the queen with a look of abject horror on his face. "I'm sorry, Your Highness, but you cannot."

"Get out of my way!" Rachæl commanded, clawing at the man. But he did not move.

"Your Highness, please, you cannot be here," said the man. A few of his nurses stood around the room, looks of shock and fear on their faces. So Gian reached for her.

"Rachæl," he said. She shoved him off as violently as she was trying to shove aside the doctor.

"Please," the doctor said to Gian. "She cannot be here. We do not know the cause of death."

"Mother," Rachæl cried again. And the sound of her voice cracking broke something within him.

"Darling," he coaxed. "Listen to me."

She did no such thing. Clambering for her mother, the doctor once again intervened.

"It is too much risk," he said, his eyes wide with some unspoken fear. And Gian understood. She needed to get out of here. It was not safe for her. Not safe for anyone, let alone the sole heir to the throne.

So Gian reached for her again, this time refusing to allow her to push him away. He pulled her away from the bed and to his chest, holding her tightly against it.

"Please," he said. "Please. We must leave."

"No!" she protested, writhing in his arms, surprisingly strong against him. "No!"

"Darling," he said, holding her fast. He gentled his voice. "Look at me."

She did not, but kept fighting him. He could feel her tiring, though. So he took her chin, forcing her to meet his gaze. "Look at me," he said again. "I'm right here, love."

Her eyes at last met his, though he could not be sure she could focus through the tears welling in hers, waiting to fall. "My love, it's all right."

"No, Gian. No," she cried, her voice breaking as the tears finally began falling. At their feet, he felt a pressure and looked down. Bear was on his hind feet, resting his front paws on Rachæl as if to console her the same way Gian was. She did not seem to notice.

"It's all right, my love," Gian said. "But we cannot stay here. It's not safe."

"I can't leave her, Gian. I can't."

"You won't, darling. I promise. No one can ever take her from you."

Those words seemed to strike something in her, for she stilled a bit, meeting his gaze. "You promise?"

"I promise. Just come with me. Please, my love. Come with me right now."

Still tightly clasped in his arms, she looked over her shoulder, past the doctor to her mother's still body lying in her bed. The queen's hands were folded across her chest, her eyes shut in what might have been peaceful slumber. But Gian knew that look. He had seen it before. Sleep that was deeper than dreaming. A stillness that was more silent than the night.

And for a breath, it was his own mother on that bed, cold and distant. For a moment, he was eleven years old, losing her all over again.

But he did not let himself weep. He did not let himself get lost in the grief that nipped at his heels. Instead, he tucked a strand of

Rachæl's hair behind her ears, pressed a gentle kiss to her brow, and led her out of the room. To his surprise, she did not protest, but let him guide her. She used him as a crutch as he led her from the room and away from her mother.

She walked thus all the way back to her chambers, dazed, silent.

Then again, so did he.

What had taken the queen's life? What had rendered her ill for so long—a silent, insidious threat that no one saw coming?

He could guess, of course. But he needed to talk to Rachæl before jumping to wild conclusions.

Gian locked her door behind him when they reached her quiet chamber. Bear scurried past them, sitting by the fire still dancing in the hearth as if he knew that's where they were headed. But Rachæl seemed to lose all strength, for she stopped, knees buckling. Gian caught her up in his arms, carrying her across the room to her settee.

"Please don't leave me. Don't let me go," he heard her plead, the strain in her voice breaking his heart.

"Never, my love," he said, wondering if she had picked up how many times he had called her his love tonight—the words spilling from him unguarded. He sat down on the settee, settling her into his lap like a babe. She curled into his arms and rested her head on his chest, breathing. Breathing. Breathing. It seemed all she could do.

So he held her and he stroked her hair and he kissed her brow again and again, muttering gentle words to console her, feeling her tears turn his shirt cold as she wept.

Bear kept his attention focused upon her, as if he understood. A poor motherless beast, just like him. Just like Gian. What a sad condition to have in common, Gian thought. After a moment, the pup made his way to the settee, standing on his hind legs and nudging the princess. She did not react though. Gian tried to shoo the beast away, but he was persistent.

When the princess did not pet his head or stroke his ears, the little bastard had the nerve to jump into her lap.

"Get down!" Gian grumbled.

But Rachæl stayed him with her hand. "No, it's all right." She let the damned thing curl into her lap, absently running her hands down his back while he licked her arm over and over again.

And thus the three of them stayed for quite a while.

"PRINCESS," Gian said, nudging Rachæl gently, though she did not stir. Still in her lap, the pup snoozed just as soundly.

"Love," he murmured again, running a finger down her cheek and neck. The motion stirred her, and she woke, blinking several times to adjust her eyes. "I think you'll be more comfortable in your bed, darling."

Rachæl looked around, squinting. "How long was I asleep?"

"Long enough that I can't feel my arms or legs," Gian said.

Rachæl moved to stand immediately. "I'm sorry," she said as Bear leapt from her lap to stretch and yawn on the rug.

"It was a joke," he said, hating that he had so abruptly stirred her from her slumber in his arms.

Rachæl sighed, stretching her back. The movement made her aware of her state of dress, which she appraised with disdain.

"I cannot get out of this damned dress by myself."

"I'll send for a servant," Gian offered.

The princess lifted a single eyebrow. "Are you telling me you don't know how to remove a woman's garments, Gian of Borras?"

He looked her over head to toe, collecting his words, his gods-damned thoughts which were taking far too many liberties at the moment. He cleared his throat before he finally managed to say, "On the contrary, I would say I'm rather skilled in the art. However, I've never removed a corset for any sort of noble purpose."

She turned, offering him the stays at the back of her dress. "I trust you."

"In retrospect, you will realize that was your first mistake," he said.

She huffed a sleepy laugh but remained with her back to him. Apparently, she really wanted him to help her out of her dress. And corset.

Shit.

Gian took a steadying breath and reminded himself that he was a godsdamned grown man and not some hormonal teenage boy with shit for brains and thread for self-control, thank you very much.

He had her dress off in no time.

"Well then, perhaps you should give up your mercenary duties and work as my lady's maid. You're much faster at undressing me than she is."

Gian swallowed about seventeen different responses to that little observation, each more depraved than the last, and instead focused on his work.

Next came her corset, which took a considerable bit more self-control to remove without resorting to his baser instincts, which were currently offering him far too many colorful, delightful, and frankly debauched ideas for what to do with her once the damned thing was removed.

It, too, was off with expert finesse.

She turned to face him in nothing but her chemise and smiled rather lazily. "See? You're the picture of gentlemanly propriety now, aren't you?"

He did not bother to point out how the fire shone through the gauzy fabric, highlighting her pert little waist and gloriously curved hips. Nor did he bother to point out that the tips of her breasts were currently beckoning him from beneath that pathetic excuse for linen. Instead, he offered her a smile that he was sure looked pained, or perhaps even pathetic, and said nothing.

Idiot.

She made her way to her bed, Bear following as if he had a damned right, and climbed in. The precocious wolf had grown enough that he could certainly climb in without her help, but she offered it to him anyway, which he seemed to accept with a smirk on his face just for Gian's benefit. And once she had sufficiently tucked him into a fluffy blanket at her feet, Gian turned. To go where, he could not say. Perhaps straight to Sheol where he belonged.

"You said you wouldn't leave me."

Gian stopped in his tracks and turned to face her. Gone was her amused but sleepy face. In its place was a somberness that ripped at him all over again. She pulled back the blanket and patted the mattress beside her.

He should have offered her the dozens of reasons why it was a terrible idea. He should have told her she'd be all right without him. He should have found a damned excuse for leaving.

But instead Gian of Borras removed his jacket, then his boots, followed by his trousers. And when he climbed into that massive bed beside her, she turned her back to him, simultaneously pulling his arm over her as if he were her personal blanket. She kissed his hand once and then sighed. Within moments, the princess was asleep again.

With the smell of her golden hair at his nose and the feel of her warm body enveloped in his, Gian slept like a babe.

Rachæl woke to the knowledge of two things: the smell of coffee and the cold despondence of being alone in a bed. She distinctly remembered falling asleep with Gian beside her, but now he was most certainly not. She rolled over, stretching her legs and toes, and scanned the room.

"Good morning, sunshine," came a familiar, irreverent voice.

Rachæl sat up, finger-combing her hair as she did. Gian was across the room, pouring a cup of coffee.

"How did you sleep?" he asked.

"I thought you stayed with me," she said in answer.

"I did," he said. He began making his way to her, two cups in tow. "Bear had some early morning needs."

"Ah." She sighed. A wave of sorrow washed over her, reminding her of the reason Gian was there at all. The reason he had stayed.

"You all right?" he asked gently, coming to her side. He took a seat beside her on her bed before handing her a cup of the steaming coffee.

She shrugged as she took her first sip.

"Good?" he asked, referring to her coffee. It was perfect—not too much cream and plenty of honey.

She nodded. "How do you know how I take it?"

"Darling, after five years of knowing you, I damn well better know how you like your coffee. Otherwise, what kind of warden would I be?"

She huffed a laugh and took another sip, the warmth welcome. Gian draped an arm around her, and she took the opportunity to rest her head on his shoulder.

"Feeling all right?" he asked.

"I feel numb, more than anything. As if it's not real. Like any moment I could walk down the halls and speak to her."

Gian nodded. "It will feel that way for a while, I reckon."

"Thank you, Gian."

"For what, darling?"

"For staying with me. For being there for me. I..." But she did not know how to finish that sentence, did not know how to put into words her gratefulness that he had been there. That he had held her. That he had reminded her again and again that he would always be there.

"I need you to do something for me," she said after a minute.

Gian seemed intrigued, cocking his head to one side in silent question.

"I need you to take me to Sachar."

Gian raised one eyebrow. "Do you know much about the town?"

"I know it is the hub of spice trade, but that is all."

Gian smirked, but offered no further explanation for his reaction. "Interested in the spice trade, Princess?"

"No. I need to know what was so damned important that my father couldn't be here for my mother's last breath. I want to see for myself what he is really up to."

Gian nodded. "It's scandalous, you know—for an unwed princess to travel without a chaperone, particularly with a known rake. And particularly to a town with the reputation of Sachar."

She tilted her head to meet his eyes. "I don't give a damn. I'm tired of playing Obedient Princess. If my father won't do what is necessary to protect this kingdom, then I will."

Gian raised both eyebrows, nodding in silence.

"Can you be ready to leave today?"

"I can be ready to leave within the hour."

It was a three-day ride to Sachar. The journey through the heart of the Majestic Mountains was uneventful, save for the beauty of the flora showing off in the sun. Bear acquiesced to the carriage with little fuss, and they only had to stop a few times to let him run off some energy. But everywhere they had stopped for the night, the wolf at their side had ensured that people gave Rachæl and Gian a wide berth.

Rachæl hadn't minded. She did not want to be recognized on this trip, which was why she had opted for her simplest dresses, no jewels or curls, no fuss. Nothing that would indicate who she was or what she was up to. So far, three days in, her plan had been successful.

"Where should we stay?" she asked Gian when they were getting close to the village.

"Sachar is not exactly a tourist attraction, love. It's a bit more rough than that."

"Rough?"

Gian seemed hesitant to answer, which let Rachæl know in no uncertain terms that *a bit more rough* was a gross understatement. "Let's just say, since this is a trade route, there are few upstanding people in the town, and a whole lot more vagrants, charlatans, and...ladies of the night. Then again, if you like gambling, illegal substances, and illicit sex, this is the place for you."

Rachæl rolled her eyes. "Sounds like your kind of town."

Gian did not offer some indecent quip at her remark. In fact, he chose to look out the window of the carriage, resting his chin on his fist as he said, "That is certainly my reputation, isn't it?"

She could not be sure, but she was fairly certain she had offended him by pointing out the obvious. She drew in a breath to say something, though she was not sure what, but Gian cut her off.

"Lucky us. Looks as if the carnival is in town."

Rachæl looked out her window to see a long train, at least fifty cars long, coming down from the mountains on the towering tracks in the distance, slowing as it rolled into the valley before them. Some of the cars were fixed with bars from top to bottom—

traveling cages filled with tigers and lions and strange creatures with impossibly long necks. Other cars were solid, offering no view of what lay inside. But the car at the front of the train looked as luxurious as a hotel, gilded with bright gold on the railings and vivid, crimson paint on the trim.

"What's that one?" she asked, pointing to the front car.

"The ringmaster's car," said Gian, but there was no delight in his eyes at the sight of the colorful train.

That's when she remembered the story he had once shared with her—of the carnival he had stumbled upon in the southern continent. "Is that...a Medinian train?"

Gian nodded. "Looks like the wonders of the carnival have made their way to our continent."

Something dark and foreboding slithered down Rachæl's spine as she watched the train come to a stop and the people on board trickle off. Such bright colors they were dressed in—crimson and ochre and cobalt. Such delight and wonder disguising something much darker.

And then she saw it, a great, woolly beast being led—dragged, really—from the largest, tallest car. His tusks were even bigger than the one Gian kept in his chambers, his head as tall as an ancient oak, his body as massive as an airship.

A mammoth.

Gian looked away—looked at anything but the sight before them.

"Are we unsafe?" she asked. At the tone of her question, Bear lifted his head from where he had been resting it on his paws. He tilted his head to one side, watching her.

"Do you think I would ever let anything happen to you?"

Bear seemed to be asking the very same question by the way he squared his shoulders, readying himself for anything.

She breathed a small laugh. "Well, I am certainly not without protection on this trip."

Gian nodded, raising a single eyebrow.

When the carriage at last came to a stop, Gian helped her step down. Her feet were not greeted with familiar cobblestone, but with mud, thick and slick, stretching out before them in a sea of brown.

"We can start with the north end of the river," Gian suggested. "It is used for trade all the way to Borras, but the majority of the merchants end up here, near Sachar."

They walked arm in arm, following the bank of the river as it wound through the valley. Rachæl let him lead as he walked purposefully through the village. He was right—nothing here looked settled or ancient. Everything in this town was new, the muddy streets peppered with crude wooden buildings and canvas tents.

"Why doesn't anyone settle here? Build something worth living in?" she asked. It seemed every permanent structure in the valley was cheap, shoddy, and a drab shade of brown.

"Because this land is barren. It has been for centuries. Terrible for farming. No minerals or riches to speak of. The river is its only saving grace. So it has become a hub of, shall we say, more *clandestine* commerce."

"Clandestine?"

"Spices are actually the ruse here. There is a whole language built around the sort of *spice* one might be in need of. For example, were I to ask the right person here for some cardamom, I would soon find myself with a treasure trove of opiates from which to choose. Or if I asked the right person for some rosemary, I could glut myself on exotic, imported tea. For illegal libation, there is a whole trove of spices one might ask for. One can purchase all manner of scandalous entertainment in this town. Hence its popularity."

Popularity, indeed. Why, the entire village was bustling with people—men mostly, Rachæl noted. Poorly dressed and equally filthy, they walked in and out of buildings and tents, on and off the steamboats and rowboats along the river. There were women, too, though they were decidedly less drab. Adorned in loud colors and outrageous amounts of ruffles, they strolled casually along the muddy streets, taking care to nod and wink at every passerby.

Ladies of the night, indeed.

Despite their brightly-colored dresses and scandalously low necklines, Rachæl did not fail to note that even the women had mud on their hems and shoes.

"Is everything here so muddy?" she asked.

Gian chuckled. "Only from the outside, darling. The true entertainment of this village lies within its walls."

In the distance, an enormous boat caught Rachæl's eye—some three stories tall, it towered above the rest in the harbor, steam puffing from two black stacks, a massive red paddle turning at its back, churning the water as it moved slowly along the banks of the Sachar River.

"What is that?" she asked, pointing.

"The wealthy who visit here in search of their favorite *spices* like to travel by paddleboat along the river."

"Shouldn't they be a bit more discreet?"

Gian chuckled. "If you ask the wrong person for the wrong spice, you'll wind up at the bottom of that river with a boulder tied about your waist. There is no need to be discreet in a place like this, because the only way you survive is if you know how to play the game."

Dread washed over her for the second time today. "Do you... know how to play the game?"

He turned his head, looking her in the eyes. "Darling, I practically invented it."

"What is my father doing here?"

"That is the question I've been trying to work out since you told me he had come here with the empress."

"Any theories?"

He nodded.

"Any of them have anything to do with noble purposes?"

"Not a single one."

"That's what I'm afraid of, too."

THEY SPENT the entire day in search of her father, but all they found was a trove of charlatans eager to peddle their spices. Rachæl had grown utterly exhausted by the sheer volume of hucksters and swindlers after the first hour. Not to mention they had *both* been propositioned by lightskirts. Gian had run off no less than a dozen within an hour of arriving.

And not a sign, not a single hint of her father. Or the empress.

"I'm beginning to wonder if my father was ever here," Rachæl admitted.

"I have a theory, but I don't think you're going to like it," Gian said.

Rachæl stopped walking, Bear stopping with her. Gian noticed a pace later and faced her.

"What?" she asked flatly.

Gian raised a single brow. "Some of the...*ladies* here deal in, shall we say, more dangerous spices."

"Ladies," she echoed, understanding his meaning. "I suppose you're well acquainted with them, then?"

"It...was a long time ago, darling." He seemed...hesitant. Maybe even bothered. As if he did not want to admit that he had probably once frequented this Sheol-hole of a place. Had once enjoyed its delights. And ladies.

Rachæl crossed her arms. "What sort of dangerous spices?"

"The expensive kind."

"That's not an answer."

He stepped closer to her, leaning in as he said, “I dare not say it out loud, darling. But I think I know where we should look.”

Rachæl released a breath. “I have a feeling I’m going to regret this.”

Gian chuckled, grabbing her hand and pulling her with him. “You say that a lot with me.”

CHAPTER TWENTY-SIX

"Gian of Borras! Do my eyes deceive me?"

Shit.

"Marjorie," he said, feigning his best smile. The prostitute poured herself onto him like hot oil, instantaneously everywhere at once. Those generous breasts of hers were a particular kind of distraction, spilling from her gown and beckoning him, like the rest of her, to a night of sin and vice. A flash of self-consciousness washed over him, and he practically manhandled her to get her off of him.

She acquiesced, stepping back. Barely. She took his cheek in her hand. "How long has it been, pumpkin? Seven? Eight years?"

"Something like that," Gian answered.

"The girls and I have missed you," she said, moving that hand from his cheek down his neck to his chest, hungry lust in her bedroom eyes. She let herself linger there, a single finger over his heart, which Gian promptly removed.

"Come inside, love. Let's pick up where we left off all those years ago."

She grabbed the ruffles of his shirt as if to pull him inside, but Gian stopped her, refusing to move. "We need your help."

Marjorie turned to face him again, realizing for the first time that he was not alone. She turned her most wicked grin to Rachæl. "Indeed, you do," she said. "You know how to pick them, don't you, Gian darling?"

"What is that supposed to mean?" Rachel's voice was cold.

Shit. Shit. *Shit.*

Why in all the realms of Sheol had he decided it was a good idea to bring the princess of Har-Navah into a brothel in the middle of the most notoriously sleazy village in the kingdom? He would never forgive himself.

Because she wanted to know what her father was up to. So did he, honestly. And this was the most likely way to find out. Never mind it was indecent. And utterly scandalous. And she was too damned good for any of this.

The prostitute leveled a knowing smirk at Rachæl. "He's always had a penchant for the innocent. Or innocent-*looking,* I should amend." She faced Gian before she continued. "Looks like she's never known a man's touch at all, this one. And so clean! How'd you find her?"

"I *look* like a virgin?" Rachæl asked distastefully.

Gian's heart was now pounding so mercilessly he was certain they could both see it beneath his shirt.

"This was not a good idea," he said, wanting to leave immediately.

"What is that thing?" Marjorie asked, pointing to Bear, sitting dutifully beside Rachæl.

"My wolf," the princess said.

"He cannot come in here."

"He goes where I go," Rachæl said without a hint of fear or hesitation in her voice. Gods help him, what that confidence did to him.

"I won't have a wolf in my brothel," Marjorie said again.

"He goes where I go," Rachæl repeated, this time more firmly.

The prostitute bristled, but said nothing, her whole demeanor melting back into her practiced seduction. She faced Gian again. "Come now, darling. Let's have some fun, shall we?"

"We're not here for fun," Rachæl said flatly.

"Then why are you here?" Marjorie asked.

"We are in search of cloves," Gian said, cutting Rachæl off from any chance of saying the wrong thing.

Marjorie froze, slowly sliding her eyes to Gian. "I never thought you'd be stupid enough to say that word aloud here."

"Believe me, I would not have come here if it were not important."

The prostitute looked him and Rachæl over once, skeptical of the entire ordeal.

"It's going to cost you."

Rachæl did not hesitate to pull a rather heavy purse from the folds of her plain yet somehow still utterly irresistible gown. She handed it to the prostitute without hesitation. "I'm sure this will suffice."

Marjorie raised a single eyebrow. "I don't know what kind of shit you're in, Gian, but if it's the kind where you let your woman carry the purse, I have a feeling I don't want to know."

"I don't *let* her do anything," he pointed out, though that tidbit was useless to Marjorie. As was the fact that Rachæl was anything but *his woman*.

She appraised Rachæl once again, and Gian used every bit of self control he had not to tear the woman to shreds for the way she looked at the princess. "If you're coming in here," said the whore with a healthy measure of disdain, "you better figure out how to look the part or you'll be eaten alive."

They should not have come here. And he certainly should not have brought Rachæl to such a place.

Marjorie turned, walking inside without waiting for them. But Gian turned to face the princess.

"You don't have to do this. I—" He was abruptly cut off by her lips, warm and eager on his. And her body—gods above, her body was supple and willing against him. She kissed him with such expertise that he forgot all about prostitutes and brothels and *cloves*... He could only taste her. Only draw her closer, wrapping himself around her and consuming her like a starving man at a feast. And gods damn him, she let him.

She broke her savage, gloriously consuming kiss and met his gaze with bedroom eyes as she said, "Just playing the part. I'd hate to be eaten alive, after all."

Then she turned and walked past, leaving him gaping and speechless. Once she was a pace or two ahead, she looked over her shoulder, extending her hand to take his. He took it without hesitation, trying and failing to find words.

"Stay close to me," she said—a request for his protection in this place she dared to brave.

"That won't be a problem."

Looking over his shoulder once, and willing himself to regain his godsdamned composure, he nodded for the wolf who dutifully followed closely behind.

Rachæl had utterly transformed herself into something... gods, what would he call it? Wanton?

No.

Brazen?

Perhaps.

Delightful?

Definitely.

She threaded her way through the gaudy halls of the brothel, pushing past grasping hands and giggles, past writhing bodies and incessant offers of indecencies as if she owned the damned place. She did not hold his hand in fear, but with a confidence and poise that left him speechless for the second time today. Her shoulders back, her chin high, she was clearly a woman on a mission to enjoy every form of entertainment this place offered. Never mind the woman had never once stepped foot in such a place. Today, Rachæl was a citizen of Sachar, not the crown princess in the midst of a harem of whores.

If he didn't deserve to burn for eternity in the fires of Sheol before, he certainly did now.

They turned a corner, following Marjorie with lazy grins, exchanging lustful glances now and then. Playing the part, indeed. Gian let go of her hand, opting to slip an arm around her waist. She let him do that, too. With any other woman he might have reveled in the fact that that she leaned into his arm, except that he reminded himself she was playacting, per Marjorie's suggestion. Regardless, when they slowed their pace to allow for others to pass in this crowded space, he used the opportunity to pull the princess close enough to press a kiss to her neck. If she could play the part, so could he.

She, however, used his nearness to whisper a question. "Where is she taking us?"

"The catacombs, if I had to guess," he offered.

She leaned her head closer, her face a picture of lustful headiness, and asked, "What are the catacombs?"

He ran a knuckle down her arm with his spare hand and pressed another kiss to the shell of her ear because he was a selfish ass who clearly had no self control. She did not tense, did not push him away, but melted into his poorly feigned affection with an eagerness that would have had him stripping any other woman naked within a matter of seconds. But he remembered who he was—and who he was not—gathered his thoughts, and answered in low tones.

"Thousands of years ago, even before Haravelle existed, there was an ancient city here. No one knows who built it or why. But it was buried long ago and Sachar was built atop it—the perfect way to disguise the real goings-on in this place. There is an entire network of ancient roads beneath us. They've come to be known as the catacombs because many go there and never return. But if your father is hiding something, he's most likely hiding it there."

He spotted goosebumps along the skin of her neck and shoulder, and wondered if his brazen lust or his story had put it there. When he realized he had been fixated on her neck for far too long, he drew a breath to clear his head and looked at her eyes again. The princess seemed to be considering all he had told her. He wondered how she would react if she knew just exactly how distracted he was by the myriad of creative ideas he currently entertained where she was concerned. But he kept her close to him, regardless. And she let him.

They walked through the winding maze of the brothel until at last they reached a dark door far, far away from the frenzy behind them.

"Keep your mouth shut," was Marjorie's only advice before she pushed the door open and ushered them into the darkness beyond.

THE STEPS DOWN into the catacombs seemed endless. The only consolation was the fact that Rachæl held onto his hand so tightly he felt their skin might fuse together permanently. They felt their way down and down and down, the few gaslamps along the way providing paltry light on the steps. The air was musty, reeking of stale mildew and the gods knew what else. Gian just wanted to be done with this endeavor, which he was currently regretting. If the king ever found out what Gian had subjected his daughter to...

Marjorie offered no conversation whatsoever, but moved down the steps like a wraith in the night. Gone was the practiced, flirtatious prostitute. In her wake was a businesswoman, well versed in clandestine operations of the highly illegal sort.

After what seemed like an hour, they finally reached the bottom of the steps, which opened into a long, dark hallway of stone, riddled with turns and forks and little else. The gas lamps that dotted the walls here and there offered weak orbs of golden light that did not help to see far.

On instinct, Gian had turned around several times to make sure Bear was behind them. The wolf hadn't faltered or hesitated once, as if he, too, was eager to keep the princess safe. In fact, there were several times that Gian could have sworn the wolf was cursing him for putting her in such a dangerous situation. He held her hand a little more tightly for good measure.

"Here," Marjorie said, her first words since descending into this gloomy darkness. "This way."

Rachæl did not hesitate to follow, and not for the first time today, Gian thought she'd make an excellent pirate, for there was absolutely no fear in her golden eyes. Only utter determination.

Gods, she was gorgeous.

After several turns down the labyrinth of dark halls, Marjorie at last stopped at what seemed like a dead end and faced them. Behind her, he saw a pile of too many crates to count, stacked to the ceiling, covered crudely by filthy canvases. "Tell me why you're looking for cloves, Gian of Borras. And don't lie to me."

Gian knew he needed a good answer to her question, and took a moment to form his thoughts. But before he could speak, Rachæl answered.

"We are not here for your advice. Show me the cloves," she said.

Marjorie lifted a single eyebrow. "I don't know who you think you are—"

Gian stepped forward, but not before Bear came between them, showing his teeth with a snarl. Marjorie seemed to hesitate. "I told you to leave that wolf out of my brothel."

"If you don't want his ire, then I suggest you do as I ask," Rachæl said confidently. "Show me what's beneath that canvas."

Marjorie hesitated for a second before releasing a sigh and turning. She lifted one corner of the canvas, exposing a dusty wooden crate.

"Open it," the princess demanded.

Marjorie could have no idea who was giving her commands, but she obeyed as if she did.

Inside the crate, surrounded by mildewed hay, sat several objects fashioned of dark metal with long, slender chambers adorned with gleaming golden crests.

"Muskets," he muttered under his breath.

"Muskets?" Rachæl asked, facing him.

Gian nodded.

"Where did these come from?" Rachæl asked Marjorie.

The prostitute seemed to hesitate. Bear apparently didn't like that, for he growled once and low, which seemed to give the woman motivation to speak. "A young man delivered them not two days ago."

"Describe him," Gian insisted.

Marjorie hesitated. "Brown hair. Average height. Skinny."

Rachæl furrowed her brows, looking at Gian and shaking her head. He didn't know who she could be describing either. It could be anyone. The young man seemed average.

Too average.

"Anything else?" Gian pushed. "Anything distinguishing about him?"

Marjorie crossed her arms. "Look, I didn't get a good look at him, all right? He was filthy anyway, the wretch. Covered in moths."

"Moths?" Rachæl asked, going very still.

So did Gian. He could not discuss it here, though. Not with Marjorie present. Rachæl seemed to understand what he was thinking, too, for she changed the subject abruptly.

"How do they work?" she asked, bringing her attention back to the crates of muskets.

"They're not regular weapons," he answered. "They're magicked. More dangerous than any bow or sword, these are guaranteed to kill with deadly precision."

"What sort of magic?" the princess asked. She let go of his hand, stepping towards the crates. Marjorie sucked in a breath to protest, but swallowed whatever she was about to say when Bear growled again, lowering on his haunches and baring his teeth.

While Rachæl carefully inspected the contents of the open crate, Gian explained them to her.

"Like any musket, there is a small projectile in the chamber, propelled by a tiny explosion. It erupts from the end of the musket to meet its mark. But these are not just regular muskets. They are magicked to minute perfection. It is rumored that the king has been quietly developing this sort of magic for years. Though I'm sure he's had help perfecting it in recent months." She met his eyes with the emphasis of those last two words, and he knew she understood his meaning. "With this sort of capability, even the most untrained soldier will not miss."

"The king could raise an army the likes of which the world has never seen, no training necessary, with just a handful of these," Marjorie added.

"Shit," Gian muttered under his breath. "Shit."

Rachæl met his gaze again. Even dimmed by the gaslamp light, he could see the worry there.

"What is he doing, Gian?"

He reached for her hand again, this time taking it not to play any part, but to let her know that he wouldn't let her face a single moment of this without him. She seemed to understand, squeezing softly.

"Thank you for your help, Marjorie," he said, giving Rachæl a look that let her know they could not speak a word more of this conversation in front of the prostitute.

She understood, turning to Marjorie. "Yes, thank you."

"That's it?" Marjorie asked. "That's all you wanted?"

"Down here, yes," the princess said. "Now we're going to need a place to sleep."

"I don't offer rooms for charity," said the prostitute.

Gian was about to retort when Rachæl said, "The amount of coin in that purse you're holding would buy us enough room and board for a month."

Marjorie merely scowled and turned back towards the stairs.

"WHAT IS my father doing with magicked muskets?" the princess asked, turning to face Gian. She'd been quiet since they left the underground area, aside from when no less than three lightskirts offered to join them tonight. She had donned that irreverent smirk that had gotten her through the brothel untouched, slipped a hand over Gian's chest, and informed the women that he was all hers tonight—and she was uninterested in sharing.

Gian had nearly passed out at that little declaration.

But faced with her worried, determined gaze now, he gave himself a shake, cleared his ridiculous thoughts, and answered her question.

"I have theories. None of them are good."

"Pray tell," Rachæl said, doffing her shawl and sitting down in the only chair in the ornately furnished yet crude room.

Gian took a seat on the bed just to steady himself, clear his head. “First of all, that obviously wasn’t a boy that delivered the weapons.”

“Do you think it was her?”

Gian nodded grimly. “If the empress can appear in any form she wants, I’d say it’s a rather convenient skill when you’re smuggling illegal weapons into the kingdom you want to overthrow.”

“You said my father has been developing that sort of magic for years,” Rachæl pointed out.

“Yes,” he said. “To no avail. Until now.”

“That was the Medinian wyvern on the crest, wasn’t it?”

Gian nodded again.

“Do you think my father understands what he’s getting into? Do you think he’s helping her?” Rachæl asked, clearly horrified.

“That’s what I’m not sure of: how much he understands what’s going on. Is he under some sort of curse? Or is he simply blinded by lust?”

Rachæl scoffed. “No man can be that blinded by a woman.”

“You might be surprised,” Gian muttered under his breath.

“What?” the princess asked.

“Nothing,” he said quickly. “The point is, whatever is going on, this is not good.”

Rachæl sighed, rubbing between her eyebrows with a thumb and forefinger. “And I’m much too hungry and exhausted to think about it right now.”

“Then that settles it,” Gian said, standing. “I shall find us something decent to eat.”

“And leave me here alone?”

Gian eyed the wolf resting contentedly at her feet, licking his paws. “I think you’re fairly well guarded, darling.”

But Rachæl did not look at the wolf, instead meeting Gian’s gaze with something unsaid in hers.

"Gian," she finally muttered. "About earlier. I was...out of line. I'm sorry."

For kissing him. For *playing the part,* as she had put it. She regretted it.

Something in his chest curled up tightly and sank low. He swallowed hard and turned towards the door, ignoring the stupid, useless disappointment threatening to show on his face. "Don't worry about it, love."

The brothel boasted a small yet bustling tavern of sorts at the back of the building. Men of all ages and states of cleanliness filled the room, women perched on their laps, tangled in their arms, or ushering them to more private nooks.

Gods.

Gian hadn't visited such a place in so long that he had forgotten the levels of desperation to which he had stooped to entertain himself. Those days seemed a lifetime ago now. And looking around, he honestly wondered what he had ever seen in such a life.

Nonetheless, he sat down at the edge of the bar and worked to gain the attention of the much-too-busy barkeep. When he finally did, the man huffed, throwing a towel over his shoulder. "What?"

"I need dinner. Enough for two," Gian said.

The barkeep didn't even bother to acknowledge the request, turning on his heel and sauntering off to a room behind him. Gian could only hope he was actually procuring something edible. The gods knew what they served in a town like this.

"Dinner for two?"

Gian turned to face the slightly familiar voice from which the question had come. He repressed a start of surprise when he saw who sat beside him.

"Lord Desperation, is it?" he asked, knowing damn well the man's name. Lord Duriel of Nehar. The insolent lord with an ostentatious mustache who had somehow gotten it into his head that he would soon be betrothed to Rachæl.

"Funny," said Lord Duriel. "Though from the looks of it, I am not the desperate one here."

"What is that supposed to mean?"

Lord Duriel grinned, showing off his crooked teeth and the lingering vestiges of whatever he had eaten for dinner in his mustache. Gods. The thought of Rachæl having to be subjected to such a man...

"What exactly are you doing in this part of the world, Lord Borras?"

Lord Borras. Only people who didn't know what to call him or were terrified to call him the wrong thing used such an asinine honorific.

"Oh, you know, a little vacation of sorts."

To his surprise, the barkeep appeared again, slopping two bowls of some sort of questionable liquid before him. Gian couldn't help but to turn up his nose at the sight.

"A vacation for two, it would seem," said Lord Duriel, eyeing the gray soup.

Gian gave the man his most irreverent smirk. "I have a tendency to wear out the finer sex. Got to keep up her strength, you know."

Lord Duriel squared his shoulders and lifted his chin. "I know what you are up to. And I know who you are with tonight."

"Don't worry, son," Gian said, patting the man's shoulder. "She's all yours when I'm done."

But the lord clearly wasn't referring to a favorite prostitute, for he leaned in close and said, "I will know if she is still a virgin on our wedding night, Lord Borras. And if she is not, I will see to it that she is hanged. Not before I am declared regent, of course."

The princess. Duriel knew she was here. How, Gian did not know. Then again, he hadn't exactly been careful today, parading her around this place like no one would notice that the king's mercenary was in the kingdom's most notorious Sheol-hole with no less than the crown princess of Har-Navah.

Shit.

"You are mistaken," Gian said stupidly. He needed to get back to their room. He needed to get her out of here. Tonight.

"For her sake, you better hope I am."

THE WOLF WAS RESTLESS. He could not seem to sit still in the room Marjorie had provided for them in the brothel. Never mind that the amount of money Rachæl had given the woman was enough to afford them the finest accommodations in the kingdom. Tonight they would settle for a lumpy mattress—only one, of course—a single chair, tattered carpets, and ungodly amounts of silk damask, draped obnoxiously over every surface of the otherwise ramshackle room.

Rachæl sighed, bending to scratch the wolf's head when he shifted again. "Me too, Bear. Me too."

Bear sat up, his attention suddenly on the door.

"I'm sure it's just Gian with dinner, darling. No need for such defense," she chuckled.

The person on the other side of the door knocked once before entering without invitation. "Hello, poppet," she said.

It wasn't Gian but a rather buxom young woman with far too much décolletage exposed for any decent person. She strolled into the room as if she owned the damned place, draping herself across the bed like a piece of fine silk.

"You've been tempting us all afternoon," the prostitute said. "You and your delicious companion. And yet I was told you demanded a private room." She ran delicate fingers along the tops of her breasts, turning her sumptuous mouth into a come-hither smile. "No need to be so selfish, poppet. There's plenty of you both to share."

"I—" Rachæl started, sure she was gaping at the prostitute like an idiot. "You need to leave."

The woman—girl, really—chuckled. "He told me you'd say that. He also told me not to listen."

"He?" Rachæl asked. "He sent you here?"

The whore smiled, beginning a slow, decadent dance of her fingers along the stays at the front of her revealing bodice. One tug, and even more of her skin was on display. "He asked me to get the fun started. He'll be along in a bit."

"I don't believe you," Rachæl said, her breath coming up short. Gian had sent her here? To have his way? With both of them?

A small part of her hated that she had been naïve enough to think that his flirtation, his attentions today had been sincere. A much larger, much more realistic part of her realized that she had been a fool to think that women were anything other than a game to Gian of Borras.

And tonight, he intended to play that game. With both a whore and the princess of Har-Navah.

Bile burned in the back of her throat.

"Leave," Rachæl commanded, standing.

The girl did no such thing, still toying with the stays of her gown. She had exposed enough skin now that she was dangerously close to baring herself. Rachæl could not stomach it.

"Get out!" she commanded.

The whore only laughed. "I wasn't going to tell you this, but he's already paid, poppet. Might as well have some fun."

Rachæl could have spit nails. "I said GET OUT."

At that moment, Gian came through the door, two bowls of something steaming in his hands. He froze at the sight of the near-naked woman on the bed, and immediately turned his attention to Rachæl.

"What is this?" he asked.

"You tell me," Rachæl growled.

Gian set the bowls aside on a nearby dresser.

"I knew you had no standards," she hissed at him. "But I never thought you'd stoop so low as to bring me into your debauchery."

"Rachæl—"

"So tense." The young woman laughed, moving to the edge of the bed. She stood and sauntered to Rachæl, running her hands up the princess's waist. Rachæl froze, shocked by the sensuality, the expertise of her touch.

"Get away from her," Gian growled under his breath.

"You need this more than I thought, poppet." The whore breathed a lusty laugh, ignoring Gian as she reached for the stays of Rachæl's gown. The princess did not know what to do—too stunned by the invasion of this woman, with her practiced fingers and uninhibited lust.

"Get your hands off of her." Gian's face was the picture of rage as he marched across the room towards them.

The whore froze, turning to face Gian. "Don't you want to play, love?"

"Get out of this room. Now." His voice was laced with frozen fury. Rachæl hated him for it—for pretending like he would protect her from a whore upon the realization that she did not want to play his game. She hated him for his lies. His two-facedness. For knowing the women in this place. For knowing that he'd likely been with each one of them a dozen times. Tears, unwelcome and hot, welled in her eyes and she ground her teeth to keep from letting them fall.

"Hmph." The whore breathed through her nose, one hand perched on her hip as he faced Gian. "I knew you were not all they claimed. I could see it the moment you walked into this place."

She sauntered the few steps to where Gian stood. "You're not who you pretend to be," she said, nearly nose to nose with him.

Gian stood as still as a statue, barely breathing, that rage in his eyes shifting to something too stunned to protest.

But the whore was not done.

"You're a liar, Gian of Borras. And a shit one at that. And your woman over there—" She nodded to Rachæl without taking her eyes from Gian. "She knows it, too. She's just too afraid to admit it."

Not bothering to refasten her dress where she had all but exposed herself, the prostitute huffed a dismissive laugh before leaving the room without another word.

Gian turned his attention to Rachæl. "Are you all right?"

"Stay away from me," she spat. She willed herself to breath. To collect herself. Those tears in her eyes pooled but did not fall.

"Rachæl, I didn't—"

"Don't you dare try to explain yourself, Gian. Don't you dare offer excuses." She was not sure she could take them. Not now. Not after today, the way he had held her, flirted with her, the way he had kissed her back. She could not take his pathetic excuses or flimsy explanations.

"Love, I swear—"

"Don't call me *love,* and don't say another damned word. Get out of my sight, Gian."

"Please," he pleaded, taking a single step towards her.

But she held up a hand, hating how it trembled, and stopped him. "Get out. Now."

Without saying another word, without so much as breathing, Gian obeyed.

GIAN WOKE to the sickening feeling of falling, followed by a hard *thud*. It took him three breaths to feel the pounding in the back of his head.

"What in Sheol are you doing down there?" The princess stood over him like a monument, her arms crossed and her brows knitted.

Gian rubbed the back of his head as he moved to sit up, righting himself from where he had fallen backward onto the floor after she had opened her door. He remembered leaning against the jamb to try to sleep, but apparently somewhere in the night, he had unfortunately shifted to lean against the door.

"I was trying to sleep," he said as he stood.

Rachæl raised a single eyebrow. "On the floor? At my door? Like a dog?"

He glanced down at Bear, who stood at her legs, wagging his tail and looking at Gian with his wolfish grin. Not an ounce of remorse, the bastard.

"Yes," Gian said.

"Why?"

"Because," he answered, knowing it would not satisfy her.

"Because *why*, Gian. And *don't* answer my question with a question."

Gian rolled his neck, stiff from his poor choice of sleeping arrangements. Then again, *choice* was not exactly the right word. It was here on the floor or in the bed of no less than a dozen whores who had offered throughout the night. A fact he was definitely not going to mention to Rachæl.

"Because I promised your father I would protect you, that's why," he said, exasperated.

She moved to march past him. "I no longer require your services."

"Where are you going?" he asked, clambering to his feet and stopping her when he grabbed her arm.

She promptly snatched it away and kept walking. "Home."

"Wonderful," he said. "I'll send for the carriage."

"You won't be needing it," Rachæl said as she marched through the quiet hall of the brothel. She ignored the bodies draped over chaises and beds, ignored the sleeping prostitutes and the few patrons who remained, stepped over anyone in her way and made her way to the front door. Gian and the wolf followed closely behind.

"Why exactly won't I be needing the carriage?" Gian asked.

Rachæl pushed open the door, the morning light assaulting them both. He squinted against it, but she was undeterred.

"You'll need to find other transportation."

"So you're not even going to let me explain," he said.

"I have nothing to say to you."

"Well, I have a lot to say to you," Gian said, walking briskly to keep up with her relentless pace.

"I'm going home. Alone," the princess announced.

"Rachæl."

She did not look at Gian, keeping her back to him as she spoke. She only paused for the briefest moment to glance over her shoulder, patting her leg once for Bear to follow. The traitorous wolf did so without a moment's hesitation.

Gian watched as she and the wolf climbed into the cab of the carriage. She did not look out the window as the driver cracked the reins. She kept her chin high, her shoulders back, looking straight forward as she rolled away.

CHAPTER TWENTY-SEVEN

"You look absolutely beautiful."

Miri smiled to herself, looking down at her dress. She *felt* beautiful in the layers of silk and decadent lace. The gown had been handmade for her by Helena as a gift for this night, perfectly tailored to flatter her swollen belly and somehow still feel elegant.

"Do you like it?" she asked her husband.

Ezra's smile was bewitching as he pulled her hand to his mouth and pressed a lingering kiss to the top of her glove. "Every time I think you couldn't be more beautiful, you go and prove me wrong."

He gave up on propriety and pulled her into his arms at the foot of the steps in the foyer, kissing her soundly as he ran his hands along her back. Her belly put a barrier between them, preventing him from holding her against the full length of his body, but his kiss was no less consuming. She did not point out to him that the babe in her womb seemed to protest his closeness, kicking rather adamantly against him. But he must have noticed anyway, for he soon pulled away, his eyes lit with unfettered delight and put both of his hands on her stomach.

"Busy little one," he mused with a laugh, eyes alight.

Joy. It was joy in his eyes at the thought of this child she carried.

Joy for the family they would soon start.

A joy she could not replicate, no matter how hard she tried, tainted by the truth that she could not bear to reveal. What would he do if he knew?

He would soon know, wouldn't he? With every passing week, her time grew closer. With every passing hour, she worried more what he would do if it were obvious the child wasn't his. What if the child's hair was a muted, drab brown like Phinehas's? Would he notice? What if it bore Phinehas's lanky arms and overly-long fingers? What if the child did not bear the telltale Kelach family traits—raven black hair, pert nose, and proud shoulders?

What would Ezra do if he had to present a lie to the world?

A knock sounded at the front door, and as if he had been anticipating it, Thaddeus appeared to open it. John Junior bounded inside ahead of his parents, Esther holding a sleeping baby Leah in her arms.

The lad's hair was as black as his mother's. As black as Ezra's. In fact, the boy could have passed for Ezra's son had no one known who his father was. And when he jumped into Ezra's arms, when Ezra lifted him from the ground and laughed with delight as he hugged his nephew close, Miri could not help but feel as if Esther's children had been born for the sole purpose of mocking her.

"Your gown is beautiful," Esther complimented Miri. "How do you feel?"

It was a question only a woman could ask with true understanding. And Miri knew the question was directed at her pregnancy and cumbersome belly, but she could not help but wonder if Esther knew more than she was letting on. Could she see the agony of the weight of her secret in Miri's eyes? Was she so bad at hiding it?

"Tired," Miri said, forcing her best smile. "But otherwise I'm fine."

Esther huffed a laugh. "You're being generous. By this point in both of my pregnancies, I was miserable most of the time."

Miri privately agreed. Her belly had grown terribly heavy, making walking, standing, sitting, laying down, even sleeping increasingly difficult. But it felt selfish to mention it, so she had kept that to herself. Even when they were alone and Ezra could so plainly read her as he always did, she would lie and tell him she was fine. That she needed nothing. That the pregnancy was not taxing.

Another knock sounded at the door, which Thaddeus promptly opened again. But instead of family on the other side, three of the most beautiful people Miri had ever seen stood there with grins on their mouths.

"Ezra, darling!" the woman in the front exclaimed. She was the most stunning of the three—dark, thick curls spilling down her generous bosom and slender waist. She looked like a painting —a picture of perfection.

"Mirabella," said Ezra with a smile. He reached for her hand, pulling it to his mouth for a kiss.

"Now, now, that's all you have for me after all this time?" Mirabella scolded. Without further explanation, she launched herself into his arms, wrapping herself around him and hugging him rather tightly. Ezra returned the gesture in kind.

"I've missed you, darling," she said.

"Are you going to let the rest of us in, or will this be a reunion for only the two of you?" This question came from one of the two men standing behind her. Mirabella scoffed but acquiesced, moving to allow them to come inside.

Like Mirabella, the men were just as polished—almost absurdly so. Not a single hair out of place. Not a single scuff on their boots. They wore top hats and tails with lush, silk cravats, one of raspberry damask and the other of brightly-colored calico florals. And like Mirabella, their clothes were of fine make, even if a bit exaggerated in style.

"Benjamin, Francis," Ezra said, reaching to shake their hands. "Thank you so much for coming. We are very much looking forward to this."

The two men removed their top hats, dipping into exaggerated bows. "At your service, Your Grace."

"Allow me to introduce my wife," said Ezra turning to Miri. He reached for her hand, which she took as he said, "Ben, Francis, Mirabella, this is my wife, Lady Miriam Kelach, Grand Duchess of Kinnereth."

The two men nodded their heads. "A pleasure, my lady."

Mirabella, however, didn't look at Miri, her stunning blue eyes remaining on Ezra. Miri wondered if she had ever seen anyone with eyes that color—impossibly beautiful, like a frozen lake glittering in the afternoon sun.

"So the rumors are true," she said. "You've broken every heart in the kingdom yet again?"

Ezra chuckled dismissively. "I'm sure you'll find a way to survive, Mirabella."

"I doubt that. You gave us all a glimmer of hope when you ended your betrothal to the princess last year. Only to destroy it all over again by marrying so soon."

Miri could not tell, but she thought perhaps the woman secretly meant what she said, disguising it with her playful, teasing tone.

"I have no doubt you'll get to know my wife and fall in love with her, too. Everyone does."

Mirabella breathed a curt *hmph*, but said nothing more.

"All right, all right. Enough, enough." Ezra chuckled. He gestured to the butler. "Thaddeus will escort you to the ballroom. The stage is ready with the set pieces you requested. Please let him or the housekeeper know anything you need."

"We should be ready within an hour, if Mirabella doesn't remain behind to flirt," said Francis.

Mirabella grinned and patted a hand on Ezra's chest. "He's not had the decency to visit our poor theatre in nearly a year. What's a girl to do?"

"It looks like he's been too busy to care," said Benjamin, gesturing to Miri's belly.

On instinct, Miri looked down, placing both hands on her stomach, willing herself to put on the face of a woman with happy news.

Ezra grinned unabashedly. "We expect our little miracle any day now," he said.

"You look positively jubilant, my friend," said Benjamin. "Marriage suits you."

"You must promise me when we are done with the show that you will regale us with the tale of how your life so drastically changed within a matter of weeks, Ezra," said Mirabella. "But for now, let us prepare. We will send your butler when the show is ready."

"We are looking forward to it," said Ezra.

THE PERFORMERS WERE as magical as she remembered. Mirabella in particular was outstanding. Her voice was clear and keen, singing out jaunty numbers and harrowing ballads with effortless finesse. And Benjamin and Francis were equally as excellent—playing off of each other's performances as if they'd done this a thousand times. Perhaps they had. Every new scene brought a new level of delight, and Miri was thrilled to be attending the theatre again, despite such an intimate setting and with such a small cast.

Ezra's Yasha gift was perfect.

Even John Junior had sat quietly through most of it, only having to be scolded by his mother a time or two in the beginning. But after about an hour, he had grown so fidgety that his father had decided it was time to give the lad a break and take him from the room, leaving Ezra, Miri, Esther, Helena, Thaddeus, Kit, a smattering of house maids and grooms, and the three soldiers—Cosmas, Vitas, and Albus. Ezra had invited everyone in the household to enjoy the show, claiming it was a waste to only have the family in attendance. Ari had not come, though, away in the southern part of the continent, no doubt speaking to the crowds who seemed to follow him wherever he went these days.

Ezra was at home among these people. At peace. These performers had seemed to be true and dear friends to not only Ezra, but Esther and John as well. When the show was over and the performers had all taken their bows several times, they had fallen into conversation with one another as if they'd done this a hundred times.

Miri had done this, hadn't she? She had kept Ezra from his friends, from his life in Shalem. From everything he had held dear, including his beloved theatre, which he and he alone had financed to keep running in such a small, remote mountain village. Indeed, the first time she had ever laid eyes on Ezra was in that very theatre, his favorite place to be.

But he hadn't been there in a year.

Because Miri hadn't been able to visit the village since she left the temple.

"You all right, Lady Miri?" Kit asked, coming to Miri's side as they stood on the edge of the ballroom, observing the chattering.

"Mmm," Miri responded.

"You seem lost in thought."

"No," Miri said. "I'm fine." She nodded towards the soldiers, currently standing near Mirabella, laughing at all her jokes and watching her as if she were the center of the universe. "Why aren't you talking to him?"

"Vitas?" Kit asked. "I can't seem to make headway where he is concerned."

"Why not?"

A shrug. "He thinks it couldn't work because he is a soldier. He says I deserve a better life than that of a soldier's wife."

"Well, isn't that for you to decide?" Miri asked. But even as she asked the question, she felt the hypocrisy of it. For hadn't Ezra asked her the very same thing over and over again? When Miri protested that Ezra deserved better than her, hadn't he reminded her that he was perfectly capable of deciding what he wanted? For Kit's sake, Miri hated that she sympathized with the soldier.

But she did.

"That's what I told him," Kit said. "But he's stubborn."

"Well, perhaps he is trying to protect you."

"I'm not so fragile," Kit said.

"No, I didn't think you were," Miri admitted.

"You don't need to be jealous of her, you know," Kit said.

Miri furrowed her eyebrows before realizing who the servant was referring to. She looked out across the room to Mirabella, laughing and resting a hand on Ezra's arm.

"He could have had her," the servant went on. "He could have had anyone he wanted. And so he did."

"What if he chose wrong?"

"The point is he *chose* you. No one forced him. I think that is the truest kind of life one could live."

CHAPTER TWENTY-EIGHT

Rachæl had been ignoring Gian for two days.

She had returned to Chesedelle Castle a half day before him, having taken the royal carriage. He, on the other hand, had had a Sheol of a time finding reliable transportation leaving Sachar, having paid no less than four cabbies, each of whom took his money and ran, before finally finding an honest one to take him home.

Her father had still not returned, and there was no word of when he would. That they did not find him at Sachar told Gian that the king—or more specifically the empress—was not done with whatever they were up to. The thought gave him great unease.

But what gave him even more unease was the princess so pointedly ignoring him at every turn. Every time he had tried to get her attention, he had been met with cold indifference. She hadn't met his eyes even once.

She thought he had sent that whore to her. She thought he had wanted a night with a prostitute. Or perhaps a night with the both of them; he did not know. It didn't matter anyway. She had believed that he could want anyone but her. Mostly because he had been so very careful over the years to make sure she believed that.

Because he had to. Because he needed to. Because he knew better than to think...

These days, he couldn't damn well remember *what* exactly he knew better.

"There you are," Gian said, unable to stop himself upon seeing the princess standing alone, leaning on the balustrade of the small, private balcony. He had searched the castle for her after dinner tonight, following her much like Bear had followed him the night he had killed the beast's mother—pathetic and fragile and alone. He wondered if he could find a way to make his eyes look as helpless as Bear's had that night. Maybe she'd show him the same pity he had shown the pup.

"I wondered where you had gotten off to," he said placatingly. She kept her back to him. "But then I thought to myself, considering the inanity of that dinner, you were likely in need of a reprieve. So here I am, bringing distraction and libation in droves like a good boy." He lifted an amber bottle as he spoke, walking towards her. At least she wasn't walking away. It was as good a sign as any.

"You all right, darling?" He knew he was rambling, but the fact that she hadn't bothered to acknowledge his presence bothered him more than looking like an idiot. He needed to talk to her. He needed to tell her the truth. She deserved the truth.

He just hoped she wouldn't hate him for it.

Perching his elbows on the rail beside her, he offered her the bottle. She did not accept, her eyes fixed on the mountains and last rays of sunlight. Her silence settled into his gut like a stone. So he took a healthy swig of the rum in his hand and said, "Please say something."

She sighed, her shoulders falling slightly. But still she did not face him.

"Did you enjoy her?"

Not the question he was expecting. "Who?"

"Don't, Gian," she said, emotion welling in her voice. She did not try to hide it. "Don't lie to me anymore, just..."

Gian moved on instinct, coming closer to her side. To his relief, she did not move away.

"Ask me what you want to ask me, Rachæl."

For the first time in days, she met his eyes. "Will you tell me the truth?"

He could only nod once, wondering if she had any idea the weight of such a question.

"You swear it?"

"I swear it," he promised.

She looked out again, her gaze on the mountains. "You are my best friend, Gian. I've come to realize that. You know me better than anyone and yet..." She hesitated, looking down at her clasped hands. "And yet sometimes I feel as if I don't know you at all."

He kept back the laugh that involuntarily bubbled in his throat at the absurdity of the observation. She knew him more than anyone ever had. Ever. Did she truly not realize it? But instead of pointing that out, he said, "What is it you want to know, darling?"

She faced him again, a resignation in her eyes that had him instantly longing to reach for her, to pull her to him. Things he should never, *could* never do.

"Tell me the truth: did you enjoy her?"

He lifted a single eyebrow, hating the hurt he saw in her face. "Who?"

She rolled her eyes, releasing a long sigh. "Please don't answer my question with a question, Gian. You swore to me you wouldn't lie."

"Darling," he said, reaching for her despite himself. He placed a hand on her arm. "I *won't* lie."

She seemed satisfied by the answer, even if she hesitated. "The woman bragging in the corridor just now. The one you took to your bed last night. Did you enjoy her? Did you take her to your bed because I stopped you from having that whore in Sachar? Or would you have been with her anyway?"

"I wasn't with a woman last night."

"Then why is that woman bragging about you?"

"I don't know," he admitted. "I've yet to figure that one out."

"What is that supposed to mean?"

He hesitated, drawing in a breath to gather his thoughts, his words.

But she did not let him. "You promised no lies, Gian."

"I have never lied to you, but you do not know the full truth." Gods. Did that really just come out of his mouth?

"What truth?"

"I will tell you if you want to know. But you must understand first: when you know the truth, it will change everything between us. There will be no going back. Not ever."

He could see it in her eyes—uncertainty. Resignation. He knew what she thought—what everyone thought. That divulging his truth would be him telling her a myriad of sordid tales of women and drink and debauchery.

Little did she know that the real story was much more shocking.

"I did not sleep with that woman last night. I did not sleep with any woman last night. Nor at the brothel." The words tumbled out of him. "The truth is, I have not been with any woman in nigh on five years."

Rachæl went very still, meeting his eyes. But her countenance gave nothing away. He had no idea what she was thinking. Whether she believed him.

"Why would she say that you have?"

"I don't know," he admitted. "I've entertained a number of ideas over the years. Perhaps it is the thrill of the story or some fear of missing out. Or perhaps most people are brazen liars and we just don't realize it. Or maybe it's a combination of all three."

"I don't understand," the princess said.

"I know," he said. "In order to explain, I must go back to the beginning. To the reason I'm here at all. Did I ever tell you that story?"

Rachæl shook her head.

Gian took another generous swig from his bottle of rum and spoke.

"I was quite content as a pirate—seeing the world, pillaging, making a name for myself. I had all that a young man could want. Women and riches and rum. I loved my life; I loved my reputation as a ruthless scoundrel more. Your father sought me out thanks to that reputation. He offered me a job taking care of a rather messy problem. The money was decent enough, but it was the thrill of the challenge that drew me to it. Could I do the king's dirty work without anyone knowing? Could I clean up a catastrophic mess that no one else seemed to be able to? It was a challenge I—a young twenty-something—gladly accepted.

"So I did the job. And the king rewarded me handsomely for it. And that was that, I thought. It wasn't until I came to Chesedelle Castle that everything changed. You see, your father offered me a job working for him full time. I wasn't really interested. No matter how much he paid, it would pale in comparison to the riches of my pirating. Not to mention the freedom. I was prepared to decline the offer when I first saw her.

"When I tell you that she was the most beautiful creature I had ever laid eyes on, I am not exaggerating. I have seen the wonders of the world. I have had every beautiful woman I wanted in my arms. But one look at her, and I forgot every bit of it. I wanted her. I wanted her in my arms and in my bed that very night.

"The problem, of course, was that she was promised to another. But in my youthful arrogance, I only saw that as another challenge—and one I was eager to take on. So I accepted the job the king offered. I took care of his dirty work for him with brutal efficiency. And in between those jobs, I found excuses to be in the castle, lurking like a spider as I watched this woman from a distance.

"She became my obsession. I had to find a way into her arms. I had to know her charms for myself. There was some reasonable part of me still intact, I suppose, because I knew it was not only unlikely but completely impossible. She could never want me. She *should* never want me. So I drowned myself in women and libation by way of distraction.

"Every night for months it was another woman. I had convinced myself that I could forget about her if I could just find the right person. But I was wrong. So very wrong. For every touch was her fingers and every kiss was her lips. Every woman I took to my bed became her.

"Within the span of only a few months, I stopped bothering. Unfortunately, by that time, I had built a reputation for myself as something of a rake. I began to hear stories about myself. I tried to squash them, to stop the rumor mill from running amok, but it was no use. The stories kept coming, each more absurd than the last.

"It occurred to me somewhere during that time that the rumors might be to my benefit, for if people were convinced of my rakish ways, perhaps they would not see where my true affections lay.

"So I indulged the rumors. Fed them. And soon they were so prolific I couldn't have stopped them if I wanted to. I began hearing stories about myself so preposterous I laughed. Stories of me and a woman on the altar at the temple of Chesedelle City. Stories of me and women on the rooftops of the city. There was even a story of me and four women and—"

"All right, I get the point," Rachæl interjected.

Gian chuckled nervously and took another drink of his rum before he continued. "The point is, I could not stop the rumors. I didn't want to either. For every new rumor, every new assumption about my life served as a diversion from my true ambition to get a little closer to the woman I wanted.

"But you see, that was the problem. For by getting to know her, I realized what I felt was more than just obsession. More than just lust. I saw her strength and her poise and her cleverness. I saw it and wanted her all the more.

"I wanted *her*. Not just her body. Her. The woman she was. Everything about her.

"But I kept my distance. I stayed away because I knew I could never have her, and even if I could, she would never want the likes of me.

"And then one day she was no longer betrothed."

Gian stopped, rolling his shoulders and taking another swig of his rum. "I knew it was stupid, foolish even, but I placed myself closer to her. I weaseled my way further into her life in the naïve hope that she would let me in.

"To my eternal shock, she did. She let me into her inner circle. She called me her friend. And I was equally elated and horrified by it, for it only caused me to want her more. To need her more. To love her more.

"And that is when I knew the bald, honest truth of it: I was in love with her. Irrevocably. For me, there would never be another. It would only be her."

He turned then, facing Rachæl at last, his hands trembling so damned hard he could barely control them. But he took her hands in his anyway and said, "It will only ever be you, Rachæl. You're the reason I'm here. You're the reason I've stayed all these years. Because I am in love with you."

He wasn't sure if she was breathing. He was even less sure what she thought of such a story, such a declaration. He wanted to shake her and force her to speak. To say anything.

Something.

Gods, why wasn't she saying anything?

She took a step towards him, silent and pensive. But she did not touch him. She only looked down, playing with her fingers and toeing an invisible stone.

"I've been terrified," she finally said, her words so small and quiet he barely heard them.

He resisted the powerful urge to touch her. To tuck a loose strand of hair behind her ear or run a finger along her jaw. "Terrified of what, darling?"

She looked up at last, meeting his gaze. There was no fear, no hesitation. Only the same kind of bald honesty he had just given her. "That I was the only one who felt this way."

She took another small step towards him, pressing her body against his and resting her hands on his chest. She fiddled with the lapels of his jacket for a second or two before she looked up to him again, searching his eyes as if asking a question.

He knew the answer.

So he kissed her.

To his eternal wonder, she deepened that kiss with such glorious expertise he could only marvel. Gods above, Rachæl.

He was kissing Rachæl.

A kiss far more consuming, far more powerful than the one she had surprised him with in Sachar.

A glimmer of common sense tugged on his soul, and he pulled away from her lips. "This balcony is not nearly as private as one might assume. Someone is bound to see us."

She raised one eyebrow. "Worried about getting caught, Gian

of Borras?"

He grinned at her, delighting in her utter lack of worry or shame. "No, it is simply that I have plans for you which would be better suited for a more private setting."

For the briefest moment, her eyes flashed with shock before melting into a delighted smile that did little to hide the blush creeping up her neck and cheeks. He bent to press a kiss to that neck as she spoke. "Then take me somewhere with fewer eyes, Gian."

He met her gaze again, searching her for any hesitancy. For a secondary meaning. He found only earnestness. So he grabbed again for the gumption with which he had so brazenly flirted with her for the better part of the last five years and said, "Your chambers are bigger than mine."

To his delight, she responded with a smirk. "So is my bed."

Rachæl knew that one day she would look back on this moment and laugh or perhaps marvel at the fact that she had walked the entire length of the castle hand in hand with Gian and barely remembered a moment of it. She knew if she could stand outside of herself in this moment and look on, she would surely scold herself for trembling so violently as she stood with her back to Gian, facing the double doors in her bedchamber that overlooked the gardens beyond, wondering what in all the realms of Heaven and Sheol she was about to do.

But there was no hesitation. Not even a bit. Not to be with him. Not for what she wanted so desperately.

No, that fear lay somewhere else—namely in the awareness that she was twenty-three years old and had never known the touch of a man. And here she was, standing in her bedchamber knowing that Gian—although he might not have had quite the prowess with every woman at Chesedelle court as she had previously assumed—certainly was no virgin. And certainly was not without knowledge of the finer details of the carnal intimacies between a man and a woman. And surely that knowledge would lead him to do one of two things: laugh at her wanton lack of skill or pity her for it.

She was not sure she could handle either.

She was brought out of that depressing train of thought and back to the present by two warm, heavy hands on her shoulders and a lingering kiss to the back of her neck. "Darling, we can take this as slow as you want to."

She faced him, searching him for a sign of regret or hesitancy or even pity. She just found Gian—her friend. This man who had become to her something so much more than that—irreplaceable and infinitely valuable. "I don't need to slow down, I just..." She trailed off, too embarrassed to finish the sentence.

But Gian took her chin, kissing her once and so painfully softly that she found her hesitation falling away. "I've never done this," she finally confessed.

"Neither have I, darling," he said.

"Yes, you have," she countered.

He lifted her into his arms at that, carrying her in such a way that afforded her the opportunity to wrap her legs around his waist. He carried her thus towards her bed, laying her there with painstaking gentleness. He climbed over her, lingering above and looking down at her with a sort of adoration in his eyes that she was certain no one had ever borne for her. And at it, her heart soared. "My darling, you are wrong. I have never known anything like this."

And then he kissed her again—a kiss more devastating, more overcoming than the one that had obliterated her there on that balcony only moments ago. He ran his hands along her waist and up her torso, lingering just below her breasts and suddenly all she could think was how much she hated her corset and wished it was not in the way of his practiced hands and exploring fingers.

But Gian must have read her mind, for his hands drifted to the stays at the back of her gown and began working them. Within a few moments he had the dress loose, sliding it down her body to expose her corset and chemise. He stopped then and removed his jacket and boots, followed by his trousers and shirt, until only his drawers remained. And in the moonlight spilling across them, she saw at last in full detail the tattoo across his sculpted chest.

Not a skull as she had previously assumed, but a stone, rough and cut in two, revealing a depthless center. Without thinking, she reached up, running her fingers along the ink. Gian shut his eyes at her ministrations, taking in a breath as her fingers trailed along his skin.

"This is the Amulet of Haravelle," she said.

Gian looked down to her fingers, watching her as she touched him. "I was obsessed with finding it in my youth. They say the man who holds it holds the power of the gods in his hands."

"Not the gods," she countered. "The legends say that the Amulet's power belongs to Providence."

He drew a breath as if he would respond, but he was cut off by a bright light. Rachæl was not sure if it came from her fingers or from his tattoo, but it was there and gone again so quickly she immediately questioned if she had seen it at all.

But she knew it had been real by the look on Gian's face when he said, "The woman who gave this to me told me it was magicked ink. Until this moment I thought she was full of shit."

She met his eyes, searching them. "Magic ink?"

"She said it would protect me or something like that. I never believed her anyway, I just wanted the amulet next to my heart."

"No one knows where the amulet is," she said. "It has been lost for centuries."

Something flashed in Gian's eyes, gone as quickly as the light had a moment ago. But before she could ask, Gian leaned down again, kissing her with such intensity she soon stopped caring about the Amulet of Haravelle.

"Enough talk of talismans, my darling." He pulled her to sit upright, reaching around her to undo the laces of her corset with expert finesse. Next, he stripped her of her chemise until she was naked and vulnerable before him. He looked her over from her head to her toes, his eyes flashing with something utterly primal.

He met her eyes again before he said, "I love you. More than I ever knew possible."

The words unleashed something within her, and she reached for the hook of his drawers, working to release it as if she had a right. As if she'd done this a thousand times before.

Gian let her. He even helped her when she could not seem to get the inner button to cooperate with her trembling fingers. And soon Gian, too, was naked, standing before her as if frozen in time, in this moment that would be forever branded in her heart.

She appraised his body with the same bald eagerness with which he had appraised her. And though she had never seen a man before, she was not ashamed. She was not embarrassed. She just wanted him—this man, this friend, this...what was the word for it? Could she define what Gian had become to her? She was lost in the inadequacies of the Har-Navarian lexicon when he climbed over her once more, pulling her body with his until they were properly lying on the bed.

He kissed her deeply and for a long enough time that she wondered if he was nervous or hesitating. When he at last pulled away to meet her eyes again, she knew she had been wrong. He wasn't nervous or hesitant. He was grateful. As grateful as she.

Her irreverent, brazen friend who could make her laugh in the darkest moments. Her thoughtful, kind companion who seemed to know what she needed before she could articulate it herself. And now, here in her arms, her passionate, reverential lover, finding every place she wanted him to be and coaxing every bit of wonderment from her. He played her body like a fiddler's tune, every movement a new note in the song they wrote together. A song of their love, grown from the tiniest seed. A song of their friendship, birthed in genuine devotion.

Melody and harmony. Verse and chorus. Song and dance.

As Gian made love to her, she understood this—the missing piece, the final note had been lingering above them all along.

Love.

True and steadfast.

This was love.

"I NEED you to teach me how to do that," she said, lying next to Gian. He played his fingers absently along her stomach, his face buried in her neck as the moonlight glinted off his glorious backside.

"To do what?" he asked lazily.

"To give you what you just gave to me," she said. "I want to know how to do it as well as you do."

Gian laughed. Laughed. And she might have murdered him for it had not a sudden bout of embarrassment washed over her like a tidal wave. "I'm serious, Gian."

He was still laughing as he spoke. "Darling, you are in need of no lessons."

"I am a virgin," she said flatly.

"Not anymore," he retorted with his signature smirk.

"You know what I mean. I don't know what I am doing. And you... I mean that was... Well, I simply want to know how to... make you feel like that."

Gian took her chin, making her meet his eyes. "You did. You do."

She did not believe him, but neither did she know how to respond.

"Darling, you haven't a clue, have you?" Gian sighed, rolling to his side and resting his head on his hand, affording himself a more comfortable angle from which to speak. "It is no secret that I have been with many women, love. Some of whom I might have fancied that I loved. I will not lie and pretend as if I've never enjoyed myself with a woman. I certainly have.

"But you... This..." He paused, gathering his thoughts as he tucked a strand of hair behind her ear. "You read about this sort of thing in storybooks and assume it's all bullshit. Wishful thinking. You spend your life looking for it anyway, all the while knowing in the back of your mind it's probably a sham. And disappointment after disappointment, you stop believing it.

"When I first met you, love, it was lust on my part. I wanted to have my way with you for the thrill of it. I suppose, as much as I loathe the bastard, I am grateful to Ezra for forcing me to keep my distance from you. It forced me to get to know you as more than just an object of desire. Forced me to see you beyond the veil of lust.

"And here I am, lying next to you now, understanding for the first time in my life that the storybooks weren't wrong. This sort of thing exists. But it starts somewhere so much more honest than in each other's arms. It starts by learning to trust each other. By getting to know each other over time. And that time and trust builds a kind of intimacy that I never knew possible.

"So you ask me to teach you how to bring me pleasure? My darling, this is a sort of pleasure I never imagined existed. This is a sort of love they write books about."

Rachæl thought she could not have said it better herself. And though her language could not provide a single word to adequately describe this *thing* between them, she knew the best things in life were the ones that defied language anyway.

CHAPTER TWENTY-NINE

The performers had stayed for a few days, laughing and reminiscing on bygone days when a young Ezra had spent most of his spare time at the theatre, making friends with every performer. They had shared a thousand stories of the shows they had put on, which ones were the favorites, how they had never been able to convince Ezra to audition. They had even shared stories of Ezra's grandfather and how much he had loved one particular show about a bird and a lion. It had done Ezra's heart good to know that so many people remembered and loved the Kelach family, particularly his grandparents.

And it had done his heart good to bring Miri into this little world of his—to bring the beloved theatre to her so that she could enjoy it again. Maybe one day, when her heart had healed enough, she'd even feel like seeing a show at the opera house again. He hoped so, anyway.

Regardless, for the first time since losing his parents and grandparents nearly three years prior, things had begun to feel settled. His life here at Massahd had found a rhythm. And with a little one on the way, the promise of a bright future loomed before him.

Ezra smiled to himself as he stood on the balcony outside his bedchamber, overlooking the lake. Miri had left dinner early, opting for a long bath to soothe her sore back from her ever-growing belly. So Ezra had come out here, the summer night particularly warm and peaceful. He had been out here since twilight, watching the stars twinkle into place one at a time.

He heard the snick of the bathing room door from inside and turned to look over his shoulder. His wife was tying the sash of her robe over her belly when she looked up to see him. That lingering sadness behind her smile had not faded as much as he had hoped. In the months since the Harvest Ball, something had remained locked deep inside her. No matter how many times he had tried, no matter how many ways he had attempted to talk to her about it, she had never explained, never elaborated.

And he still had not figured out what to do about it.

Miri approached the glass doors separating the dark bedchamber from the balcony. Only a single candle glowed within, making the room dark in comparison to the moonlight. "Stargazing?" she asked as she pushed open the door.

Ezra only nodded, coming to her. Mother of kings, she looked so beautiful standing there with her wild flaming curls spilling down her breast and a hand under her belly. He slipped his arms around her and pulled her close. She rested her head on his shoulder, sighing deeply.

"Tired, Wildfire?"

"Always these days."

Ezra kissed the top of her head. "We should retire," he said, offering her his hand. She took it, letting him lead her back inside.

"I never properly thanked you," she said.

"For what?" He took a seat in his favorite chaise in the sitting area that faced the windows, moonlight spilling across the velvet upholstery. He gestured for her to sit in his lap. To his delight, she did, settling into his arms.

"For the theatre," she answered. "It was so beautiful. And the performers were wonderful—particularly Mirabella."

"She is gifted, that's for certain."

"I don't think she's very fond of me, though."

"Why do you think that?" he asked, playing with a strand of her curls that had spilled across his chest.

Miri shrugged. "I think she resents that *I* ended up as your wife and not *her*."

Ezra chuckled. "She was never a prospect."

Miri chuckled, too. "Please don't ever tell her that. I'm not sure her ego could survive it."

He smiled. "No doubt."

Miri's words grew softer. "I suppose there are many women who feel that way."

He tilted his head, trying to read her face. It was impossible from this angle. "Why are you thinking about this?"

She toyed with the signet ring on her left hand, turning it over and over. "I don't know. Do you ever wonder if your life would have been less complicated if you had chosen someone else?"

"No, I don't."

"You've given me more than I ever deserved. You've given me a dream, Ezra. One cannot help but wonder how she could ever give you so much in return."

Ezra sat up, turning so that he might meet her eyes. "You do, Miri. Every day. Our life. Our love. Our family," he added, placing a hand on her swollen belly. "I'm the one indebted to you. Miri, I've never been happier."

Miri shook her head, a tear falling down her cheek as she looked down to her stomach. She covered it with both hands but said nothing.

"Did you know?" he asked. "I never really considered fatherhood until I saw John hold his son for the first time. It was the first time I was ever jealous of him. I wanted that—the look in his eyes. The utter adoration for his child and for his wife for making him a father. The way he fell even more deeply in love with my sister because of it. I suppose it was the birth of John Junior that first set my heart on a new trajectory. It was the first time I ever wanted more for myself than the life I was being offered.

"And now, here I am sitting with my best friend who happens to be my wife. And she carries our child, who we'll get to meet any day now. And I could not be happier. I could not be more grateful. This life...it is sweeter than I ever imagined. So you're wrong, Miri. I am the one who will forever be indebted to you. I am the one who will never be able to give you enough."

"Ezra." She tried to speak, but her words were clogged by her tears, and she shook her head, silent.

So Ezra took her chin and kissed her softly. Miri deepened that kiss, turning to face him more fully, a task not easily accomplished thanks to her cumbersome belly. When she was at last comfortably sitting astride his lap, he smiled, running hands along the side of her waist, loving the feel of their child pressed between him.

"I love you, Ezra," she said, her words so earnest it nearly broke his heart. "I love you more than I'll ever be able to explain."

"I know, Wildfire," he said. "I can feel it."

"I don't want you to forget it," she went on. "No matter what, never forget that I love you."

"You're branded on my heart, my love. There is no turning back now."

She kissed him again, even more deeply this time, beginning to work loose the knot of his cravat. When next she began undoing the buttons of his shirt, he reached to untie the sash of her robe, slipping it from her shoulders and kissing his way across the skin he exposed. She did the same with every button, and Ezra made love to his wife by the light of the stars.

The morning light woke him. He stretched lazily under the blankets, letting a smile curl his mouth at the memory of his night of little sleep. His eyes still shut, Ezra reached across the bed to pull his wife close, only to find cold, empty sheets.

He sat up, rubbing his eyes before getting out of the bed. He reached for his robe to cover himself, fully intending to remove it the moment he found his wife again. He made his way to the bathing room, pushing gently on the door.

"You in there, Wildfire?"

There was no response, and the room was empty. Ezra glanced toward the balcony, but it, too, was empty.

Someone knocked at his door.

"Come in," he said.

Kit emerged, bright-eyed. "Morning, my lord!" she said.

"Good morning, Kit," he said amiably. "Will you do me a favor and tell my wife that I will join her downstairs for breakfast momentarily? She must have slipped out of bed without my realizing."

Kit tilted her head to one side, furrowing her brow. "She is not at breakfast, my lord. I thought she was sleeping in with you."

"Hmm," Ezra said. "Well, she must have gone for a walk. It's such a beautiful morning. I'll dress and find her. I'm sure she's in the gardens."

Miri was not in the gardens. Nor was she at the stables or the lake. Back inside the castle, Ezra did not find her in any of the libraries either.

"Have you seen her, my lord?" Thaddeus asked, approaching Ezra in the main foyer.

"No," Ezra said, shaking his head. "But she could not have gone far. The groom said no one has taken a horse today." He thought of her swollen belly. He thought of the way she had paused several times in their night of pleasure, shutting her eyes and breathing through painful tightening fits. Her time was close. They both knew it, though she did not speak of it. "I'm worried it might be her time," he went on. "She must have gone for a walk or something. She probably needs help somewhere."

"I have searched the bedchambers, and Kit has searched each of the private gardens," said the butler. Something like fatherly concern shone on his long face. "I have contacted General Albus to search the grounds, but he has not reported back."

"I'm sure she's just somewhere we haven't thought of, Thaddeus," Ezra said, attempting to reassure him. "No need to worry."

Helena bustled into the foyer a moment later. "There you are," she said. "I've been looking for you." In her hand, she waved a piece of paper. "I found this."

She handed it to Ezra, along with his grandmother's signet ring.

"The ring was with the note," she said.

"Where?"

"In your study," she said. "On your desk. I did not read it."

Ezra looked down at the small, folded piece of paper in his hand. Something in his gut went very, very still as he slowly unfolded the note.

Only truth between us. Do you remember our promise?

You deserve to be happy. You deserve the kind of love you've given me. But it can never be so because I have not given you the whole truth, knowing it would devastate you.

I have betrayed you in the deepest sense. I have robbed you of your dream of our family and you never knew it. I have lied to you every day since the Harvest Ball. Thanks to that night, I will never know who the child's father is.

I meant it when I said that I will love you forever—that was never a lie. But you deserve better than this.

I'm so sorry.

~Wildfire

Ezra fell to his knees, his heart screaming out as he read the words over and over again.

Only truth between us.

The truth, for the first time, stared him square in the face. That silent sorrow in Miri's eyes. The words she would not say. The cold darkness that had swept over them the night of the Harvest Ball.

He understood.

For the first time, Ezra understood the real truth of what had happened not just to him that night, but to his wife.

"My lord?" Thaddeus asked.

At his side, Helena knelt, a hand on his shoulder. "What's wrong, darling?" she asked in her motherly voice. "What happened?"

Ezra swallowed against the lump in his throat, fighting back tears of rage as he finally managed to speak. He could only utter a single name.

"Phinehas."

End of Book II

ACKNOWLEDGMENTS

These get harder to write every time. And today as I'm penning this, life has thrown us a curveball, as it so often does. It has reminded me in no uncertain terms that life is precious, family is everything, and love is worth the fight. So for these acknowledgments, let me just say this: I had no idea when I started writing Ezra and Miri's story just how much it would mirror my own. It's almost prophetic, really. Not in the specifics, but in the journey they take to find that quiet, unassuming magic that comes in the waiting, in the hurting, in the pain, and in the sacrificing. It's the very moments in life that we think we cannot handle that are the moments that define us. Shape us. Make us better.

God, thank you for giving me these books. I had no idea how much I'd need them. May they give just one person the same hope they've given me.

Side note: sorry for the cliffhanger. Again. Apparently I really like them.

ABOUT THE AUTHOR

So let's just be real here... My name is Morgan and I'm a chronic over-achiever and avid binger of *The Office.* When I watch *Lord of the Rings,* I watch the extended versions, and they're still not long enough. I won arguments in elementary school by out-quoting everyone with my vast knowledge of *The Princess Bride.* So yeah, I'm kind of a big deal.* I used to have a mohawk‡. And once I had purple bangs‡. But I try not to let that dictate my current fashion choices, which are just as confused, I confess. Bless.

In my spare time, I write. A lot. Songs, stories, articles, novels... It's just this thing in me that I have to get out. The book you're reading, part of *The Chalam Færytales,* is sort of a magnum opus of all the things that have been stirring in me from the time I was a kid—musing about the existence of humanity, pondering the wonder of God and the ongoing work of redemption...you know, kid stuff. I'm real proud of it. (That's my Texan coming out. Fight me.) I'd be honored if you left a review of it somewhere on the interwebs. (Consequently, I'm convinced that novel writing is just an acceptable form of psychosis, but it's definitely a beast within me that roars to be freed. So I pet it and feed it and let it dictate my fingers on the keyboard without regrets.)

But even if you don't ever read another one of my novels or listen to one of my songs, I can't thank you enough for reading this one. I hope I can bring a little magic to your world in some way.

The art in me manifests in various forms—from my books, to my music, to my digital art and even the occasional article. I get confused about what I should call myself: author or musician or songwriter or graphic designer or armchair theologian. I think it's probably safe to say I'm just an artist at heart exploring the magic around us. Thanks for exploring with me!

*This is sarcasm.

‡This is not sarcasm.

facebook.com/morgangfarris
instagram.com/morgangfarris
youtube.com/morgangfarris
pinterest.com/morgangfarris

ONE WORLD. TWO TALES. ONE THOUSAND YEARS APART.

THE CHALAM CHRONICLES begin with the Færytales, a 5-book series set in a medieval fantasy world full of monsters, magic, and all the witchy forest wonder your little heart desires.
Oh yes, and flying horses.

FÆRYTALES (VOL. 1) // COMPLETED VOLUME

Once you've read the Færytales, it's time to start the Legends. Beginning with The Stag at Hand, the Legends are set 1000 years in the future of the same world: a victorian-gothic fantasy with hints of steampunk and carnival opulence.
Oh yes, and there are still flying horses, don't worry.

LEGENDS (VOL. 2) // INCOMPLETE VOLUME

EXPLORE MORE OF THE CHALAM WORLD, INCLUDING AN INTERACTIVE MAP!

CHALAMCHRONICLES.COM

ALSO BY MORGAN G FARRIS

THE CHALAM FÆRYTALES:

The Promised One (Book I)

The Purloined Prophecy (Book II)

The Parallax (Book III)

The Perdurables (Book IV)

The War and the Petrichor (Book V)

THE CHALAM LEGENDS:

The Stag at Hand (Book I)

The Song in the Shadows (Book II)

MUSIC:

Find covers and original songs at Youtube.com/MorganGFarris

ART:

Shop curiosities at Etsy.com/shop/Minor5Emporium

FAERYTALES (VOL. 1)

LEGENDS (VOL. 2)

SIGN UP FOR THE NEWSLETTER

I don't send out newsletters a lot. Honestly, it's a pain. But I do use them from time to time to update you when things are releasing, or when something new is happening, or when I set out on another out-of-the-blue artistic endeavor. So that being said, I don't do the whole spammy, weekly, buy my stuff email thing. It's obnoxious.

When you visit my site, this annoying pop-up shows up asking you to sign up. Just add your email there. Use the QR code below, or just visit my website.

Morgan G Farris.com

www.ingramcontent.com/pod-product-compliance
Lightning Source LLC
Chambersburg PA
CBHW021957040826
48979CB00046B/2657/J

* 9 7 8 1 7 3 7 9 4 7 9 6 7 *